No One Like You

Read More Kate Angell

Sweet Spot (Richmond Rogues)

No Tan Lines (Barefoot William)

Unwrapped (Anthology)

He's the One (Anthology)

No Strings Attached (Barefoot William)

The Sugar Cookie Sweetheart Swap (Anthology)

No Sunshine When She's Gone (Barefoot William)

No One Like You

KATE ANGELL

KENSINGTON PUBLISHING CORP.
www.kensingtonbooks.com

KENSINGTON BOOKS are published by

Kensington Publishing Corp.
119 West 40th Street
New York, NY 10018

All Kensington titles, imprints, and distributed lines are available at special quantity discounts for bulk purchases for sales promotions, premiums, fund-raising, educational, or institutional use.

Special book excerpts or customized printings can also be created to fit specific needs. For details, write or phone the office of the Kensington sales manager: Kensington Publishing Corp., 119 West 40th Street, New York, NY 10018, attn: Sales Department; phone: 1-800-221-2647.

KENSINGTON and the k logo are Reg. U.S. Pat. & TM Off.

ISBN-13: 978-0-7582-9130-1
ISBN-10: 0-7582-9130-2

First Kensington Trade Paperback Printing: May 2015

10 9 8 7 6 5 4 3 2 1

Printed in the United States of America

First Electronic Edition: May 2015

ISBN-13: 978-0-7582-9131-8
ISBN-10: 0-7582-9131-0

To dog lovers: I hope you enjoy Atlas and gang. I had a Great Dane named Banshee, and many of the big boy's antics are portrayed in this story.

To Alicia Condon, my editor: we've worked together for fifteen years. I value your insight, positive energy, and patience. You are the very best.

To the ladies in my life who remain constant and supportive: Jina Bacarr, Marion Brown, Stella Brown, Debbie Roome, and Sue-Ellen Welfonder. I thank you!

Barefoot William Sun **Classified Ads:**

Live-in personal assistant: eight weeks
Appointment scheduling
Maintaining and updating contact lists
Dinner parties
Travel planning
Dinner reservations
Personal shopping
Tickets to entertainment events
Manage invitations
Culinary ability
Interaction with fans, family, and teammates
Light housework
Pet sitter/dog walker
Salary: negotiable with room and board
Contact: RCates@CatesMgmt.com

One

D*og playing dead in the middle of the road.*
  Beth Avery couldn't believe the black Great Dane had stopped, dropped, and rolled onto his side. He had a mind of his own and was testing her patience. She shook her head. She should never have applied for the personal assistant position. Dog walker wasn't on her résumé.

The big boy couldn't be coaxed or talked from the crosswalk at Center Street and Egret Way. Nothing worked. He'd lain down and stayed down. All one hundred and fifty pounds of him.

The situation was hopeless.

Beth tugged gently on the leather leash attached to his harness. "Up, Atlas, *up,*" she pleaded again.

Not a flicker of his ears. He even closed his eyes. What if he was sick or hurt? She stared at his chest. The rise and fall was slow and peaceful. Had he fallen asleep?

Atlas was the alpha dog of the four dogs she was walking. Dismayed, she watched the golden retriever and two dapple dachshunds follow his lead. They, too, settled on the asphalt. The dachsies, Oscar and Nathan, turned onto their backs so the sunshine could warm their bellies. They stretched, yawned, looking way too comfortable.

What was she to do? Beth clutched the loop handles on the leashes so tightly they left an imprint on her palm. For a beat, she thought about letting go. See what they would do. It couldn't be any worse than watching them sunbathe on the road. She wasn't a dog person. She favored cats. So how was it that she found herself in this predicament at ten a.m. on a Monday morning?

She knew why. She was so desperate to find work, she'd somehow missed the dog walking requirement in the ad. She was so excited she'd been called back for a follow-up interview with Rylan Cates for the assistant position, she didn't dare tell him she had no experience with canines. He'd met with people all week and had narrowed his choices to three women, herself included.

The final applicants went on to walk, feed, and bathe his dogs. She had no idea how the other ladies had fared before her, although Atlas smelled profoundly doggie. Beth shook her head to clear her thoughts. She wasn't doing all that well, either.

She'd walked the pack for close to an hour, up and down the streets of Olde Barefoot William, where the homes were handed down through generations. She'd fallen in love with the beachside town, which was as eclectic in its architecture as it was harmonious. William Cates had founded the community. Here lay the inner circle. The old Florida-style cottages were quaint. The houses were shingled and shuttered, with wide porches. They'd withstood hurricanes and time. A few had had minor facelifts.

Enormous evergreens lined the narrow two-lane road. Ancient moss clung to the cypress. The sun cast shadows through the scarlet-flowered branches of the Royal Poinciana trees that cornered the street. The scent of plumeria, gardenia, and hibiscus was heavy on the air. Sprinklers on automatic timers kicked on, watering lawns.

Only three blocks from Rylan's house, Beth sighed heavily. The neighborhood was momentarily quiet. No cars and no joggers. No one to witness the sleeping dogs.

Thank goodness. How was she going to explain she'd fallen off schedule because Atlas pulled a Rip van Winkle? Baths needed to be given to the dogs before noon. Ry had handed her a canine cookbook for their food. They ate organic. A blender and baking were involved. Lunch would be late.

Determined to find a solution, she transferred the leashes to one hand, and then patted the back pocket on her cutoff jeans with the other. She had one trick up her sleeve she'd yet to play. She'd purposely changed her clothes and had dressed down for the walk. Had to. Drool stained white linen slacks. Dirty paws would leave permanent marks. She couldn't afford cleaning bills. Not in her current economic state.

Sweetening her tone, she tried, "Atlas, treat? Yum, yum." She smacked her lips.

Treat didn't get the slightest reaction from the Dane, but the other dogs perked up. The two dachshunds scrambled to their feet and the golden retriever looked at Atlas then back to Beth. Rue was slow to make her decision.

"Oatmeal-apple biscuits," Beth said, enticing the golden with a handful of snacks she pulled from her denim pocket.

Rue sniffed the air, then nudged Atlas with her nose, but the Dane wouldn't budge. The retriever slowly rose.

Three up, and one to go. *A minor victory,* Beth thought.

The dachsies and golden ate their snacks, then eyed Atlas once again, waiting for him to make his move. Or not. Beth agonized over the moment until inspiration struck. Looping the leashes over her wrist, she crouched down near the big dog. There, she quickly tied her retro red Keds. Atlas had stomped all over her feet when he'd spotted a squirrel. She'd tripped twice over the loose laces.

Leaning forward, her cutoffs rode up and snugged her bottom. The fringe tickled the tops of her thighs. Her bright blue crop top had shrunk in the dryer making the back hem even with her sports bra. The sun kissed her bare skin.

She didn't care if she looked ridiculous, whispering to the Dane. She needed this job. She drew in a breath and started making promises that she never planned to keep, sweet-talking him. "No organic food for you, Atlas. I'll cook you a big, juicy steak if you'll get up."

The Dane cracked his eyelids, a good sign that he was listening.

"You can have the entire couch to yourself. I will stand for the remainder of my interview."

His tail thumped.

"We could even skip your bath." She had dreaded it anyway. The shampooing might not be so bad. Rinsing him off would drench her. What other enticements could she offer?

"He doesn't take bribes," said a man from behind her. His voice was deep and concerned. "I've tried."

Rylan Cates's sudden arrival took her by surprise. Beth sat down hard on the asphalt. Small rocks jabbed her bottom. She jarred her tailbone. Winced. His shadow loomed over her, larger than life. She turned slightly, tilted back her head, and worked her gaze up his body.

Navy flip-flops. Long legs dusted with brown hair. Gray board shorts. Lean hips. A hint of his package. Defined abs beneath a T-shirt scripted with *I Came to Play*. Muscled arms. Solid shoulders. A scruffy chin in need of a shave. A masculine mouth that tipped up at one corner. Straight nose. Eyes so blue they made the sky jealous. His hair was dark blond and shaggy. He looked more surfer than professional baseball player.

He was way hotter than she remembered. Or was it because she'd barely looked up from her hands folded in her lap during the interview? Interviewing was new to her.

She'd been incredibly nervous then, and was even more so now.

He cleared his throat, shifted slightly, breaking her stare. He extended his hand, and she took it. He helped her up. His grasp was strong. His palm callused. He squished her fingers. She shook out her hand when released and brushed pebbles from her thighs and butt cheeks. Tugged down her top then faced him.

Her stomach tightened, her mind working overtime imagining what he must be thinking. Where had he come from? she wondered, glancing along the street. She hadn't heard him approach, but soon understood why. He drove a McLaren. The black sports car was built for stealth and speed and was good for sneaking up on someone. Especially someone walking his dogs. He could easily spy on her. It was parked against the curb, looking shiny and pricey against the backdrop of aging homes.

He ran one hand down his face. "Why is Atlas sleeping in the street?"

"He needed a nap," was said with more snark than she'd intended. She had never been more frustrated.

"He can't stay there all day," he told her. "Traffic picks up closer to noon."

She tried to read his expression. Was he amused or angry? She couldn't tell and released a short breath. "I'm open to suggestions."

He stuck his hands in the pockets of his board shorts, rocked back on his heels. She couldn't believe he had the balls to debate helping her.

Moments passed before he said, "Give him Rue's leash so he can walk her home."

A dog walking a dog? Her eyes widened. Surely he was joking.

"The big boy likes to be in control," Rylan explained as if she should have known that and adjusted her dog walking style. "He's had a crush on Rue since they were puppies. She won't mind." Ry paused, looked her in the eye. His lips twisted. "Staring at me like I'm crazy won't get him up."

She blushed, embarrassed by her inability to manage Atlas. He hadn't taken to her, but it hadn't been for lack of trying. She wondered if the other applicants had won him over. Perhaps this job wasn't meant for her after all. A position stocking shelves at Crabby Abby's General Store or scooping ice cream cones at The Dairy Godmother might be a better choice. At either place she wouldn't have to contend with scooping dog poop.

Rylan nudged her aside and took the leashes from her. Separating Rue's hot pink lead from the others, he held it up for Beth to see the teeth marks—big indentations made by a big mouth—on the curved handle. No mistaking the Great Dane's signature bite. "Watch this. Atlas, take Rue home," he instructed the Dane.

Atlas stood up so quickly, Beth swore the earth moved.

Rising on his back legs, the dog put his paws on Rylan's shoulders. They were eye to eye. Ry smiled and scratched the dog's floppy ears. Atlas barked. It was a sight she'd never forget.

Dropping back down, Atlas snatched Rue's leash from Ry's hand and gripped it between his teeth. His tail whipped wildly. He was happy and attentive. He took off at a trot, dragging Rue several steps before she balked. He then slowed his stride so the golden could keep up and they headed down the sidewalk.

Beth stared after them, utterly blown away. She wouldn't have believed it, had she not seen it. She needed to catch up to them, she realized, or her chances of landing this job were long gone. They were already a half-block ahead of her. The dachshunds had short legs. She decided to scoop them up and carry them, tucking each under an arm. Like footballs.

She left Rylan standing on the crosswalk, not daring to turn around to see if he was watching her. She was already so embarrassed, she didn't want to mess this up, too. No doubt he was observing her every move. His judging her did not sit well. People in her past had taken her to task, and she'd not enjoyed the criticism.

Jogging, she caught up with Atlas and Rue. Ry trailed behind them in the McLaren. Apparently he didn't trust her to cover the three blocks alone. Not that she blamed him. What dog owner wanted to see his animals sprawled out and asleep on the asphalt? It was not a pretty sight.

Rylan's two-story cottage sat west of Center Street on Manatee Way. The heavily wooded lot provided him privacy. Only hints of gray paint and white shutters could be seen through the trees.

Slowing to catch her breath, Beth followed the lime rock driveway that wound between tall hedges. She pulled in her gut and kept going. She was determined Atlas and company weren't going to get the better of her. The problem was, they knew the terrain, and she did not.

She nearly turned her ankle on a loose stone in her attempt to keep up with the lead dogs. She winced, wanting to stop and rub her foot, but they had picked up the pace and were headed for their water bowls aligned in a row on the porch. The dachshunds squirmed in her arms, wanting down. Once on the ground, they scrambled up the steps.

Tires crunched on the driveway behind her, and she heard Coldplay on Ry's car radio before the engine cut off. Exhaling, she pushed back the hair falling into her eyes and straightened her top. She barely had time to adjust her shorts before Rylan joined her at the front of the house.

He looked down at her. She tried not to notice that his light eyes looked tired and he hadn't shaved this morning. He seemed to have a lot on his mind. Perhaps the man needed an assistant more than she'd realized. She hoped it would be her.

"You made it back okay," he said.

She nodded. "Just in time to—"

Be slobbered on. Oh, no. Atlas had drunk deeply, then jumped off the porch, coming straight to her. He wiped his muzzle on her denim hip. She was his towel. Drool spread from her crotch to her thigh. She flinched.

"Sorry about that," Rylan apologized as he tugged off his T-shirt. "Let me dry you off."

"No, I'm fine—"

"I insist."

He touched her. She should've remained wet. His hands were large and rough; the fabric of his shirt soft from wear. His bare chest brushed her breast as he bent toward her hip. The warmth of his breath blew across her belly. His rubdown was fast, thorough, and disturbingly intimate. He didn't seem affected, but she nearly came out of her skin. Goose bumps rose.

She waved him off. "I'm okay, really," she managed and moved away from him, only to walk into Atlas. The Dane still invaded her space.

Rylan smiled, appearing relieved. "He likes you."

She found that hard to believe. "He wiped his face on me."

"He's playing with you."

"Then why am I not having fun?"

"You'll get used to him."

His words gave her pause. He would have to hire her for that to happen. She wasn't sure she could live with a dog the size of a pony and the stubbornness of a mule.

"I'm not certain this job is for me." She was being honest with him and herself, even if it meant the interview ended right there. Being broke was no longer an option. She hated to let the job go, but she didn't want to get in over her head. Been there. Done that. Her past hadn't played out well.

Her hesitancy had Rylan narrowing his eyes. He did the unexpected. Throwing back his head, he released his inner beast. He howled. The sound cued the dogs to do the same. They howled so loudly, Beth covered her ears.

"What are you doing?" she asked once the racket eased.

"We're talking you into staying."

She shook her head. "You're crazy."

"I'm also smart, practical, and tend to be too serious, according to my family," he told her. "I'm an animal lover and a decent ballplayer."

Decent ballplayer? She'd Googled him before she applied for the job. Statistics showed he ranked among the best. He was a gifted athlete.

She needed to come clean with him. "I lied on my résumé," she confessed. She figured her admission would put him off.

"I know," he surprised her by saying. "I checked your previous employers and references. If you worked where you said you did, you were invisible."

"Why did you let me slide?" she asked, confused.

He shrugged. "I'm honestly not sure. I trust my dogs' instincts. Atlas is an excellent judge of character. He wouldn't let anyone in the cottage who didn't belong. He joined you on the sofa during your first interview and you didn't freak out. I had one applicant leave the house screaming."

"He is rather large."

"Large, but harmless," Ry assured her. "He's still growing. He's just two years old."

Still growing. Her heart nearly stopped.

"The job is only for eight weeks. It starts a week before

spring training and ends a week after," he reminded her. "I have a permanent assistant in Richmond. She's just gotten married. I gave her time off for an extended honeymoon in Cancun."

The timing is ideal, Beth thought. Free of her previous obligations, she didn't want to stay in one place too long. She had a lot of country to explore. She wanted to lose herself in her travels. Returning home was not an option. She wouldn't be missed.

"It's a busy time for me," Rylan continued. "I'll have personal and professional obligations. I'll need someone to keep me on track."

Beth swallowed hard. Some days she lived chaos, all on her own. Could she keep his life and her own running smooth? That was to be seen. Organization could be challenging.

To her surprise, he took her silence as holding out for more money. "You'll receive a salary and a household budget. You'll have a business credit card for emergencies. Should you come up short for any reason, just let me know."

The man was trusting. Perhaps overly so. She didn't want to disappoint him. She quickly gave the job a final assessment. The pay was enticing—she'd make more money in eight weeks than she had made the previous year. The cash cushion would be nice—she could take a short vacation once she left town. She wouldn't be forced to immediately seek another position.

She had one final question for him before she accepted. "You had far more qualified applicants. I couldn't be your first choice. So why me, Rylan? Besides the fact your dog likes me."

Because I'm not attracted to you. He didn't admit that to Beth; he didn't want to hurt her feelings.

Plain and simply put, she wasn't his type. He didn't have a lot of time to date, but when he did, he favored tall, slender, savvy blondes. The two other women he'd interviewed had turned him on. He didn't need the distraction or the erection. No work would've gotten done.

Beth Avery had *quirky* written all over her. Her brown hair was curly and unruly. The tip of her nose turned up slightly. She pursed her lips a lot. She had a chin dimple. She couldn't be more than five foot two.

Her style in clothes was mismatched. She'd shown up to her first interview wearing a lavender prairie flower print top, a flowing ankle-length green skirt, and white cowgirl boots with silver scrolling. Peace sign earrings had dangled from her ears, and a crocheted and beaded bracelet had wrapped her wrist.

Her amazing eyes had gotten her a second interview. Rain cast in color, the blue-gray reminded him of the Gulf of Mexico before a summer storm. He'd noticed that the hue changed with her mood. Blue dominated when she was relaxed. Gray indicated her frustration. Atlas had aggravated her greatly. Her eyes had turned gunmetal gray.

Ry was polite when he informed her, "I'm going on gut instinct alone in hiring you," he admitted. "You seem nice, have an ability to adapt, and if you screw up, Atlas will let me know."

"Atlas looks like a tattletale," she agreed with a glance in the dog's direction.

"I need someone immediately," he added. "You're standing before me. The job is yours if you want it."

No hesitation. "I'll take it."

"How soon can you start?"

She glanced toward her PT Cruiser parked at the curb. "I travel light. I'm temporarily living out of my car."

She lived out of her car? That made him blink. He had no

room to criticize her. He'd taken road trips in college. He'd lived free and easy until responsibility had forced him to grow up. Playing professional ball aged a man.

"I'll grab my suitcases," she said, cutting across the yard.

"I'll help you." He was right behind her. Atlas came, too.

"Will I get a ticket parked at the curb?" She cast a look over her shoulder. No other cars were on the street.

"I'll get you a city parking sticker later today." He saw the pained look on her face and guessed the reason. "There's no charge."

She released a breath. "I would've needed an advance on my pay otherwise."

"You're broke?" slipped out before he could stop himself.

Her lips thinned. "I'm on a tight budget."

Before he could ask her any more questions, she jumped the dwarf Natal Plum hedge near the curb, and he was surprised she cleared it. He didn't take her for athletic. He and Atlas hopped over it next. She circled to the rear of the vehicle, pulled a keyless remote from the side pocket of her shorts, and popped the hatchback.

He noticed her out-of-state license plate. She'd listed her permanent residence on her application as White Bear Lake, Minnesota, yet she had Missouri plates. A HIKE MICHIGAN bumper sticker and Arizona flag decal trimmed her bumper. VIRGINIA IS FOR LOVERS and PROPERTY OF IOWA, HAWKEYE STATE stickers noted her travels. The lady was a nomad.

The pieces to her puzzle didn't quite fit.

He was intrigued.

She pulled two suitcases from the Cruiser.

Rylan stepped back. He'd been so involved in reading her stickers, he nearly forgot his manners. He hung his T-shirt over his shoulder, and took the suitcases from her.

Dingy gold hardware hinged the battered, scratched, and ancient brown leather. A man's name was barely visible near one handle. Lou Vui. *Her father, brother? Husband?* He glanced at her left hand. She wasn't wearing a wedding ring.

The cases were surprisingly light. He had expected heavier. She would settle in quickly.

"I inherited my house from my grandparents," he told her as they headed up the driveway. "Frank and Emma lived here for twenty years before they moved rural. The empty lots on both sides belong to me, too. The cottage has four bedrooms—two up, two down. You can have the connecting rooms on the first floor. Bedroom, full bath, and office. My dogs have the run of the place. Close your door for privacy. Atlas is known to twist a doorknob with his mouth. He'll also paw and scratch to get your attention." The Great Dane could be pushy and persistent.

They climbed the steps to the porch and entered through the double doors. The dogs followed them. The dachsies and Rue took to their plush corduroy dog beds in the living room and waited patiently. They had manners. Atlas, not so much. The big dog was bumping Beth from the back. He was hungry and hurrying her along. It was close to lunchtime, and he expected her to feed him.

Rylan noticed it with a wry smile and looked around the entryway. His home was his sanctuary. It was where he could exhale and hang out with his dogs. He never took the peace and quiet for granted. The floors were dark Florida pine, as was the staircase to the second floor. The walls were stark white. "This way," he said, moving down the hallway.

He nudged open a door with his foot and set her suitcases inside. He was pragmatic and didn't buy anything he didn't need. Except his McLaren. The splurge came from bonus money when he'd been traded from the St. Louis

Colonels to the Richmond Rogues. It was his dream vehicle. He also had a Range Rover with washable mats to
haul his dogs. He kept it parked in the garage.

He glanced around the guest room and wondered if
Beth would feel at home. He'd furnished the room with a
queen sofa sleeper, but had no idea if it was comfortable.
She would find out at bedtime. A mirrored dresser leaned
against the wall and a yellow-cushioned fan back chair sat
in one corner.

"There are a few hangers in the closet," he told her. For
those few clothes she might need to hang up. Again, that
puzzled him. "The dresser once belonged to my sister
Shaye. The drawers have scented liners. Smell like flowers."

"Nice. I like flowers."

"Sheets, a comforter, and two pillows are stored in the
old seaman's chest used as a bedside table."

"No gold or treasure?" she asked.

He shook his head. "Shaye had it refurbished. It once
belonged to my great-great Uncle Cletis. He was a commercial fisherman."

"I like antiques and family history." Beth smiled. For the
first time. A soft smile while she scrutinized the dresser
with the decorative carved mirror. It was old, and the bottom drawer was slightly warped. But at least it closed.

He went on to show her the bathroom situated between
the bedroom and the office. Functional, but not fancy. He'd
supplied a set of blue towels. Shaye had suggested pear
shampoo, a neutral olive oil soap, and a natural sea sponge.

Rylan next entered the office. Atlas followed Beth in.
She didn't seem to notice that every step she took, the
Dane tracked her. He didn't let her out of his sight.

He had connected with her, Ry realized, although she
had yet to bond with him. In time she would, he hoped.
Rylan's closest friends and his entire family found the dog

likeable. But clumsy. Because of his size, Atlas didn't get invited to many social functions.

Rylan turned to catch Beth's reaction to the work area. She was completely engrossed by the setup. He'd chosen an L-shaped, space-saver desk. Roller chair. High-end technology. A big-screen TV hung on one wall. Television relaxed him. He had several staged throughout the house.

"Check out the desktop. My password is *Rogue*. You'll find a file labeled Obligations. My baseball and hometown commitments should be self-explanatory. I'm hosting a late-afternoon picnic at my house this Saturday for family, a few close friends, and team members. E-mail invitations were sent. Sixty guests, give or take. All adults. You'll need to put it together. Five days should be enough time."

She gave a slight start, but was quick to recover. "Do you want updates as I make the arrangements?"

He shook his head. "Not necessary, unless you hit a snag." As an afterthought, he added, "Contact Shaye Saunders should you need assistance. My sister is good at planning. She's coordinated charity benefits and board-walk events. Her phone number and e-mail address are in the computer file marked Family."

"Appreciated." Beth breathed easier.

"I have a main house line and a business iPhone," he went on to say. "I prefer text over a call when I'm away from the house. I'm not a man to talk on the phone for any length of time."

She nodded. "Text it is." Her gaze lowered then, lingering a second too long on his bare chest. Her eyes were a soft blue.

He didn't mind her looking at him as long as she wasn't into him. He had no designs on her. He stretched, scratched his stomach, and wrapped up the meeting. "As far as feeding the dogs, choose a recipe from the Organic Canine Cookbook. The dogs like all the meals." He turned then. "I need to get cleaned up. I'll be back shortly." He nearly tripped over Atlas on his way out. The Dane had dropped down beside Beth's chair, still eyeing her every move.

Rylan took the stairs two at a time to the second floor. He planned to stick around long enough to get Beth through lunch. He didn't care if the dogs got a bath or not, but food was a necessity. Especially for Atlas. He lived to eat.

Ry tossed his T-shirt in the clothes hamper, then dropped his board shorts and kicked off his flip-flops. He went into his bathroom, stepped into the shower, and set a hot, pulsing spray. Water sluiced and heated his skin. Loosened his muscles. He exhaled, giving thought to his afternoon. He had a lot to do.

A stop by the Rogues spring training facility was at the top of his list. He needed to meet with Jillian Cates—his sister-in-law, married to his older brother Aidan. She worked as the community liaison for the club, sponsoring and promoting events that brought fans and players to-gether. Spring training was the ideal time for fan appreci-ation. She wanted to discuss upcoming activities with him.

Ry was team captain, not by player vote but by execu-tive board decision. He had played for the St. Louis Colonels for twelve seasons and then been traded to the Richmond Rogues during their rebuilding year. At thirty-four, he was considered the old man. The average age of his teammates was twenty-five.

It wasn't easy being leader to players who had their own agendas and believed their own press. He'd worked his ass off, earning their respect. It had taken an entire season for the team to mesh and become a cohesive unit.

They had finally hit their stride last fall during the race for the pennant. They'd landed a Wild Card slot in the

National League East. Only to have the Atlanta Braves take the division championship. Rylan and the majority of players had stayed in Richmond during the off-season. They had watched film and honed skills. Built camaraderie. Focused on their future. A new season was upon them.

Those who hadn't stayed over the winter had filtered into town slowly.

My town, Rylan thought. He valued his family's heritage.

The majority of the players were a week ahead of schedule. Shortstop Brody Jones was the only married man on the team. The single guys wanted to check out the beach, boardwalk, and pier; then locate the nighttime hot spots.

The Chamber of Commerce boasted that the sun shone three hundred and sixty days during the year—which was a slight exaggeration. They discounted the rainy season. But Barefoot William was a sunbather's paradise despite the summer showers. No place on earth could compare to the coastal sugar sand and turquoise water.

Specialty shops with adjoining walls and multicolored doors lined the cement boardwalk, selling everything from Florida T-shirts and penny candy to designer jewelry, while kiosks on the long wooden pier offered sunglasses, sharks' teeth, shells, and hula hoops. Food carts served hot dogs, funnel cakes, cotton candy, and chili-cheese nachos.

Amusement arcades and carnival rides enticed the tourists further. A century-old carousel whirled within a weatherproof enclosure. Its walls of windows overlooked the Gulf. The whirr of the Ferris wheel was soothing, while the swing ride that whipped out over the waves sent pulses racing. The roller coaster had children raising their arms and cheering their bravery. Just beyond, metallic black bumper cars raced and collided on a metal floor.

The bars on the boardwalk flashed a lot of neon. The Blue Coconut and Lusty Oyster opened at noon to serve parched and sunburned patrons. Dress codes were obsolete. String and thong bikinis and swim trunks were as common as sportswear. The scent of coconut suntan lotion mixed with the piña coladas.

The crowd remained polite during the day, but got rowdy once the sun set. Wherever the ballplayers gathered, they would be followed. Female fans would stroke their egos and other parts of their anatomy. The guys dated with the same dedication they played ball. Fast, intense, and scoring big.

Couples connected on the morning side of midnight. The men went through nightly hookups and morning breakups like clockwork. It was a sexual cycle that caused female tears, some cursing, and the occasional knee to a player's groin.

Ry couldn't keep track of what the guys did on their own time. His main concern was that they showed up at the stadium with a winning mind-set. Preseason was crucial. They played in the Grapefruit League and needed to start out strong. To make a statement. If confidence and swagger won games, the Rogues would take the pennant this year. They just couldn't get too cocky.

The team was housed at Driftwood Inn, a hotel near the stadium. Each man had his own room. Ry had gotten permission from the general manager to alternate his own nights between the inn and his cottage. He liked his home. He needed to keep an eye on his dogs, even with Beth in attendance. Atlas could be a handful.

Taking a glycerin bar of eucalyptus soap from the plastic container on his shower rack, he scrubbed down his chest and arms. He washed his groin, then down his legs. The woodsy scent cleared his head. He continued mapping his day.

A stop at Barefoot William Retirement Village was a must. He wanted to see his grandfather Frank. His granddad had recently moved from his rural cedar stilt house built on one hundred acres to a condominium in a gated community. The change had been difficult for him. Ry hoped a game of gin would brighten the older man's day.

He owed Shaye and her husband Trace a visit, too. They were a power couple. Shaye ran Barefoot William Enterprises while Trace was CEO of Saunders Shores. They worked together on many building projects and both towns thrived.

Trace had fought to bring major league baseball to the Gulf Coast. Once the county commissioners unanimously voted to build the park, Trace had courted the team as did the bigger cities of Tallahassee and Jacksonville.

After several months of intense negotiation, Trace won over club owner James Lawless and his executive board. It would be a huge economic boost for the adjoining cities to have a major-league team start its season in southwest Florida.

Rylan added two final stops to his list before stepping from the shower—the bank and the barber. Theodore's was an old-fashioned barbershop on the boardwalk, specializing in classic, hot lather shaves, haircuts, and shoe shines. The shop had three vintage barber chairs and a striped-pole out front. Theodore Cates had been in business for forty years. His place was an institution. Appointments were required. Ry grinned. How many times had he squirmed in that barber chair as a kid? More times than he could count.

Standing on the vinyl floor, he toweled off. Finger-combed his hair. Once back in his bedroom, he crossed to his dresser and chose a pair of boxer-briefs. He dressed casual, selecting a light blue pullover and khaki slacks. Dark brown flip-flops were as close to going barefoot as he could get. He wasn't a man for shoes . . . if he could avoid them.

Returning downstairs, he found Beth and his dogs in the kitchen. It was the only room in the house that he'd renovated. His brother Aidan had done the work. He was a contractor. They'd bumped up the room's roof to double height for a soaring ceiling. The tongue-and-groove boards resembled nineteenth century planks. New oak beams acted as structural cross ties.

The large, all-white room was clad in bead board cabinets with nickel hardware. The modern range had a white enamel finish and vent hood. The apron-front sink had been a steal at an antique show. The center island was topped with old chestnut boards salvaged from the floor in the upstairs closet. Vintage red soda fountain stools surrounded the island where Rylan enjoyed his morning coffee. Old subway tiles completed the countertops. Clerestory windows flooded the kitchen with light.

Beth stood in a pool of sunshine. A red bandana held her wild hair. Her movements caused her crop top to creep up her back, flashing smooth skin and a narrow waist. She'd kicked off her sneakers and wore a pair of short pink and yellow floral socks trimmed in turquoise.

He squinted to read the writing at her ankle. *I Think I Can.*

She caught him staring. "My positive message socks. They're similar to a mental mantra, but on my feet. Not as good as yoga, but they keep me balanced."

He believed in staying positive. Life could shift and shake at unexpected moments. Stability was important to him.

Beth had located the organic cookbook and gathered the ingredients: ground turkey, carrots, apples, and broccoli. Atlas barked at her to move faster then nudged her thigh with his nose, making her laugh. Her laughter was light, feminine. Contagious.

Ry couldn't help but smile.

Beth handed Atlas a carrot, which he scarfed down. The Dane liked his vegetables. All but peas. He had the ability to find a single pea in his meal and spit it out. That had always amazed Rylan.

"How's lunch coming along?" he asked, crossing to her. Standing close, he felt the heat of her body. Despite having walked his dogs, her scent was fresh and very female. "Need any help?"

"I'm feeling confident," she said, stuffing the food processor with the fruit and veggies. She secured the top and then flipped the switch. The blades whirred and chopped. She went on to combine the ground turkey with the mixture. Then blended in two raw eggs. She scooped the ingredients into a rectangular baking pan and popped it in the preheated oven. Atlas stood before the stove, not moving except for his tail wagging back and forth.

Beth set the timer for twenty minutes before turning back to Rylan. "You received five calls while you were in the shower." She tapped her finger on a white sheet of paper near the microwave. "I printed out your messages, and also sent them to your iPhone."

"Read them to me, please." He was running late and could listen far easier than if he took the time to read each one.

Beth relayed the messages. She spoke quickly, precisely.

He paid attention. The first two calls were from his family. His older brother Dune invited him to stop by his volleyball clinic. Dune's wife Sophie offered to drop off groceries. No emergencies. He'd get back to them later in the day. If not tomorrow. The third and fourth calls were from his teammates.

"Halo Todd needs the name of a good tattoo artist. He, uh"—Beth's cheeks warmed—"wants to ink his groin."

Ry rolled his eyes, but wasn't surprised. Halo was keeping to Rogue tradition. Players of previous years had such tats. The right fielder would set the bar. His teammates would be inked before opening day. All but Rylan. He didn't always conform, either on or off the field. He believed in live and let live as long as the players got the job done.

"Esme at Inkcredible Tattoos on Breakaway Wave Drive does nice work." Or so he'd heard from his brother Zane. Zane had *Hurricane Hunter* on his left bicep. He'd felt no pain. However a tat to the groin could prove tender.

"Landon Kane wants to know where he can get the best deal on tires," Beth said, checking her list. "His Porsche has a flat."

When had he become Google? Ry wondered. The third baseman had an iPhone. Barefoot William had only one tire dealership. It was easy to find. "Send him to Rubber and Rims."

Beth looked at him to see if he was serious, then chuckled. "You made that up."

Lady was quick. "It will take Land a few hours to figure that out."

"What if he calls back?" Her concern was genuine. He liked that—having an assistant who looked out for his teammates was crucial to him. Even if the men drove him nuts sometimes.

"Tell him Gray's Garage on the southeast corner of Sunshine Drive carries tires at a good price."

Beth wrapped up with, "Your last call was from Ava Vonn."

Ry's grin came easy. He didn't try to hide his pleasure at hearing her name. She'd been one of the applicants for the PA position; a hot blonde with full breasts who spoke her mind. She'd flirted with him. Shamelessly. He'd been flattered but in the end, feared mixing business and pleasure.

"Ava would like to meet for drinks and dinner," Beth told him, keeping her voice professional, though he noted a hint of curiosity creeping into her rain cast eyes, "to compensate for her not getting the job."

Compensation worked for him. "Call Ava back and see if she's free tonight. Apologize for the short notice. If she's available, make a reservation for seven at The Pier House in Saunders Shores. The restaurant is popular and often booked a month in advance. Tell the manager I'd appreciate a table. He should be able to accommodate us. A view of the Gulf would be nice."

"Got it," Beth said.

"Then schedule an appointment at Theodore's Barber Shop for four, if possible. Shave and a haircut."

"Will do." She scrunched her nose. "Don't get your hair cut too short. You look good now."

Her compliment surprised him. He took it to heart. He eyed her, then suggested, "Shouldn't you be writing this down? iPhone, or there's a pencil and notepad in the drawer by the dishwasher."

She tapped her temple with her forefinger. "I have an excellent memory."

He could only hope she did. He didn't take her for the cerebral type, but he'd been wrong about women before. He wondered if there was more to Beth than met the eye.

He didn't have time to contemplate her secrets. The timer on the stove went off, and Atlas did his dinner dance. He turned in a circle. Once, then twice, and then stood there with his tongue hanging out. There was no denying the dog his lunch. Now.

Beth grabbed a pot holder from the counter, then removed the pan from the oven. Her mouth twisted as if she didn't know what to do next, and she glanced at Ry for guidance.

He reached beneath the sink and produced four dog

bowls in assorted sizes. "Dish up the food, but let it cool for a few minutes. Atlas gets half the batch. Rue gets the next largest portion and the dachshunds receive the smallest."

He pointed to two elevated metal food stands by the wall. Neat, perfect, and ready. "Atlas and Rue eat there; Oscar and Nathan by the back door. You can set their bowls on the floor. Keep an eye on Atlas. Don't let him steal anyone's meal. Rue nips him to back off. He overpowers the dachs."

Beth nodded and then proceeded to follow his directions. She'd held her own during the meal prep. Rylan was pleased.

He stayed in the kitchen while the dogs ate. There was one more thing left to do. He removed a white dish towel from a drawer and tossed it to Beth to prepare her. "Atlas wears his lunch."

The Dane went directly to her after he'd eaten. He tried to wipe his mouth on her shorts once again. She intercepted him with the drool towel—which he took as a toy. He grabbed it and started tugging. Tugging hard.

"Is he always so playful after he eats?" she asked, her voice breathy.

"Wait until you give him a bath," he warned.

She pulled a face but didn't let go of the towel.

"Don't hurt your back," Rylan said as she fought to keep her footing. Her socks slid on the hardwood floor. She leaned over so far he was afraid she'd fall. The back of her shirt fluttered, and he glimpsed her lavender bra. Her shorts rode up her butt cheeks. She had a tight little ass.

He averted his gaze. "Give it up, Beth. Once you release the towel, he'll lose interest."

The moment she let go, so did the Dane. "Good boy, Atlas," she praised, visibly relieved.

Ry pretended not to notice how exhausted she looked

after the tug of war. Her bandana had loosened and her hair sprang free. Wildly so. Her face was flushed. The Dane outweighed her by at least forty pounds. Words instead of force were her only way to control him. He hoped Atlas would listen.

"Stand firm with him," Ry said to Beth.

She looked at him dubiously.

"He's smarter than he looks."

"He has more expressions than a cartoon character."

That he did. Ry glanced at his watch. It was almost noon. He didn't have time to fix himself lunch, so he grabbed a Marathon protein bar from the cupboard. His meal on-the-go. "I'm leaving," he told her, ripping off the wrapper. He quickly went over his plans for the day, finishing with, "Text if you need me. I'll stop by the house later this afternoon to change clothes for my date tonight. I'll see you then."

The dogs trailed him to the front door. He patted each one then singled out Atlas. "Behave," he said firmly. "Later, Beth," he called before he slipped out.

"Have a good day." Her voice rose over the clatter of metal dog bowls as she loaded them in the dishwasher. "We'll be fine." She sounded competent.

Fine didn't last long. He wasn't surprised to receive a text from her before he reached the end of the block. Seemed there was a tiny war going on at his place.

Atlas is chewing on the leg of the living room couch.

Then another text. *Is he still hungry? Should I feed him again?*

And finally, he could almost see her frantically typing on the keypad. *Where are his toys?*

Two

Beth's stomach sank. She was going to be fired; she could feel it in her bones. The moment Rylan walked out the door, Atlas morphed into Jaws. He dropped down beside the living room sofa and began gnawing the front leg on the only piece of furniture in the room. His bites weren't small; he'd taken the entire wooden leg in his mouth. Chips flew from his lips. The couch wobbled. Tipped forward. One green overstuffed cushion slipped off. Atlas attacked it next. Ripping one corner before returning to the sofa leg.

The golden retriever and dachshunds barked excitedly, encouraging his bad behavior. Beth shook her head. She couldn't believe that gentle Rue and little Oscar and Nathan would side against her. Where was their loyalty? She'd made their lunch. How quickly they'd forgotten.

The barking didn't stop. Beth cupped her hands over her ears. How could three dogs make so much noise? Their barks bounced off the walls. Echoed down the hallway. She debated shouting, but doubted she would be heard. They were that loud.

Standing beside Atlas, she clutched her hands at her sides and raised her voice. "Stop that! No, Atlas, *no.*"

No fell on deaf doggie ears. She needed to find another way to get his attention. Circling to the opposite end of the couch, she gripped the armrest and attempted to scoot it away from him. In her socks, she had no traction and didn't get far. Her feet slipped, and she fell down on one knee. Pain shot up her thigh. There would be bruising.

Back on her feet, she put her weight behind moving the sofa several inches before Atlas got distracted. His ears suddenly pricked as if he'd heard something. Something she had not. What was up? Beth grew suspicious when he went from destroyer to deceivingly innocent. In seconds.

He trotted to his quilted burgundy dog bed along the far wall. There, he lay down, his chin resting on his paws. The other dogs gathered around him, too. They'd all gone quiet. The transformation was amazing to watch.

Beth stared at them and they stared back. She swore Atlas raised one brow. And that Rue winked at her.

She bent down and evaluated the damage to the couch and cushion. Sandpaper and paint wouldn't fix the crooked leg. The sofa was on a permanent tilt. The foam stuffing in the cushion spilled out. She flipped it over, but couldn't completely hide the tear. The cushion would need to be reupholstered.

She shook her finger at the Dane. "How could you, Atlas? You're making me look bad." Was that a gleam she saw in his eye? Or was she just imagining it?

Beth glanced toward a single bookshelf, secured to the wall below the wide-screen television. That gave her an idea. She crossed to it. Brown brick bookends supported mystery paperbacks and several hardbound biographies of famous baseball players.

She reached for a copy of Josh Hamilton's *Beyond Belief.* Perfect. It appeared the right thickness to balance the couch. For the time being, anyway. Until she could find a furniture repairman.

She was about to fit the novel under the leg when Rylan's voice stopped her cold. "Not Hamilton's biography."

She spun around. Her heart nearly failed. How long had he been leaning against the door frame, watching her? She hadn't heard him come in. She'd bet the batch of dog biscuits she planned to bake later that afternoon that Atlas had the hearing of a bat. He'd recognized the McLaren pulling into the driveway and never warned her. The big dog had gone from difficult to manageable with Rylan's return. Atlas had played her. Again.

Ry looked at her for a long moment, then shook his head at Atlas. Who did he blame for the mess? Her or his dog? She couldn't tell from his expression.

He moved then, crossing to the shelf. He made his own selection and tossed it to her. "*Planet of the Umps* will work better."

Her body tensed as she caught the book. It wasn't as thick as Hamilton's biography. She muttered a nervous "Thank-you" and quickly inserted it under the lopsided leg. The sofa still sloped somewhat. She returned Hamilton's bio to the shelf.

Ry crossed to the Dane. His expression pained. "What's with the chewing? This isn't like you, Atlas."

Beth watched as Atlas rolled onto his side, closed his eyes, and played dead. Fortunately, they were at the house and not on a walk, she thought. She bit back a smile, amused by the fact Atlas hadn't singled her out, and that he gave Ry a hard time, too.

"Don't ignore me, big boy," Rylan said on a sigh. His dog paid him no mind. Whatsoever.

"Where are his toys?" Beth asked, hoping to gain the dog's attention.

"They're in the hall closet." The tone of Ry's voice indicated he wasn't pleased by the Dane's pranks. "Atlas knows exactly where to find his wooden barbell, football, and tug toys. I put them away at night so I don't trip over them. He usually retrieves them at first light. He lays them all out on the living room floor."

"You mentioned he could open doors," she recalled. Atlas had skills. "What about the other dogs? Do they have their own toys?" The dachs were smaller than a football. They would have problems dragging it around the house. Even if it was deflated.

"Rue and the dachshunds aren't big chewers. Atlas will share his toys if one of them has the urge to gnaw. He plays dead to get attention at the most inopportune times." Ry rubbed the back of his neck and added, "You were hired to organize my life and keep the dogs company while I'm away. For whatever his reason, Atlas acted out. I don't get it, but I don't have time to figure it out. I have a tight schedule from one o'clock on today and can't stay long."

"Did Atlas cause your Richmond assistant any problem?" She was curious and hoped it wasn't just her.

Rylan shook his head. "Atlas pretty much ignored Connie. He ate and slept the day away when she worked."

Interesting. Beth took it all in. She strengthened her resolve to work through the big dog's theatrics. She cleared her throat, promised, "I won't bother you again. I refuse to let Atlas get the better of me."

"Do the best you can," Rylan said, supporting her. He then cut his gaze to the Dane. "He owes you an apology."

"He's sleeping."

"He's faking." Ry stood over Atlas. "Tell Beth you're sorry," he said in a firm tone.

Atlas cracked his eyelids. He blew what sounded like raspberries, then slowly rose. With his head bowed low, he came toward her, and Ry followed. The Dane sat before her, and Rylan circled behind her. The dog tilted his head to one side, appearing repentant.

Beth found it hard to believe, but she listened as Atlas

made a rumbling sound deep in his throat. She wasn't quite sure if he was actually apologizing or still griping at her.

She reached out and scratched his ear. "Forgiven," she said, expecting that would be the end of it.

It wasn't.

The Dane had spring in his hind legs and, before she could step aside, he jumped up and put his paws on her shoulders. Startling her. His sudden weight knocked her backward. She landed flush against Rylan.

She was short and Ry was tall. Her shoulder blades scraped low on his chest and her bottom bumped high on his thighs. She accidentally elbowed his balls. He sucked a sharp breath as she slid down his body. He caught her before she hit the floor. His left hand curved her hip and his right cupped her breast. His thumb brushed her nipple as he tightened his grip.

His heat spread over her. His scent was pure male. The back of her head pressed his groin. His abdomen flexed. His dick stiffened.

They both went still. Barely breathing.

Now what? Beth was afraid to move.

Atlas's bark broke them apart. His tail wagged. Almost as if he was pleased with what he'd done. Crazy dog.

Beth scrambled to her feet. She took a stumbling step away from Rylan, just managing to stay upright. It wasn't easy. She could still feel his hands on her. She looked down. Suddenly self-conscious. His touch affected her. Her nipples were visible points beneath the cotton of her top. Could he hear the rapid beat of her heart?

Rylan stared a second too long at her chest. He clenched the hand that had held her breast. He started to say something, but stopped. She didn't know if it was the puzzled look in his eyes or the way he worked his jaw, but her stomach fluttered as if something between them had changed. Something small but significant. Something she didn't quite understand.

Before Beth could ask him what was on his mind, he shifted his stance, then called to his dogs as he took his leave, "Try to be good." Was that frustration in his voice? Or something else?

Barks and a howl from Atlas followed him out the door.

Beth sighed with relief over his departure. She needed to focus on the tasks at hand. The picnic needed her immediate attention. She returned to her office. Booted her computer. Then sat scrunched on her chair as the four dogs settled on the floor around her. Jockeying for the best position, they didn't allow her much space. Atlas dropped down on his haunches and placed his paw on her left knee.

"Pretty sure of yourself, aren't you?" She gave the Dane her raised-eyebrow look. He nudged her forearm with his nose. She gave in and petted him.

She then returned Halo and Landon's phone calls before opening dozens of files. She scanned Rylan's online photo album. There were pics and captions of family gatherings from when he and his siblings were small. He was the fourth youngest son of Barbara and Robert Cates, and one year older than his sister Shaye. Beth smiled to herself over one photo in particular. Rylan as a toddler gripped a Louisville Slugger that was bigger than he was. He'd been destined to be a baseball player even at an early age.

He fascinated her. She was surprised by her curiosity. And unnerved by her attraction. That wasn't like her. She was cautious when it came to men. Her past relationships had fallen flat. She'd learned deception was the kiss of death.

Searching further online, she found photographs that depicted team parties. Whether at a bar, a club, or a restaurant, the Rogues could barely be seen for all the beautiful women surrounding them. Beth tugged on her cotton top. Plain and practical. Comfortable. Unlike the ladies in the photos. They all had long hair, deep cleavage, and curvy bodies. Their lips parted for kisses; their manicured fingers splayed on the men's shoulders, arms, chest, and places the camera dared not go.

So much for her close encounter with Rylan. He could never be interested in her. She wasn't his type. Not that he was her type either. She'd never dated an athlete.

Beth went on to skim a succession of pictures that focused on community events. Rylan participated in the Chalk Walk, where fans paid money to produce colorful chalk drawings alongside their favorite players on a long stretch of sidewalk in downtown Richmond. A class of sixth graders surrounded Ry. He was their hero.

The action shots came next. An amazing photo showed Ry scaling the centerfield wall. He'd grabbed a high fly ball and averted a home run. The man had jump. That must be his super power.

It didn't take Beth long to realize that Rylan Cates was immensely popular. A man in demand. Not only by his family, but by the community and his fans alike. Such was the life of a professional ballplayer, she gathered. She sensed there was more to him than that, however. He seemed a man of substance.

Looking over his schedule, she noted he did his best to accommodate all those around him. Ry didn't have a lot of free time. A few hours here and there didn't make for much of a private life. No wonder he needed an assistant.

"Back to work. No more excuses." She had a picnic to plan.

The truth was she was scared that she'd mess this up. She drew in a breath. Held it. Dispelled all negative thought. A previous mishap shouldn't affect her present. She was starting over. Beginnings were always good. She'd gotten the courage to leave her old life, strike out on her own, so surely she could plan one little event.

"I Think I Can," she chanted, repeating the mantra from her socks. She then typed Picnic, and started a Word file. Her fingers trembled over the keyboard. Organizing the get-together shouldn't be too tough. Rylan wanted late-afternoon casual. She didn't have to worry about ballrooms, bakers, caterers, decorations, photographers, entertainment. Or five hundred guests. Not even a self-centered bride and a drunken groom. Only the weather might give her pause since it was an outdoor event.

She shouldn't have a problem in southwest Florida, but Mother Nature could be fickle. Such unpredictability had arrived in a thunderstorm the previous summer. Her career as a party planner had died a slow, rainy death. She cringed, remembering everything that had happened so fast that June day in Potomac, Maryland, then moved beyond her control.

One moment the sky was clear and bright blue. The next, the day darkened to a nightmare shade of black. The air cooled. People shivered. No one had time to run for cover.

An unforgiving wind ripped across the waterfront lawn, tearing the romantic gauze drape from the outdoor reception tent. Lifting and sending it flying over the Potomac River. The strings of twinkling lights in the trees sparked and popped.

Heavy rain followed, drowning the canapés on the buffet tables. Delicate puff pastries squished like sponges. The goat cheese became paste. It was not a pretty sight.

Severe gusts pushed the bride and groom toppers on the wedding cake facedown in the buttercream fondant. The pink handmade sugar flowers dissolved. Crystal vases arranged with white and lavender roses tipped, spilled, the velvet petals torn from the stems.

*No one escaped the downpour. The society wedding ended
with drenched guests standing in ankle-deep water. The ladies'
satin party dresses and Giuseppe Zanotti heels were ruined. The
men's formal jackets drooped at the shoulders. Neck ties shriv-
eled. Their pants hung baggy at their butts.*

*The bride blamed Beth for the bad weather as if she'd released
the storm herself. Words were exchanged that could never be
taken back. That was only the beginning. Accusations about the
groom's infidelity soon flew around. The bride was horrified and
humiliated. Worse, the groom identified Beth as the other
woman in the couple's divorce.*

She shook her head, shaking away the painful memories
of the hurtful words that still rang in her ears. Truth be
told, she and the groom had once been involved . . . up
until the time he'd betrayed her. The man had dumped her
for the bride. He'd quickly come up with the maddening
story about having an affair with Beth—which was a total
lie. Yet no one had believed her. Everyone had turned
against her. She'd been his scapegoat.

He'd snuck around and sought her forgiveness six
months into his marriage. She couldn't believe his arro-
gance. She'd refused his advances.

Fortunately, those days were behind her. She had a pair
of maroon and brown checked socks in her suitcase with
the positive lime green message *When the Past Calls, Let it
go to Voicemail. It has Nothing New to Say.* She believed that
to be true.

She was fortunate that Barefoot William was a city of
sunshine and moderate temperatures. She would keep an
eye on the local forecast. She didn't need any surprises.

Returning to work, she proceeded to type a prep list for
the picnic.

She'd noticed a lawn maintenance service in Ry's con-
tacts and wondered if the backyard needed to be mowed
before the gathering. She decided to take a look. Carefully

pushing back her chair, she gently slipped Atlas's paw off her knee and stepped around the two sleeping dachs. Rue peeked at her as Beth left the room. Only Atlas followed her out. She had to smile. As far as he was concerned, they were joined at the hip.

The front doorbell chimed before she made it to the yard. Chimed and chimed. Someone was impatient. She went to see who was leaning on the bell. One ring would've been sufficient.

Atlas beat her to the door and pressed his nose to the narrow glass pane.

Beth peered around him. Two tall men stood outside on the porch, intimidating in their size. Muscular arms and seam-stretching shoulders. They were fit, firm, and superfine.

She let out a sigh of relief when Atlas woofed and wagged his tail. He seemed to recognize them. They looked familiar to her, too. From Rylan's online photo album with all the captions, she recognized them as Ry's teammates, right fielder Halo Todd and third baseman Landon Kane. Pictures didn't do them justice. They looked even better in person.

She cracked the door, only to have Atlas bolt past her. The door hit her in the hip. A sharp pain slammed through her. She pulled a face. That was her second bruise of the day.

"Atta-Boy," said Halo. He held his own as the Dane charged him. He bent and rubbed his knuckles over the dog's head. The scrub must have felt good. Atlas's eyes rolled back and he drooled. He leaned heavily against the man's leg.

Beth took the men in. Richmond Rogues baseball caps shaded their eyes. Light blue T-shirts were tucked into jeans worn low on their lean hips. She couldn't help but smile when she read the navy inscriptions.

Hello, My Name is Halo Cates.
Hello, My Name is Landon Cates.

She eyed them curiously. "You're not Cateses. What's with the shirts?"

Halo removed his cap and ran one hand through his thick black hair. He looked down at her; his eyes were dark green and scheming with humor. "We had the shirts made before we left Richmond," he told her, grinning. "Ry's our team captain. Being Rogues makes us brothers. The Cates family owns Barefoot William. We decided to have a little fun. We had shirts made for the starting lineup. It's good to be family."

The shirts had entertainment value, she had to admit. She wondered if Rylan would find them as funny as his teammates. She hadn't known him long enough to gage his reaction.

Halo gave her a body scan, slow and easy. He smiled. "You must be Beth, Rylan's PA. We spoke earlier." His voice was as deep as his dimples. He had the sexiest mouth she'd ever seen.

Landon winked at her. "I can see why Ry hired you."

Landon's wink would set female hearts racing, Beth thought. He had light brown eyes and a face so handsome women would hate to blink.

She wondered what Landon saw in her that she didn't see in herself. She'd qualified for certain aspects of the job, but not for all of them. She was definitely scoreless when it came to her looks. But Rylan's confidence in her motivated her to do her best. She would learn as she went.

Landon shot a look into the house. "We came to see Ry. Is he here?"

She shook her head. "Sorry, no. He had meetings and errands." And a date tonight, which she kept to herself. She needed to make Ry's dinner reservation, then confirm the time and place with Ava.

"When will he be back?" asked Landon.

"Late afternoon." Rylan hadn't been specific.

"How long have you worked for him?" Landon was curious.

She glanced at her watch. It was one o'clock. "Two hours and thirty-seven minutes."

"How's it going?" Halo asked. "Getting a lot accomplished?"

A sigh escaped her. "So far I've walked the dogs and made them lunch." Her activities didn't sound like much, but they had been time consuming.

Landon eyed Atlas. "Still eating organic?"

The Dane woofed.

Landon lowered his voice. "I'd sneak you a Milk Bone, buddy, but Ry would chew my ass."

"The dogs only get homemade treats," said Beth.

"Can't break Ry's rules," said Halo.

"I'll be baking peanut butter biscuits for them later."

"Lucky you, Atlas," Landon said.

The dog wagged his tail.

The conversation slowed. Beth had nothing more to say. She waited patiently for the men to leave. Still they lingered.

"So . . ." Landon said.

From Halo came, "So . . . Ry's not home. What should we do?"

"How about the beach and boardwalk?" she suggested, hoping to move them along so she could get back to work.

Landon shrugged. Indifferent. "I'm not feeling it."

"Me either," said Halo.

There was a lengthy pause before Landon asked her, "What's on your agenda, Beth?"

"I'm planning Rylan's picnic."

Picnic caught their attention. The men exchanged a

look. A long look. Their silent communication spoke volumes. She grew uneasy. Halo's eyes soon glinted, and one corner of Landon's mouth tipped up. She sensed that they had come to a decision without consulting her.

Leaving was ruled out. The men settled in. For the duration. Halo hiked his hip onto the porch railing. "Our day is free. We could help you."

Landon crossed his arms over his chest and leaned one broad shoulder against a post. "We know what Rylan likes in food, beer, and entertainment."

What was happening? Beth was at a loss. Were they restless and bored or did they have an ulterior motive? She felt it might be the latter, given their smug expressions.

They looked far too comfortable. Too solid. Too immovable. Too sure of themselves. They gave her little choice. They were there to stay.

She bemoaned that fact. What to do? Interacting with his teammates was part of her job description. She didn't want to be rude. She had only one choice. She would keep them. And put them to work.

She crooked her finger for them to follow her. "I was headed to the backyard when you arrived. The picnic will be outside. I wanted to see if the grass needed to be mowed."

Halo hopped off the porch railing. "We can advise you."

Landon pushed off the post. "I'll mow if it's needed. If not, we can sit on the porch and watch the grass grow."

Beth didn't want them sitting. She wanted them working.

"Let's cut through the house." Halo entered through the front door before Beth could object.

"He knows where he's going," Landon assured her. "We've been here once before. Not by invitation. We dropped by yesterday unannounced. Ry didn't even offer us a beer."

"Perhaps you caught him at a bad time."

"I don't think there's a good time with him when it comes to us."

Beth mulled over his words. "Maybe you should call ahead."

"Warn him we're in the neighborhood? He'd never pick up." Landon held the door for her. "Let's find Halo." He placed his palm low on her spine; came in behind her.

To her surprise, Atlas made a low sound in his throat. Not quite a growl, but more of a grumble. He butted between her and Landon, separating them. Beth bumped her hip on the door frame. Bruise number three. The Dane stuck to her side. Guarding her.

Landon lowered his hand and eased back. "What's up with that? I've never seen him so territorial. He doesn't want me near you." He raised his hands, palms out. "No touching, big boy, promise."

The Dane barked his approval.

They moved through the living room. "Ry still needs furniture," Landon observed. "I've never known anyone to live with so little." He stopped at the sofa, studied it. "Teeth marks. Slight tilt."

Beth glanced at Atlas. "He had a moment."

The dog turned in a circle, barked as if proud of himself. Rue and the two dachshunds wakened from their nap. Stretched and stood. Spotting Landon, they got all wiggly.

"Sweet Rue and the weenies." He bent to pet them.

After he gave them plenty of attention, they moved toward the kitchen.

They soon found Halo on the back porch, surveying the lawn. He'd taken off his baseball cap and shaded his eyes with one hand. "The grass is above the ankle. I say we mow. I've met Ry's family. His sister Shaye likes to go barefoot. So does his older brother Dune."

"This is one big yard," Beth admired. The size would accommodate numerous afternoon activities and conversation areas. A buffet table would fit nicely on the porch.

"We can also cut back a few tree branches," said Halo. "No one wants to get poked in the eye. Maybe trim the rose and gardenia bushes, too."

Beth wasn't sure that was a good idea. "Trimming is an art. Do you know what you're doing?"

Landon grinned. "We learn as we go. We could turn the boxwood hedge into a train topiary."

"No train."

Her anxious expression had Halo saying, "Nothing will be ruined. Besides, nature grows back."

They looked determined. For whatever reason, they'd taken on Rylan's picnic preparations as their own. It was a bit disconcerting.

"Tell us what you're planning," Landon said.

"We'll make it happen," said Halo.

She claimed the moment and shared her thoughts. "I want everyone to feel comfortable. Each guest will know someone at the picnic. There should be areas to gather and talk."

"Ry's family is pretty cool," said Halo. "His hometown friends that we've met are nice, too."

"We need to make sure everyone has a good time," Beth continued. "I scanned Rylan's online photo album and noticed Shaye likes croquet. There was a photo of her playing on the beach. Dune played pro-volleyball. There's plenty of room in the yard for a court. I want to set up both games." She stared at the enormous banyan tree that shaded the porch. "A wraparound trunk bench would draw people to sit and visit. Picnic tables are a must. Maybe a couple porch swings. I'll locate a rental service."

"I'll haul the outdoor furniture, if the company doesn't deliver," Halo said, donating his time. "I have a pickup truck."

Beth appreciated his offer. "The picnic starts at four on Saturday. I'll have soft drinks and beer available. Food will be served at six. People can eat and run or hang out. It gets dark by seven. I'll need lighting of some kind."

"Tiki torches," suggested Halo.

Beth shook her head. "No fire."

"Christmas tree lights?" asked Landon.

"Too holiday." She bit down on her bottom lip, decided. "Large solar lanterns would work well. I can hang them in the trees. I'll set them out in the sunshine during the day and they'll glow brightly at night."

Halo scratched his chin. "How do you know this party stuff?"

Beth had loved planning parties for as long as she could remember. Tea parties for her dolls and stuffed animals. Birthday parties for her friends. Decorating for high school dances. Becoming entertainment chairman for her college sorority. Hosting small family gatherings. Then opening her own business. Sadly, failure had come with her first society event. The bride's family was old money. Influential and powerful. The community was small and tight. Gossip was their second language. No one wanted to hire her after the wedding fiasco.

She'd yet to gather her courage to start over in a new city. Although she hoped to someday. She looked up at Halo. "I visualize, then create." It was as simple as that.

Landon scanned the yard and pointed to the far corner. "There's a shed. Let's see if Ry has a riding mower and garden tools. If he does, we're looking at an hour max." He jumped off the porch.

Halo took the wide wooden stairs. They headed for the shed, which appeared a hundred years old. It leaned to the left as if blown by a mighty wind. Perhaps it had even withstood a hurricane. The roof slanted dangerously. The glass in the solitary window was cracked.

Landon pushed on the door. The rusted hinges stuck. He put his shoulder to it, and it creaked open. The two men peered into the darkness, then stepped inside.

Beth gave a shiver. They were braver than she was. How many spiders called the shed home? she wondered. Snakes? She suddenly felt a little guilty that she hadn't shared with the guys that Rylan had a lawn service.

She shrugged. The two men had stepped into her day and seemed intent on staying. She'd let them clip and mow. Then send them on their way.

Atlas still stood by her side, she realized. Rue and the dachshunds had stretched out on the wide porch. The golden was attentive. Oscar and Nathan snored.

"Hot damn. A classic push mower," Landon shouted from the shed. He sounded excited. He appeared moments later, pushing a manual reel mower. "My granddad belongs to an old lawn mower club in Milwaukee. This model is rare. The handle's solid, but the blades need to be sharpened. I'm hoping Rylan has a sharpening stone in the garage."

Halo was right behind Landon. "The edge shears need to be oiled. I'll check for tool lube. The pole pruner seems okay, although the rope's twisted."

The lawn equipment was ancient, Beth thought. They'd be putting brawn and muscle into cleaning up the yard. It was a project that would last longer than planned. The weather was temperate, yet they would still work up a sweat.

She couldn't believe these elite athletes were choosing yard work instead of the beach. They would be instantly recognized the moment they stepped onto the sand. Women's fingers would itch to rub suntan oil on their bodies. They would've gotten lucky.

Instead of bikinied babes and slick skin, they cornered the cottage on their way to the garage. The two moved around Rylan's property as if they owned the place. Beth wondered what Ry would think of such familiarity. She hoped he wouldn't mind.

Halo and Landon were hyped to work when they returned to the yard a short time later. They had slipped on heavy duty leather work gloves to avoid blisters. Landon carried a sharpening stone and Halo a rusted can of WD-40.

Once the equipment was in working order, Landon called to her. "We'll start at the back boundary and progress toward the porch. We should have enough room for the volleyball and croquet courts."

We. It had become a group project. The guys were being supportive. Her initial angst left her, yet niggling suspicion lingered. She still felt they had a hidden agenda for being at the cottage. If so, it would eventually be revealed.

Beth went inside, Atlas on her heels. The big dog sat down in the kitchen and stared at the stove . . . as if he was waiting for food to come out of the oven.

"I owe you biscuits, don't I? I could make them now."

Atlas gave a happy bark.

She retrieved the doggie cookbook from the counter where she'd left it, scanned the index, and flipped to the Treats section. The recipe for peanut butter biscuits had a big star in the upper right-hand corner of the page. She figured it was a favorite of the dogs.

She preheated the oven and lightly greased a baking sheet, then selected a large mixing bowl and located a spatula. She went to work. Atlas rested his chin on the counter, sniffing as she measured and stirred together the egg yolk, peanut butter, and honey. Once the ingredients were thoroughly blended, she added the rice flour and wheat germ. Atlas smacked his lips.

She next turned the dough out on a floured board and rolled the mixture to a one-quarter inch thickness. Using a medium-size dog-shaped cookie cutter she'd found in the cupboard, she cut out the shapes and set them on the baking sheet. Before putting them in the oven to bake, she brushed the tops with egg white.

Atlas tried to snag an uncooked treat. He would've eaten the batter raw had she let him. She did not. She held the baking sheet over her head—which was awkward. She wasn't going to let him get the better of her. She opened and closed the oven door without his interference. She patted him on the head, praised his patience.

Cooking time was twelve minutes, followed by cooling on a wire rack. He would have to wait a while longer.

Beth headed for her office. She could accomplish a lot in a short time. She settled on the edge of her chair and Atlas settled at her feet. She turned on the computer and went to e-mail. According to the information listed under Ry's brother Dune, besides professional volleyball, he also ran a local volleyball clinic.. She took a chance and sent him a message, asking to borrow a net, poles, and volleyballs for the picnic. She fired off a second e-mail to Shaye, hoping she had a croquet set. If neither responded, she'd move to Plan B and rent the necessary equipment.

Beth was surprised when Shaye and Dune responded within minutes. Both would be in the neighborhood shortly and could drop off her recreational requests. Beth was relieved, clicked on REPLY, and thanked them.

She then called Ava Vonn and extended Rylan's invitation to dinner. The woman gushed her acceptance and shared her relief at not being hired. She confided that Rylan would never date his employee. The woman planned to see him often—which was more information than Beth cared to hear.

She told Ava she would get back to her once the reservation was set. By the time their phone call ended, Beth had a knot in her stomach. Ava made her uncomfortable. She sounded possessive. And far too sure of herself.

The scent of peanut butter drifted in from the kitchen. Atlas woofed and trotted back to the stove. Beth had two phone calls yet to make—to the restaurant and the barber shop. She would get to them shortly. She didn't want the dog treats to burn.

She shut down the computer, slipped on her discarded Keds, which were under the desk, and left her office.

Halo and Landon burst through the back door just as she was removing the biscuits from the oven. She set the hot tray on a wire rack to cool then looked at the men. Sweat dampened Landon's brow. Leaves stuck to Halo's T-shirt. They smelled like the outdoors—mowed grass and sunshine.

Rue and the dachshunds trailed in behind them.

"I could use a beer." Landon removed his gloves and crossed to the refrigerator.

"Peanut butter cookies look good." Halo popped a warm dog treat into his mouth before Beth could stop him.

Atlas grumbled loudly.

"What's with him?" asked Halo.

"You, uh, ate one of his biscuits."

Halo's chewing slowed, but he didn't spit out the treat. "Organic?"

"The ingredients won't hurt you."

Halo swallowed. "Not bad." He broke a second treat in half to make sure it had fully cooled. "Here big guy," he said, handing it to Atlas. The Dane took it.

"Cold one?" Landon asked Halo.

Halo nodded, and Land tossed him a BrewDog.

"Do you want a glass?" Beth offered.

"Bottle's fine," said Halo.

"We haven't had lunch," Landon said next. "Any chance of a sandwich?"

Beth looked up from feeding the dogs their treats. The tray of biscuits was almost gone. Atlas scarfed three treats for every one consumed by the other dogs.

The Dane went after Beth when he'd finished his snack. She was ready for him, dish towel in hand. She cleaned off his face before he could wipe his mouth on her cutoffs. Atlas wagged his tail.

She crossed to the refrigerator, nudging Landon aside. Rylan ate as healthy as his dogs, she noted. There were lots of fruits, vegetables, cheeses, along with a Ziploc of organic sliced chicken breast. She pursed her lips, debated what to fix the men. A quick look in the bread box, and she decided on eight-grain bagels with melted cheese.

"That's it? One grilled cheese bagel and a pear?" Halo grunted when she passed him a plate. He sat next to Landon on a soda fountain stool at the kitchen island. His face was pinched as if he was starving to death. "I'm a growing boy, sweetheart."

"I'll feed you but I won't fatten you up," she said.

"I'd work better after two sandwiches," Halo insisted

"One." She stood firm. She had no idea how Rylan would react to her feeding his teammates or to their drinking his imported beer.

Halo was on his second. The guys tended to take over, whether they meant to or not.

The chiming of the doorbell sent Atlas scrambling. He beat Beth to the front door by the length of his tail. She looked through the glass. A pretty blonde with curly hair and rainbow-framed sunglasses stood on the porch. A rectangular wooden storage box labeled CROQUET was propped against her hip. Shaye Cates-Saunders had arrived.

Beth opened the door, and Atlas once again bounded past her to get to Shaye.

"Hello Big Lug," Shaye greeted the dog. Atlas danced around her. She smiled at Beth. "I'm Shaye, Rylan's sister."

"I'm Beth Avery, Ry's PA."

Before the women could speak further, a white van pulled into the driveway. CATES VOLLEYBALL CLINIC was highlighted in black on the panel door. The rear doors were cracked, and metal poles were visible. A red flag hung from the ends.

A very tall, lean man in jeans and a gray T-shirt climbed out. His shirt had a picture of a volleyball and the script *Go for the Kill.* He walked around the hood and opened the passenger side door. A pretty, petite, very pregnant woman in a light green sundress stepped out. The man curved his arm about her shoulders and held her close as they crossed to the porch. He matched his longer stride to her shorter steps.

"My brother Dune and his wife Sophie," Shaye said as the couple approached. "This is Beth Avery, Rylan's assistant."

Sophie gave Beth a soft smile. "Rylan is a busy guy."

"My brother's organized, but his life can be overwhelming." Dune appealed to Beth, "A confidential request, please. I'd consider it a personal favor if you could find an hour or two for him to relax each night. Close off his life to the public." It was obvious Dune cared about his brother. Recently retired from playing professional beach volleyball, Dune understood the importance of privacy and downtime. Of exhaling and rejuvenating.

"I'll do my best," Beth said.

"Hey, look who's arrived." Halo appeared in the doorway. He crossed to Dune and thumped him on the back. He smiled at Shaye and said, "Hi, Mom," to Sophie.

Sophie blushed.

Shaye caught sight of Landon as he came to stand behind Halo. "Look who's already here." She raised one eyebrow over their T-shirts. "*Family,* really?"

"Ry-man is like a brother to us," said Landon.

"A brother who's not home." Shaye eyed the men suspiciously. "So why are you here?"

"We didn't know he was away when we dropped by," Halo said. "We hadn't planned to stay long, but Beth begged us to help with the picnic."

Shaye glanced at Beth. "She did, did she?"

"Begged them on bended knee," Beth said straight-faced.

That made Halo smile. "She got us to volunteer."

"To do what?" asked Dune.

"Yard work," said Beth.

"Landon's mowing and I'm trimming," said Halo.

Dune looked uneasy. "You trust them with a mower and trimmer?"

"It's a push mower and rope operated pole saw," Beth informed him.

"Still, there are blades," said Shaye.

"We're being careful." Landon glanced at the van. "Can we help you unload the volleyball equipment?"

Dune nodded. "There are poles, a net, two volleyballs and a pole hole digger. There's a tape measure in the glove compartment to mark off the court. I picked up bags of mulch to mark the side and back lines."

"I'm on it." Landon went down the steps two at a time and jogged toward the van.

Dune gazed fondly down on his wife. "Go sit inside, Sophie. Put your feet up."

She nodded, and he went after Landon.

"I've got the croquet set." Halo took it from Shaye. He shouldered the box; headed back through the house.

The women remained on the front porch. "When is your baby due?" Beth asked Sophie.

Sophie placed her hand on her tummy, smiled. "Mid-July. You'd think I was delivering today the way Dune hovers."

The man was protective of his woman. Beth liked that fact. "Boy or girl?"

"Dune said he didn't have a gender preference, but when the doctor announced we were having a boy, my husband jumped as high as he once did when spiking a volleyball for match point."

"Congratulations." Beth held the front door open for Sophie and Shaye. "You're welcome to sit on the couch, although it's a bit lopsided," she said to Sophie. "Or you might prefer a kitchen stool."

"A stool is fine," Sophie said as she entered the house. "I'll have a good view of my husband and the yard."

"Are you all moved in?" Shaye asked Beth as they passed through the living room. "Do you need anything?"

"I'm in and settled. I'm comfortable," Beth assured her. Her wants were few. She could survive most anything for eight weeks.

The women reached the kitchen. Atlas continued to stick to Beth's side, bumping her as they walked. The other dogs had returned to the back porch. All three were awake and actively watching the lawn work and the construction of the volleyball court.

Shaye stood at the door. "Halo set the croquet box near the banyan tree," she noted. "Should I set it up for you? I know the spacing and dimensions. I have a free hour."

Beth liked Shaye. Her assistance was appreciated. "That would be great. I can check croquet off my list."

"Is your list long?" Shaye asked. "You seem to be going all out. Rylan's previous picnics were eat and run. He grilled hot dogs and hamburgers, and we stood and ate. There was small talk, but no activities."

Beth questioned herself. "Am I doing too much?"

"You're putting together the perfect picnic." Shaye sounded confident. "Volleyball is a big sport in our family. I kick butt in croquet."

Beth was relieved. She didn't want to overdo it.

Shaye tilted her head, looked out the kitchen window. "Halo and Landon like to play; they're not usually so helpful. Makes me wonder why."

"They haven't said. I'm sure we'll find out soon enough."

"Rylan is an actual grown-up in a sport of overgrown boys. He and Brody Jones are the most stable players. Ry's the oldest team member and Brody's married. All the players get serious on game day, but trouble always follows Halo and Landon from the ball park."

Beth smiled. "I can believe that."

"How are you doing with the dogs?" Shaye next asked.

Atlas looked up at Beth as if he understood Shaye's question.

Beth scratched his ear. "We're slow to reach an understanding. I'm trying to fit in."

Shaye stared at her then, a curious, yet evaluating look in her eyes. "You'll be fine. Rylan wouldn't have hired you if he didn't believe you could do the job."

"I hope you're right," Beth said softly.

"I am." Shaye turned to her sister-in-law. "Sophie, do you need anything before we head outside?"

Sophie's lips twitched. "I'm capable of getting a glass of water on my own."

"Yes, you are," Shaye agreed. "However, take advantage of family. We want to pamper you."

Shaye motioned Beth onto the porch. Atlas went, too.

He gently latched his mouth onto Beth's wrist and tugged her forward.

"What?" Beth asked. The dog's teeth grazed her skin, but he didn't bite down.

"Follow him." Shaye recognized the dog's request. "He won't let go until you do."

Down the steps they went.

Atlas led her to where Dune was digging holes for the metal volleyball posts. The Dane stopped and eyed the small pile of dirt. He released Beth's hand and began to dig his own hole. He was an earth-mover.

"A little wide and way too deep," Dune said when the dog's shoulders could barely be seen. "We're not tunneling to China."

"Atlas, over here." Beth encouraged him across the court to the X that Dune had marked with mulch. To where the second pole would be set. "Let's try a smaller hole here."

Everything Atlas did, he did in big way. There was nothing small about the next hole either. He dug faster than a backhoe. Dirt flew, and Beth watched as Rylan's lawn took a beating. She was about to call Atlas off, when he suddenly retreated from the hole on his own.

He looked around as if he sensed someone or something that Beth didn't.

That someone was Rylan Cates. He stood at the corner of the cottage, partially obscured by an overgrown gardenia bush. His stance was wide; his hands jammed into the pockets of his khakis. Atlas ran toward him. Rue and the dachshunds dashed down the porch steps and barked their greetings. Ry petted and spoke to each one of them as if they were his kids.

Once again, Beth wondered how long he'd been there. Watching what was going on. Taking it all in. He had a way of showing up without her hearing him. His profile was sharp, serious. His stance, tense.

He nodded to his brother and sister. They waved back.

He then narrowed his gaze on Halo and Landon.

Beth hesitantly walked toward him. Her heart skipped, missing beats. "You're home early." It was three o'clock.

"Apparently not soon enough." He paused. "What's the deal with Halo and Landon?"

"Picnic prep. They stopped by, looking for you."

"I wasn't home."

"They—" *stayed.*

Rylan sensed her reluctance to rat them out. "Made themselves at home." He knew them well.

"They've been working hard. Mowing and trimming."

"Not so hard now." His blue eyes darkened. "Landon's juggling volleyballs and Halo's playing croquet."

Three

Rylan noticed his teammates' T-shirts when they crossed the yard to speak with him. Landon tossed a volleyball in the air as he walked, and Halo swung a croquet mallet by his side. Ry wasn't surprised by their shirts. They ran with a thought without ever expecting repercussions. What they saw as funny, he found mental.

"Hello, *brothers*."

"We got a shirt made for you, too," said Landon.

"I'll pass. I already know who I am."

"We like being Cateses," Halo said.

"I bet you do. You're making yourselves at home, I see."

Halo side-eyed Beth. "We came to see you, and she begged us to stay. We're planning your picnic."

Beth scrunched her nose, but didn't out Halo. She appeared calm, yet her eyes gave her away. The color was more gray than blue. Frustration? Possibly.

"You're damn lucky we stopped in," Landon said. "Otherwise there'd be a wading pool, slip and slide, and bounce house in your backyard on Saturday. Beth can be such a kid. We talked her into volleyball and croquet."

Rylan shook his head. The men were all tongue-in-cheek, teasing her. She had yet to say a word—which only pushed them further.

"She fed me peanut butter dog treats," came from Halo.

"She forced us into that creepy shed to get the yard equipment," Landon added.

Beth rolled her eyes at that.

"You could've called Lawn Rangers," Rylan said to her. "It would've made your life easier."

"And mine, too." Halo rested the mallet against his leg, slipped off his work gloves, and held up his right hand. The skin was red between his thumb and forefinger. The leather hadn't prevented a blister on his palm from using the hedge clippers. He glared down his nose at Beth. "There was no mention of a lawn service," he growled.

"You took over before I could tell you about it." Her eyes were blue—the color of satisfaction.

Halo slapped his gloves across his palm. His face was hard, then hinted at a smile. "Touché, babe. Game on."

She shook her head. "Game over."

Landon lobbed the volleyball to her, and she tossed it back. "We like her," he said matter-of-factly.

The approval was unexpected. Beth would be dealing with them on occasion. They could be difficult. Pushy came naturally to them. They were used to getting their own way. Which she had witnessed today. Somehow she'd withstood their company. A good sign as far as Rylan was concerned.

How did *he* feel about her? Ry asked himself. He self-consciously flexed his hand. The feel of her breast still lingered on his palm. Soft, warm, full. Long after he'd caught her.

He wasn't a man to capture moments. That wasn't like him.

"Give us five minutes?" he requested of her, shifting his attention to his teammates.. What he had to say to Halo and Lander, he preferred to do privately. Word of their night out had reached him. The guys had screwed up. He wanted to hear their side of the story before he passed judgment.

Beth nodded and took off with the dogs. She chased Atlas across the yard toward Dune. Rue, Oscar, and Nathan returned to the porch. His brother had worked fast, Ry noted. The poles and net were set and Dune was measuring the sidelines.

Atlas tore open a bag of mulch before Beth could stop him. Mulch flew in all directions. *"Sit!"* she commanded.

Atlas looked at her with a mouthful of twigs. He sputtered, spat, and tried to wipe his mouth on her cutoffs. She jumped back, and he dropped down on his haunches. The big boy had behaved.

Rylan smiled to himself. There was a first time for everything. He felt inordinately pleased.

He turned to Halo and Landon, only to find them staring after Beth. She held their interest.

"Is she yours?" Halo asked Ry.

"She works for me."

"Then she's available," Landon assumed.

Rylan wasn't sure he wanted Beth dating his teammates. "Clear it with Atlas."

The men glanced at the Great Dane.

Seriously? Rylan thought. *They'd better not try to bribe Atlas with a Pup-peroni stick.* He moved on. "Tell me about your altercation last night at the Lusty Oyster. You promised my cousin Ron Nash that you'd reimburse him for damages. He just texted me. You've yet to pay up."

"The afternoon's young," Halo said. "We'll get to Ron soon enough. I plan to compensate him, even though the damages weren't my fault."

"It's never your fault, Halo."

"This time it really wasn't." Landon came to his buddy's defense. "Some guy's date came on to Halo. She straddled his lap. Tried to slip him her tongue. Her date was drunk. He got mad and took a swing at Halo. Halo warned him off. The guy didn't listen. He gave Halo a shove. Halo's chair rocked back, and he and the woman knocked into a table. The table tipped, taking out a second chair. Halo's chair broke when they hit the floor. The table was chipped.

"There were only six people in the bar. Few witnessed the incident. Ron escorted the dude and his date to the door. I cleaned up, and Halo offered to pay for the table and chair."

A muscle ticked along Rylan's jaw. Ron's accounting differed from Landon's. His teammates were creative. They formulated excuses to counter whatever trouble they might face. According to his cousin, the bar had been packed. He'd turned away customers. Halo had pursued the brunette from the moment he walked through the door, while her date played darts. They'd slow danced to music from the juke box. Pressing bodies and making out like lovers. They'd drawn a lot of stares.

Once the dart game ended, the man came looking for his date. He found her with Halo, who had his hands up her shirt. The man back-tackled Halo. The brunette was taken down along with the men. She rolled to the side. Saved herself. The crowd stepped back. Punches were thrown, knocking the men into tables, chairs, and bar stools. Beer was spilled, shot glasses broken, and baskets of pretzels upended. The man left the bar with a black eye and split lip. Halo walked away without a scratch. He was damn lucky the man hadn't darted his ass.

Rylan hoped to avert another bar fight. He eyed Halo's T-shirt. "Wear the shirt, walk the walk. There are a lot of available women in town. Avoid one with a date."

"What if she's really, really hot?"

"Take a cold shower."

"We came by your cottage to make amends," said Landon.

Ry had figured as much. They'd tried to get back in his good graces. "Yard work doesn't make up for a busted bar."

Landon presumed, "We thought it might."

"Think again."

"It sucks to be the black sheep of the family," Halo said.

"At least we got to meet Beth," said Landon.

All three men looked in her direction. Rylan ran one hand down his face, concerned by what he saw. Atlas had sunk his teeth into a volleyball. His jaws were clamped tight. Beth was bent over, her bottom in the air, trying to retrieve it. Her ass wiggled with her attempts. Her cutoffs barely covered her butt cheeks.

"Blessed Mary," Halo muttered under his breath.

Landon whistled low. "I like, a lot."

Rylan was about to call to her when Dune announced, "You owe me a volleyball, Ry."

"Atlas!" Rylan got the Dane's attention. The dog trotted over to him.

Beth came, too. She held out her hand for the ball. Atlas dropped it at her feet. She picked it up, squished, deflated, and damp with drool. "Your bite is worse than your bark," she said on a sigh.

Sophie Cates appeared on the back porch just as Dune finished outlining the perimeter of the volleyball court with mulch. He collected the pole hole digger, the empty plastic bags, and crossed to her. "Ready to leave?"

Sophie's smile came softly. "I'm ready for my nap."

"Me, too." Dune's whisper carried. "We'll rest together." He slipped an arm around his wife, bent low, and kissed her—without regard for those looking on.

Rylan liked the fact his brother was so affectionate with her. She was so taken by her husband's kiss, she clung to his arm.

"We're gone." Dune waved to them.

"Thanks for the volleyball equipment," Beth said gratefully.

Dune gave her a thumb's up. "I'll bring an extra ball on Saturday. Atlas can keep the one he crushed."

Shaye was also ready to leave. The wooden storage box in hand, she stopped by the group on her way out. "Croquet is all set," she told Beth. She took the mallet from Halo and put it away. "I'll put the box in the garage on my way out. Let me know if there's anything else you might need." She gave Rylan a sisterly hug, bumped fists with Halo and Landon, then took off, too.

"Dune and Shaye were very helpful," Beth told Ry.

"So were we," Halo reminded her.

"The yard looks decent." Ry shaded his eyes against the late afternoon sun. "What's with the hedge?"

Halo looked at his handiwork. "Can't you tell? It's a topiary. A train."

"Can't see it," said Ry.

But Beth could. She tilted her head and said, "The engine and caboose are recognizable."

"It's what's in-between that falls short," said Landon. "The cars look like camel humps."

"You could do better?" Halo challenged him.

"Look at the yard," Landon pointed out. "Lawn striping. A ballpark grass pattern."

It did look good, Rylan had to admit. He also liked the way the volleyball court was set up in the far corner. And how the game of croquet would be played beneath the banyan tree. There'd be lots of shade. The picnic was taking shape. Far better than he'd expected.

Halo shifted beside him, growing restless. The man seldom stood still. He had energy to burn. He worked out three times a day. He made his teammates nuts in the dugout during a ball game. He never sat down. Instead he paced. Sport-driven.

He glanced at his watch. "It's after three. We're done here. We need to go by the Lusty Oyster." He grinned. "Just in time for Happy Hour." He nudged Beth with his elbow. "Join us, babe?"

She shook her head. "Thanks, but no. I'm still working."

"Another time, then," said Landon.

There was a glint in Halo's eyes when he said, "Ry can be a slave driver. Come work for me. I could use a personal assistant."

"Yeah, so could I." Landon clearly liked the idea. His grin came slowly. Deviously. "Any chance we could steal you from Rylan?"

"We'd pay you more than you're making now and offer better benefits," Halo enticed. "I could be part of your benefit package."

"We're better looking than the old man," said Landon. "And a whole lot more fun. What do you say? Join us?"

Rylan was about to say something, but decided against it. How would Beth react to their offer? He was about to find out.

She had their number. "Neither of you needs an assistant," she said flatly. "You're impulsive and competitive. You want what Ry has. At the moment that's me, working for him. Am I right?"

Halo put his hand over his heart. "You wound me."

"She saw right through us," said Landon.

"My job is for eight weeks," Beth told them. "The length of time I'm in town. It fits me perfectly."

Rylan listened when Halo asked, "Then what? Where will you go after spring training?"

She shrugged a slender shoulder. "Here and there. Anywhere and everywhere."

"The lady is elusive," said Landon.

"We have two months to learn her wicked ways," Halo teased.

Beth rolled her eyes. "I have no wicked ways."

"Hang around us and you soon will," said Landon.

"Your play date is over, guys," Rylan said, moving them along. "I met with our community liaison, Jillian Cates, this morning. Tomorrow we're putting our footprints in cement at the stadium plaza. Jill's set up media coverage. Photos, followed by interviews."

He paused, continued with, "It's tourist season. The snowbirds have arrived. There's a lot going on in town. The Gallery Walk opens to the public late Tuesday afternoon. International and local artists display their photography and paintings along the boardwalk near the pier entrance. Shaye organized the event. Try and make an appearance. Be supportive. Buy something."

"Anyone paint nudes?" asked Halo. The man had *naked* on his brain.

Rylan shrugged. "Doubtful, the event is family oriented. But see for yourself."

"We're gone." Halo handed Beth his work gloves.

Landon gave her his gloves, too. "Later, sweet Beth."

"What about the lawn equipment?" Rylan called after them. "It needs to be put away." The men had left the mower and tools where they'd last used them.

"Not it," Halo cast over his shoulder.

"Not it," Landon quickly seconded.

"I'm it," Beth muttered.

"It's your turn to go into the shed," Halo said from the corner of the cottage. "Watch out for bats." Both men disappeared down the driveway.

Rylan shook his head. "Idiots."

"*Your* idiots," Beth said. "I didn't mean to eavesdrop, but your voices carried. I heard them apologize for the bar fight. They respect you."

The respect was not always evident.

"We all have our own way of righting a wrong," she added.

"The guys are wrong a lot," he stated. "They're like kids. Sorry about something at least once a day. I don't want them making amends at the cottage whenever they get disruptive in town."

"You're all family, or so their T-shirts say."

"They'll take advantage of being Cateses while they're here, and they'll be obnoxious about it. I don't need any more brothers. I grew up with three."

"Dune seems like a nice guy," she said. "I hope you don't mind that I contacted him and Shaye. Picnics need games. I'd rather borrow than rent equipment. They were quick to respond."

"Working with them is fine. However, next time Halo and Landon show up, don't answer the door. They're aimless until spring training starts. They can't camp out on my porch."

He scratched his jaw, felt the stubble. "I'm headed to Theodore's Barber Shop for my shave and a haircut."

He could tell by the immediate change in her expression that something was wrong. It was.

"Oh, no . . ." she murmured. Her face was pale. Her eyes were wide. She clutched her hands before her. The work gloves slipped through her fingers.

Atlas picked one up, shook it, and held it in his mouth. Ry snagged it from him before he could gnaw a hole in the leather. He then picked up those on the ground.

"I didn't make your appointment," Beth confessed. "Halo and Landon showed up, and time got away from me. I'm so sorry."

He could live without a haircut. What about the dinner reservation? "The Pier House?" he inquired, already knowing the answer. The look on her face said it all.

"I can try for a table now," she offered. "The manager knows you. He might squeeze you in."

She spun around, had taken two steps, when he reached out and stopped her. His hand fully curved her upper arm, and her soft skin teased his callused palm. His knuckles brushed the outer swell of her breast. His thumb came in contact with her nipple. Once again.

Rylan swore beneath his breath. What was with his hand and her breast? He seemed out to touch her every chance he got. That wasn't his intention. It was embarrassing. Yet he was slow in removing his hand. Noticeably slow.

Beth was in profile to him, and her unmanageable curls shadowed one eye. Her cheek and nose were sunburned. The shade trees had not protected her from the heat of the day. Her lips were parted. Her breathing was uneven. The pulse point at the base of her throat beat too fast. He made her nervous. Awkwardly so.

He released her then. Eased back. "Forget the reservation. There are lots of restaurants on the boardwalk. I'll find somewhere else to take Ava." He paused. "Did you call her?" He hoped so.

Beth nodded. "Ava accepted your date, but I never got back to her on time or place."

"Okay, I'll handle it from here."

"I'm really sorry, Rylan."

"You've already apologized."

"I can do better." *Please don't fire me.*

He heard the worry in her voice. He had no intention of letting her go. Atlas and crew liked her. A mistake was a mistake. Halo and Landon had shown up and taken over her day. He couldn't fault her for their distraction.

All in all, he had to admit that the yard looked amazing. The trees were trimmed back and the grass was perfectly cut. Only the train topiary had derailed. Otherwise the guys had done a decent job.

He glanced down at Beth's socks and read the positive message for the second time that day. "I think I can?"

"I know I can."

"I have no doubt."

Her shoulders sagged with relief. "I can give you that shave and a haircut."

He was reluctant. "There's an art to the barber shop shave. How many men have you shaved?"

"One."

"One besides me or one including me?"

"I gave my father his morning shave when he was bed-ridden. Cardiac arrhythmia." Her sigh was heavy. "I had sixty-three shaves to my credit before he passed away."

"I won't need a box of Kleenex to stanch bleeding?" He attempted to lighten the moment.

"Maybe a styptic pencil."

"Let's get through the shave; then I'll see about the hair-cut." One thing at a time.

She was agreeable. "I'll collect the lawn equipment while you call Ava and get your shaving kit. I'll meet you in the kitchen."

"I'll help you first." There was no reason for her to clean up by herself. His teammates had left out the mower and tools.

"You can fight off the bats," she said, a quirky smile lift-ing one corner of her mouth. She was teasing him.

His own grin came easily. "Beware of red eyes."

One sweep of the yard was all it took to gather the items.

Rylan pushed the mower just inside the door. Beth set the tools on the closest shelf. Atlas stuck his head inside, sniffed the air. It was musty, and the Dane sneezed. A big old sneeze that sprayed Beth. Her cutoffs were once again wet.

They crossed the yard together. Atlas beat them to the back door. Beth waited in the kitchen while he took the stairs two at a time to get his shaving kit. He gave Ava a quick call from the upper landing. They set a time for him to pick her up. She promised an evening to remember. He anticipated seeing her.

He went on to grab a bath towel to drape over his shoulders and returned to the kitchen in minutes. He drew a retro stool near the sink. Sat down. Then laid his Edwin Jagger shaving kit on the counter. The double-edge safety razor, aloe vera shaving cream, and sandalwood aftershave had been a gift from Dune. A welcome back to town.

His dogs settled around him. So close, he wasn't sure Beth could squeeze in to shave him.

Somehow she managed. She stood beside him at the sink and dampened a dish towel. "Can you tilt your head back, just a little?"

He had good balance and made the adjustment.

She went on to gently place the cloth beneath his nose and under his chin. "Too hot?" she asked, concerned.

Steam rose like a sauna. He didn't complain. "I'm fine." His voice was muffled beneath the towel. He closed his eyes as the heat penetrated his skin, softening his whiskers. The warmth felt surprisingly good.

She removed the cloth after several minutes. Moistened it once again. Wringing it out, she primed his skin for a smooth shave, repeating the process four times.

He heard the slide of her socks and the slight shift of the dogs as she stepped back so he could relax. He liked the fact she wasn't a woman who hovered or made small talk.

He was comfortable with silence. He was half asleep when she removed the final cloth.

His thoughts drifted to his Uncle Theodore. Old-fashioned shaves were his specialty. He mixed his homemade lather in a porcelain bowl, applied it with a badger-hair shaving brush, and then scraped off the stubble with a stainless steel straight-edge. Theodore had a steady hand and immense patience.

"Do you shave once or twice a day?" she asked him.

"Twice most days." He had a heavy beard.

"My dad enjoyed a facial massage," she said reflectively. "He had little to look forward to at the end of his life. I took extra time with his shave." Her touch was warm and gentle; her application focused. She pressed her fingertips to his temple and massaged slow circles between his hairline and eyebrows. After tracing the inner corners of his eyes and the side of his nose, she moved to his earlobes and the rims of his ears.

Ry appreciated the same attention. His ears were sensitive. He held back a moan.

She next stroked his cheeks and chin. He grew so relaxed, his jaw went slack. The gentle slide of her thumbs down his neck was soothing.

He peeked at her when she leaned across him and snagged the tube of shaving cream. He side-glanced down on his dogs. Atlas followed Beth's every move. The four had tightly trapped her between the counter and his stool.

She pressed fully against him.

Her breast brushed his shoulder.

His elbow nudged her abdomen.

Her hip touched his thigh. All warm and womanly.

He forced himself to sit still and not shift—which took a concentrated effort. He reminded himself that she wasn't his type. That wouldn't change.

Beth was a little shaky, Rylan noticed, when she squeezed a small amount of shaving cream onto her palm and then slowly rubbed her hands together. He again shut his eyes, letting her know that he trusted her.

She applied the shaving cream up and down his face and neck. The aloe vera scent was clean and refreshing. His face was soon covered with thick, creamy lather.

He heard her turn on the tap at the sink, then listened as she rinsed off her hands and picked up his razor. She used the fingers on her non-shaving hand to pull his skin taut near his sideburns. He inwardly tensed, and hoped it wasn't outwardly noticeable.

Beth wasn't fooled. "I promise not to take off an ear," she whispered. There was humor in her voice.

He couldn't help but smile. The movement of his mouth had him tasting shaving cream. The gentle brush of her thumb along his lower lip removed the excess lather. There was an inexplicable intimacy to her touch. Electric seconds of awareness passed between them. His palms prickled. He clasped his hands over his groin, making sure his zipper was covered. He avoided tenting.

He sat perfectly still with her first downward slide of the razor. He was impressed. Beth knew what she was doing.

She used long, light strokes, rather than pressing down into the skin. Her method was as good as his uncle's. She shaved over the same area twice, rinsing the blade with warm water between strokes. She gave him an incredible shave.

Afterward, she stood between his legs, her bare outer thighs rubbing his inner khakis. Heat sparked. His thigh muscles flexed. He shifted on the stool. Tried to appear nonchalant. It was difficult to remain indifferent.

She ran her fingers over his face when she was finished. "Smooth as polished stone. No nicks, cuts, or razor burn."

He rubbed his knuckles along his jaw. "Nice." He was pleased.

"Aftershave?" she asked.

Why not draw out the moment? "Sounds good."

She took a small amount of aftershave balm in her hands and lightly patted it where she had shaved. The woodsy and balsamic fragrance was subtle. Pleasant.

She surprised him by placing a light kiss on his forehead. That had him opening his eyes. He stared at her. She blushed deeply and was quick to explain, "I always kissed my father on his brow when we wrapped up. It was habit. One I haven't broken. I'm sorry."

He wasn't sorry. Her lips were warm, soft, full. Her kiss had relayed a fondness once shared between father and daughter. "My sister Shaye always drops a kiss on my grandfather Frank's cheek when she says good-bye. I understand."

Beth appeared relieved. After washing and drying off her hands, she went on to ask, "What about that haircut now?"

"You said you liked my hair longer." Why the hell had he said that? He didn't want her thinking that her opinion mattered to him.

She pursed her lips, momentarily thoughtful. "You have your own look—casual and unkempt, but very cool. You have a date. A light trim wouldn't hurt."

"There's a comb in my shaving kit. You'll find a small pair of scissors in the drawer left of the sink."

She retrieved both. Wetting the comb, she ran it through his hair with slow, measured passes, starting at his scalp, running down to the ends.

Having a woman comb his hair felt nice, Ry had to admit. His mother had been the last person to do so when he was a child.

A slight tug on his scalp, and Beth combed upward in the back, then snipped the ends. She continued, taking part of a just-cut section between her fingers so she could use it as a length guide. Finishing the right side, she leaned across him to finish the left. Her breasts were so close, he could've rested his chin in her cleavage. Each release of his breath fanned the neckline on her top. He eased back slightly.

She pressed her fingertips near his temple. "You have one strand that won't lay flat," she muttered as she clipped near his left eye. The snipping went on and on. Too long. She eventually held up the scissors, scrunched her nose, and sighed. She seemed uneasy. Her eyes were an unsettling gray.

He raised an eyebrow. "Problem?"

"How fast does your hair grow?"

"Pretty fast, why?"

"I got carried away with your cowlick."

"I don't have a cowlick."

"Two sections of your hair went in opposite directions."

"Two?" She had to be kidding. "You're standing on my right and cutting left. Your perception's off."

"Possibly . . ."

It wasn't what he wanted to hear. "How bad is it?"

"A comb-over might help."

Comb-over meant bald spot.

"Don't look in a mirror."

Atlas stood and backed up, staring at Ry as if he didn't recognize him. Rue gave a short bark. The dachshunds made squeaky toy noises.

Crap, Rylan thought. The shave had gone so well. The trim not so much. Hot date. Bad cut. Maybe Ava wouldn't notice. He needed to check for himself.

He drew the bath towel from around his neck and shook it over the garbage can under the sink. Significant hair loss, he noted. He caught his reflection in the window above the sink and couldn't believe his eyes. He'd always brushed his hair back, out of his eyes. Only one side fell back now. The other side was shorn. Short spikes and visible scalp.

Punk. A-symmetrical. Awful. Rylan wasn't a vain man. He'd had the occasional bad haircut over the years, but this was the worst to date. He clutched the edge of the sink; dropped his chin to his chest. Breathed deep.

Minutes passed before he turned to Beth. Atlas and Rue flanked her. The dachsies had pushed up to their full height—which wasn't all that tall. They sensed his irritation and her unease. They wanted to protect her. *From him.*

Any other time, he would've thrown back his head and laughed out loud. However, he had a date tonight. Presentable was important to him. He didn't look his best. Not by a long shot.

Tomorrow he would face fans and media at the stadium plaza. Reporters would question "his new look." His teammates would gain amusement at his expense. Not that he cared. Not much, anyway.

He rubbed the back of his neck and focused on the positive. Beth hadn't poked his eye with the scissors. Or snipped the tip of his nose.

She still held the scissors and comb. Her throat worked. She had difficulty swallowing. The lady was nervous.

Atlas took that moment to bark at him. A gruff sound. Smart when he wanted to be, the big dog awaited Rylan's apology. He expected Ry to forgive Beth. Ry could do that. Life would go on. He wasn't as upset with her as she was with herself. "Not my best look," he slowly said, "but I can live with it. Don't beat yourself up."

"I think you look edgy."

That surprised him. He'd been called handsome, stable,

and straightforward over the years. All-American, too. No one had ever called him *edgy*. His dogs came to him. Atlas rose on his back legs and sniffed Ry's head. Then dropping back down, he returned to Beth's side.

Ry watched as Beth slipped the comb into his shaving kit. Dropped the scissors into the drawer. She slapped her palms against her thighs, uncertain as to what to do next.

He had plans for the rest of the day. A visit with his grandfather at the retirement village was a must. He needed to get going. "I'd like you to meet my granddad," he said to Beth. "I'm going to be busy with spring training shortly, and won't be able to spend as much time with him as usual. Any chance you play cards?"

She nodded. "Gin, two-man solitaire, spades, war, crazy eights."

"Gin is good. How about cribbage?"

Another nod. "Also backgammon."

"Great." That worked out well. "I was asked to speak to the seniors as part of their lecture series. I'm scheduled for Wednesday. You can come with me then."

"I'd like that." She looked down on the dogs. "They'll be okay without me?"

He appreciated her concern. "Atlas will babysit."

Beth grinned. "Does he get paid for his services?"

"In dog treats."

Atlas loved his snacks. He could be insistent. When Connie forgot to bake, Atlas would drag the canine cookbook off the kitchen counter and drop it on her desk. Drool and all. Beth seemed more in-tune to the Dane than his Richmond assistant. The doggie cookie jar would always be full.

Ry stared at her, for no apparent reason. Her rain cast eyes were more blue than gray. Her smile held, only to slip the longer he held her gaze. Her breath caught, and her breasts rose. His left hand instinctively flexed. He had the unexpected urge to touch her. That would be a major mistake. He mentally kicked himself for being so stupid.

He needed to get going. "I'm taking my dinner jacket and shoes with me now. I won't return until late. I'll see you in the morning."

She licked her lips and hesitantly asked, "Will there be two of you at breakfast? Should I make myself scarce?"

"I don't bring dates to the cottage," he said to ease her mind. He never had. It was a personal rule. He wasn't an overnight date, either. He needed to get home to his dogs. They were his priority.

Not every woman understood his leaving. A few had argued with him. And lost. He had yet to meet someone who could fit seamlessly into his life. Someone who would love him . . . for himself. Not because he was a professional ballplayer. And a Cates.

Someone who could live with his crazy-ass schedule.

Someone who was an animal lover, too. That was an absolute must.

"Have a good evening, Rylan." Beth gave him a nudge.

"Thanks." He lingered a moment longer over his dogs. Then addressed Atlas on his way out. "Don't wait up, big guy."

Atlas had a habit of lying just inside the front door until he returned. He guarded the cottage. Ry doubted that would be so tonight. He'd bet his dogs would follow Beth to bed once she called it a day. He hoped Atlas wouldn't crowd her on the queen sofa sleeper. The big dog liked to stretch out and chase rabbits in his sleep. He kicked. Hard. There was a chance Beth would end up on the floor.

Beth woke up facedown on the floor. Sunlight streamed through the window, filtering across her blanket and the dark pine boards. Soft snores rose from the dachshunds camped beside her. She'd dragged their dog beds into her bedroom and they had curled up comfortably. Atlas and Rue had taken to her bed the moment she'd shut off the bedside table light. It had gotten crowded fast.

She'd curled into a ball, allowed them to stay, and slept fairly well. She couldn't recall exactly when she'd been shoved off the mattress. Sometime after three a.m., she figured. Shortly after she'd gotten up for a drink of water. She had less room when she'd climbed back into bed than when she'd left it moments before.

The floor was hard and uncomfortable. She had a slight crick in her neck. Her left elbow was sore. She rotated her right ankle to relieve the stiffness. She yawned. Twice. Then glanced at the alarm clock on the seaman's trunk. Six-thirty.

She wondered what time Rylan had gotten home. She was surprised the dogs hadn't wakened with his arrival, then joined him upstairs. She had yet to see the second floor. She imagined his bedroom was larger than her own.

She sat up slowly. Rolled her shoulders. Stretched out her arms. Straightened her short cotton nightgown. What to do first? She debated. She'd yet to set a routine. She could grab a quick shower while the dogs still slept. Then take them out for their walk. Followed by their breakfast. She'd work on the picnic afterward. She hoped to catch Rylan before he left for the day, to see if he had a list for her.

Twenty minutes later, showered and dressed in navy walking shorts and a powder blue tank top, Beth harnessed the dogs. She had her hand on the doorknob, about to leave the cottage, when Rylan made an appearance. He came down the stairs, bare chested and barefoot, wearing gray athletic shorts. He had a nice chest, lean and defined. His hair hadn't grown overnight, as she had hoped. But his chin stubble had. He looked sexy, in a bed-head, sleepy-eyed way.

The dogs charged him.

He greeted each one. "Have a good walk," he told them.

They returned to Beth, and she fitted their leashes. Atlas tugged her out the front door, then took the lead. His leash was longer than the rest. It was a beautiful morning.

She had never minded getting up early. She usually beat her alarm.

Used to an active lifestyle, the exercise felt good. She had a grip on Atlas's antics. For the moment, anyway. She breathed easier when they passed the crosswalk where he'd played dead the previous day.

On the way back, she turned Rue's leash over to him when they were two blocks from the house. Oscar and Nathan were dragging by the time they reached the driveway. The dachsies picked up their pace when they spotted Rylan sitting in a redwood Adirondack chair on the front porch, sipping a glass of orange juice.

"Keeping an eye out for us?" she asked.

"I wanted to make sure there wasn't a problem," he said easily. "I'd have given you five more minutes, then come looking."

She appreciated his concern. "We managed just fine."

He glanced down on her feet, and smiled when he read the hot pink message on her purple socks. *Baby Steps*.

She scuffed the toe on her Keds. "Another mantra I chant," she confessed. "Slow and steady wins the race."

"Giant steps come later?" he asked.

"Soon enough," she answered.

Rylan helped her unhook the harnesses. Atlas shot to the kitchen once he was freed. He dropped down near the stove and waited for his breakfast. The other dogs trailed more slowly.

Beth grabbed a paper towel from the roll on the counter and wiped perspiration from her brow. She glanced through the back window, then wondered aloud, "Why haven't you fenced the yard?"

"I use the yard for social gatherings," he told her. "I like to keep it clean, if you know what I mean."

She understood, but still suggested, "A doggie door and sturdy fence on the shady side of the cottage might work. The dogs would have an opportunity to be outside at times other than their walks. Atlas has pent-up energy. He needs to run."

"You could jog with him."

She shook her head. "He'd pull me off my feet. Fly me like a kite."

Ry laughed at that. "E-mail my brother Aidan. He's a contractor. Actually, his company built the Rogue's stadium. He might have extra fencing on a job site. He knows the size of my lot. See if he has time for the project."

Beth couldn't believe he'd gone along with her idea. "I'll get to it after breakfast."

Breakfast drew a gurgle from Atlas, and he started to drool.

She went to the cookbook and decided on organic beef and vegetable patties. It was a quick fix. Cooking time was twelve minutes.

Rylan had made coffee in the electric percolator by the time the patties went in the oven. He poured her a cup. She drank it black. So did he.

"Can I fix you something to eat?" she asked him.

"What were you planning to have?"

She hadn't thought that far ahead. "Whole wheat waffles." She'd noticed a waffle iron in the cupboard. She had her grandmother's recipe memorized. Ry had the ingredients.

"Waffles sound good. I prefer warm honey instead of syrup."

So did she.

Rylan read the newspaper while she made the waffles. The timers on the oven and waffle maker *dinged* simultaneously. Rylan set his paper aside, pushed off his stool, and grabbed a pot holder. He removed the tray of patties, setting them on an iron trivet to cool. Atlas sniffed the air, trying to inhale his breakfast.

Beth warmed a cup of honey and served Ry the first waffle topped with fresh blackberries. She next set out the dogs' dishes. Another minute, and she counted patties into their bowls. Four for Atlas. Three for Rue. And the dachsies each got one. She placed their food at the designated spots. Atlas ate surprisingly slow as if he was savoring each bite.

She turned her back on the dogs to fix her own waffle.

"Dish towel," Ry called, warning her of Atlas's approach.

She snagged the towel just in time and wiped the Dane's mouth before he could smear her walking shorts. Damage control.

She placed her waffle on a plate when it was ready, added a few berries, then took a stool across from Rylan at the island. Meals had always been a social time when she was growing up. She'd cherished those moments she spent with her parents.

Sadly, her mother had passed away when she was thirteen. Her father had remarried. His second marriage had been stressful, and put him in an early grave. He'd suffered a heart attack when she was nineteen. Two days before her twentieth birthday. There'd been no celebration. Only tears.

Her life had never been the same. She was an unwanted member of the family, scrambling to please a stepmother who faulted her for breathing.

Beth closed the top on her memory box and moved on. She attempted upbeat. "How was your date?" she casually asked Rylan.

"I was home by eleven," he said between bites.

That didn't sound good. She'd gone to bed at ten and hadn't heard him come in. She'd figured he'd had a late night. Apparently not. He had no reason to share with her; she was his PA, not his confidante. They barely knew each other. However he seemed willing to talk. She was there to listen.

He began with, "The anticipation was better than the actual date. That's a first for me. She hated my haircut. She called me minor league."

"That wasn't very nice."

"No, it wasn't," he agreed. He scratched the sheared side of his head. "Seems she was more into my looks than my personality."

Beth stared at him over the rim of her coffee cup. He had a strong face. The asymmetrical style sharpened his features. He looked fierce.

She made a suggestion. "I could trim your right side to match the left," she slowly said. "Even it out, if you like."

"I don't like." He was firm. "I'll live with it." He leaned his elbows on the island, steepled his fingers, and commented further on his date. "The night went downhill fast. Nothing pleased Ava. She doesn't like crowds. I've never seen as many people on the boardwalk as I did last night. It's tourist season, and all the beach bistros were packed. Most had a ninety-minute wait. We ended up at Molly Malone's Diner. The tables always turn over quickly there."

"Family dining at a fair price." Beth remembered the sign that hung on the door. "That's where I ate my first meal when I arrived in town. A hot meatloaf sandwich. It was delicious. Casual atmosphere."

"Casual was the killer," he confessed. "Ava had dressed

up. She looked hot. She didn't fit with the locals and beachgoers. She wanted fine dining; I gave her home-cooking. She called the diner a dive."

Ava sounded difficult. Superficial, too, Beth thought. The woman had expected candlelight, wine, and intimacy. Instead, she'd sat in a vinyl booth and sipped her beverage from a plastic glass. Noisy conversations had swirled around her. The polka music from the carousel would have entered with each customer.

Ry's frown appeared permanent as he finished off his waffle. "Ava pushed her Cobb salad around her plate for twenty minutes before she called it a night. She told me to call her when I could deliver what I'd promised. She left the diner before I paid the bill and hailed a cab. I stood on the curb. Saw taillights."

Beth's stomach cramped. She'd forgotten to make the dinner reservation and shouldered the blame. It was heavy. "I can fix this," she rushed to say. "I'll call Ava and explain the situation. Then schedule another date." Ava had *wanted* him. She'd told Beth so on the phone. Yet because of his haircut and the diner, she'd desired him less. "I'll reserve the best table at The Pier House. You have Wednesday night free, according to your calendar."

Ry stretched his arms. Shook his head. "Pause that thought. I'm not certain I want a second date."

"Of course you do." Beth tried to convince him.

He gave her a long look. "Don't assume, Beth." His tone was tight. "Ava wasn't my best date, but neither was she my worst."

"Not your worst?" She found that hard to believe.

"It's true," he admitted. "I once dated a woman in Richmond who did a strip tease from my living room to my bedroom. Sasha left a trail of clothing, which Atlas took for new toys. He chewed the toes on her suede stilettos and gnawed the clasps off her garter belt. He tore the underwire from her bra. She never did find one of the removable cups."

"Oh . . . Atlas," Beth murmured, fighting a smile.

"Oh . . . Atlas is right. I gave her five hundred dollars."

"Expensive date."

"Atlas paid me back from his allowance." Ry was joking, and Beth grinned.

Rylan finished with, "If Ava wants to see me again, she knows where to find me. It's her move. I told her about the footprint event and Media Day. The Gallery Walk." His expression mellowed. "Last night ended well. I stopped to visit Shaye and her husband Trace after Ava split. Aidan built their beach house. It's enormous. My sister has the coolest Quaker parrot. Olive talks like a person. I chatted longer with Olive than I did with Ava."

"You're not disappointed then?" Beth needed to be sure.

"What's meant to be, is. What's not, isn't. That's my brother Zane's philosophy."

"Zane is the family hurricane hunter?" She'd seen his photo in the online album, standing next to a Lockheed-Martin WC-130J aircraft. Big and burly, he had a buzz cut. His expression was hard. His eyes piercing. His jaw granite.

"He's the daredevil and lives each day as if it was his last." That said, Ry slid off his stool, picked up his plate, and put it in the sink. "A quick shower and I'm headed to the stadium. The team has a full morning ahead." He gave her further instructions. "I keep a running grocery list on the computer. You'll need to stock up once a week. Best place to shop is Harvest Farms, north of town. Crabby Abby's General Store carries my personal items. I have an account."

"Got it." She pursed her lips. "There's no problem with me leaving the dogs alone while I do errands?"

"They'll sleep while you're gone. Be home by noon to

feed and walk them. Otherwise Atlas will send up a smoke signal."

She grinned. "I'll keep an eye on the sky."

"Keys to my Range Rover and the cottage are on a metal ring in the drawer below the coffeemaker. Drive my vehicle, there's no need to put extra miles on your Cruiser."

She nodded. Feeling grateful. She'd traded in her Mini Cooper at a used car dealership in Atlanta, then gone on to purchase the PT Cruiser. It was her third car swap since leaving Maryland. She didn't want anyone following her.

The odometer had turned one hundred and twenty thousand miles on her trip to Florida. The car still ran well, but she didn't want to push her luck. She didn't need any red lights flashing on the dashboard.

"Have fun with your footprints," she said as he turned to leave. "Fans will go nuts."

"The stadium will be crowded. It's Media Day. We'll do a Q and A. Baseball stats soon take second place to personal info."

"What kind of information?" She was curious.

"Drop by the park around ten-thirty and see for yourself," he suggested. "There's a player's pass hanging from the rearview mirror on the Rover. Park in the team lot. Remove and clip the pass to your top. You'll have full-access to the day's events."

Rylan Cates as a Richmond Rogue. Definitely worth her while. "I'll see you there." Afterward she'd shop for groceries. She didn't want the fresh produce to sit overly long in the SUV.

Ry headed upstairs, and she finished her waffle, giving Atlas the last bite. The dog had a way of looking goofy and grateful at the same time. She collected their bowls and rinsed them at the sink, then stuck them in the dishwasher. She'd run a load of dishes later in the day.

She walked to the office. The dogs trailed behind her. She settled in to work. Turning on the computer, she pulled up the file for the picnic. First item on her list was locating the solar powered lanterns. Where to look? Hardware store, lamp shop, or party rental? She'd check out local business websites. Next came the outdoor furniture. Then she would plan the menu.

Eight o'clock, and Rylan stuck his head in the door, letting her know he was leaving. He looked handsome in a maroon and white Henley pullover and khakis. The dogs barked and Beth waved him on his way.

She worked steadily for an hour, making phone calls and sending e-mails. She approached Aidan Cates on fencing. He promised to send one of his crew to take measurements. The work would be done by the end of the week. Before the picnic. The thought of Atlas and gang having extra room to play pleased Beth greatly.

She soon discovered that no one in town carried the lanterns, so she ordered them online. They were expensive, but Rylan could use them again and again. She saw them as an investment. The company guaranteed two-day delivery, which fell within her timeline.

She jumped along with the dogs when a horn honked in the driveway. Someone leaned on it. Loud and insistent. The noise sent her to the front door with Atlas on her heels.

Who in the world . . . ?

Halo Todd stood beside his silver metallic Hummer H3T pickup. A beast of a truck. His arms were crossed over his chest. He faced her in a T-shirt scripted with *To Be Continued, Babe,* jeans ladder-ripped over his right thigh, and a big, old smirk. He appeared proud of himself.

What had he done? she wondered.

Atlas nearly knocked Beth over getting to Halo.

The man greeted the Dane with the affection of the previous day.

Beth approached Halo more slowly. "What's up?"

"I found a circular bench for the base of the banyan tree. Perfect for the picnic."

"You did?" She was stunned with the delivery.

"The Cates name opened doors. I borrowed the bench from Porch and Patio. Rylan can buy or return it after the picnic."

"How many pieces are there?"

"Six individual. It's an easy set up. The redwood sections curve and lock. I'll do it for you now."

Now? "You're supposed to be at the stadium," she reminded him. "Footprints and Media Day." Rylan had left for the training facility an hour ago. Halo was late. "I don't want you to get in trouble on my account."

He had the balls to laugh at her. "I appreciate your concern. Don't worry. I'll plant my footprints before the cement dries. Reporters always ask the same questions. I get bored." He worked his jaw. "Fifteen minutes, and I'll have your bench together."

Halo was procrastinating. Big time. She narrowed her gaze on him. Tapped her foot. "Talk to me, Halo."

"You're sounding like Rylan."

"I'm waiting."

He kept her waiting while he dropped the tailgate on the Hummer and unloaded the bench section by section from the covered cargo area. He then hefted one curved piece onto his shoulder and headed down the driveway toward the backyard. She hurried to keep up with him. Atlas ran ahead of them both.

Halo broke his silence at the corner of the cottage. "I picked up a woman last night at a hotel bar. She'd had a terrible date and I consoled her. We later got a room. It was a night of little sleep. The sun rose and so did I. No man denies his morning erection. Twice."

"Too much information."

"Even running late I did you a solid," he insisted. "I located the bench."

His reasoning became clear to her. She wanted to punch him. "No way, Halo. I won't be your excuse for being late."

"Come on, be a sport."

"No."

"Rylan won't be nearly as mad at me if he knows I've helped you."

"No, tell him the truth."

"That sex with Ava—"

"Ava?" Beth startled.

"Ava Vonn. Do you know her?"

"No, can't say that I do." She had, however, gotten an earful on the woman at breakfast. Ava had left Ry at the diner, only to hookup with Halo at the bar. However coincidentally.

She didn't want Rylan caught off guard in the locker room should Halo brag about his conquest. She needed to avert the conversation. But how? She finally came up with a solution. She'd give them something else to talk about.

She waited until Halo connected the last wraparound section on the bench before she approached him. The spot looked comfortable and inviting. A conversation starter.

He met her halfway with enough strut for six men. "Cover my ass?" he questioned her a second time.

"I'll have your back on one condition."

"Conditions are never good. What's yours?"

"I give you a haircut."

Four

"We're fuckin' twins," Halo Todd cursed as he entered the Rogues locker room.

Not twins, Rylan thought. But they had the same haircut. Both were bad. Halo's hair was worse than Ry's . . . if that was even possible. Ry at least had short spikes. Halo had a visible bald spot. He would've smiled had Halo not looked ready to kill someone.

Rylan finished buttoning his navy jersey and tucked it into his baseball pants. Then threaded his belt and asked unnecessarily, "Who's your barber?" Somehow he already knew.

Halo stood two lockers down. He tugged his gray T-shirt over his head. His voice was muffled through the neck hole. "Beth took scissors to me."

"You saw her this morning?" *When?* Ry wondered.

"I located the wraparound bench she wanted for your picnic and delivered it early." Halo tossed his shirt on the floor of his locker, then heel-toed his athletic shoes. He stood in his socks. "You and I passed at the corner. Didn't you see me? I waved."

Waved? His ass. Halo's Hummer was hard to miss. It took up two parking places in the players' lot. Rylan drove defensively. There hadn't been another car on his street this morning, and only minimal traffic on the highway to the stadium.

"I only planned to stay a few minutes," the right fielder continued, "but once I unloaded the redwood sections, Beth begged me to put the bench together. Right then, right there."

"Begged you like she did yesterday with the yard work?"

Halo shrugged. "More or less."

Ry figured less.

"She's a hard woman to refuse."

"The setup took two hours?"

"Time got away from me."

Two hours was a lot to lose. Rylan didn't believe for a second that Halo had spent that length of time at his cottage. "The reason for your cut?" He'd yet to figure that out. "Mine was a mistake."

Halo winced. "Mine was on purpose. Beth mumbled something about 'team unity,' and that haircuts were better than tattoos. I had no idea what she was talking about." He glanced at Rylan. "But now I do. She got to you, then came after me. The woman can't be trusted with scissors. She's not my favorite person at the moment."

Team unity. Ry's chest warmed. He appreciated Beth looking out for him. She'd slipped up with his cowlick, yet deliberately sheared Halo. She'd taken the focus off him on Media Day. Her loyalty meant a lot.

Ry had received strange looks from his teammates when he'd first entered the locker room. There'd been a few raised eyebrows, but only one smirk. Landon Kane stared the longest, looking confused, but no one had questioned him. They'd waited for him to explain. He'd yet to do so.

Silence had held until the last uniformed man left for the plaza. The footprint ceremony was about to begin. Rylan had remained in the locker room, waiting for Halo. Where could he be? Ry had wondered.

Late and unconcerned, Halo had finally made an appearance. In his own good time—which was inconsiderate. And irritating.

Ry practiced patience.

Clubhouse manager Walter Atwater made the locker assignments. As a veteran player, Ry had seniority and was given two lockers so he could spread out and be comfortable. Space was important to him. He was adjacent to the lounge and food cart and had easy access to the showers.

Halo's locker adjoined Ry's. Walt had hoped by placing Halo next to him during spring training that Rylan's stability would rub off on the rule breaker, even a little.

Ry had his doubts. He pitched his wallet and keys on the top shelf of the empty locker that separated them. Halo already coveted his real estate. Landon Kane's locker was next to Halo's. The starting lineup filled the row against the south wall.

Rylan was still curious about Halo's whereabouts prior to his stop at the cottage. The truth lay in what had happened *beforehand*. Stopping by his home was a half-assed excuse. Beth knew the importance of today and wouldn't have allowed Halo to linger. She would've broomed his ass.

The man's personal life was his own, unless it affected team events. It had interfered today. Ry wasn't aware of an all-night poker game. He usually got an invite. Or a dusk-to-dawn party under the city pier. He figured a woman was involved.

Rylan dropped down on the gray-enameled bench, pulled on his logo crew socks. His cleats came next. Contracted with New Balance, he had four boxed pairs stacked in his locker. Facing a grueling one hundred sixty-two game season, he sacrificed the metal grip and wore their plastic cleats. Plastic lessened the wear and tear on his joints. He chose the oldest and most scuffed pair for stepping in cement.

Several feet away, Halo unbuckled his belt, unsnapped, and unzipped his jeans. He dropped and stepped out of them. He wore his boxers low on his hips. He made a grab for his baseball pants, hanging on a hook.

Ry stood, stretched, and was about to ask Halo one final question, when the answer flashed before him. Wicked red scratches scored Halo's upper butt. His lover had talons. Her fingernails had dug deep to draw out her passion. He would have scars.

Rylan's jaw worked. The outfielder lived by untruths and ulterior motives. Beth hadn't made him late, as Halo had sworn. Sex had. Halo knew the team rules. Those spoken and unspoken.

"Who scratched your ass, Halo?" asked Ry. "I hope she was worth the fine."

Busted. Halo contorted to check out his backside. Heat circled his neck. "Shit. Cut me some slack, Ry-man. It's preseason."

"This is a scheduled Rogues event."

Halo swore beneath his breath. "What-the-fuck-ever." He finished getting dressed.

The locker room door swung open. Landon Kane called to them. "What's holding you guys up?" He blinked. "Damn. First Rylan and now you. What's with the haircut, Halo?"

Halo rubbed his bald spot, grumbled, "Team unity."

Still Land was skeptical. "We voted on tattoos."

"Cuts now. Tats later," said Halo.

Landon wasn't convinced. He ran a hand through his hair. "I like one length."

So did Rylan. Had he been Land, he would've headed for the door and not looked back.

Halo hedged a little more. "Unifying the team is a huge undertaking." He made it sound as if he had the Rogues' best interest at heart. "Call it preseason initiation. Cuts precede the first pitch of spring training."

Landon shifted. Uneasily. "Have all the guys committed?"

Halo rubbed his chin. "Pretty much so."

"Not fully." Rylan had to be honest.

"Stand with us, dude," Halo pulled Land in.

Reluctantly, Landon said, "Maybe later. There's no time—"

"We'll make time," Halo said. "I have an electric shaver in my locker. What's another five minutes?"

That was exactly how long it took Halo to trim Land's hair. The two men were tight. What one man started, the other man finished. They always had each other's backs. Even when it came to bad haircuts.

"How's it feel?" Halo asked Land once he finished.

Landon touched the side of his head. His expression was pained. "Lopsided." He glanced in the mirror set between the lockers. "I look like shit."

"Edgy." Ry recalled what Beth had said.

"Whacked," Landon grumbled.

Three of nine starters were now buzzed. There were six players to go. Ry wondered how the remaining dominos would fall. No man would be pressured. He wouldn't allow it, although Halo had a way of convincing people to do things they might not ordinarily do. He was a one for all and all for one kind of guy.

Rylan grabbed his baseball cap and moved toward the door. "Let's go. We're really late."

"We?" Halo caught Rylan's eye. "Fines all-around then? Not just on me?"

Ry glared at him. "You held us up in the first place, remember?" How quickly Halo could forget.

"Yeah, but we're three bad haircuts facing Media Day. You're not alone, dude. That should count for something."

It counted for little. "I'll think about it," was all Rylan would commit.

"Landon," Halo called to the third baseman. "Mirror, mirror on the wall, your hair hasn't grown at all. Move your ass."

Land followed them out. They were met by two security guards who escorted them along the fan walkway toward the front of the facility. Jillian had initiated the winding sidewalk the previous year when the stadium was under construction. The promotional event had honored the fans and their continued support. She'd invited the ball players to leave their footprints for future generations. No other spring training facility had a fan walkway. It spread goodwill throughout the community.

Rogues Plaza was located near the entrance of the stadium. Dirt squares had been prepped for the event. A cement truck beeped as it backed up, pulling close to the concrete finishers. Once the 'crete was poured, the players would step up and leave their prints.

The crowd was enormous, Ry noted. Excitement shimmered like a mirage. A semicircle of collapsible bleachers provided seating. Several rows were roped off for media, city officials, and the Cates family. Fans squeezed together; it was standing room only.

Jill approached Rylan the moment she spotted him. "Where have you been?" she asked, her voice tight. She glanced at Halo; her mouth pinched. "I should've known he'd be the one to hold us up."

Halo curled his lip. "It's not always me."

"Oh, yes, it is." Jill knew otherwise. She ran her gaze over them. "Seriously?" she muttered. "Trend or angry barber?"

"Unity," said Halo.

"I got roped," said Landon.

"A long story," said Rylan.

Jill let it drop. Taking Ry by the arm, she led him to the first prepared square. The masons had spread the fresh cement. They awaited his cleats.

"You're up," she said to him. "It's quick drying, so make it fast."

He left his prints for posterity. Jill then passed him a pencil to sign his name. Whistles and applause echoed on the air. News cameras zoomed in. Individual photos were snapped. A young boy held a garden hose nearby. Ry lifted each foot so the kid could spray off his cleats. The boy was all smiles when Rylan autographed the bill of his Rogues cap.

He walked to the sidelines and watched the festivities.

He avoided the spotlight, while Halo sought attention. The outfielder caused a roar from the fans when he hunkered down, ready to leave his butt print. Jill was quick to intervene. She tugged him from the square. And not too gently.

Ry rolled his eyes. Halo would've been taught a lesson had he sat down. The quick-drying concrete would've set around his backside. He'd have difficulty getting up. Chipping cement off his ass wouldn't be pretty. It might have taught him a lesson.

The footprints took forty minutes. Rylan tipped back his ball cap and scanned the bleachers while he waited. He quickly spotted Dune and Sophie. His grandfather Frank. Shaye and Trace. Then Beth. He felt an unexpected relief that she'd made it. Shaye had made room for her in the family section, sitting next to his sister. The two women chatted like old friends. Ry liked the fact that they got along. He stared at her until Halo and Landon joined him.

The men were playing *hottest babe in the crowd*. Alternate versions of their game were hottest babe in a restaurant or at a bar. In a store or crossing the street. On the beach or at the movie theater. The guys just liked to play. Wherever.

Halo nodded left. "Behind the cameraman. Blonde in the white tank top."

"I'd tap her," Land agreed. "Bleachers, third row right. Redhead in the low-cut blouse."

Halo moaned his interest. "Nice."

"Hey, there's Beth." Landon was first to spot her. "She's a contender."

Ry again glanced her way. Her yellow top was as bright as the sunshine that streaked her hair. She was one of few without a tan. She talked with her hands and smiled easily.

He'd give her *cute,* but *a contender*? Were Halo and Landon humoring him? Possibly. They seemed to like Beth. Both men had wanted to ask her out. He stared at her a moment longer. She was even more animated than a second ago.

He watched as Shaye threw back her head and laughed at something Beth said. Beth was laughing, too. Rylan found that he was grinning for no apparent reason.

"Who are you looking at, dude?" Land asked, craning his neck. "Share her."

"No one in particular," was all Ry would admit. "I'm enjoying the day. Clear skies, big crowd, nice press coverage—it's perfect."

Shortly thereafter, Jillian directed clubhouse assistants to set up tall stools in the center of the plaza. As team captain, Rylan sat in the middle. Halo Todd and Landon Kane flanked him. The other players fanned out. First baseman Jake Packer, left fielder Joe "Zoo" Zooker, and catcher Hank Jacoby went right. Shortstop Brody Jones, second baseman Sam Matthews, and pitcher Will Ridgeway were seated left. They were ready to face the media.

National and local television stations were well represented, as were newspapers and sports magazines. Introductions soon followed. Jill detailed each man's career. Rylan was the veteran and had the longest list of accomplishments. He was also the hometown boy, and was embraced wholeheartedly. The applause was deafening.

Halo leaned toward Rylan and spoke from the corner of his mouth. "You had a .321 batting average last year?" He feigned awe.

"I clubbed a few," was all Ry would give him.

Jill may have read his numbers off a paper, but Halo knew Ry's stats by heart. The man tried to best him at every turn and always came up short. But not by much.

"You sure you have three Golden Gloves?" Halo pressed him.

"Jill just said as much." Rylan had posted three errorless seasons with the St. Louis Colonels.

"I think she padded your stats."

"Go back to your padded cell."

The Q&A came next. The crowd quieted, intent on listening.

The majority of the questions were lobbed to Rylan.

Halo snorted, swore he was invisible.

The reporters aired their concerns. *"Are the Rogues ready for the season?"*

Ry never referred to himself, but always spoke for the team. "The team's strong, focused, and prepared for whatever comes our way."

"How does the team stack up against last year?"

"We're all a year older and wiser," he said, staying positive.

"Any injuries?"

Two of the men played it light. Landon answered first. "Does stubbing my toe in the dark last night getting a drink of water count?"

The reporter smiled.

Zoo came next. He put his hand over his heart and said, "I have a broken heart. My girlfriend just dumped me."

Females sighed, sympathizing with him.

"Winning projections?"

Rylan held back. Predictions often bit a player in the butt. He was cautious in answering. He wasn't psychic. He had no idea where the Rogues would be in the fall standings. He could only hope they'd be sitting at the top of the National League East.

Ry cringed when Halo looked into his crystal ball. The outfielder stood up, pumped his arm, and announced, "We're going to win the World Series."

There was a heartbeat of stunned silence before the crowd crowned Halo their hero. Their cheers would be heard all the way to the beach. He was always a fan favorite, but today he ruled.

He sat back down, and Rylan muttered "Idiot," just loud enough for him to hear.

"A popular idiot, wouldn't you say?"

Popular or not, Halo had put a target on the team's back. The National League would be gunning for them—to prove him wrong. It would be balls to the wall all season.

Rylan sucked it up. He hoped Halo was right. If not, Halo would eat his words before the media and MLB. No man wanted humble pie as a main course.

The next question was tossed out to the men at large. *"How do you like the new spring training facility?"*

"I like the new locker room smell," said Landon—which drew laughter.

That newness would fade after their first game, Ry knew. Sweat and dirty uniforms would require air fresheners.

"Our Florida park is as nice as our home in Richmond," he responded, paying a compliment to the community. "We're glad to be in Barefoot William."

A sports editor singled him out. "This being your hometown, do you have more to prove than your team-mates?"

"Not necessarily," Ry responded. "My bat speaks for me. Playing consistent is my goal."

"Mine, too," added Halo.

"Me, three," said Landon.

The rest of the lineup chimed in with "Me, four" all the way to "Me, nine." The fans loved it.

A female reporter from *Weekend Warrior* magazine was brave enough to get personal and ask about their haircuts. Halo was quick to give his unity speech. He likened the cuts to other teams growing beards or fully shaving their heads. He stated that the Rogues were unanimous in their decision.

A few of the men groaned, but no one challenged him. Not publically, anyway. Brody Jones cut Ry a *what-the-fuck* look. Zoo nearly fell off his stool. Throats were cleared. Sam punched his fist into his palm. Will snorted. Discussion would continue in the locker room. No doubt loudly.

Rylan glanced up at Beth to catch her reaction to the media event, thus far. He found her staring at him, fasci-nated, and taking it all in. The moment meant something to her. The corners of her mouth tipped in a small smile. She was enjoying herself.

Moments later, he saw her check her watch. She slowly stood, spoke to Shaye, and then scooted from the row. She carefully picked her way down the bleachers, avoiding the people who sat on the aisle steps. He watched her clear the gate. A part of him wished she could've stayed. But she was his assistant and had responsibilities.

Most important, his dogs expected lunch and a walk. Atlas had an inner clock. He would read her the riot act if she was late. The Dane could be critical.

Clouds shifted overhead, and fans stretched on the

bleachers. The fun part of the morning came next. Jillian drew several kids forward so they could ask the players questions. A boy of ten inquired about their walk-up songs. That was the music played when the hitter left the on-deck circle for the batter's box. Or the pitcher walked to the mound or bullpen. Entrance music defined the man.

Halo was a shock jock. His song intimidated. He'd chosen Screamin' Jay Hawkins's "I Put a Spell on You." He would point at the opposing pitcher when Hawkins blurted out the line after the title, "Because you're mine." Fans would shout it out, right along with Hawkins.

Landon preferred "Game On" by Pitbull.

Ry kept the same song he had in St. Louis. John Fogerty's "Centerfield." The rest of the players rattled off their preferences, too.

A freckled-faced girl asked Rylan if he was a dog or cat person. His teammates answered for him. They barked.

Favorite cars, first jobs, workout routines, downtime activities, and were the men single or married were some of the questions. Jill let as many children as she could step up. An infatuated teenage girl blushed as she requested a hug from Rylan. He obliged. The crowd whistled its approval.

Media Day was to have ended at noon, but continued until one. The players didn't mind. Not a bit. The fans supported them, and the team gave back.

Security ushered the crowd through the main gate once the event was over. The players returned to the locker room.

Zoo found Halo standing beside the food cart, peeling an orange. Zoo chose an apple, tossed it in the air, and cut to the chase. "What's with the haircuts?"

"Unity—"

"Bullshit." Zoo was not taken in.

"You don't believe me?"

"Reality check, dude," said Zoo. "Don't conspire behind our backs. You should've consulted us first."

"Damn straight," echoed Sam Matthews.

Male dominance filled the locker room. Chests puffed
and lips curled. Fists clenched. Landon moved to stand by
Halo. Both men crossed their arms over their chests. Stiffened their stances.

Rylan shook his head. They were making more out of
the haircuts than the cuts deserved. "Use your words,
girls," he called to them.

Halo flipped him off.

"We're good with the tattoos," Zoo growled. "That's it."

Halo rolled his tongue in his cheek. "Do or don't.
Doesn't matter to me."

"It's about to matter to all of us," Zoo stated. "You
rolled a snowball into hell. Chances are good that hun-
dreds of our loyal fans will show up with the same cut on
opening day. We'll appear to have lied to them if we don't
go along with your scheme." He glared at Halo. "All your
fault, dickhead."

"Not his, but mine." Rylan stepped up before further
argument ensued. He needed to clear the air.

"Yours?" Zoo was disbelieving.

His teammates gathered around him. Halo offered him
a section of orange, which he ate. Ry would've liked to let
Halo take the blame, but truth was important to him. He
did a quick recap of how his PA had trimmed his hair,
mistaking crisscrossed strands for a cowlick. Beth then got
hold of Halo. Halo went after Land.

The players shook their heads, but accepted his expla-
nation. Most men laughed. Only Zoo rolled his eyes.
"The moral of the story is to stay the hell away from
Beth."

"She's smokin'," said Landon. "Check her out at Ry-
man's picnic on Saturday."

Rylan wasn't sure he liked the idea. Beth was responsible for the afternoon running smoothly. She didn't need to be tripping over ballplayers. "She'll be working." And keeping track of his dogs. Atlas would be beside himself, having so much company. He'd need a handler.

"Slave driver," came from Halo.

"I pay her salary," Ry reminded them.

Zoo shot Halo a condescending look. He spoke on behalf of the remaining players. "We'll get the cuts, but you'll owe us big, bro."

"How big?" Halo didn't like owing anyone anything.

"You'll super-size when the time comes."

"Super-size what? What the hell does that mean?"

"Whatever we want, whenever we want it." Zoo left it open-ended.

"Shit." Halo hated being left in the dark.

Halo had been warned, Rylan mused. He turned his back on his teammates. They drifted off. He unbuttoned his jersey, slipped it off. He untied his cleats, kicked them aside. Off came his baseball pants and on went his khakis. He slipped on his Henley pullover and leather flip-flops and was off. He left the locker room with several other players. Including Halo.

Rylan had parked his sports car in the far corner of the lot. Away from the other vehicles. A safety factor against dents and dings. Why Halo had angled his pickup near the McLaren was beyond Ry. He had a hundred spaces to choose from. Landon had left his Porsche by the south entrance, near the gate attendant.

Halo and Rylan matched strides. "What are your plans for the rest of the day?" Halo asked.

Ry wasn't sure if the man was making conversation or hinting at stopping by the cottage. "I need to prepare a speech. I'm presenting a program at the Barefoot William Retirement Center tomorrow afternoon."

"Maybe I'll stop by."

"Maybe you won't."

"I like your gramps."

"Frank's yet to pass judgment on you."

"We could get better acquainted."

"Don't go there. Find someone else to play with."

"I have a lunch date," Halo boasted. "With Scratches."

"Take Neosporin," Ry advised; the man didn't need infection. As an afterthought he added, "Don't forget the Gallery Walk."

"We'll be there."

"Later, then." The men parted ways at their vehicles.

Beth slept longer than she had planned. She'd stretched out on the sofa after lunch to watch her favorite soap opera and drifted off. Her legs felt warm and a bit numb. She soon realized why. Atlas had joined her on the couch. He lay on her calves. She couldn't feel her feet.

She turned slightly and nearly came out of her skin. Rylan stood over her. He'd caught her napping on the job. She struggled to sit, but the Dane held her down.

"Atlas, up," Rylan said with authority.

The dog yawned in his face.

Beth gave the big boy a push. Atlas didn't look pleased. He made a rumbling sound in his throat.

"Let me move and you can stay," she bribed.

Atlas gave her an inch.

Her legs tingled as she swung her feet to the floor. Sharp prickles shot to her hip. She rose too fast, and her legs gave out. Ry reached for her. His firm grip on her shoulders eased her back down. Her bottom bounced on the cushion.

"My legs are asleep," she told him, rolling her ankles.

"Let's wake them up."

He rounded the end of the sofa, crouched down before her. There was no hesitation in his touch. He started with her right foot, massaging her sole through her sock. He rotated her ankles in a circle. Then rubbed upward.

Beth tensed. "I haven't shaved my legs."

"I thought I'd caught a splinter."

She cuffed his arm.

He laughed. The man had a sense of humor.

Beth gave an inward sigh. Rylan should've been a masseur. His hands were big and strong. Unsettling tingles came from his touch. Her calves were no longer asleep. Her whole body was awake. Her skin heated. Could legs blush?

"I enjoyed my hour at the stadium," she initiated.

"I saw you in the stands."

She'd seen him, too. He'd stood out among his teammates, a man of quiet strength and seriousness. His haircut captured his athletic fierceness. He filled out his uniform like a sports hero. She'd loved every minute.

"Halo's quite a crowd pleaser," she noted.

"Give him an audience and he has ready dialogue."

Ry's hands worked higher. A sinfully steady pressure.

Her mouth went dry. She could barely speak. "Three of you now have the same cut."

"Two were by the same barber."

That barber would be her. Apparently Rylan knew she'd taken scissors to Halo. Did he know the reason why? "I wanted to level the playing field," she admitted.

"You did." He chuckled. "Halo then went after Landon in the locker room. The starting lineup will look alike on Monday."

"An initiation into spring training?"

"You could say that." He took a moment and concentrated fully on her knees. He found pressure points that should've relaxed her further, but didn't. His thumbs pressed deep, sending pleasure straight to her crotch. She shifted uneasily.

Concerned, he asked, "Am I hurting you?"

He was turning her on. "No, I'm fine."

Rylan rocked back slightly. Met her gaze. "Halo mentioned delivering a bench."

She nodded. "He arrived at nine-fifteen." She remembered the time. "He insisted on putting it together."

Rylan scratched his chin. "Makes sense. He was already late when he came by the cottage."

She bit down on her bottom lip. "I tried to hurry him along. Really, I did."

Atlas barked, supporting her. Beth patted his backside.

Ry again focused on her knees.

She could've told him to stop anytime, but she didn't. What would a few more minutes hurt? His massage felt too good to quit.

"Halo made you his fall guy," Rylan said.

She had expected no less.

"The truth did come out though."

"How so?" she asked.

"Let's just say some woman left her mark on him."

Some woman. Rylan apparently didn't know her name.

But Beth did. Ava Vonn. Apprehension slowed her breathing. What should she do? Loyalty to her boss came into play. Was it her place to tell Rylan that Halo had hooked up with Ava? Or should she let him find out on his own? The moment turned awkward.

She grew even more uneasy when she realized the placement of his hands. His fingers were beneath the hem of her walking shorts and his thumbs grazed her inner thighs. She'd been so relaxed that she hadn't been paying attention. Apparently neither had he. She was wide-eyed. And shivery.

His hands stilled with her goose bumps. He pulled back and pushed to his feet in one fluid motion. He held out his palms as if defending himself. "Sorry about that."

She wasn't sorry at all. His touch seemed natural. No part of her body could've slept through his massage. Her calves tingled, but for a very different reason than before. She'd liked his hands on her. "We're good," she told him. She kicked out her legs. "I could dance now if there was music."

He looked down at her. "What kind of music do you like?"

She was thoughtful. "I take after my mother. She loved music that filled her soul and made her heart race. I'd walk into the kitchen after school when I was a kid and find her dancing while baking cookies. She had a favorite oldies mixed disc. She would grab my hands with her floured fingers and spin me around. My dad would enter, and we each moved to our own beat. My mom sang along—she had the best voice." She smiled over the memory. "Whitney Houston's "I Wanna Dance with Somebody," Tina Turner's "Proud Mary," and "Last Dance" by Donna Summers were on that mix."

Beth celebrated her past. "We would dance until we dropped. We'd collapse on café chairs, out of breath and laughing so hard we had tears in our eyes. Once we could breathe again, Mom would serve us glasses of milk and whatever she had baked. Most times it was double-chocolate chips. Warm, gooey, and delicious."

"Sounds nice," Rylan said.

"It was while it lasted." Sadness slid in where her happiness had been. "My mother developed bone cancer when I was twelve. Our dancing days were over."

"I'm sorry."

"So was I." Her heart had broken. Her last year in middle school passed in a blur. "My dad and I never played the mixed tape again." Not after watching Mom live out the rest of her life in a wheelchair. "I haven't danced since." By her own choice.

Ry was thoughtful. He raised an eyebrow, and one corner of his mouth tipped, too. "Care to dance now?"

Surprise had her saying, "We have work to do."

"What's a few minutes here or there?"

She liked a man who took time to have fun. She just wasn't sure she could join in.

"Atlas likes to dance," he said over his shoulder as he downloaded several songs, then connected his iPhone to a speaker docking station on the bookshelf. He appeared nostalgic when he said, "I surfed at every opportunity when I was young. I lived in the Gulf. For me, no band can compare to the Beach Boys. The sand and sun is in every beat of their music."

"Fun, Fun, Fun" began to play. Atlas climbed off the couch, turned in a circle. Rue barked her excitement. The dachshunds did their own short-legged bouncing.

Beth watched as Rylan clapped his hands to the music while two-stepping among his dogs. His moves were concise. But cool. He supported the Dane's front paws when Atlas jumped up on his hind legs. The dog kept his balance. He took several forward and backward steps before dropping back down. The big boy wiggled, proud of himself.

Beth was amazed. "He makes a good partner."

"You should see him in a Conga line." Ry was teasing her.

The image made her grin.

Ry motioned, encouraging her. "Join us, Beth."

The music filled the living room, alive and beckoning, yet her smile faded, and the past held her still. Her heart weighed heavily. What she'd thought would be fun moments before no longer appealed. Her arms were leaden. Her feet refused to move. Her voice caught when she said, "I'll watch."

"Watch me dance with my dogs?" He shook his head.

"Not on your life." He stood at one end of the couch, holding out his hand, expecting her to close the distance between them.

She could not.

Atlas came to her then. He sensed her apprehension. He took her hand in his mouth and gave a gentle tug. He forced her to take that first step toward Rylan.

Baby steps, she told herself. She could do this. She had to. Additional steps followed until she reached Rylan. Atlas handed her over to him.

Ry twined his fingers with hers. "You made it."

Yes, she had.

"I Get Around" played next. Ry smiled down at her. "You can do this," he encouraged. Ry spun her beneath his arm before she could dwell further on her memories. Around and around she went. He then captured her against him until she could catch her breath.

No man should have a chest that solid, she thought, leaning into him.

He held her loosely, widened his stance, and muscles flexed in his thighs. The flat of his hand rested low on her spine. His scent was soap, sunshine, and masculinity.

They danced together. Slowly at first.

Her joints felt rusty. Creaky. They took short steps to "Kokomo," until she was able to relax and her body became more fluid. He then eased back and let her move on her own.

Somehow she managed. She let the music sift into her. Felt each note in her heart. Made a new memory with Rylan. She swayed, her feet finding their own way. No push, no hurry, she let it happen. In her own time.

The song ended, and Rylan cleared his throat. "One more to go. A surprise."

His thoughtfulness brought tears to her eyes. "I Want to Dance with Somebody" had her closing them against the

NO ONE LIKE YOU

pain. She pictured her parents and felt their love. Her body responded to all that she'd once known, and all that she had lost. She became one with the lyrics.

She danced.

She wished the music could've lasted forever. Unfortunately it ended too soon. She crossed her arms over her chest and held on to the moment. She didn't want to open her eyes. Ever.

When she did peek through her lashes, she found Rylan standing at the corner of the couch. The dogs sat near their beds. They all watched her. Rylan's stunned expression made her question her dance moves. Had they been that bad?

"Did I embarrass myself?" she finally managed.

Ry continued to stare at her. He seemed as lost in the moment as she had been. "You were amazing," he said sincerely.

She squeezed herself tighter. "I let myself go."

"Your soul took over. Impressive, Beth."

Atlas barked his agreement. The dogs came to her then. Nudging, nuzzling, and demanding that she pet them. She dropped down on one knee and loved on them. For the first time in ages, she felt part of a family. Even if it was a canine household.

The doorbell chimed, drawing Ry to the entrance. She heard him talking, but couldn't distinguish his words. He returned shortly. "A man from Aidan's construction company is here to take measurements for the fence. I'm headed outside to show him the layout."

"I'll be in my office."

"I'll find you later." He turned and left.

She realized with his departure that she hadn't mentioned Ava Vonn. A touchy subject, for sure. She didn't want him blindsided. Telling him was all in the timing. She'd wait, pick the right moment. If there was one. No man wanted to hear that his date had hooked up with one of his teammates.

She rolled her shoulders and debated baking a quick batch of dog biscuits before settling at her computer. Atlas seemed to read her mind. He head-butted her toward the kitchen. The boy was a bottomless pit.

Rylan walked into the kitchen just as she opened the oven door and released the scent of sweet potato chips. Atlas howled his excitement. Ry joined in. Beth shook her head. Man and beast celebrating snack time.

The other dogs came at Atlas's call. Beth had hoped to save some chips for the cookie jar. Once cooled, they were devoured in two minutes flat. The Dane didn't believe in saving a few for later. He wanted them all now.

"Sweet potato breath," Beth teased Atlas when he tried to wipe his mouth on her. She'd gotten quick with the dish towel. She caught him before he drooled on her.

Rylan took an apple from the fruit bowl on the counter and tossed it in the air. Atlas looked ready to jump and retrieve, but Ry was faster. He caught it over his head. Then took a bite. The Dane waited for him to share. Ry searched out a knife, then sliced off a piece. The apple was crispy, and the big dog chewed loudly.

Ry discussed his afternoon between bites. "I need to gear up for my speech tomorrow at the retirement center. I'm going to make some notes. I'd appreciate it if you'd type them for me."

"Happy to," she agreed.

"Then there's the Gallery Walk." He paused, looked thoughtful. "Have you been on the boardwalk?"

"Only briefly," she confessed.

"Join me tonight then? Unless you have other plans."

No plans at all. Still, she hesitated. He was Rylan Cates. Elite athlete. Hometown sports hero. A super sexy guy with an edgy haircut. "Sure there isn't someone you'd rather ask?"

He shook his head. "I want to kick back and relax tonight. You're easy company." He paused, finished with, "I need you to call Evelyn Wells. She owns Galler-E. Let her know I'm looking for a painting. She knows my taste."

"The dogs?" They were her first concern.

"We won't be gone that long."

"I'm in," she agreed. Only to add, "If you change your mind between now and then, I'll understand." She gave him an out.

"I don't break dates." He shot her a self-deprecating smile. "I just get dumped."

Dumped. By Ava Vonn. He'd given her an opening. Maybe this was a good time to tell him about the hookup. Beth was about to, she had every intention of doing so, until his iPhone rang. He slipped it from his side pants pocket, glanced at the incoming ID, and accepted the call. His voice warmed when he answered. "Hello, Jillian."

Beth recognized Jill as the team's community liaison. No doubt calling on Rogues business. She left the kitchen so Ry could speak privately.

Her office shrank in size when the dogs joined her. She heard Rylan take the stairs to his room above, and she expected the dogs to follow. They didn't. They seemed content to squeeze together around her chair. The temperature in the room rose ten degrees. She fanned herself with a file folder.

An hour passed, then two. It was after four by the time Rylan appeared at her door. Yawning. He held a yellow legal pad in his hand. "I love talking about the Rogues, but I'm not much of a public speaker. I need notes. I'm not good at winging it."

"I'm sure you'll be great."

He laid the pad on her desk. "Two pages. Bullet points. Let me know if you can't read my writing or have any questions."

She scanned what he'd done. She had no problem deciphering his handwriting. It was neat and precise. "I'll type this now."

"Once you're done, we'll head out."

"The dogs need to be fed and walked first."

"I'll take care of them."

She started. "It's my job."

"I don't mind helping when I'm home and on my own time. That's the case now. Next week the gang is all yours. My sister sent me an e-mail with a new organic dog recipe that I've wanted to try. Ground Round Rice Balls."

"Sounds yummy."

"I'm having a sliced chicken and sprout sandwich. Care to join me?"

"Some other time." She pursed her lips. "I've got my heart set on junk food on the boardwalk. My eyes will be bigger than my stomach."

He frowned slightly. "Not healthy, Beth. You'll get a stomachache."

" 'Plop, plop, fizz, fizz . . .' "

"You have Alka-Seltzer?"

"I bought a box today at Crabby Abby's when I picked up your items."

"Don't bellyache to Atlas later tonight. He's not sympathetic."

"I'll suffer in silence."

Ry ran his hand through the longer side of his hair. "I'll meet you at the front door in one hour."

"I'll be there." She started typing his notes.

Afterward, she took a quick shower and changed her clothes. She decided on a pale pink tank top, skinny black jeans, and a pair of white socks with red hearts. The positive message read *Heart of a Champion*. She slipped on her Keds.

She met Rylan in the entrance hallway with a minute to spare. The dogs had gathered around him. He spoke softly to them. She caught the words *behave* and *I'll be back soon*. They listened intently, their ears flickering.

She took a moment to admire the man. He filled out his clothes nicely. He'd tucked a light blue T-shirt designed with a row of colorful surfboards into stonewashed jeans. He wore his leather flip-flops.

Going out with him seemed surreal. She was afraid to talk, afraid to let her excitement show. She was his PA. She'd known him only one day, yet it felt like months. She'd settled into his cottage. He'd made her feel at home.

"We're taking the Range Rover," he said as he locked the door behind them. "I don't take chances with my McLaren. There'll be lots of traffic and overflowing parking lots. My sports car stays home tonight."

Ry's prediction of a large crowd was accurate. He found a parking spot two blocks from the beach, and they walked from there. The Gallery Walk drew tourists and locals, and the evening hummed with activity. Beth took it all in.

Rylan was a local celebrity and easily recognized. People stared, smiled, and stopped to chat with him. The man was polite. He signed autographs. He made small talk. Kids idolized him. Men admired him. Women were into him.

Fans put a wedge between them. She eased out of the way. She wasn't dependent on Rylan and decided to do the Gallery Walk alone. Long sections of the boardwalk were set up as an outdoor gallery, showcasing photos and paintings. The artwork beckoned to Beth. She moved comfortably among the patrons and those merely browsing.

The majority of the paintings cost more than she could afford . . . at the moment, anyway. In her previous life, she would've chosen several beachscapes to decorate her home. Tonight, her shoulder bag was light on cash. The money she carried would be spent on junk food.

She sat on a bench before a display of black-and-white photographs and ate a basket of chili-cheese fries. Sipped an orange soda. The Before and After photos fascinated her. The photographer had chosen weather as his medium. Tsunamis, earthquakes, volcanic eruptions, blizzards, and more. The three-scene sequences transitioned from normality to disaster. Seamlessly.

One tragic print of Atlantic City made her swallow hard. Here was a witness to Hurricane Sandy. The photo struck home. The October progression started far left with a stretch of boardwalk and beach in filtered sunshine. Advancing, a sweep of stormy skies, high winds, and surging waves darkened the middle panel. The right side revealed the aftermath. A toppled Ferris wheel and lost storefronts. A man sat on his roof with his head in his hands. People waded through standing water. It was heartbreaking.

Beth finished her snack, tossed the paper basket and soda can in a trash receptacle, then moved closer to the display. Disaster and depression surrounded her. A stand of smaller unframed photos caught her eye. Most were eighteen by twelve inches. She felt drawn to study each one.

She traced a glossy corner of the island of Leyte in the Philippines. Once forested and mountainous, it lay devastated in the wake of Typhoon Haiyan. In another, a lone farmhouse in North Dakota stood stark against a winter sky. Light snowfall whipped into blizzard. The smoke from the chimney disappeared in the white-out.

She thumbed further into the stack. The sixth photograph stopped her cold. She came face to face with her past, and it stared back hard. She felt disoriented, out of time, out of place. All noise on the boardwalk faded. She stood in silence, oblivious to the people around her.

The Statton wedding. The photograph came alive as she relived each moment. To the left, the sun sparkled on a fairytale tent, manicured lawn, and wedding party. Absolute perfection. Until the storm crashed the reception. Mother Nature glared at her from the middle section. Black sky, thunder, and lightning. No amount of old money could've kept the rain away. The sky opened, and it had poured.

She gazed right, to the final frame. To the screaming bride and sobbing bridesmaids. To the swearing groom and distressed guests. *To her.* Standing wet and weary near the wedding arch. Her hands covered her face. Her linen summer suit had lost its style and sheen. Her shoulders slumped in defeat.

She was grateful that no one would recognize her, unless they knew her well. She'd changed since that day. Physically and mentally. She'd cut her hair, lost weight, and no longer hung her head. She'd moved on.

Her initial urge was to place the photo at the back of the stack. To hide it. Yet a different part of her wanted to buy it. On the off chance it would sell to someone else.

She slid her fingers nervously around the edges. Her eyes rounded. How had she missed the famous photographer's name at the bottom of the photo? Gerald deVasi. She'd hired the man for the videos and stills of the wedding. She never imagined that he would take the worst day of her life and smear it on film. She was disheartened.

She held the photo between her finger and thumb, careful not to crush the corner. She looked over the crowd, trying to locate the man. She couldn't find him . . .

He found her. "Elizabeth Avery?" Gerald called to her as he cut through the crowd. He was a hard man to miss with his prematurely white hair, pleated tuxedo shirt, and black pants. Reaching her, he touched her cheek. "Is it really you?

To acknowledge or deny? Everyone had a twin. Could she fool him? Doubtful. He was a photographer with a discerning eye. He'd also been her friend. Once upon a time.

"It's been too long," he said. "I'd heard you left Maryland. Are you living in Barefoot William now? Does your family know you're here?"

She took a step back. He lowered his hand.

"Hello, Gerald." She kept her voice even. Her life was private. No one knew her whereabouts. She planned to leave him and his questions in a matter of seconds—once he explained the photograph. She held up the wedding progression. "What's with this? Why would you embarrass me? How dare you make money off my misery?"

His brow creased, but he showed no remorse. "It was a miserable day, wasn't it?" he mused. "For both of us."

"Who gave you permission to use the print?" She had to know.

"They're not your negatives, Elizabeth," he said firmly. "The photos belong to me. I never got paid. Not even for the video shoot before the storm."

That made her feel bad. He'd deserved compensation. "Sorry about that, Gerald. You spent a lot of time working with a difficult bride."

"Difficult?" he snorted. "You're being nice. Nothing and no one pleased her. Her mother was the definition of rude."

"I know . . ."

"I know you do."

"Still, I hate to have you selling me at my worst."

"It's not about you, sweetie. I captured Mother Nature bitch-slapping the Stattons. That's priceless."

She glanced at the photo, then back to him. "How many prints did you make?"

"Just this one."

"How much?"

"You want to buy it?"

"I don't want anyone else to ever see it."

"Not many people would know it was you." He was sincere. "You're in the background. Your hands are over your face."

"But I know, Gerald."

"You know what, Beth?" Rylan Cates came up behind her.

She said the first thing that came to mind. "That photography is an art, and Gerald is incredibly talented." She hoped Ry would accept her answer.

He did. Rylan took a moment to scan several pictures. "You have an interesting style," he said to Gerald. He glanced down at Beth's hand. "Did you find a photo you wanted to buy?"

"Possibly." She hesitated. "Depending on the price."

Gerald eyed them curiously. He seemed interested in their relationship. Beth had no intention of clueing him in.

"Let me see the photo," Ry requested.

Her hands began to sweat. Praying he would not recognize her, she placed her thumb over her face in the image and held up the print. Ry tilted his head and looked at it thoughtfully. "I'm not sure I understand what you see in the photo," he commented. "Weather can be unpredictable. It ruined someone's big day."

That it had, Beth thought. Both the bride's and her own.

Rylan slipped his wallet from his back pocket before she could locate her checkbook in her handbag. She was hesitant to write a check. It had her old Maryland address on it. "Let me buy the photograph for you," he offered. "A welcome to Barefoot William."

She shook her head. "I can't let you do that."

"If not from me, would you accept a gift from Atlas?" His mention of the Great Dane made her smile.

"You make it hard for me to say no."

"The big boy's become attached to you. He'd want you to have the print," Rylan insisted. He turned to Gerald. "What do I owe you?"

Gerald debated. Beth could almost hear his mind work. None of his photographs had a price tag. Some people appeared able to pay more than others. She figured Gerald priced them when he sold them. Had he recognized Rylan Cates? Everyone else on the boardwalk seemed to know him. If so, the price of the photo was about to go up. She refused to let that happen.

She took a chance and said, "You mentioned I was the first to take interest in this particular photo." She hoped to devalue Gerald's dollar.

"That you were," Gerald replied honestly. He held her gaze until he came to his decision. "It's worth five hundred dollars, but I'll let it go for fifty."

"Twenty," Beth countered.

"Let's split the difference. How about thirty-five?" Rylan paid the photographer.

Gerald took the print from Beth, slipped it into a protective cardboard envelope, and passed it to her. Instead of a hug, he squeezed her wrist. "I wish you sunshine."

She understood. He hoped her rainy days were behind her. So did she.

Rylan took her hand and drew her into the crush of the crowd. It was a friendly gesture. The stream of people was never-ending. "Have you eaten?"

"Fries and a soda."

"Did that fill you up?"

"I've room for cotton candy." She grinned. "Maybe a funnel cake." She pointed two storefronts down. "There's a fudge shop ahead."

"You're making my stomach hurt."

His heart was about to hurt, too, Beth realized, given

the group walking their way. The foursome was hard to miss. Halo Todd, Landon Kane, and their dates. The men wore their Cates T-shirts and seemed at home on the boardwalk. The ladies hung on their arms. She pegged the blonde as Ava Vonn.

Face or avoid them? That was the question.

Rylan had yet to see them. A fan had stopped him, requesting an autograph. His back was to the oncoming four.

Leave it to Halo to spot them. To flag them down. "Ry-man, Beth, are we having fun yet?"

Five

Rylan heard Halo shout for him. He'd barely finished signing his name on the shoulder of a young boy's baseball jersey when Beth grabbed his hand once again. Her urgent squeeze warned him something was up. She rose on tiptoe, her words low and rushed. "Halo's dating Ava Vonn."

What the hell? Was she serious? "You know this how?"

"He mentioned it this morning when he delivered the bench."

"And you're just telling me now?" A little warning would've been nice. He hated being the last one to know.

Her face was pale. Her eyes, a distressed gray. She squeezed his hand so tightly, he lost circulation in his little finger. "I wasn't sure it was my place."

"Trust me, this was worth sharing." Still, he couldn't fault her. She'd just started working for him. They'd yet to set boundaries. He didn't want her feeling bad, so he suggested, "Tell Atlas next time. He loves to gossip."

She managed a small smile. Eased off her toes.

He appreciated her concern, but she shouldn't have worried. His older brothers had taught him to man up in any awkward situation. To take control.

His game face in place, he glanced down the boardwalk. Seeing Ava with Halo gave him a moment's pause. It was unexpected, but not hurtful. It was what it was. He had escaped some serious scratches.

Beth's intentions suddenly became clear. Halo's haircut didn't reflect team unity. It was all about the man's hook-up. Sticking up for Ry, she'd snipped Halo's hair. Better than his balls.

Rylan moved beyond the foot traffic and found a place along the blue metallic railing that separated the boardwalk from the beach. He double-squeezed Beth's hand, signaling that all was well. Or as good as it was going to get at the moment. She eased her grip, but only slightly.

Easygoing worked for him and he smiled to himself over their silent communication. She got him.

Ava Vonn did not. The lady was high maintenance. Her purple satin jumpsuit, sparkling jewelry, and stilettos proved his point. She was a peacock amid Florida casual.

Halo seemed inordinately glad to see him and Beth. He greeted Ry with a complicated fist-bump. Landon did the same. Ava couldn't meet his eyes.

"Hello, Ava." He played it straight. His greeting seemed to surprise her.

Halo, too. "You know each other?"

Ry nodded. "Ava interviewed for my assistant position." It was important for him to clear the air. "I invited her to dinner when she didn't get the job."

Ava narrowed her gaze on him. Looking spiteful.

Her reaction meant little to him. He was most concerned about Halo. He had a season ahead with the right fielder. He didn't believe in hiding the truth.

Halo turned to Ava, his expression puzzled. "You've dated Ry-man?"

Ava ran a long, lavender fingernail down Halo's arm. "Just to show there were no hard feelings. We didn't click."

Halo frowned and questioned his date. "Who doesn't get along with Ry?"

"Me, for one," Ava said, more sharply than she may have intended.

"He's a great guy," Halo insisted. "You missed out."

Ava shrugged a shoulder. "My loss."

Rylan watched and listened to their exchange. Halo wasn't pleased by her response. A muscle ticked in his jaw. Rylan had never expected his teammate to take his side. It was a surreal moment.

"You could do worse than Ry-man," Halo told her.

Ava arched an eyebrow. "I'm debating that now." Her comment was cutting. "You all look alike."

"Same haircuts." Halo winked at Beth. "We're trending." He went on to make the introductions. "Beth Avery, this is Ava Vonn."

She pinned Beth with instant dislike.

Beth didn't flinch. She was polite. "Nice to meet you."

Ava's lips pinched. "Or not."

Landon nodded to his date. "Gia, meet Beth and Rylan Cates. Gia's a friend of Ava's. Ry's a Rogue. Beth is his PA."

Everyone now knew everyone else. Ry figured that was as far as it would go. The men might be tight since they were teammates. He didn't foresee friendships forming among the women.

The throng thickened around them. Loud voices and laughter rose on the night air. Sunlight faded and pole lights came on at dusk. The nighttime entertainers emerged. Jugglers, magicians, and guitar players. Slow-moving stilt walkers, and unicyclists joined the Gallery Walk. Pedicab service stalled. The fringed rickshaws were swallowed in the crowd.

Beth hadn't moved from his side. Clutching her photograph to her chest, her left shoulder brushed his chest, and her hip leaned against his thigh. Halo and Landon seemed interested in the sights. Ava and Gia were visibly bored. They wanted to go shopping. They would return in an hour or so they said. They left the group and strolled south toward Saunders Shores.

The Shores was as high-profile as Barefoot William was honky-tonk. Waterfront mansions welcomed the rich and retired. Yachts the size of cruise ships lined the waterways. Private airstrips replaced commercial travel. Forbes listed Saunders Shores as the wealthiest resort community in the country.

The designer stores and fine dining at the Shores contrasted sharply with the T-shirt shops and food carts of Ry's hometown. He preferred his side of Center Street where people were carefree and down to earth. Life was lived at its own pace. Going barefoot was accepted. Vacationers never wore a watch.

He decided it was time to locate the Galler-E display. A local resident and admired talent, Evelyn Wells would have a prime spot. Chances were good she'd set up at the entrance to the pier. That was his destination. He squeezed Beth's hand, made his move to leave. "We're off."

Halo wasn't ready for them to go. He looked curiously from Ry to Beth. "You two together?" He was always blunt.

Ry was always honest. "We're both attending the art event."

Landon scrubbed his knuckles along his jaw. "Looks more like a date."

"We're here as friends."

"Friends don't hold hands," Halo kept on.

"It's crowded, and we got separated earlier," Rylan patiently explained. "It took me a while to find her."

Halo snorted. "Beth lost? Get real."

"A hot babe stands out," said Landon.

Beth shifted uneasily beside Ry. She didn't take compliments well. The men had embarrassed her.

Ry stated the obvious. "She's short."

Halo wouldn't let him off the hook. "I'd have seen her."

Landon nodded. "Yeah, me, too."

What's with them? Rylan wondered. Could they be more annoying? "Go find your women," he suggested.

"We'll let them find us," said Landon.

"They're not Beth. We want to spend time with her."

Not time with *him,* Rylan realized, but with *her.*

That didn't set well. They both had dates. He had his PA. "You were headed north when you spotted us, and we were walking south," he reminded them.

"Easy fix," said Halo. "We'll turn around."

"Beth won't mind if we tag along, will you, babe?" Landon asked her.

She sighed. "Can you behave?"

Halo looked down at his T-shirt. "We're Cateses and can do no wrong."

"That's reassuring," she muttered.

The guys dogged them, reminding Rylan of Atlas. Constantly on his heels. He'd wanted to spend time alone with Beth; to get to know her better. That had become impossible. Three Rogues together were a target for autographs and photos. Somehow Beth got pushed to the side. Once again he lost sight of her.

When he did locate her, he saw that Halo had taken her hand and was leading her toward the amusement arcade. He heard Landon ask if she played foosball. She never had. Land called her a foosball virgin.

Ry's annoyance spiked. His baseball buddies were sucking all the fun out of his night. And he couldn't make a big deal out of the situation or the men would assume he liked Beth, that he wanted her to be more than his assistant. He did not. Assumptions were a bitch. Then why did he feel left out?

Beth stopped the men at the Galler-E display. She slanted a glance over her shoulder and caught Rylan's eye.

He appreciated her consideration. He wanted to buy a painting. He caught up with them to seek her opinion.

Halo gravitated toward *Two Nudes,* an abstract of flesh tones, squares and ovals without physical form. He stood before the painting, tilting his head, trying to see more in the artwork than was actually there. Beth laughed at him.

Halo pulled a face. "I don't get it."

"Me, either," said Landon. "I think that small circle in the corner is a boob."

"I think not," Beth disagreed. "Use your imagination. See the intimacy."

Landon squinted. "They're doing it?"

"Hot and heavy," she told them.

Rylan listened to their exchange and smiled to himself. The guys were staring so intently at the painting, they missed the twinkle in her eyes. She was teasing them. They'd yet to catch on.

"The woman's on top, right?" Landon sounded unsure. "The oval's humping the square."

"I see missionary," said Halo.

"It's Kama Sutra," Beth said.

"More than one position?" Halo was amazed.

"They're about to break the bed."

It was then that Halo and Landon realized she had played them. They glared at her, then grinned. Devious grins that promised retribution.

Rylan liked her humor and how she fit in.

So did Halo. "You're good, babe."

"You had me going, too," said Landon.

"Abstract art is a personal experience," Beth told them. "We all see things differently."

"I'm going to buy the painting and study it further." Halo went to find the artist.

Landon went off on his own, viewing the mixed media of watercolors, acrylics, and pastels with a discerning eye.

Rylan watched as his teammate paused before *City Park*. The painting portrayed a triangular-shaped face wearing mirrored sunglasses. A gray cloud floated as hair. The nose spread like a tree trunk. Tiny joggers formed the mouth. Skyscrapers were reflected in the lenses.

Weird, Ry thought.

But Landon seemed to like it. A sleek woman dressed in a tunic and yoga pants joined him at the easel. She looked artsy. She pointed to the painting and made a comment, apparently speaking Greek, given Landon's expression. He blew out a breath and concentrated harder.

Rylan turned to Beth. "Do you see anything you like?"

"I'm a fan of abstracts," she told him. "Evelyn has quite a selection."

Close to fifty acrylics, if he'd counted correctly. He followed Beth as she wandered from painting to painting, still hugging her photograph to her chest. The black and white photo seemed important to her. He hadn't taken her for someone who liked washed-out weddings. Those pictured looked outraged. Bitter. Unforgiving of the weather. Not pleasant people to hang on her wall.

Evelyn Wells spotted him a moment later. She parted the waters to reach him, greeted him with a hug, then welcomed Beth warmly. Ry had always liked Evelyn. Flamboyant and close to seventy, she was a local talent with international patrons. She favored landscapes and intense colors. Her abstracts hung in private residences, business offices, Mediterranean villas, and a Scottish castle. She could've lived anywhere in the world, but she called Barefoot William home. The community considered her family.

She smiled when she said, "Beth called me. I have just the piece for you, Rylan. In fact, I painted it with you in mind. It's at my gallery." She hooked her arm through his, then nudged him to take Beth's hand—which he'd planned to do, even without her encouragement. "A short walk on a gorgeous night."

She spoke briefly to her assistant before they turned a corner and headed down the sidewalk. They soon ended up walking single file against the flow of people streaming toward the boardwalk. The Gallery Walk was well-received, attendance at an all-time high. His sister Shaye would be pleased.

Located two blocks from the beach on White Sands Way, Galler-E showcased struggling and emerging young artists. Several renowned watercolorists owed Evelyn their start. Open to the public, the most expensive pieces hung on cameo pink walls protected from the press of the crowd and the salt air. A hostess greeted patrons at the door.

An associate served iced glasses of sparkling water and trays of canapés. Rylan tried cream cheese and smoked salmon on a thin round of French bread. He finished it in two bites. Beth chose a cucumber finger sandwich with whipped Feta and sun-dried tomatoes. She ate it so slowly, Ry thought she'd never finish. The lady could savor. She flicked her tongue to the corner of her mouth, then swept her lower lip.

His blood surged. He had the strangest sensation of her licking him. His chest, his abdomen, lower. It was unnerving. His body tensed when she accepted a second canapé. He shifted his gaze away from her lips, yet the feeling lingered.

Culture and festivity met at the gallery. Paintings were walking out the door as fast as patrons could purchase them. It was a profitable night for Evelyn Wells.

A short time later, Evelyn directed them to a private room. Rylan let Beth pass ahead of him. He saw her eyes widen and her lips part when she spotted the large painting. It covered half the far wall. She was in awe. But then so was he.

The abstract had his name on it. He made the decision to buy it the moment he laid eyes on the piece. Evelyn invited them to sit on Queen Anne chairs placed at a proper distance before the powder blue seascape with curled waves and a spiral sun. A surfboard with a broken fin leaned against a weathered wooden fence.

"Azure." Evelyn told them the name of her painting. She then left the room, closing the door behind her.

Seated beside him, Beth released an appreciative breath. "Rylan, if you don't buy this painting, I will."

He wasn't sure she could afford it. "How do you think it would look in my living room?"

"Fabulous." She was excited. "You could add pieces of furniture to pick up the colors in the painting."

That he could. Perhaps it was time to select a new couch and a couple chairs. He would no longer have to fight Atlas for a place to sit. The big dog preferred the sofa to his dog bed.

Beth leaned her shoulder against Rylan's. An unconscious move, but he liked the feel of her against him. She tilted her head and took in the texture and colors of the painting. Her wild curls brushed his jaw. Pear shampoo scented her hair.

She flexed her ankles, wiggled her feet. "I can feel the wet sand between my toes with the incoming tide."

Ry wasn't quite there, but the overall impression was appealing. The fact that Evelyn had chosen the painting for him pleased him greatly. Even better, Beth liked it, too. Somehow that cemented his purchase.

He had never shopped with a woman. No female opinion had mattered, not until hers. She could help him set up his living room, then share it with him for a short time. Eight weeks would fly by. He barely knew her, but the thought of them eventually going their separate ways bothered him. More than it should.

Atlas would miss her.

Evelyn gave them plenty of time to view the painting. She returned, smiling, looking hopeful. "What do you think?" she asked Ry.

"When can it be delivered?" He hoped soon.

"Tomorrow," she assured him. "My assistant will call ahead. I'll send experts to mount the painting."

"Make it after three, if possible," he requested. "We have an early afternoon engagement." He would be speaking at the retirement village. Beth would accompany him. He didn't want Atlas meeting the delivery truck.

He stood then, and Beth rose, too. He slipped his wallet from his back pocket, removed his American Express black card, and handed it to Evelyn. She hadn't quoted him a price, but he had faith it would be fair. "Add a donation as well. You help starving artists. Let's offer an art scholarship for a year. Make it anonymous."

Evelyn got tears in her eyes. "You are a good man, Rylan Cates. I have someone in mind who could use your assistance."

"Do you frame in-house?" he asked the gallery owner.

Evelyn nodded.

He went on to say, "It's a black and white photograph, not a painting."

Evelyn was accommodating. "Still something we could do."

He turned to Beth. "I'd like to frame your wedding photo."

She started. "Whatever for?"

"To be nice."

"You bought the picture, and I thank you. That's enough. There's no need to spend more money on me."

"Can I see the photo?" Evelyn inquired.

Beth had a white-knuckle grip on the protective cardboard envelope.

Ry wasn't sure she would give it up. Her hand shook when she passed it to Evelyn. She made a nervous fist afterward.

Evelyn carefully unwrapped the photograph, held it up by one corner, and took it in. "A deVasi," she said admiringly. "I've met Gerald. He's made quite a name for himself." She glanced at Beth, went on to ask, "Do you know these unhappy people?"

Beth didn't give her a direct answer. "I was fascinated by the storm."

"Weather can be controversial," Evelyn agreed. She smiled at Beth. A small, almost secretive smile as if something private passed between the women that didn't involve Ry.

That made him curious. He didn't like being out of the loop.

Evelyn was contemplative. "Should you allow me to frame your photo," she said to Beth, "I would suggest a border in mauve or pale turquoise to soften the subject matter."

"It is rather. . . . harsh," Beth agreed.

"Thunderstorms devour. Sunshine nourishes," said Evelyn.

"Florida is the Sunshine State."

The women exchanged a further look that went deeper than their words. Rylan had no idea what was going on.

However Beth understood perfectly. She released a soft breath. Visibly relaxed. Decided on the color. "Let's go with turquoise."

"Good choice." Evelyn inserted the photograph back into the cardboard envelope. "Give me two days on the frame."

"I'll pick it up," Beth said. "There's no need to deliver."

"I look forward to seeing you again." Evelyn went to ring up Rylan's sale and returned for his signature.

Ry took Beth's hand as they left the gallery. He was happy with his painting. He felt good about the night ahead, too. He wanted to show Beth the boardwalk and the pier. This was his home. He never got tired of the carnival rides and arcade. Amusements where he could let his inner child out to play.

People collected on the sidewalk, talking, showing off their purchases. Lots of smiles and laughter. Shadows played between the pole lights. Stars patterned the sky.

They stopped at the corner of Center Street and the boardwalk and Beth asked, "I wonder what happened to Halo and Landon." She sounded concerned.

Ry wasn't the least bit worried. "They create their own fun." Wherever they landed. "Anything in particular you'd like to do?" He left the decision to her.

"Am I too old to ride the merry-go-round?"

She'd typed *thirty* on her résumé, but age didn't matter. "The ride is timeless. Grandparents ride with their grandkids."

Big kids rode the carousel, too, Ry was soon to find out. Halo and Landon were jockeying for the brass ring. Great. Just great. His teammates waved to them.

"Yee-ha," howled Halo.

The ride slowed, came to a stop, and the men dismounted. They headed for the ticket booth and purchased four passes. Landon motioned to Beth. "Ride with us, sweetheart. The old man can come, too."

Beth noticed their dates were missing. "Where are Ava and Gia?"

Ry was wondering the same thing.

Landon shrugged. "We got ditched."

"They chose shopping over us," added Halo. "Go figure."

Neither man seemed to care. They had a way of springing back.

Ry wasn't about to let Beth ride without him. Not with

his teammates on board. He led her beneath the orange scalloped top and across the polished wooden platform. He caught their reflections in the mirrored center panels. Beth was wide-eyed as she took in the purple and white horses standing three abreast. Each mount had jeweled amber eyes and a gold saddle. Their legs were bent, ready to race.

Halo thought he was the Lone Ranger. He chose a white horse, showed off. "Hi-ho, Silver." He faced the rear of the horse, his hands on its rump, and jumped—but not high enough. He didn't clear the wooden tail. Profanity colored the air. A guttural groan followed. He dropped like a bag of sand. Sucked air. Was down for the count.

That count lasted several minutes. Rylan felt his pain and signaled to Oliver Ray, who managed the carousel, to hold off starting the ride. Only two other adults were on the carousel. Both young women. They sat horses diagonally across the platform, their expressions concerned.

Beth released Ry's hand and took a step toward Halo. Rylan held her back. A man needed time alone after he'd slammed his groin into a horse's tail. He'd be sore and bruising. Her sympathy wouldn't be welcome. However well-intentioned.

Halo slowly crawled to his feet. Took several deep breaths. He wasn't about to let the horse get the better of him. His face was pale and his lips were pinched when he stepped into the leather stirrup. He grunted, tugged himself up. Once mounted, he stood stiff-legged in both stirrups, unable to sit on the saddle. He looked like he was *posting*. Rising to a trot.

Landon eyed Halo from the platform. "Dude?"

"I'm no fuckin' cowboy," Halo ground out.

"You've lost your giddy-up."

"And my sex drive."

"Let's cut," Landon gave him an out.

Halo gritted his teeth. "I'm riding the beast."

Beth picked her horse next. She was short, yet chose the tallest lavender steed. She couldn't reach the stirrup and needed a boost. Landon came to her rescue, but Rylan glared him off. Land took two giant steps back and swung onto a deep purple racer.

Beth was small boned and a lightweight. Ry wrapped his hands about her waist, and his fingertips touched over her navel. He had her up and settled before she was aware her feet had left the ground. She straddled her mount, clutched the pole. She was ready to ride.

Rylan's horse was the color of a dark plum. Its amber eyes sparkled. Calliope music set the carousel in motion. The horses went up, down, and all around. They picked up speed.

Beth smiled at him. "This is fun." Her voice rose above the Beer Barrel Polka. "I haven't been on a merry-go-round since I was eight, when my parents took me to the state fair."

"I'll get you a monthly amusement pass. You can ride to your heart's content in your free time."

"My free time?" She seemed surprised.

"I don't expect you to work twenty-four-seven. Although Atlas might," he teased her. "My only weekend obligation is the picnic. After that, give me a head's up when you want a day off."

She looked thoughtful. "I have nowhere to go," she slowly admitted. "I like your cottage. Your dogs."

How did she feel about him? he wondered. Strange that he would even care. He liked being around her. He hoped she felt the same way. He didn't have many women friends. Most wanted to date his brains out.

A thought crossed his mind, and he asked her a question that hadn't come up in her interview. "Do you even like baseball?"

She nodded as her horse went up and his went down.

"My grandfather does too. I'll need you to drive him to my games when Shaye's not available to do so. Frank is my biggest fan."

"I'm looking forward to meeting your granddad."

"You will tomorrow."

"I'll set up a schedule with him then, so we can meet and play cards."

"He aims to win. Prepare to get beaten."

"I'm a good loser."

The carousel slowed, stopped. The music continued, but on a softer note. Landon hopped off his horse.

Halo was slow to dismount. He struggled. His face screwed in pain. "No rootin' tootin' tonight," he told Rylan. "I need to ice." He walked bowlegged to the exit.

"Halo's my ride. I'm gone." Landon followed him out.

The two women on the carousel disappeared, too.

Rylan was off his horse and ready to assist Beth. She swung her right leg over the pommel and slid off quicker than he expected. He wasn't ready for her. She landed against him, and he caught her. Tucked her close.

She was warm and curvy.

Her breasts flattened against his chest.

Her belly softened against his six-pack.

Her hip bones rubbed his groin.

Her thighs parted over his sex.

One of her ankles curved the back of his knee. Hooking him to her.

Their breathing slowed. He breathed in. She, out.

Her lips parted.

His throat tightened.

She looked into his eyes and her expression reflected his own. Awareness. Apprehension, too.

Affection was not in their forecast. Beth was nice. Cute, even. Getting involved with her went against his work ethic. He needed a PA more than a lover. She wasn't his type. But his body had a mind of its own.

A man couldn't hide his erection. He'd held her too long.

He eased her down. Then stepped back. Forced a smile. "Cotton candy, funnel cake, fried Oreos? What's next?"

Her eyes brightened. "Pop Goes the Corn."

He took her hand, held it loosely, and they left the carousel behind. He led her through the crowd toward the popcorn shop.

They entered the buttery yellow door. The old-fashioned popper produced as fast as people ordered. One line was to buy boxes of theater butter, the all-time favorite. The second line formed before a glass counter, displaying a dozen other flavors. Beth chose caramel-macadamia nut. Ry preferred cheddar cheese.

All the café tables were filled. People lounged in no particular hurry so they took their popcorn outside and located a bench near the boardwalk railing. They faced the Gulf. The moon's reflection was captured in the mirror-smooth surface.

High tide grabbed the ankles of beachcombers. Seagulls did their night fishing, plunge-diving into schools of small redfish. A yacht cruised off-shore. The running lights were white to the stern of the boat, red to port, and green to starboard. They looked like Christmas.

The Gallery Walk had thinned considerably. The early burst of buyers took their artwork home. Ry hunched his shoulders, discouraging conversation or requests for autographs. He wanted to get to know his PA. Without interruption.

"What's your story, Beth?" he initiated. "Something that wasn't on your résumé."

She slowly ate her popcorn, hesitant to talk about herself. She wasn't going to be in town long. She wasn't there to make friends. While Rylan Cates was an attractive man, she wouldn't act on his appeal. But neither would she be rude to him. She'd been brought up better.

Her mouth was dry when she said, "There's not much to tell."

"I've learned your taste in photography. Downpours and drenched brides."

"I prefer happier endings."

"What was the attraction then?"

"The photo is a reminder of how quickly life can change." For the worse, in this case. She saw no reason to explain her involvement in the wedding. It was her past. "I know now that you like abstract art."

"I like to interpret my paintings in my own way."

She liked his imagination. He looked beyond his eyes. They munched their popcorn. Listened to the conversations around them. The laughter. The night seemed to smile.

"Ever played One or the Other?" Rylan asked her.

She shook her head.

He offered her a choice. "Pick one—Great Dane or Chihuahua?"

She couldn't help but smile. "Great Dane."

"Atlas would never have forgiven you had you said *Chihuahua*."

"How would he have known?"

"I'd have told him."

"He is your buddy."

"And your sidekick."

True enough. Atlas kept his eye on her. The big dog was afraid she'd bake treats when he wasn't looking and he'd miss out.

"Snow or sunshine?" Ry tossed out.

She wondered if he was trying to pinpoint her hometown. She had no plans to return to Maryland. Her answer was open-ended. "I like seasons."

He nodded, kept it simple. "Books or movies?"

"Books." She loved to read.

"Mysteries, thrillers, romance?"

She drew in a breath. "Self-help."

That set him back. His brow creased. She knew what he was thinking. It was written on his face—did she have issues? Was she carrying the weight of the world on her shoulders or merely trying to improve herself? She wasn't ready to tell him more. So she let him wonder.

"Psychologist or psychic?"

"I've never studied ink blots or stared into a crystal ball."

"We have a fortune-teller on the boardwalk," he told her. "My aunt, Madame Aleta, has the 'sight.' " He used air quotes. "Stop and see her sometime."

"Do you get readings?" Beth asked, surprised. Rylan seemed more logical than paranormal minded.

"Aleta predicted my home runs to within one last year."

Her lips parted in surprise. "That's amazing."

"Halo keeps trying to schedule an appointment with her." Rylan chuckled. "But she needs a calm mind to make a connection. He's wired."

"That I believe."

"Song in your head or do you hear voices?"

"Does the Meow Mix commercial count?"

"Better than a monkey clanging cymbals."

"Or a bongo-playing dog."

"Atlas," they said simultaneously. Then grinned at each other.

"Do you follow your heart or your head?" Ry asked.

"I listen to my gut."

"I live by my intuition, too."

They finished off their popcorn within a bite of each

other. Rylan stacked the boxes, then made a long dunk shot into the distant trash receptacle. Beth admired his technique. Walking the boxes to the garbage can covered her skills. She wasn't very athletic.

Not wanting their conversation to end, she continued with One or the Other. "Climb a mountain or trek the desert?"

"Surf the Gulf," he replied, opting for his own answer. "Morning or night person?" he shot back.

"Morning. I'm up with the sun."

"Atlas gets up early, too. The sooner you're up, the quicker he eats. Rue and the dachs are more patient. At-las has his own inner alarm clock." He leaned forward, rested his elbows on his knees. "House, condo, apart-ment?"

"I like your cottage."

"So do I," he agreed. "Traveler or homebody?"

"I've been on the road a lot recently."

He side-eyed her. "Touring the country or running away?" he snuck in.

Too personal. He'd hit a nerve. She hedged. "A little of both." She had no place to return. She would drive until she relocated.

"What about family? Your parents have passed away. Do you have relatives?" He seemed concerned for her.

The thought of her stepmother and stepsister pressed heavily on her chest.

Rylan sensed her vulnerability, reached over, and took her hand. He held it lightly, rubbing his thumb across her palm.

Beth cleared her throat. She found it difficult to speak. Yet somehow she managed. "My dad remarried after my mom passed away. My stepmother put on a good face and pretended to like me while my father was alive. Once he was gone, she showed her dislike. Daily." She shrugged. "I found my own way."

"I'm glad you landed in Barefoot William."

So was she.

"Wallflower or life of the party?"

"I have a strong back for holding up walls."

Ry squeezed her hand. "I would have gotten to know you," he said sincerely. "My parents taught their boys to mix with all the girls. Not just the popular and pretty ones. Their advice led to female friendships over the years, which I might have overlooked otherwise. A woman who likes my dogs holds a place in my heart." He stretched, rolled his shoulders, and stood. He tugged her up beside him. "Let's head home."

The Gallery Walk came to an end. Artists were closing down their easels and packing up their paintings. Rylan and Beth had the boardwalk to themselves, yet continued to hold hands. There was comfort and companionship in his touch. She didn't feel alone.

He bought her an elephant ear and a candied apple on their way to his SUV. She ate the cinnamon-sugar fried bread on the ride home. She would save the apple for tomorrow.

Atlas and gang greeted them at the door with an exuberance that crushed Beth against Rylan. He curved his arm about her shoulders and supported her against the onslaught. She turned her face into his chest when Atlas tried to lick cinnamon sugar off her cheek. She breathed Ry in. Night air and man. Nice.

The Dane sniffed her candied apple through the paper bag she held.

She wasn't sharing her treat. She walked quickly to the kitchen and put it in the refrigerator, nearly closing the door on Atlas's nose. He was that close to snagging her apple.

"Walk?" Rylan offered his dogs.

Atlas and Rue spun in circles. The dachshunds bounced low. She collected their harnesses and helped hook them up. "Mind if I come with you?" she asked, not wanting to intrude on his time with his pets.

"You're one of us, Beth. You don't have to ask." He handed her Rue, Oscar, and Nathan's leashes. He kept Atlas on a tight lead until they reached the end of the driveway. Street lights were numerous. The night was bright as day.

"Atlas and I are going to jog." He added length to the big dog's leash. "Six blocks down to the cul-de-sac and we'll loop back." He grinned. "We'll meet at his Rip Van Winkle corner."

Dog playing dead in the middle of the road. A memory she would never forget. She gazed after the two of them as they took off down the street. The Dane's ears flopped and his nose was in the air, sniffing the breeze. Rylan was fluid. Athletic grace. He picked up his pace at the first cross street. Atlas bucked and charged alongside him.

Rue whined and the dachsies barked. They wanted their walk, too. Off they went. Beth easily controlled the three. She didn't have Atlas pulling on her arm.

They strolled the neighborhood. Driveways and yards were well-lit. Front window curtains were drawn back, and she caught sight of family gatherings. Groups sat around tables, possibly playing cards or a board game. Perhaps catching up on the events of the day. Or enjoying evening coffee and dessert.

Homey, she thought. *Togetherness. Sharing.*

Nostalgia gave her a hug. She missed her parents always, but tonight the feeling was doubly strong. She was an adult, yet memories of her mom and dad made her feel like a kid again. Sadness and loss had her slowing her steps.

The dogs sensed her mood. They stopped and stared up at her. Beth swiped her palm across her eyes. Her chest felt tight, and her throat closed. She refused to cry. Tears wouldn't bring her parents back.

A man rolled a garbage can to the curb.

A young boy rode his bicycle into the driveway next door.

A dog barked behind a fenced backyard. Rue and the weenies responded. A continuous chorus of howls erupted along the street.

"I heard you coming," Rylan called to her as he and Atlas rounded the corner. He was running full out. Atlas ran circles around him. It was a sight to behold.

The Dane saw Rue and came to a skidding stop before her. He nuzzled her, and she nuzzled back. Ry bent over to catch his breath. Atlas turned his foam-flecked jowls on Beth.

Beth shook her finger at him. "Don't you dare," she firmly said.

They stood toe to paw. Instead of wiping his face on her, Atlas shook his head. Foam flew, getting her equally as wet. He head butted her hip until she scratched his ear.

"You're doing laundry tomorrow," she told him.

"He adds too much fabric softener," said Ry. "He's not great with fluff and fold."

His comment made her smile. She passed Rue's leash to Atlas. "Take her home."

And he did. Rylan scooped up Nathan and Beth carried Oscar. They arrived at the cottage in no time. There, they unharnessed the dogs.

Atlas stood waiting for Beth.

Beth waited for Rylan. "Do you have anything further for me to do tonight?"

He shook his head. "I'm headed upstairs for some computer time. E-mails have piled up." He lightly touched her arm. "See you in the morning." He took the stairs two at a time.

At the top, he called down to her. "One or the Other. Giving speeches or listening to someone talk?" He sounded concerned about his presentation.

"I like listening. Your speech will be great," she assured him.

Six

Everyone in the audience was asleep. Including his grandfather.

Rylan Cates gazed at the senior citizens gathered in the lecture hall at the Barefoot William Retirement Village. One hundred folding chairs were set in rows of ten, only half were occupied. Of those seated, all had their eyes closed. Their heads were bent and their bifocals slid down their noses. Many snored. One man snored so loudly his body shook.

His grandfather had suggested the engagement a month ago. Frank had bragging rights on his grandson playing major league baseball and was proud of Ry.

Rylan had agreed. Yesterday, he'd put together a thirty-minute presentation.

His granddad had been the first to yawn, but the last to nod off.

Ry stepped from the spotlight and hopped off the small dais. Not a single person would miss him if he took a short break. Or even a long one. The snoring only grew louder. How could people sleep on metal folding chairs? he wondered. They had to be uncomfortable.

He'd planned to hand out Richmond Rogues T-shirts at the end of his talk, but he was no longer so sure. He'd brought large and extra-large sizes. Most of the men appeared to be medium; the women leaned toward small. They would drown in the cotton. Maybe the shirts would shrink in the wash. He could only hope so.

He located Beth at the back of the room and walked down the aisle, needing to speak with her. She was dressed in the same clothes she'd worn to her interview. Prairie flower top, long skirt, cowgirl boots. Her curls went every-which-way, her eyes were a dark gray, and her lips were pursed. She was concerned for him.

His speech had bombed. He was embarrassed, too. He wished he had done better. A part of him had wanted to impress her. Unfortunately, he had not. Tongue-in-cheek, he asked her, "How'd you like my speech?"

She leaned toward him, whispered, "You only spoke for fifteen minutes. Why didn't you finish?"

"I couldn't be heard above the snoring."

She sighed. "I'm sorry your audience fell asleep." She meant it. "I spoke to the residents on their arrival. One of the ladies mentioned pasta salad was served for lunch. Carbs relax the brain."

He rolled up the sleeves of his white shirt to his elbows. Then stuffed his hands in the pockets of his gray slacks. "They zonked." He couldn't get the image out of his head.

"They should be stirring shortly," she assured him. She reached for the circular switch on the wall and dimmed the overhead lights. "I don't want the brightness to startle them when they open their eyes." Her gesture was kind.

They moved to the lobby, which was only a few yards from the lecture hall. Sunshine streamed through the wide windows and domed skylight, and danced across the hardwood floors.

The area was bright and cheerful with its sand-toned furniture and lavender accents. A collection of dwarf palms stood six feet tall in natural ceramic planters in one corner.

A deep purple impatiens plant added color to the counter at the reception station.

Beth picked up a pamphlet off a corner table. She flipped through the pages; found it informative. "The brochure lists all the monthly events and activities, including the speakers for the month of February. You're one of many."

"I'll be the one remembered for putting everyone to sleep." He ran his hand down his face. "Was I that boring?"

She lightly touched his arm. "I loved your speech. However, judging from the brochure, the interactive presentations appear to work best."

"I should've tossed around a baseball?"

She looked thoughtful. "That might have proved strenuous, but film highlights of the Rogues season might've worked."

"Hindsight is twenty-twenty."

"Earlier this month, a florist demonstrated flower arrangements. Those who attended got to plant African violets in clay pots."

"What else?" he asked, curious.

"A nutritionist offered herbal remedies for colds, arthritis, and other ailments."

Rylan would have enjoyed that lecture. He took vitamins. Nutrients built up his body. Staying strong was important in sports.

"Then there are the therapy dogs."

He heard the smile in her voice.

"Three golden retrievers are brought in once a week. The seniors can walk, pet, and play with them." She tapped one corner of the page, drawing his attention. "One of the dogs had cancer as a puppy and has only three legs. His name is Tripod." She showed Ry the dog's picture then pursed her lips. "Atlas could be a therapy dog."

Ry had his doubts. "Not without a ton of training. He's

not aggressive, he's just big. A head butt or brush of his tail would knock someone over. The women I've seen are frail."

Beth read on. "The petting zoo brings Dalmatian guinea pigs for a visit. They're white with dark spots. They weigh three pounds and are a foot long. Malcolm and Morris are quite the snugglers." A further photo showed the guineas curled on an older lady's lap. She sat in a rocking chair, smiling.

Rylan took it all in. He couldn't arrange flowers or discuss herbs, but he did understand the appeal of pets.

He checked his watch and decided it was time to return to the lecture hall. Beth followed. He scanned the room. "Is everyone still breathing?" He had his concerns. One of the men in the back row was slumped low on his chair; his breaths shallow. "I'm tempted to stick a mirror under their noses."

Beth rolled her eyes. "You put them to sleep, not to death. These people are in their eighties. They deserve a nap."

His granddad was eighty-eight and a widower of twenty-two years. Frank still missed his wife. Emma was and always would be the love of his life. He was fortunate to have friends at the village—those old-timers who'd grown up in Barefoot William. Many had roots as deep as the Cates family.

Frank had avoided retirement for a long, long time—up until his citrus grove became a burden. There'd been days his bones had ached and his feet shuffled. He would fall asleep in his easy chair with both the television and living room lights left on.

Frank's family had checked on him often, making certain his stilt home was clean and that he had plenty of groceries. His loved ones came together, anxious and concerned, when he'd fallen off a ladder while cleaning the outside gutters. It was a job too big for one man. He'd fractured his ankle.

A second fall on his front porch steps had shaken Frank thoroughly. He'd slipped on a puddle of rain water. That's when he'd agreed to the move. The retirement community was perfect for him. It was the finest facility in Southwest Florida.

The village was gated and self-contained. Cars were obsolete. Golf carts and adult tricycles with big baskets provided outdoor transportation. Inside, the seniors rode motorized scooters or leaned on walkers and canes. Like Frank, a few still managed on their own.

The west wing of the facility was anchored by a small grocery store. A gift shop, hair salon, pharmacy, and library were also open for business. A medical team was on staff, and a hospital was close by.

The condominiums were large and comfortable. The seniors could move from their lifetime homes and still have room for their memories. Every condo had a kitchen, although most residents chose to eat in the main dining room. Meals were social. After-dinner decaf and dessert stretched into the evening hours.

All those in residence considered themselves related, whether they were or not. They were one big extended family. They faced aging together. That was their common bond. They held tight to each other and the years they had left.

Beside Rylan, Beth pointed to the front of the room. "Cora Salvo, the lady with the apricot hair in the third row, is wakening. Morton Potter, sitting next to her, has opened his eyes, too. I saw him yawn."

It amazed Rylan that she remembered their names. She'd stood in the back and greeted everyone at the door while he'd set up in front. The exchanges had been brief, yet she recalled each one.

She gave him a nudge, suggested, "Go back to the podium. You don't want anyone feeling bad that they fell asleep during your talk."

She was right. Her concern for the residents touched him. He never wanted to disappoint his grandfather. He headed for the low stage while Beth turned up the lights. Applause broke the moment he stepped in the spotlight. The noise woke everyone still sleeping. Those in the front row gave Ry a standing ovation.

He appreciated their enthusiasm, even if they hadn't heard his entire presentation. He had purposely cut it short when they'd all fallen asleep. He finished up with, "I have Richmond Rogue T-shirts, should anyone want one."

Beth came down the aisle and joined him on the dais. She helped him pass out the shirts. "Morton Potter," she whispered from the corner of her mouth as a brown-eyed man with a shock of white hair approached.

Puffing out his chest, Morton inquired, "Do you have an extra-large?"

"Morty played college football." Cora Salvo wasn't far behind him. "He likes sports."

"You could use a double extra-large, Morton," Beth said to him. "You have such broad shoulders."

The man grinned. He still had all his teeth, either that or a solid set of dentures. Morton carried himself taller with Beth's compliment.

Cora was a little bit of a woman. She was dressed smartly in a starched white blouse and dark pleated skirt. She added a wrinkle to her brow when she asked, "Any chance I could have two shirts? One for me and one for my roommate Lana Arnett. Lana wasn't feeling well, so she went to lie down after lunch."

"Two is fine." Rylan handed them to her. "I hope Lana feels better."

Cora lowered her voice, shared, "It's gas from the Italian dressing on the pasta salad. A tablespoon of Pepto-Bismol and she'll be back to her old self."

A woman with copper-colored hair introduced herself before Beth could make the connection. ""I'm Grace Mayberry. I'm ninety-six and the oldest resident at the village."

"A proud distinction," said Ry.

"Grace has a birthday next week," Beth informed him.

Grace smiled. "February sixteenth. You're invited, Rylan Cates, if you'd care to come. Your pretty assistant, too."

"Thank you. We'll check our schedules."

"Don't let spring training stand in your way," Grace said. "My birthday will be great fun. Parties are held in the activity room. There'll be cake and ice cream. Even chocolate. There will be dancing, too. You can box step, can't you, young man?"

Rylan nodded. He could manage the square.

"I'll save you a dance then," promised Grace. "I don't cha-cha anymore. It throws out my hip." Her shirt in hand, she leaned on her cane and walked back down the aisle.

A tall, thin woman with thick glasses came next. She narrowed her gaze on Ry. "What sizes are your shirts?"

"Large and extra-large," he told her.

She squinted further. "What sizes did you say?"

He repeated them to her.

"Small?" she tried again.

Beth intervened. She raised her voice and called the woman by name. "Turn up your hearing aid, Iris."

Iris proceeded to do so. "Better now," she said after making the adjustment.

Ry glanced at Beth, keeping his voice low. "How'd you know?"

"Her hearing aid is small, discreet, but I saw it when she straightened her glasses and the arms pushed back her hair.

His assistant was observant.

Once Iris could hear, she asked one final time, "The sizes?"

"Large is the smallest we have," Beth told her.

Iris contemplated. "I could wear the shirt with a gold belt, couldn't I? Fancy it up a bit."

"That you could do," Beth agreed.

Iris accepted her shirt and stepped aside.

The remaining Rogues shirts were quickly passed out. The room soon emptied, until only his grandfather remained. He was a tall man and still carried himself well. His face was weathered, but he had a full head of gray hair.

"Beth." His gramps cordially shook her hand before giving Ry a fist bump. Man to man. "I'm so proud of you, son. You're the best speaker this month."

Ry wasn't going to debate him. Everyone felt better after a nap. Life moved on. He would make sure each resident at the village had a ticket to at least one home ball game, should he want to attend. He'd have Beth check with the events coordinator tomorrow. Set up transportation to and from the stadium.

"Thanks for inviting me to speak. How about a shirt? I have a few left," he offered.

"I have several," his granddad replied. "I wear your number sixteen jersey on game day. Rogues fans gather in the TV room during the regular season. We cheer you on with popcorn and root beer floats."

Ry felt a lump in his throat. Frank honored him. For as long as he could remember, his grandfather had brought his own baseball glove to the park. He always liked sitting in the centerfield stands. He backed Ry's position.

Rylan would do his best to hit a home run over the wall during spring training. He'd airmail Frank a ball.

His granddad cleared his throat, lowered his voice. He put his hand on Ry's shoulder. "I overheard Grace Mayberry invite you to her birthday party. Don't feel obligated. I'll buy her a gift and sign the card from all three of us." He included Beth.

"She seems to like sweets," said Ry, recalling her comment on ice cream and cake, chocolate.

Frank frowned. "Sweets don't always like her. Grace is diabetic and needs to monitor her sugar. We all keep an eye on her."

"I'll be at Grace's party, even if Rylan can't make it," Beth decided on the spot. "I'll request the night off."

Ry would give her the time, whether he attended or not. He had several evening obligations scheduled.

"What's on your agenda for the rest of the day?" he asked his grandfather.

"Bingo," said Frank. "You can stay and play if you like. We're allowed guests at all activities."

Ry gave it some thought. It had been ages since he'd played Bingo. Not since he was twelve. He glanced at Beth. "We have a free hour. It's up to you."

"I'm in," she was quick to say.

Frank offered his arm to Beth, and she took it. A gentlemanly gesture. He smiled down on her. "Rylan mentioned you play cards."

"You name it, I play it. Or I'll learn how."

"I play for quarters."

"I'll bring a roll next time."

"We'll get along just fine."

Rylan packed up the box of shirts. "I'll run these out to my SUV and be back in a minute."

Frank nodded and included Beth when he said, "We'll save you a seat at our table in the recreational center. Take the main hall—we're third door on the right."

Ry watched his granddad and Beth walk down the aisle. Frank had been an active man all his life. His steps might be slower, but he was steady on his feet. Beth listened attentively as his grandfather relayed a story. They smiled at the same time. Ry found himself grinning, too.

The moment stood out in his mind. Beth and his grandfather. It felt good, right. He carried their image with him out to his Range Rover and back inside. He found the game room easily.

A gong sounded on the hour, and the wide hallway filled with seniors, electric scooters leading the way. It appeared a parade.

Bingo drew a big crowd. No one dallied. The commotion and noise as they entered the room sounded like a bunch of kids rather than a group of elderly citizens.

A square card table stacked with laminated, large print bingo cards—black letters and numbers on a white background—stood just inside the door. The residents took their time choosing their lucky cards. Those with poor eyesight played one card while others managed more. Ella Mayberry went with twelve.

A wicker basket held jumbo erasable daubers used to mark the cards. Ry noticed the women preferred neon glitter while the men chose standard colors. Kleenex tissue cleaned the surface after each game.

Twenty long tables were placed evenly. Chairs were spaced for elbow room. Rylan located Beth and his grandfather at the second table. Beth had saved him a place on her right.

He pulled out the chair, took a seat. "Only one card?"

"I'm a guest."

Ry grinned. "I took six."

"I've no intention of winning."

"I plan to."

"You're related to Frank. No one will mind if you shout 'Bingo.' "

That was true. He planned to keep an eye on her card, too. Make sure she blotted all numbers called. He'd call out for her if she won. Winners got a dollar.

Morton Potter sat on the far side of his grandfather. The two men discussed the weather; moved on to the shuffle-board tournament the following week. Both were going to participate.

Ry was glad his gramps remained active.

Within minutes, two middle-aged women addressed those gathered. Social director Miriam Myers introduced herself to those she had not met. Diane Norman was the recreational therapist, and available to anyone needing assistance.

Miriam crossed to a table set front and center. She rested her right hand on a black wire cage that stood securely on a holder, making it easy to turn and mix up the wooden balls. A drop sleeve released one ball at a time.

Miriam hooked up her microphone and went on to announce the first game—a line or diagonal. She cranked the cage, and it spun. A ball soon appeared. She called out the number with the letter. The ball then went up on the master board for clarity and easy tracking.

Ella Mayberry won the first game. She filled in her Bs. Morton Potter won the next, by forming an X. The games continued.

After a while, Rylan paid minimal attention to his cards, realizing there were times when watching someone play was more fun than participating. He eyed Beth once, then twice, and found he couldn't look away. It was self-defeating to try.

He liked the way she brushed her hair off her cheek, only to have the curls bounce back. Sometimes they covered one eye. Or tipped the corner of her mouth. Her brow creased as she squinted in concentration. The players were going for a blackout. Her hand hovered over the Os, her silver dauber poised. She dotted perfect little circles when a matching letter-number was called.

"You're missing squares," she told him without looking his way. Her cheeks were pink. He'd made her blush.

"How would you know?" he had to ask.

"I have excellent peripheral vision."

So she was aware that he was watching her. Had been for a good long time. "Do you mind?"

"That you were staring?" She sighed. "Either tell me why or look away."

One or the Other. He chose to tell. "I was admiring your focus."

"Which you've now broken."

He smiled to himself. He hadn't meant to rattle her, but he liked the fact he affected her. He had no idea why that pleased him so much. It just did.

"Bingo!" his grandfather called out, startling them both.

Ry jerked, and Beth nearly fell off her chair.

He leaned around Beth. "Congratulations, Gramps."

"Not me, son. Our Beth."

Our Beth. Frank had already taken to her. Rylan's chest tightened. He didn't want his granddad to get too attached. Her stay in their town was short-lived.

Beth looked down on her card. It wasn't fully covered. She had three spaces open. "I've several squares to go," she told Frank.

"I kept an eye out while my grandson was distracting you." Frank dabbed blue ink on the clear spaces. "You won, girl, despite Rylan's flirting."

"Flirting?" Her voice was soft, unsure. "A man like Ry doesn't flirt with a girl like me," she corrected Frank. "I work for him only." She stood then and walked her card forward to be verified.

Rylan was stunned by her comment.

Frank, not so much. "You were dallying."

His stare made Ry uncomfortable. His gramps knew him better than his parents. Even his own brothers. He never judged or criticized. He was always supportive.

Rylan couldn't hide anything from him. "It didn't mean anything." Or did it?

"Maybe not to you, but perhaps to her." Frank set down his dauber, snagged a Kleenex, and cleaned his card. "Beth is a sweet girl; she has a tender heart."

"You learned that in thirty minutes?"

"I listen when someone talks. There's always an underlying message." He paused, added, "What you see as casual, she may take seriously."

"Are you lecturing me, Gramps?" It would be a first. Ry wasn't offended, just curious.

"Merely giving advice. Take it or leave it."

One or the Other. Frank was seldom wrong. He saw people and situations from all angles. He'd raised concern because he cared about Ry. And Beth apparently, too.

"Point taken," Ry said.

Beth returned to their table a moment later. She waved a single dollar bill at him, smiled. "I'm the blackout champion." It was the last game of the day.

The social director walked around the room, collecting the cards and daubers. The residents headed for the door. It became a race. Two ladies interlocked the legs on their walkers. Two men on electric scooters collided at the exit. Fortunately no one was hurt.

"They're headed to the television room," Frank explained. "*Forever and a Day* is about to start. The soap opera is as old as we are. It started out on radio in nineteen thirty-two, then went to TV. Ella Mayberry heard the very first broadcast."

Rylan grinned at his granddad. "I didn't take you for a fan."

"My wife got me hooked when we were first married," his grandfather admitted. "I've followed the show ever since."

Beth opted into the conversation. "I left the show when sisters Betsy and Clara Walton became pregnant."

"By the same man." Frank knew the story line. "That episode was"—he mentally calculated—"six or seven months ago."

"Seven," Beth told him. Her voice was soft, nostalgic, as if she'd counted each passing day.

"The show moves slowly," Frank said. "Come join us anytime. You know where to find me."

"I'll see you soon," said Beth.

Rylan gave his grandfather a hug. Frank felt thinner than Ry last remembered. His shoulder blades seemed sharper, too. "See you at my picnic?" He wanted to be sure his granddad would attend.

"I'm riding with Shaye and Trace." Frank took his leave.

Rylan watched his grandfather until he cleared the door.

"You look worried," Beth commented.

Ry was honest. "He's getting up there in years."

"We all age."

True. "He likes to stay busy."

"He's also competitive. He's out to win the shuffleboard tournament. He has a side bet with Morton."

Ry understood competition. He'd like to watch his gramps compete, if time allowed. He turned to Beth "Ready to head home, Bingo champ?"

"Champ . . . I've never won anything."

"Feels good, doesn't it?"

"Yes . . . it does." Her smile lasted all the way home.

Beth gasped when they pulled into the driveway at his cottage. "The fence is up!" She was so excited that she hopped from his Range Rover before he'd come to a full stop. She walked so fast to the side of the house, her feet barely touched the ground. She clutched the six foot chain-link as if it was a personal gift, and not solely meant for his dogs. "They're going to love it. I bet Atlas watched the men work from the window. Can we let them out now?"

Rylan was impressed by the fence. Aidan's men had worked quickly and done a great job. He owed his brother big time. They would settle up soon. For now, his dogs would enjoy their freedom. They would still get their walks, but the fenced area was large enough for Atlas to run. Or at least gather speed down the straightaway.

"The fence was your idea," he said to Beth. "Introduce the dogs to their new yard."

She dashed into the house. Her skirt swayed and the heels of her boots tapped on the hardwood floor. He went in behind her. Atlas woofed his greeting, then nudged her for attention. Rue and the dachsies gave her love, too.

His dogs came to him second. Ry found it amusing. He scratched their ears and under their chins. "Lead the way," he said to Beth.

She whistled and became the Pied Piper. Rylan pulled his iPhone from his pocket and started the video. This was a memory he wanted to capture. Atlas was bucking and bouncing and Rue was barking at him to behave. Too darn funny.

Beth reached the kitchen and cracked the side door that opened into the fenced yard. "Ready?" She built the anticipation.

Atlas howled. He was tired of waiting.

She swung the door wide and stepped back. Atlas shot out as if he were blown from a cannon. Rue went more slowly. Nathan and Oscar were cautious on the steps. At-las had run a dozen laps by the time the other three realized their freedom. They all began to play. They looked like children on a playground. Tugging ears, nipping feet, and chasing each other. Ry filmed every minute.

He turned his iPhone on Beth. He found her leaning against a fence pole, her shoulders slumped, and her hands covering her face. Her posture was familiar, but he couldn't place the pose. *Where?* he wondered. *The Gallery Walk?* Possibly. The moment eluded him.

She glanced up then, all teary-eyed and happy. He hadn't realized a simple fence could draw such strong emotion. Her sensitivity touched him. She was genuine and compassionate, always looking out for him and his dogs. He was glad he'd agreed to the enclosure.

"They're having a great time," she said, her words watery.

Atlas was presently on his back, his legs pointed toward the sky, as the dachshunds climbed on his belly and rolled off the other side. Rue lay under a tree. Peaceful.

Ry realized he was content, too. It was a nice feeling, and one he'd never shared with anyone outside his family. "Should you have any more suggestions on home improvement, let me know. I'm open."

"Furniture?" she asked him.

He replied, "Overstuffed and comfortable. Dog resistant."

"I'll offer you options. Before or after the picnic?"

"After. I want to be the one to break in my new couch and chairs. Otherwise Halo and Landon will leave their butt prints first."

Beth understood. "They tend to make themselves at home."

Atlas's ears pricked, and he barked.

Ry listened, too. "A vehicle's pulled into the driveway," he said, leaving the backyard for the front door.

Four-fifteen, and his abstract painting had arrived. Two

men carried it into his living room. They carefully un-
boxed *Azure*.

"Which wall?" the taller of the two asked him.

Ry debated, then called for Beth to ask her opinion.
"What do you think?" he asked when she joined him. The
dogs followed her inside.

She did a full circle. Thoughtful. "South wall. The abstract is big and needs plenty of space to show off the
colors."

"Good choice," he agreed.

The installers hung the painting.

Once the men departed, Rylan shoved the lopsided sofa
across the room. He motioned for Beth to sit with him
and admire his new acquisition. He took one end of the
couch and she was about to take the other when Atlas
dove onto the cushion Beth had chosen. The only spot
that remained was beside Ry. She eased down slowly. The
golden and the dachs settled on their dog beds.

Their sides touched. Her arm rested against his. Their
hips bumped. Their thighs brushed. Atlas stretched out
farther, and Beth was pushed closer to Rylan. Her softness
pressed him fully. Ry cast Atlas a look. The big dog's head
bobbed. Rylan swore Atlas had planned the seating
arrangement. The Dane was sneaky smart.

Sitting next to Beth was nice. Together they shared
Azure. Even Atlas had his eye on the abstract, but his attention didn't last long. He'd gotten his exercise in the
yard and settled in for a nap, dropping his head onto Beth's
lap. Closing his eyes.

His dog had moves, Ry thought. Beth was considerate
and wouldn't disrupt his sleep. They could be sitting there
for a while—which appealed to him. He had a night off,
for once.

"I love your artwork," Beth said softly. She kept her

voice low, as if savoring the moment. "The painting is so . . . you."

He took a moment and studied it. She had imagination. "Evelyn said she had me in mind when she painted the abstract. Where am I in the painting? A curled wave?"

Beth settled deeper into the couch cushion, leaned her head back. She was relaxed when she said, "You're the broken surfboard."

He blinked. "That's how you see me?"

She laughed at him. "Are you seeking a compliment?"

A little ego stroking never hurt. A man liked to know a woman saw him in a good light. "A kind word wouldn't hurt."

"Vital."

"What?"

"I gave you a word."

She was teasing him. He wanted more. "Vital, huh?"

She gave him what he wanted to hear. And more. "I took an art appreciation class in college years ago. A spiral is one of the oldest geometric symbols. Some consider it the symbol of a man's spiritual journey. An evolutionary process of learning and growing. Your life path passes the same point over and over again but from a different perspective. The spiral stands for coming into being."

A deep perspective, Rylan thought, but one he understood. He leaned forward. Rested his elbows on his knees. He kept his gaze on the painting as he asked. "The curled waves?"

"They curve tightest at the highest peak," she noted, "protecting themselves against the break. Man often hides within his own identity. Not letting others see his inner self."

He could identify with that. He was serious most days, even when he was the most relaxed. "The surfboard? Fence?"

"My speculation only, but the fence is old, weather-beaten. That often represents the past. The broken board, a part of your life you've given up for something better."

Baseball was the better. He'd thought about professional surfing in his teens, but there'd been no security in the sport. No matter how much time went by, he'd never been able to shake the baseball glove from his hand. He played to his strengths. He could live without surfing, but not without America's favorite pastime.

He liked how Evelyn saw him. How Beth did, too. His assistant had depth. Her interpretation pleased him. It was inspiring. But then so was she.

She stroked Atlas's shoulders without conscious thought. The big boy was content.

Ry straightened slightly, asked, "Where did you study art?"

"Barnard College."

New York City. He'd never have taken her for big city. She appeared smaller town. Someone sheltered. Perhaps he'd misjudged her. Education was another piece to Beth Avery's puzzle.

He leaned back, stretched his arm along the back of the sofa. Atlas began to snore. The dog's muscles flexed, and he gained another few inches of couch space, pushing Beth flush against Ry. One more push by Atlas and she'd be sitting on Rylan's lap.

Her color was already high.

He felt her heat. Breathed in her scent. Fresh and feminine. He liked their closeness. "Comfortable?" he asked her.

She shifted slightly. "My leg is damp. Atlas is sleep-drooling."

"He must be dreaming about food."

"I'm guessing so. It's almost dinnertime."

Moments later, Rue and the dachsies' stomachs growled.

The golden retriever crossed the room and nudged Atlas with her nose. The Dane came out of a dead sleep, nipped her gently, then rolled off the couch. They all headed into the kitchen and sat down before the stove.

"Guess that's my cue." Beth stood up. Her skirt had stuck to her bottom and thighs, and she shook it out. Stomped her feet for circulation.

"You want help?" He'd gladly pitch in.

"Thanks, but no. I need to earn my paycheck." She hesitated, then added, "You could always join us. We could talk in the kitchen."

He would like that. The sofa suddenly felt too big and empty. Atlas had taken up most of the space, but it was Beth's presence he missed most. They'd connected over his painting.

He took a stool at the island counter. "What are your plans for tonight?"

"I'll be finalizing your picnic. How about you? There's nothing on your schedule."

A free night. "Do you need me for something?" he asked.

"Maybe . . ." Her back was to him as she stood before the refrigerator, choosing vegetables for the canine chicken stew.

Atlas had his face in the door, sniffing. He was attracted to the paper bag with her candied apple on the second shelf. She moved the apple to a crisper drawer. Out of sight, but not out of mind, the Dane stared a hole in the drawer until Beth closed the door.

She glanced over her shoulder, spoke to Ry. "Just a thought, that's all. Your dogs need to be bathed, so they'll smell nice for your weekend guests." She looked away. Baths. It was the part of her job that she'd been avoiding, possibly even dreading.

He wasn't going to let her off the hook, but he could

compromise. "I'll wash Nathan and Oscar in the laundry room sink. Rue's easy to do. Outside with the garden hose. The water runs warm. You can do Atlas."

"Or you could do Atlas and I'll take the other three."

"Or not."

"I've never bathed a dog." She wasn't whining, merely clarifying her position.

"There's always a first time. Atlas will show you how it's done, once he's had dinner."

"I bet he will," she mumbled.

"Wear your swimsuit. You're going to get wet."

Rylan had finished bathing Rue. She smelled like cherry blossoms. He'd toweled her off in the laundry room, and she stretched out on the porch beside the shampooed dachshunds.

He handed Beth a leash, a bottle of aloe vera shampoo, a stack of towels, and the hose. "Go for it," he said. He stood off to the side and watched.

The bath went downhill from there. She should've leashed Atlas first, that was her initial mistake. Instead, she set the shampoo bottle on the ground near the hose and draped the towels over the fence, only to have the big dog pull them down and run off with all three. She went after him. Atlas shook them, tore one in half, before giving them up. When she went to retrieve the shampoo, a strong spray blasted her backside.

Beth was drenched. Head to toe. Atlas was trotting around the backyard with the hose between his teeth. He'd triggered the plastic spray gun. Water came down like rain.

Atlas continued to prance around her. Water shot out the corner of his mouth. His ears flopped wildly. He made sure he'd soaked her. She didn't have a swimsuit. She'd changed into a tank top and cutoff shorts. She was barefooted. The grass was slippery.

Atlas went on to pull the garden hose the full length of the yard. He now ran through the puddles. Beth took hold of the hose and tried to reel him in. She tugged, and he pulled back.

It was a tug of war she couldn't win. The Dane was too strong.

Frustration rose. The only way to get to Atlas was through his stomach. "Treat?" she called out. He'd recently eaten dinner, but there was always room for an organic biscuit.

Atlas skidded to a stop, as she had hoped he would. He came toward her, watering the yard along the way. She happened to glance at Rylan. His Rogues T-shirt and jeans were dry as he comfortably leaned against a metal fence post. His arms were folded over his chest; one ankle crossed the other. He looked relaxed, as if he was enjoying himself. He was far too amused.

She wanted to turn the hose on him. *Live and learn,* she thought.

She lassoed Atlas with the leash when he got close enough then removed the spray gun from his mouth. She momentarily had control. She needed to make the most of it.

Surprisingly, once he'd calmed down, Atlas didn't mind his bath. He didn't like having his ears washed. He fidgeted when she did his paws. She sprayed him off, toweled him down. She tickled his sides, and he got wiggly.

Atlas needed a nail trim. That was a two person job. She turned to Rylan, hoping he would help her. "Nail clippers?"

Ry was reluctant. He ran one hand down his face. "I usually have a veterinary technician clip them."

"He could easily scratch someone. We're here now."

"Let's give it a try." Ry entered the house, returned with a pair of clippers.

Atlas eyed Rylan with suspicion. He began shifting.

"Treat," Beth whispered near his ear. To Ry she said, "I'll sweet talk him. You do the trimming."

Rylan bent down on one knee. He white-knuckle gripped the clippers and started with a back paw. "What's the worst that could happen?" he mumbled.

They soon found out. The Dane angled his head down, tracking Ry's moves. He didn't like his feet being touched. He kicked out like a mule, barely missing Ry's balls. He then threw back his head, popping Beth in the face.

Pain hit her hard. She staggered. Her eyes watered. She saw stars.

Her low moan brought Ry to his feet. He dropped the clippers and gently tipped up her chin. Atlas nudged her hip. He didn't understand what had happened. He started whining.

"It's okay," Beth reached out, patted him on the head.

Atlas wasn't satisfied. He jumped up, his paws on Ry's right shoulder, supporting himself. He looked Beth in the eye, whined again, and tried to lick her face.

"Not now, buddy." Ry rolled his shoulder, nudging him down.

Rylan cupped her face and gently ran his thumb over her left cheek. Down her nose, across her jaw. Concern darkened his eyes. "No flatness to your cheek," he noted. "No blood in the side of your eye. Any visual issues?"

She blinked. "A little blurry, but not bad."

"Can you move your jaw?"

She could shift it with minimal pain.

"I'm not a doctor, but I've witnessed sports injuries. I don't think anything's broken," he concluded. "But you're going to have a shiner."

"It could've been worse," she managed. "He could've broken my nose."

Ry leaned forward, spoke low. "He broke mine when

he was a puppy. Jumping up unexpectedly. Fortunately, it healed well. No bumps or scars."

He kissed her on the forehead; tried to make her feel better. "Let's get some ice. Otherwise your cheek's going to swell."

"The hose, shampoo, and towels?" She didn't want to leave them behind.

"I'll pick them up once I've taken care of you." He wrapped his arm about her shoulders and led her toward the house.

Atlas followed them inside, still whimpering.

"I need a shower and change of clothes," she said in the kitchen. She was soaked to the bone. Goose bumps rose. She felt chilled, despite the warm evening.

"Clean up and come back. You can stretch out on the couch."

She headed to her bedroom and closed the door behind her. The knob soon rattled. Twisted. A faint click, and Atlas peeked in. He didn't charge her as was his usual manner. He stood with his head down.

Beth dropped on her sofa bed. Her cutoffs dampened the sheet. She didn't care. Atlas came first. She patted her thigh. The Dane padded to her. He sat at her feet. Rested his chin on her knee. She scratched his ear. "You have a hard head, big guy. It was an accident. I'll live."

The low rumble in his throat sounded like an apology.

She hugged him. He leaned hard against her as if he was hugging her back. She stood slowly. "Shower time." She left Atlas sitting at the foot of her bed.

She took a quick shower. Her head ached and her cheek throbbed by the time she finished. One look in the mirror, and she sighed. A bruise covered her entire cheek and the lower rim of her eye. She looked like she'd been punched.

She dried off, wrapped a towel around herself, returned

to her bedroom, and tripped over a deflated football. She kicked it aside, took in the floor. Her heart hitched, then warmed. Atlas had brought her his toys. They were scattered from the door to the dresser. Tug toys, deflated balls, a thick rubber Kong, a wooden barbell, and so many more. She didn't have a free inch to step.

He lay in the doorway, looking at her, awaiting her reaction. Tears backed her eyes. He was being generous, offering his playthings. She picked up the red Kong, held it to her chest. "I feel better already," she told him.

He barked a deep, happy sound. His tail wagged. She laughed.

A knock on her door brought Rylan to her room. He scanned the floor. "My boy is *really* sorry," he mused. "I've never gotten more than two of his toys. You're definitely special."

"I feel special," she softly returned.

He lifted his gaze, taking in her bare feet, exposed thighs, up to her shoulders and face. Her hair was wet and subdued. For the moment.

She wasn't embarrassed, standing there in her towel. It was Ry's look that confused her. He stared intently, as if seeing her for the first time. She didn't look her best, yet he didn't seem to care. He rubbed his brow as if trying to clear his head.

She broke the moment, saying, "Atlas, I have something for you, too." She went to the top drawer on the dresser and removed two socks. They were black and blue, just like her cheek. *Howl with Happiness* was scripted across the toes. Stuffing one sock inside the other, she made him a sock toy. "Be gentle," she told him, then offered her gift.

Atlas sniffed, nuzzled the socks with his nose. He took them in his mouth and trotted off. He had his bounce back.

"Hopefully he won't swallow them," she said as an afterthought.

"He won't," Rylan assured her. "Trust me, he'll have those socks long after you're gone. He's a pack rat."

You're gone. She would be leaving. That was a given. There was no permanence with Rylan Cates. Still, the thought was unsettling. She waved him out. "I need to get dressed."

"I'll do a quick sweep of the backyard," he informed her. "I've got an ice pack ready for you. Meet me on the couch in five."

She took ten minutes and arrived in the living room wearing an old Barnard College T-shirt and a pair of yoga pants. Soft, loose and comfy. Cuddle up on the couch clothes.

She dropped down on the sofa. Sighed heavily. She felt suddenly tired. Atlas spotted her. He left Ry's side in the kitchen and joined her. Instead of hopping on the couch, he lay down by her feet. She scratched his shoulder with her toes.

Rylan brought her a dish towel and a Ziploc bag filled with crushed ice. She took both from him, leaned her head on the back of the sofa, and closed her eyes. She positioned the dish towel over her cheek, then placed the bag over it. The coldness seeped through quickly. It hurt and felt good at the same time.

Ry eased down beside her. He took her hand, said, "This was my fault, and I'm sorry. I should never have insisted you bathe Atlas."

"The baths were originally my idea."

"So . . . more your fault than mine?"

"We'll each shoulder the blame."

"Next time we hire a mobile groomer."

"Bathing them is part of my job."

"Not anymore." He was firm. "My cousin owns Hair of the Dog. He'll come to the house. I'll get his number for you."

She wasn't going to argue with him. She opened her good eye, whispered to him. "Atlas never got his treat."

"The boy's not starving. He'll survive until morning." It dawned on Ry then that they hadn't eaten. "What would you like for dinner?"

"Pizza."

"I'll call for delivery."

"Half meat lovers, half vegetarian." She'd split it with him.

Ry made the call. "Here in twenty minutes," he told her. "Watch for the pizza guy," he said to Atlas.

The dog moved to the front window.

"He's taken the cardboard box out of the delivery man's hand. The man likes me to meet him at the sidewalk from now on."

Atlas barked a short time later. Ry went to pay for the pizza. He fixed her a plate, included a soft drink. They sat side by side on the sofa and ate until they were full. None of the dogs begged for a bite. Ry rewarded them by slicing an apple. Juicy and crunchy. "Not your candied apple," he reassured her from the kitchen. "It's still safe." He cleaned up.

She smiled at his consideration. Her thoughts ran to the picnic and all she had left to do.

She started to get up, but Rylan had returned and put his hand on her shoulder. "Where do you think you're going?"

"My office. I've work—"

"Not tonight you don't." He shook his head.

"I want your picnic to go off without a hitch."

"It will," he assured her. "What's on your list?"

"I need to clean the house."

"Hire a cleaning service."

"The menu—"

"Find a caterer."

He'd cut two more of her duties, which was kind. However, she didn't want him taking away so many that she was out of a job. "I'd planned to cook and clean," she told him. "Keep within my budget."

He narrowed his gaze on her. "Screw the budget, Beth. Make it easy on yourself. I don't want you in the kitchen during the picnic."

"Where am I supposed to be?" *Dog sitting?*

He seemed surprised by her question. "Outside with everyone else, meeting my family and friends, and enjoying the day."

That set her back. "But I'm your assistant."

"It's my picnic. I want you there as my guest."

His guest. That was the nicest invitation she'd ever received.

"Let's relax and have a good time on Saturday."

She could do that. Happily.

"Care to watch some television?" he next asked her. He located the remote on the bookshelf.

She removed the ice bag, blinked. Her vision was clear. "For a while."

"Any chance you like westerns? There's a marathon tonight. *Gunsmoke, Big Valley, Bonanza, Rifle Man?*"

"I'm a fan of rope opera," she said.

He took the Ziploc from her, emptied it at the kitchen sink. Returning to her, he sat down, his body flush against hers. She liked their closeness. She made it through an hour episode of *Gunsmoke* before her eyelids grew heavy. She stirred awake, only to have sleep overtake her completely. She sagged against Rylan. He wrapped his arm around her. Tucked her to his chest.

She slept until morning.

Seven

Rylan woke to a wet nose against his cheek. He cracked his eyes and saw Atlas. Staring at him. The other dogs were lined up, too. Waiting, watching, curious.

What time was it? he wondered. A twist of his wrist and he checked his watch. Seven-thirty. He didn't remember when he had stretched out on the couch, shifting positions. From sitting beside Beth to spooning her. His hand had found her breast in sleep—which didn't surprise him. He was drawn to touch her. She felt good in his arms— soft, curvy, feminine—as if she was meant to be there. But for how long?

He removed his hand, but her warmth remained on his palm. He rested his chin on the top of her head. Her springy curls tickled his nose. He was afraid he might sneeze. Raising on one elbow, he tried to get a peek at her cheek. How bad was the bruise?

Really, *really* bad, he was soon to discover. Half her face was dark with color. He noticed a slight split in her bottom lip that hadn't bled the previous evening, but was evident by morning's light. He instinctively held her tighter. Feeling protective. Accidents happened. He felt bad that his insistence she bathe Atlas had ended so poorly. The big dog would never purposely hurt her. Atlas had accepted her as his temporary human.

"Rylan?" Beth spoke softly as she slowly wakened.

"Right behind you." Sporting a hard-on that was painful. He was pushed as far back against the couch as he could get. Yet one roll of her hips, and she would *feel* him. There was no hiding his erection.

"The dogs need to go outside," she mumbled.

He would have to get up to let them out. The idea of a doggie door crossed his mind. That might be nice. If he could find one to fit Atlas. The gang could go in and out at will, when either he or Beth was home. He'd take measurements and check out the prospects today.

"Can you sit up for a second?" he asked Beth. Hoping she'd lean forward and not back.

No such luck. She rocked back first, and found what he'd tried to hide. His boner pressed her bottom. Spots on her neck and cheek that weren't bruised blushed a bright pink. The lady was colorful.

"I'll take care of them." She rose quickly. Atlas head-butted her hip for attention. She scratched his ear as she walked to the kitchen.

Rylan groaned as he sat up. He adjusted himself. He'd pulled his jeans on without his boxers. His dick scraped against his zipper. He'd have teeth tracks if he wasn't careful.

A cold shower would calm him down. His other alternative was sex . . . but not with Beth. She was not an option. He had a few women he could contact for an early morning bootie call. He'd have to go to one of them, however. Not here.

It seemed too complicated at the moment. All he wanted was release. He could always take care of himself. Not his first choice.

He heard pans clanging and the refrigerator door open and close. Beth was preparing breakfast for the dogs. She would feed him, too, should he make the request. A part of him enjoyed sharing food and conversation with her. However a second side of him needed to escape.

He liked Beth Avery. He was surprised by how much. His feelings were confusing. He'd felt her pain when Atlas slammed his head into her cheek. She hadn't screamed or cried, yet he'd sensed her vulnerability. He wished he had the power to heal her. Staring at her afterward, he'd seen her inner beauty. Her compassion and caring. Her big heart.

He'd held her on the couch throughout the night, and it had been incredible. Her body had curled into his and fit perfectly. He'd slept deep, which he didn't do often. He always had one ear for the dogs.

He had no idea how Beth felt, although her gaze warmed whenever she saw him. He valued their friendship, yet anything further would mess up their working relationship. Perhaps it was time to listen to his grandfather and take a step back, now instead of later. Give them both some space.

He had the option of staying at Driftwood Inn with the team or sleeping at home next week. A few nights at the hotel might give him the distance and perspective he needed. He'd give it some serious thought.

"Veggie omelet?" Beth called to him, offering breakfast. "I've started the coffee."

It sounded good. He liked her cooking for him. So did Atlas. The dog's food was in the oven and his nose was an inch off the door. The scent of his morning meatloaf had him drooling.

Ry rose from the couch, his erection still evident, but no longer unbearable. He made it to the kitchen and located a tape measure in a top drawer. He took down the dimensions for the side door. A shower and shave were next. "I'll catch breakfast in town," he told Beth when he returned the measuring tape. "I have a lot of errands."

"Anything I can do for you?" she asked.

"Stay home and take it easy if you can."

"I'm expecting deliveries today," she noted. "Several picnic tables and the solar lights."

"Have the men unload by the garage. Otherwise Atlas will want to help, and he'll only get in the way."

She gave him a thumb's up. "Got it."

"Ice your face, too. There's swelling under your eye."

"Will do."

He was slow in taking the stairs, slower still in getting ready for his day. His thoughts remained on Beth, downstairs with his dogs. Feeding them, then cooking her own breakfast. Sharing a bite or two of her eggs with Atlas and crew.

Maybe he should've joined her.

Then again, maybe he was smarter not to.

He texted Shaye and asked if she would stop by his cottage and check on Beth while he was away for the day. Perhaps Shaye could suggest a house cleaning service and a caterer, too. There wasn't much time before the picnic. Beth seemed competent, but the Cates' arm stretched long. Shaye could pull some strings and make things happen.

His sister's return text indicated that her day was scheduled to the second. She would try to squeeze out a few minutes to visit Beth. There was no guarantee.

Rylan backtracked, reworked his day. He would grab a quick bite at Molly Malone's Diner on the boardwalk then stop by the hardware store and buy a doggie door. He'd swing back home to install it. He had some handyman skills. He could see how Beth was doing. He was her boss. She was his responsibility.

He cleaned up and took off. He drove his Range Rover to the beach, parked behind the diner. His cousin Violet greeted and seated him. He slid onto a blue leather booth in the corner.

The place hadn't changed over the years. The colors reflected the beach, aqua and sand tones. Continuous foot traffic had yet to scuff the brown-tiled floor. One wall was decorated with restored vintage photos, each one depicting the growth of Barefoot William. One black-and-white photo showed the original fishing pier under construction. Another pictured the boardwalk with only three shops. In the largest of the photographs, ten big boats were scattered offshore. Commercial fishing had supported the town for fifty years.

Ry was drawn to the older photographs. He thought about mixing a few framed prints with his abstract painting. An eclectic blend of artwork. He liked different. He wondered if Beth would feel the same. She might even have some suggestions of her own. He was open to her ideas.

A waitress set a menu before him. He studied it and chose a vegetarian omelet and coffee, the same breakfast Beth had offered him earlier. He should've let her cook for him. It was one of her duties. He'd let her fix him lunch.

His server suggestively flirted with him. She got off work at two. He appreciated her interest, but didn't act on it. He could still feel Beth pressed against him when they'd lain on the couch, as if her backside had left a permanent imprint. He flexed his hand and shook it for good measure. He had to stop cupping her breast.

He watched customers come and go. He waved at his sister-in-law when she entered the diner alone. Jillian joined him in the booth. He flagged down his waitress for another menu and place setting.

Jill smiled at him once they'd ordered; she went with French toast and hot tea. "How's my favorite Rogue?"

"I'm fine, but don't let Halo and Landon hear you say that. They'll swear you love them best."

She sighed. "Let them think what they will."

"You won't convince them otherwise." He unwrapped his silverware from the folded napkin. "What's happening in your world today?"

"I'm waiting for a big delivery at the Rogues Store. The truck is late. Team memorabilia is flying off the shelves." She winked at him. "You're a popular player, Rylan. I can't keep your jersey in stock."

The waitress brought her tea. Jill took a sip, then went on to request, "Stop by the shop tomorrow if you have time and sign your photographs. Baseball caps, too."

"That I can do."

"What are your plans for today?" She showed interest.

"I'm running errands," he told her. "I have a new fence and now need to buy a doggie door."

"Do they make them big enough for Atlas?"

"I'll need to make some adjustments."

Their food arrived, and they dug in. Rylan's omelet tasted good, but not quite as good as Beth would have made it. He chewed thoughtfully. He needed to stop making comparisons.

Violet Cates-Davis walked by their table.

"Join us?" Rylan invited her.

"I could use a break." Vi took a seat next to Jill.

Rylan had always liked Violet. She'd married her high school sweetheart Brad. He'd been dirt poor when he left town after graduation, only to return a wealthy man. Flipping small businesses had made him a fortune. He'd bought the diner when Molly decided to retire, making Vi the new owner. She was vibrant, happy, and always knew the latest boardwalk gossip.

Violet rested her elbows on the table, said, "I'm looking forward to your picnic on Saturday."

Jillian finished one of three slices of her French toast before agreeing. "Me, too."

Surprisingly, so was Ry. He'd dreaded such occasions over the years, but not this spring. "Beth's putting it together."

"She's working out okay, then?" came from Jill.

Far better than he'd expected. "She's doing great."

Violet smiled at him. "I hear your PA is a looker."

"Who told you that?" he couldn't help but ask.

"Both Halo and Landon," Vi told him. "They've been taking their meals here. Nice enough guys. They're still wearing their Cates T-shirts. My waitresses love them. They're entertaining and leave a big tip."

Rylan's inquiring mind wanted to know. "What, exactly, did they say about Beth?"

Vi tapped her temple, thoughtful. "That she's smart, quirky, fun to be around, and easy on the eyes."

Ry had to agree. The guys had left out the fact she was good with his dogs, had a mysterious past, and would only be in their lives eight weeks.

Jill nudged Violet with her elbow. "Beth sent out a general e-mail, telling everyone to dress comfortably. There will be volleyball and croquet. The Cates men have already challenged several of the Rogues to volleyball. Competition will run high."

"What are you wearing?" Vi asked.

"A sundress. No volleyball, but I can still play croquet."

Rylan tuned out the girl talk. His mind wandered once again to Beth. He couldn't help himself. He wondered what clothes she had in her closet. Her suitcases had been light. She hadn't asked him for additional hangers. She'd already worn her interview clothes twice. Her cutoffs several times. Did she need something new?

Her cheek wouldn't be healed by the weekend. Eggplant purple would be her color of the day. A contrasting outfit might be nice. The decision to shop for her came with his second cup of coffee. He could also use a woman's opinion. Violet was working. Perhaps Jillian had a few minutes to spare.

He waited until Vi left the booth before he approached his sister-in-law. "Atlas needs to make amends with Beth. He sent me to buy her a gift."

Jill arched an eyebrow. "What did the big boy do?"

He detailed the Great Dane's bath and how Beth had been popped in the cheek. "She has pale skin and bruised instantly. She must have been in a lot of pain but didn't complain once."

"Strong lady," Jill admired. "I'm sorry she got hurt."

"Me, too. Atlas gave Beth his toys, but he needs to do more."

The corners of Jill's mouth twitched. "How much does your Dane wish to spend?"

"Whatever's appropriate. You tell me."

Jill contemplated. "More than a gift card but less than a car."

"That's a wide range to consider."

"What do you know about her? What does she like?"

"Abstract art, progressive photography, junk food, my dogs." That he knew for sure. "I'd like to go with clothes."

"Do you know her size? Favorite color?"

He could only guess. "She's shorter than you, but your bodies are similar. Any color other than black and blue."

"Will Beth be working the picnic?"

"I'd prefer she didn't. I told her to hire a caterer."

"Will she listen to you or be stubborn and do it herself, because it's her job?" Jill asked.

Ry hadn't thought about that. "I don't honestly know." He could only hope that she had made a few calls, inquired about menus, and wouldn't tackle the cooking herself. He had a gut feeling she was doing more than she should be.

"I frequent several boutiques in Saunders Shores," Jill said. "Upscale and good quality. Let's see what we can find."

Rylan paid for their breakfasts. They left the diner for the boardwalk. Headed south. He was glad Jillian took the lead, otherwise he'd have been lost in the designer stores. He wasn't into fashion. He'd never bought a woman clothes, which put him at a disadvantage.

They entered Eclipz, a boutique owned by designer Melody Sommers. She greeted Jillian warmly and shook Rylan's hand. Jill explained their shopping mission, adding that the gift was a reward for an employee's dedication and hard work.

"Let me show you a few new pieces." Melody motioned them to the back of the shop. "My clothes mix hues and textures and have sleek lines."

Rylan looked around the boutique as he followed the women. The shop's decor played off the theme of lunar eclipse. The moon moving into the earth's shadow was painted on the main wall. The designer's logo *Step Out of the Shadows* was scripted above the artwork.

Melody offered them seating near a three-way mirror. His chair was brocade and delicate. Ry wasn't sure it would hold his weight, so he opted to stand. Jillian settled comfortably.

The designer entered the dressing room and drew out a clothing rack with six outfits. "Spring inspired."

"Beautiful colors." Jillian admired them.

Melody held up and described each one. "A-line, décolleté, raglan, and Jackie-O."

Rylan followed only half of what she said. *Chic, unique, current, must-have,* made more sense to him. He breathed deeply. He couldn't be specific as to what he wanted for Beth. He only knew none of the designer outfits felt right. They didn't look like Beth.

Melody left them for a moment to explore other options in the back room.

Ry couldn't help noticing that his sister-in-law was taken by a sage green satin blouse and a pair of dark blue wide-legged pants. Her gaze had returned to the outfit a dozen times.

Melody had used the words *breezy polish, jeweled neck,* and *shirred forward shoulder seams* to describe the blouse. The pants were *European inspired.*

He bent toward Jill, kept his voice low. "Try on the green and blue," he urged her.

Jill listened, went on to warn him. "I won't wear the ensemble exactly like Beth. She's petite. I have several inches on her."

He cleared his throat. "You're not wearing it for Beth. You'll be wearing it for yourself."

Her lips parted. "Ry, I don't understand."

"Nothing appeals to me," he explained honestly. "I can't picture Beth in any of these clothes. Melody's been nice. I'd like to buy something. You're here; let's do it."

Jill touched him on the arm. "You're not obligated to make a purchase," she assured him. "Many times I've dropped in to browse. Melody's not pushy."

Ry nodded toward the dressing room. "Go."

She went. Moments later, she modeled the garments for him.

"You look hot," he told his sister-in-law as she stood before the mirrors. "Those clothes should inspire a dinner date with your husband."

Jill grinned at him. "I think so, too."

He gave Melody his credit card, and the designer

wrapped the two pieces in silver gauze paper, then put them in a gift box. Jill hugged Rylan at the door, obviously thrilled.

He hoped whatever he found for Beth would thrill her, too.

They walked the length of Saunders Shores, entering shops, only to walk out without a purchase. Jill soon glanced at her watch. "It's almost eleven. Sorry, but I need to get back to work. The deliveries won't check themselves in."

"I'll walk with you. Barefoot William shops may not be as fancy as the ones in Saunders Shores, but several stores sell 'chic and current.' " He grinned as he quoted Melody.

Jill agreed with him. They strolled north, soon stopping at a shop with a bright red door. RICHMOND ROGUES stood out in block letters.

She kissed him on the cheek. "See you Saturday." Then left him on the boardwalk.

He stood alone. Debated his options. Three Shirts to the Wind sold beachwear. He decided to feed the local economy and buy something for himself. His cousin Jen owned the T-shirt shop. She was married to Mac James, a retired pro-volleyball player who had partnered with his brother Dune on the tour. Jen promoted Dune's line of designer beach shirts. Rylan planned to buy several. Also new board shorts. He entered through the tangerine-colored door.

Jen was at the cash register, ringing up a sale. She smiled her greeting. "Be right with you," she mouthed.

There were no other people in the store. He'd stopped at a good time. Three Shirts carried everything from plain white cotton tees to brightly colored polos. Some had caricatures while others had decorative designs. A few naughty slogans raised eyebrows. Most sayings were funny and silly. Overhead clotheslines stretched the width of the ceiling, displaying a line of Barefoot William attire. Dune had his own designer corner.

"Dude." Jen joined him shortly. She was blunt and honest and openly stared at his haircut. "Halo Todd said you're 'trending.' I personally think your barber had a slip of the scissors."

"I'd say you were right, but keep it to yourself."

"My lips are sealed." She nudged him with her elbow. "Shopping for yourself or for someone else?"

"Me today," he told her. "Dune's shirts fit me well. Size large."

Jen went to the rack of short-sleeve button-downs and selected two. "My all-time favorites from his collection," she said, holding them up.

He liked both. Colorful sea shells, starfish, and sand dollars decorated a black background on the first. The pattern was intricate, but masculine. A sunrise rose over the pier on the second. He went on to shop for board shorts. Chose four pairs in solid colors.

"Flip-flops?" Jen asked him as they returned to the front of the store. "I've a new roped design you might like. A twist of black and brown leather form the Y between the toes. Very durable."

He nodded. "I'll take a pair. Size twelve."

She carefully packed up his items and placed them in a waterproof nylon drawstring bag, given to special customers. He paid, paused, asked her, "Unusual women's clothing, where would you shop?" Her surprised expression had him elaborating. "Not for me. For a female friend."

"Do I know her?" Jen was curious.

"My PA. You'll meet her at the picnic."

"You're shopping for her because—?"

He gave her the condensed version of Atlas and Beth's bruise.

Jen was sympathetic. "You might try Vintage Attic," she suggested. "It's one of the dozen small shops located on the street behind the boardwalk."

Ry knew the area. His family owned the property, but the stores were rented to outside entrepreneurs. Shaye screened each shop owner to be sure the stores wouldn't compete with those on the boardwalk.

He cut through Three Shirts, went out the back door, and walked across the alley to the next street. Vintage Attic held a corner spot. The window was decorated with antique clothing. He was drawn inside.

"I'm Naomi." The woman who appeared as old as the clothing introduced herself when he entered. She wore a long black dress with a lacy shawl. "Look around, ask questions."

He stood and stared and slowly took it all in. He admired the curio cabinet with antique jewelry, the stack of felt and feathered hats, the shelves of shoes and boots, the purses and luggage. Clothing hung on hangers pegged to the walls. Small signs were discreetly placed, identifying the clothing by date. Time fell away beneath cascading floral tops, nostalgic skipper and prance skirts, flapper and swing dresses, pin-up girl shorts, bell bottoms, acid washed and distressed jeans. The past was well represented.

"There are contemporary items in the back," Naomi told him. "Customers will oftentimes combine the old with the new. Every vintage piece of clothing has been dry cleaned."

A mannequin stood near a glass case of old-fashioned glasses frames. The upper half of its body showcased an exquisite white blouse.

"What can you tell me about that piece?" he asked Naomi.

She came to him. "One of my buyers brought it back from London. It's a Victorian lace cap sleeve blouse with the original glass buttons. Delicate and feminine. Sheer, but not see-through."

It reminded him of Beth. "Exactly what I'm looking for. Does it go best with slacks or a skirt?"

"A formal occasion?" she asked.

"No, casual. Outdoors."

"Might I suggest a vintage pair of Levi 501 jeans? A classic in the original state of wear and distress. High-waisted with a slightly tapered leg. The button fly is classic, even for women. There's a tear below one knee. They can be cuffed. Each jean is unique and one-of-a-kind, which we handpick from a limited stock."

The jeans worked for him. "Let's do it."

"They have a vintage size tag that differs from the modern size. I have personally measured and sorted each pair into contemporary proportions. What size would you need?"

He wasn't sure. His hands had encircled Beth's waist when he'd helped her off the horse on the carousel. Not totally accurate, but it gave him a rough idea. "Maybe twenty-six inches. She's short, small."

Naomi smiled at him. "I would allow an exchange, should the jeans not fit her." She went on to choose a pair for him.

Rylan exhaled his relief. Shopping for a woman was not easy. He reminded himself he was doing this for Atlas. The surprise on Beth's face would be worth the trouble.

He had to admit the Levi's had Beth's name on them. He could picture her in the lace blouse and jeans. She would look amazing.

"One final thought," Naomi said. "Retro Zodiac boots. Nineteen eighties, and still very popular. I have a knee high pair in burgundy tones, suede base and leather upper. A beautiful patina. Stacked wood heel."

Ry liked boots. Sexy or kick-ass, they drew a man's eye

to a woman's legs. A stacked heel would give Beth height. Choosing the right size worried him a little. He'd massaged her feet when they had fallen asleep. He took a wild guess. Holding up his hand, he said, "Palm to index finger tip and add two inches. Do you have her size?"

Fortunately, Naomi did. "A beautiful, offbeat, individual look," she complimented as she hung the blouse and jeans in a protective garment bag. The boots came boxed.

Ry paid for the items, then moved toward the door. On his way out, he happened to notice a display of vintage suitcases artfully arranged by the wall. They weren't in great shape, showing worn leather, battered handles, and rusted hardware. Still, they were distinctive. The designer was Louis Vuitton.

Naomi crossed to him. "Aged, but still useable. Quite valuable. Clients refurbish them. They speak of class and wealth."

Ry's gaze lingered on Louis Vuitton. The name stuck in his mind. It took him several seconds to remember where he'd seen it last. It hadn't been the full name, only partial letters. *Lou Vui* was on Beth Avery's luggage. The remainder of the name had been scratched off.

Was she a collector of old suitcases or was it a hand-me-down? Her past didn't fit with the woman she seemed to be. She'd yet to come together for him. He'd keep trying to figure her out.

He returned to his SUV, then headed for the hardware store. He bought a plastic-rimmed door that could be inserted behind the heavier wooden one. The lower half had double flaps for easy access. Atlas should be able to clear it. Ry could easily install it himself.

Home came next. He pulled into the driveway, stepped from the Range Rover. He hooked the hangers of the garment bag over one finger. Tucked the boot box beneath his arm. Clutched the drawstring bag in his other hand. He climbed the steps and entered the cottage.

He stopped in the entryway, looked around. Beth had been busy. She'd located his cleaning supplies in the laundry room. The Swiffer WetJet had left the floors clean and shiny. The scent of citrus lingered. His cottage smelled like sunshine. It was spotless.

"Atlas, no dust bunnies!" He heard Beth scold from the kitchen. Her tone was firm.

He set the items on the sofa then followed her voice. He stopped short of announcing he was home. Instead, he rested his shoulder against the wall and stared. He slipped his iPhone from his pocket and snapped a photo. *For posterity,* he mused. He would refer to the picture whenever he needed a smile.

His Great Dane was sitting on his haunches before the refrigerator. His front paws pounced on the dust bunnies Beth swept from beneath it. She was on all fours, her bottom in the air, a whisk broom in one hand. A dust pan sat between them. She swished as fast as he stomped. Her cutoffs rode above the lower curve of her ass. Firm and curvy flashed him.

Atlas's tail wagged. He liked playing with the dust bunnies. Beth's butt wiggled with the stretch of her arm. Rylan couldn't believe she was going to such great lengths in cleaning his house.

"We have to be ready in case it rains," Beth said to Atlas.

The Dane tilted his head as if he were listening.

"The meteorologist said seventy degrees and sunny on Saturday, but I don't trust Mother Nature. She's been mean to me."

Mean to her? That caught Ry's attention. How so?

She didn't elaborate. "We need Plan B. Rylan doesn't have much furniture, but between the back porch and the living room, we'd have plenty of space should we need to move inside."

The last of the dust bunnies escaped, and Atlas barked them to death.

Beth whisked them onto the dust pan. "All done." Back on her feet, she dumped the contents in the garbage can beneath the sink. Her back was still to Ry.

He pushed off the wall and approached her. Atlas had yet to give him away. The big boy didn't seem to care he was home. His eyes were on Beth.

She'd yet to straighten the hem on her shorts. Rylan glimpsed the feminine crease between her thigh and bottom. There was no bra line beneath her tank top. Her breasts were free.

His groin tightened. Unexpected and untimely. His last few steps were awkward. He drew a settling breath, which Beth heard. She spun around, dust pan raised, ready to fend him off. Silly woman. Had he been an intruder, Atlas would have nailed him to the floor. Still, he'd scared her. Her eyes were wide and gray, and her lips parted. Her cheek was a serious blue. Dust streaked her forehead. Her clothes carried the same scent as the cleaning supplies. It was evident who had done the work. Not a maid service. Atlas even had lint on one ear.

Rylan circled her wrist with his fingers and eased her hand down. He chose not to let her go. Her back was to the sink. He had her front. He leaned into her.

Her chest rose and fell. Her breath caught. Her nipples flirted with his shirt. Her crotch pressed his thigh. Her heat stroked him. It was difficult to lecture her when they stood so close. Her body was a distraction.

He'd given her permission to hire a cleaning service, but apparently Beth preferred to do the work herself. She could be stubborn, he realized. He kept his voice even when he said, "I wanted you to take it easy today. Not exert yourself. Your face is still swollen, sore—"

"My cheek hurts whether I'm dusting, sweeping or sitting on the couch." She stopped him before he could finish. "I needed to be productive. It took my mind off the pain."

"I saw Atlas was helping, too?"

She gave him a small smile. "He chased the dust bunnies and I chased him. Rue and the dachshunds grew tired of the game. Pine-Sol made Nathan sneeze. I let them outside. The fenced yard came in handy."

He looked around the kitchen. "The place looks amazing."

"Atlas and I made a good team."

"The big boy sent me on an errand. He has something for you," Ry told her, ready to spring his surprise.

Atlas was steps ahead of him. The Dane had already spotted the garment and nylon bags and shoe box on the sofa. He'd gone to check them out. He was curious. Destructively so. He'd loosened the drawstring and shaken out Rylan's beach attire. The shirts and board shorts were spread across the sofa and floor. The sunrise shirt hung over his neck. He trotted around the living room with the garment bag in his mouth. He'd found a prize and was proud of himself.

Rylan sucked air. He should never have set the items on the couch. A very stupid mistake. Anything low was easy access for Atlas. Ry didn't want the dog tearing the bag. The present was for Beth. He whistled for the Dane. A sharp, commanding whistle. Atlas's ears pricked.

Rylan released her hand, then patted his thigh. "Bring it here," he said to Atlas.

He knew from experience that if he had gone after her gift, Atlas would have taken it as an invitation to play. Possibly rough. The lace blouse wouldn't stand a chance against him. The Great Dane would chew the Levi's like a piece of beef jerky.

"Atlas?" Beth called him, too.

He responded, delivering the garment bag—which she accepted.

Ry snagged his shirt. It wasn't Atlas's size. He set it on the tiled counter. "The gift is for you. From Atlas."

Hearing his name, the dog barked and wagged himself in a circle.

Beth was slower in sharing his excitement. She stared overly long at the bag. "I don't understand," she finally managed, uncertain of Ry's motive.

Rylan seldom felt self-conscious or insecure, but he did so at that moment. He went on to explain. "You deserved more than Atlas's toys for the bruise you're sporting. A present seemed appropriate."

She touched her cheek. "It's not necessary. I'm healing."

"We like you, and wanted to do something nice."

"But you didn't have to," she insisted.

He'd thought to make her happy; instead she got teary-eyed. She held the garment bag to her chest. A tear escaped, slid down her bruised cheek.

He reached around her, snagged a piece of paper towel from the roll on the counter. Passed it to her. She dabbed at her eyes. Atlas stuck his head between her arm and hip. Looked up at her. She choked up even more.

Ry felt helpless. He needed to turn the moment around. Fast. "One or the Other," he initiated. "Leather or lace?"

"Lace." The word was barely audible.

"Pants—cotton, silk, or denim?"

"Denim. My cutoffs and jeans have seen better days," she admitted. "I wear them all the time. The more worn, the better."

He was batting two for two. He moved on to the third question. "Flip-flops, sandals, shoes, or boots?"

"I don't own a pair of flip-flops. Sandals either. I wear my message socks alone or with my Keds and cowgirl boots." The inspiration scripted on her orange and gray paisley socks with the piano key toes said *Play Your Own Song.*

He was down to two final choices. "Canvas sneakers or boots?" He needed to know her preference.

Her eyes were dry when she said, "Boots make me taller."

Exactly as he'd figured. He knew her better than he'd thought. A part of him was pleased. The other part was nervous that he'd pegged her so well. Familiarity brought people closer. How close did he want to be with Beth? He had yet to decide. He'd take one moment at a time.

"Have a seat at the island," he suggested. It was clear, clean, and an easy place to open her gifts.

She placed the bag carefully on the polished chestnut surface. Then perched one hip on a stool. Atlas sat beside her and rested his chin on her thigh. Beth's hands trembled slightly as she unzipped the garment bag.

Beth Avery was afraid to open her gift. Kindness made her cry. It always had. Years had passed since she'd been given a present. The last one she remembered had come from her father. Right before he passed away. He'd given her an antique necklace. Aquamarines winked from a thin gold chain. She'd cherished the piece and kept it secured in a velvet pouch. She'd tucked the small bag in the top drawer of her dresser. Safe beneath her socks.

Rylan cleared his throat.

She realized that he and Atlas were waiting for her to unzip the bag. She did so, slowly, inch by inch. Her breath stilled when she saw the vintage lace blouse. Elegant, classic, it spoke of poetry and courting. Of romance and falling in love.

"Clothes?" she murmured in surprise.

"Something new for the picnic," said Ry.

She looked down at her tank top and cutoffs. She tugged down the hem on her shorts. They were old. A few holes and white seams. "I'd planned to buy a new outfit when I got paid tomorrow." She bit down on her bottom lip. "I would never embarrass you."

"No embarrassment, ever," he said. "Atlas was apologetic. That's the reason for the gift."

Slowly, she slid the blouse from the garment bag. She held it up and admired the delicate lace and glass buttons. Vintage beauty. Her heart gave a squeeze, and her stomach went soft. She laid a hand on the dog's shoulder, then caught Rylan's eye. "You have good taste, big guy."

The Dane woofed. Ry smiled.

She hung the blouse on the corner of the island, explored the bag further. "Button fly Levi's." Her voice broke. "Oh . . . Atlas."

Atlas raised his head, sniffed the denim.

She spoke to the Dane. "What am I going to do with you? Both of you?" she added, including Rylan.

"One box to go," Ry told her. He pointed to the sofa. "Retrieve, Atlas."

The dog moved so fast, Beth swore the kitchen shifted. He charged into the living room, skidded to a stop before the couch, and brought back the box, along with another of Rylan's shirts. She'd never known the Dane to be so gentle. There wasn't a tooth mark on the large, square box. Or a tear in Ry's shirt.

"They can be exchanged," Ry told her as she lifted the lid.

Her eyes rounded. Why would anyone want to return such beautiful boots? She prayed they were the right size. She took them out of the box. Then hopped off the stool and immediately tried them on over her message socks. She sighed her relief. The knee high boots fit as if they were made for her.

She walked around the kitchen, loving their feel and texture. Atlas trailed her. They did three laps around the island before she approached Rylan. She found him staring at her legs, and she took advantage of the moment. Happy and grateful, she wanted to thank him. Words didn't seem enough. She did what came naturally. She rose on tiptoe, went to kiss him on the cheek.

Atlas gave her a last minute bump, and her ankle rolled. She fell against Rylan. She grabbed his arms. Held steady.

His big hands curved her waist. His fingertips touched at the small of her back.

She felt weak in the knees.

Ry stood stiffly.

She tipped back her head and met his gaze.

His indecision was evident. His desire, surprising. Expectancy passed between them.

She held her breath.

He released his own. His body relaxed.

Her uncertainty about kissing him was banished by his mouth coming down on hers. He'd made the decision for her. It was one she could live with.

Trust and curiosity came with his kiss. It was closed-mouth, but meaningful. He was experienced. Time fell away to sensation.

Her emotions were heightened. Vulnerability and awareness. A sense of belonging stirred the strongest.

Warmth spread in her chest. Her heart raced.

Her nipples imprinted his shirt.

She affected him, too. His erection was a dead giveaway.

He ended their kiss just as she was getting started.

She wanted more, but he denied her.

Rylan rested his forehead against her own. His eyes remained closed. She'd thrown off his breathing. That pleased her. Greatly.

Their moment slowly passed.

She knew in her heart that his kiss meant more to her than it ever would to him. No matter, she would hold tight to the memory. "Thank-you for everything," she whispered against his cheek. *Everything* covered his kiss and her clothes. As well as the hope in her heart.

Eight

Rylan had hoped his picnic would go well. He hadn't expected it to be perfect. But Beth had been surprisingly adept at pulling it all together. The chaos of the morning had turned calm by afternoon. It amazed him.

Atlas followed her around as if he was part of the planning committee. Rue and the dachsies sought a quieter spot and headed for her office. Beth checked on them often, offering treats and chances to go outside.

The invitation to the picnic indicated four p.m. as the start time. However, by three-thirty his guests began to arrive. Several of his teammates couldn't tell time and had shown up early. The entire starting lineup wore their Cates T-shirts. His family, not by blood but by scheme.

A sign near the front door directed everyone down the driveway and toward the backyard. There would be no cutting through the house. Atlas stood before the front window, his nose pressed to the glass. He barked his own personal welcome. The ballplayers all barked back.

Beth stood behind the short buffet table set up near the corner of the cottage, greeting and introducing herself to each arrival. Two huge galvanized metal buckets packed with ice anchored the ends, offering beer and soft drinks to get the picnic rolling. It got moving really fast.

Ry stood on the porch where he could keep an eye on

her and still catch the incoming crowd. She'd checked the weather channel a dozen times throughout the day, making sure rain wasn't in the forecast. He'd overheard her praying for a nice day. Her prayers had been answered.

The sun shared the sky with a stream of white clouds. The temperature sat in the low seventies. His friends and family conversed on the circular bench beneath the banyan tree. Redwood picnic tables offered additional seating. His grandfather sat on a cushioned Adirondack chair in the shade of the garage. A game of volleyball was already underway.

His sister Shaye soon played the first round of croquet. She had the Cates competitive gene. "Back off, Halo or I'll take you out at the knees," she said when the right fielder crowded her near the sixth wicket. She swung her mallet at him.

Halo took her warning to heart and let her hit through. He was still recovering from his groin sprain. He didn't need a second injury.

Beth had added a last minute activity to the yard. One with his grandfather in mind. Her thoughtfulness stuck with Ry. She'd contacted a local sports company and ordered a regulation size stowable shuffleboard court. Two employees had assembled the interlocking playing surface on a slab of cement between the garage and shed. The game came with four fiberglass cues, eight regulation Nemar tournament disks, four black, four red.

His grandfather's gaze had gone straight to the shuffleboard court upon his arrival, and he'd grinned from ear to ear. Beth had made the older man's day. Frank immediately had asked her to be his partner when they took on Shaye and Ry later in the afternoon. Beth warned him that she'd never played. Frank paid the warning no mind.

Rylan turned his attention to Aidan and Jillian as they approached. "Thanks for getting my fence up so quickly."

He was appreciative. "It's made a huge difference to the dogs. Send me a bill."

Aidan rubbed the back of his neck. "Let's call it even, bro. I appreciate the outfit you bought Jill, even though it's costing me expensive dinners." He grinned. "She meets me at the door after work, dressed up and wanting to dine out."

Dune flagged down Aidan from across the yard, and Aidan went to speak with him. That gave Jill a moment to lean close to Ry and say, "Your PA is adorable. I'm not the only one who thinks so. Several Rogues haven't made it past the entrance table."

Ry was aware of the bottleneck. Zoo, Will Ridgeway, and Jake Packer were taken with his assistant. Will and Jake had gone ahead and gotten the *trending* team haircut. Zoo would hold out until the last minute. He tended to be vain.

"You found Beth the ideal gift," Jill complimented him. "Not every woman could pull off that lace blouse, but she can. And she looks cute doing it. I haven't seen 501 Levi's in forever. Beth's attracting a lot of attention."

Beth looked hot, Ry had to admit. She was also personable and complimentary. She'd researched each player on the Internet and was informed on their careers. The men were proud of their accomplishments and would be drawn to her knowledge and praise.

Jill left Ry and went to join her husband.

Ry next talked to several hometown friends. He caught up on local news.

Zoo approached him shortly thereafter, swaggering up the porch steps, looking smug. "Beth sent me for another bucket of beer. It's in the laundry room."

Ry stalled him. "I'll get it for her."

"She asked me," Zoo insisted.

"My laundry room."

A frown came from Zoo before his smile flickered. "That's the way of it, is it?"

Ry responded with, "What way?"

"Your picnic, your beer, your PA. All yours."

Pretty much so, Ry thought, but didn't let on. Instead, he went with an excuse. "My dogs are inside. I don't want them getting out."

"I've blocked Atlas in the past when we've played touch football. He won't get by me."

Rylan narrowed his gaze, stared Zoo back a step.

"Fine." The left fielder shrugged. "I'll guard the door while you shoulder the bucket."

Ry turned and entered the cottage. His Great Dane met him in the kitchen with a series of low grumbles. He read Ry the riot act for keeping him inside when there were so many people to meet. But set free, the Dane would be disruptive.

Rylan rubbed the dog's ears. "Not now, big guy. Maybe later." Once the crowd thinned.

Atlas jumping for volleyballs or knocking into his grandfather Frank would ruin the afternoon. Atlas already added one deflated volleyball to his collection of toys.

Ry located the ice bucket, hefted it. Bottles of Heineken clinked against Coors Light. Landshark tapped Snow Bear. Beth had made the selections. She'd covered everyone's taste and then some.

Atlas trailed him to the door. "Stay," Ry said.

Atlas sat and whined. Pitifully.

Ry shook his head. The boy had a future in acting.

Rylan carefully took the steps, crossed the yard, and made his delivery. Beth stood alone for the first time that afternoon. He momentarily had her all to himself.

She looked up, broke into a smile. "I sent Zoo and got you." Her eyes were a soft blue. She was glad to see him.

"How's it going?" he asked.

"I've met everyone," she told him. "Your friends are fun, your teammates, insane, and your family couldn't be nicer." She touched the side of her face. "I look awful, but no one except Halo has mentioned my bruise. He kissed my cheek; said he had healing lips."

That sounded like Halo.

"I'm glad I haven't had to explain what happened."

"That's because I explained it for you."

She blinked. "You did? When?"

"Texting is quick and efficient. Two sentences, and word spread. I didn't want you facing a lot of unnecessary questions."

She breathed easier. "Thank you. I hated to blame Atlas."

He studied her face. "Your bruise has faded. You look more jaundiced than black and blue."

She blanched. "That's appealing."

"Yellow seems to be my teammates' favorite color today," he teased her. He wondered how many of the guys had made a move on her. Had asked her out. He didn't want her dating any of them.

Not since their kiss in the kitchen.

Atlas's nudge had landed her in his arms. Her eyes had widened in astonishment. He'd taken up where she'd left off. He'd kissed the surprise from her parted lips. He'd kept the kiss soft, light, tentative. She'd responded with a shy intimacy that gave him a hard-on.

His physical reaction had stopped him short. He could have lifted her onto the kitchen island or walked her backward to her bedroom. Kissing her all the way. Turning her on.

Instead, he'd stepped back. He knew in his heart that was for the best. He wasn't certain she was ready for him. He wasn't yet sure he was ready for her, either. Acting on attraction was not wise. But was any man ever smart when it came to sex? Debatable.

Beth turned toward the yard, took in the activities. "Did you expect everyone to show? Were there any cancelations?"

"I counted heads a few moments ago," he told her. "The gang's all here."

"I need to set out munchies," she said. "We have two hours before the main meal."

"What are you serving?"

Her eyes sparkled. "Wait and see." She sounded secretive.

Fine. He hadn't seen much of her the past two days. He'd had town and team obligations, and she'd kept the house in order. She'd texted him with messages and updates. They'd passed in the kitchen at first light, then again right before bed.

He hadn't noticed any major food prep or lingering scents of her cooking, so she hadn't slaved over a hot stove, but she had something up her sleeve. He'd enjoy her surprise with the rest of his guests.

"I'll help you with the snacks," he offered.

She nodded toward the crowd. "Shouldn't you be mingling?"

"I've known most of these people all my life. We stay in touch. There's nothing new going on. I'll keep an eye on my teammates so they don't get rowdy."

Remarkably enough, the guys drank in moderation. Respect for Beth limited their intake. Ry noticed Halo and Landon had switched to soft drinks after a six-pack. He wouldn't have believed it, had he not seen it.

Additional buffet tables were set up along the front of the porch, to the left of the steps. He and Beth filled and brought out straw baskets of chips and sides of dip, mixed nuts, and vegetable platters. She'd kept it simple, so no one would spoil their dinner. Atlas got a treat, too. She sliced an apple for the boy. His howl of appreciation echoed into the backyard.

The Rogues ate the snacks as if they hadn't seen food for a week.

Typical, Ry thought. His heart squeezed when Beth prepared a small plate of vegetables for his grandfather and took it to him. She pulled up a beach chair, sat, and engaged him in conversation. Frank appeared pleased to see her. The corners of his eyes crinkled. His gramps was a meat and potato man, yet he ate the celery and carrot sticks as if they were a regular part of his diet.

"Ry-man, v-ball?" Landon called to him once the snacks were consumed. "Four Rogues against Dune and Mac." Ballplayers against pro-volleyball's world champs? Why not?

Ry crossed to the court. Dune grinned at him. "I like your duds."

So did Ry. He wore the sunrise-over-the-pier designer button-down with a pair of solid brown board shorts. He didn't need a Cates T-shirt to know who he was. Barefoot worked for him.

Zoo, Landon, Will Ridgeway, and Rylan made up the Rogues' side of the net.

"No Halo?" Ry asked. The right fielder loved competition and was always in the mix.

Zoo smirked. "The man who'd do anything for tail is standing down," he said, referring to the horse on the merry-go-round. Word had spread about Halo's mishap. "There's too much jumping and diving on the court. Halo's barely walking. He's sticking with croquet."

Ry got in position. Dune tossed him the volleyball; he would serve first. He glanced at Beth and his grandfather from the corner of his eye. They'd turned their chairs toward the court and watched the action.

Athletes liked to shine, even in a sport in which they weren't adept. Ry bemoaned the fact his first serve landed in the net. His second cleared it by half an inch. The Rogues played with a winning passion. There was taunting between the sides. Most was friendly. Rylan made some nice plays. Will could dive. Zoo had jump. Landon, a decent spike. At the end of forty minutes, volleyball's best won by a score of twenty-one to sixteen.

"We've still got it." Dune high-fived his professional partner, Mac James.

"You'll never lose it," said Rylan.

"Killer final point," Zoo said to Dune. "Damn, dude, did you have to aim for my feet?" He'd played barefoot.

"You hopped around like a girl," Landon said as he left the court.

Zoo defended himself, "I could've broken a freakin' toe."

"Not a break, but a sharp sting," said Dune.

The men wanted to cool off. They headed toward the ice buckets for something to drink.

Ry stopped to speak with Beth and his gramps. "How'd I do?" he asked Frank.

"Don't give up your day job."

Rylan laughed. He patted his granddad on the shoulder. "Dune has the monopoly on volleyball."

Beth's voice was soft when she said, "I thought you were wonderful."

"Wonderful when?" he teased her. "When I hit the volleyball out of bounds or stepped outside the lines multiple times?"

"When you spiked the ball into Mac's chest."

"Yeah, that was a good shot," he agreed. He glanced

down on his grandfather. "How about that game of shuffleboard?"

Frank rose, his energy defying his age. He held out his hand to Beth. "Young lady, ready to send the biscuit?"

She took his hand, stood, her expression reluctant.

"We'll go over the terminology and rules before we play," said Frank. He then called to Shaye, who was wrapping up another game of croquet.

She'd kicked Halo's ass once again and pumped her mallet in the air. Halo wasn't looking all that happy. He complained of being beaten by a girl.

Frank led the way to the shuffleboard court.

Everyone at the picnic followed. They clustered around the edges. Frank raised his arms, flexed his elbows, said, "Give us room." Family, friends, and teammates granted his request. They took one giant step back.

His grandfather passed out the sticks, called tangs, that would push the weighted disks, referred to as biscuits. Beth listened intently as Frank went over the object of the game and the scoring.

"We'll start at one end and alternate play," the older man said. "Horse Collar is the name of the game. We'll play to twenty-one."

The four of them each took a practice shot to get used to the tang and biscuit. Rylan admired his grandfather's concentration and skill. Frank had every intention of beating his grandkids. He took his stance and sent the biscuit to the opposite end of the court, toward the pinnacle of points. Zones were divided into four numbered subzones, the numbers representing point values.

Ten points was awarded to any player who could land the biscuit within the small triangular tip zone without touching any part of the border. The second tier was worth eight points. The third, seven. If the disk stopped within the rearmost section, the sender lost ten points. If the disk touched the edge of any section, the player lost five points.

All the practice disks but Beth's sailed to the opposite end. Hers only made it halfway down the court. She frowned, appearing defeated before the game even started.

Rylan stepped up, settled her down. He ignored the amused glances and silent speculations on their relationship. Let them assume what they would. His concern was solely for Beth. She needed to relax and enjoy the game.

"What do your socks say?" he whispered near her ear.

She gave him a small smile. *"You can. You will."*

"Do it then," he encouraged her. "Remember what my grandfather told you. Aim, focus, two-step delivery, stroke, follow-through. Don't overthink it." He gave her shoulder a quick squeeze and backed off.

Shaye eyed him as curiously as the rest of the crowd.

His grandfather nodded his approval. That meant a lot.

Halo stood off to his right. His grin split. "Good pep talk, Ry-man. Wish you'd be that nice to me in the dugout."

"Rub my shoulders before my next at-bat and I'll guarantee you a double," said Zoo.

"Sweet words would go a long way toward me hitting a home run," added Landon.

His teammates chuckled. Beth blushed.

Jerks. Rylan didn't take the bait. He ignored them.

"Everyone ready?" Frank asked.

Nods all around got the game underway.

Frank shot first. His disk glided to a stop on eight. Shaye went second and gained seven points. Beth came next. She drew in a breath and sent her biscuit down the elongated court. It landed on the ten, perfectly centered. She blinked, couldn't believe her eyes. Whoops and applause followed.

"A ringer," Halo shouted.

His granddad raised an eyebrow. "Hidden talent, I see."

Beth exhaled. "Beginner's luck."

Her luck held, even after Ry knocked off her ten. He got booed. Loudly. *What the hell?* He wasn't going to cut her any slack. He was out to win. Beth's second ten dared Ry to go after her again. He tried, but he wasn't successful. Shaye was forced to deduct five points each time she landed on a numbered border. Their score went downhill fast. Two of Rylan's disks fell off the end of the board into the alley. Not to his liking.

"Too much power in your delivery," his gramps pointed out.

Rylan's arm was strong enough to throw a baseball from center field to home plate. He lessened the thrust on his next turn. Grounded a seven.

Frank and Beth made a good team. They won the first game. Shaye and Ry took the second by a single point. The tie-breaker went to his gramps and Ry's assistant.

Beth had gained a fan base. His family and teammates hugged her. Zoo left his arm around her overly long.

"I worked up an appetite watching the game," Halo commented from the sidelines. "When do we eat, Beth?"

"My stomach will be grumbling louder than Atlas if it's not soon," said Landon.

Beth glanced at her watch. "Anytime now," she promised.

As if on cue, four catering vans pulled into the driveway. An assembly line of servers entered the backyard. The guests stopped what they were doing and stared at the amount of food being delivered.

"I need to direct traffic," Beth said, cutting through the crowd toward the buffet tables.

The picnic turned international, Ry noticed. Beth hadn't cooked; instead she'd brought in a variety of food. Italian, Mexican, and Chinese were served alongside All-

American hot dogs and hamburgers. The tables rapidly filled with serving trays and covered pans. Rylan stood to the side and watched as his guests formed a line. They gathered silverware, then loaded their plastic plates.

Lasagna, spaghetti, tacos, burritos, chow mein, sweet and sour chicken were just a start. He'd never seen so much food at a picnic. Beth had outdone herself. His teammates could have seconds or thirds and not make a dent. He was feeling hungry himself and moved to the end of the line.

A hint of dusk crept across the yard. It would be dark by seven. The large solar powered lanterns did their job. He'd held the ladder for Beth when she'd hung them from branches on the banyan tree, the corners of the garage, and across the overhang on his roof. The lighting lent a softer mood to the evening. Activities would continue, but at a slower pace.

Rylan soon filled his own plate, then looked around for Beth. One sweep of the yard, and he realized she was no longer outside. He let himself into the kitchen.

There he found her, preparing dinner for his dogs. He leaned against the door and watched her work. She was talking soothingly to Atlas, who was quite put out at having been stuck inside. She promised him a walk after he ate. Ry's throat tightened. Beth had willingly left the picnic to care for his pets. He would walk with them. No one would miss him.

Beth started when she saw him. "We're getting ready to eat, too," she told him. "Breakfast for dinner. Barkin' Turkey Omelets." She continued her preparation. Atlas helped, too. He nudged her to hurry up.

Ry crossed to the island, sat on a stool. "You haven't eaten," he noted.

"I'll grab something later."

"Or you could share my plate." Tofu lasagna and vegetable brown rice. Baked and healthy. "Thanks for thinking of me when you planned the menu."

"It is your picnic." She smiled at him over her shoulder. "The spaghetti and meatballs are for me."

He ate a bite of lasagna, complimented her. "You're good at planning, Beth."

"I tried."

"You were successful. Have you ever thought about capitalizing on your talent?" he asked her. "Become a party planner? Start your own business?"

Her shoulders tensed as she thought over his suggestion. She fried up the omelets and let them cool before answering him, "Something to consider." She sounded wistful.

He didn't understand her apprehension.

Atlas soon gave Beth his most persuasive look, pushing her to scoop his dinner. He crossed to his raised dog bowl. Wagged his tail. Rue joined him. Oscar and Nathan took their places, too.

Beth fed them.

Ry enjoyed watching her care for his dogs. She'd accepted their habits.

She backed up against the sink and had a dish towel in hand when Atlas turned toward her. The big dog had flecks of egg on his whiskers. Beth cleaned his face. He then leaned heavily against her. She adjusted her stance to support the big boy's weight.

"Walk?" she asked them, once they finished their meal.

They charged the front door.

She collected their dishes and set them in the sink. "They licked their platters clean."

Ry pushed off the stool. "I'm going with you."

"What about your guests?" she asked.

"I'm not worried about them. Those who want to stay,

will stay. Those who want to leave, will leave." He met her gaze. "I'd rather be with you."

"You would?" Surprise parted her lips and widened her eyes.

Atlas paced before the door. Made a rumbling sound.

"He says you're good company," Rylan translated for her.

"I'm becoming quite fond of him," she admitted. "Rue and the dachshunds, too."

"We're a misfit bunch, but somehow it works."

"I'll get the harnesses." She went to collect them from the closet.

Once hooked up, the dogs were off. Laugher from the backyard brightened the night. Rylan heard Halo's warrior whoop and figured he'd finally beaten Shaye at croquet. His teammate would've played all night to best his sister. He was that competitive.

Atlas balked at the end of the driveway. He tugged the handle of his leash from Rylan's hand and took it to Beth. Beth then passed Ry the leads on the other three dogs.

Ry shook his head. "Can't believe he likes you more than me."

She smiled. "I bake his treats. He moaned today over peanut butter pumpkin cookies."

"The way to a dog's heart is through his stomach."

"He's a growing boy."

"He's the size of a pony already," said Ry. "When he rides in my Range Rover, I vacuum the ceiling for fur. It takes three people to get him on the scale at the vet's. He licks dishes that are in the sink. One time Dune put donuts on top of the refrigerator. I came home to find powdered sugar on Atlas's nose. Shaye once held him straddled between her legs when the doorbell rang. She took a short, fast ride straight to the door."

"He is a handful," Beth agreed.

"He's as gentle with you as he is with anyone."

He heard her sigh, and her words were barely audible when she said, "I need gentle in my life right now."

Had her past been difficult? he wondered. How so? He wanted to make her time with him enjoyable and easy. He'd work on it.

They stopped at a street corner. Two cars passed, and the drivers called to Atlas. Atlas barked back.

They crossed the road in silence. The street lights clicked on. Beth stood in a fluorescent glow. She'd tamed her curls for the picnic, but they'd turned wild once again. Her expression was reflective. Her shoulders slightly slumped. Atlas looked up at her as if he expected her to share her innermost secrets. She didn't, but he got a pat on his head.

Rylan went to take her free hand. Her fingers slipped between his. Her palm was small, warm. "One or the Other," he engaged her. "What makes you smile in hard times?"

"Memories of my parents. You?"

"My family. My dogs." He paused, considered his next question. "Do you fight against adversity or do you withdraw?"

She was honest. "Withdraw, and wait for the right moment to wrap my head around the situation." She cut him a glance. "You have face-and-fight written all over you."

"I deal with situations as they arise. Problems get resolved quickly."

She dipped her head. "I let things linger."

"Are those things eating you up inside?" He hoped not.

"Less now than before."

"If you ever want to talk—"

"Atlas will be there for me."

He chuckled. "The big boy listens. I'm not so sure about his advice."

She tipped her chin, side-glanced at Ry. "Easygoing or a firm plan of action man?" she asked.

"Low key in my downtime. Action man when I play ball."

"Any daredevil in your soul?"

He responded with, "I took some crazy chances in my surfing days. I'm a Libra, so at heart, I like security and permanence."

Beth wanted that, too. Stability was important to her. She'd been living her life on a tilt ever since her parents had passed away. She wanted to stand on solid ground. So very badly.

Thirty minutes later, they'd finished their loop and were a block from home when Atlas stopped and eyed Rue's leash. He wanted to walk her the rest of the way.

"Not tonight," Rylan told him. "I don't want you running loose. Not with a backyard full of people."

Atlas grumbled, sat down on the curb. Rylan blew out a breath, said, "Don't cop an attitude with me."

The Dane turned his head away. Snorted.

Beth bent, whispered near the dog's ear, "Good boys get ice cream."

Atlas's ears flickered.

"Vanilla," she tempted him.

He was suddenly up and tugging her toward the cottage. Her feet flew along the sidewalk. She put all her weight into hanging on.

Ry was close behind her. "We don't have any ice cream at the house," he reminded her. "The dogs can tolerate dairy, but it's not all that healthy."

"How about low-fat frozen yogurt?"

He gave in. "A small cup wouldn't hurt, I guess. Are you running to the grocery store?"

"No, I'm having it delivered."

The tinkling of a distant bell grew closer. Headlights

fanned them as the vehicle rounded the corner. Dessert had arrived. The ice cream truck pulled into Ry's driveway beside the catering vans.

"You are unbelievable," Rylan said to her. "I'm surprised Foster's Frozen Treats agreed to come by the house. Last time the vehicle was in the neighborhood, Atlas got out, and the kids scattered. My boy chased the truck for blocks before I could catch him. Alfred Foster didn't have much business that day. I gave him fifty bucks."

"Atlas is on his best behavior now," Beth said as she tapped on the service window.

A man slid it open, stuck his head out. Seeing the Dane, he leaned back inside.

"Three small cups with one scoop of vanilla yogurt each," she ordered. "One larger cup with two scoops." She grabbed a handful of paper napkins. Atlas would eat his yogurt with gusto.

Alfred fixed her order. He passed her the smaller paper cups first, which she set on the lawn. Rue ate daintily. The dachshunds dove in. Atlas's bigger cup came next. He gobbled and slurped his dessert. All the dogs had white muzzles by the time they'd finished. The napkins came in handy. Ry helped her clean their faces.

Guests from the backyard soon drifted around the corner of the cottage. Excitement over the ice cream truck grew with each order. Beth kept a firm grip on Atlas's leash so he didn't charge or jump on anyone. He was exceptionally good. Rue sat quietly as well. Rylan carried Nathan and Oscar inside. They were tired from their walk.

Beth listened as everyone ordered. Shaye chose an orange Creamsicle; her husband Trace got a Fudgsicle.

Dune decided on an ice cream sandwich. His pregnant wife Sophie wanted two scoops of strawberry shortcake.

Halo Todd had a Chipwich.

Landon Kane a blueberry snow cone.

Zoo opted for a Snickers Ice Cream Bar.

Grandfather Frank had a butterscotch sundae with whipped cream and two cherries.

The guests were soon full and moving slow. The caterers wrapped and refrigerated the leftover food, then departed. The ice cream truck backed out of the driveway shortly thereafter.

Beth put Rue and Atlas in the house. The Dane groused all the way. She then stepped back outside. Rylan's friends, family, and teammates were letting their meals settle. They sat on chairs and benches in the backyard, talking quietly. Some stayed another hour; others, two.

"Best picnic, ever, Rylan," Shaye said to her brother when he joined them on the porch. "I had a great time."

Beth was seated next to his sister. She was surprised, but pleased, when he settled on the wide wooden arm of her Adirondack chair. His thigh brushed her arm. He leaned his elbow on the back curve of the chair. He sat so close, his heat and scent seemed a physical touch.

"The picnic was all Beth," Ry said, giving her the credit.

"She's missing her calling, working for you, dude," Halo commented as he climbed the porch steps, then hiked his hip on the railing.

Shaye pursed her lips, said to Beth, "I have a boardwalk luncheon scheduled in two weeks for shop owners and city councilmen. Can I borrow you?"

Rylan spoke for her. "Don't borrow Beth—hire her. She's starting a side business."

She was? Beth didn't want to contradict him; it would be impolite. However, she wasn't certain she was ready for a second event. One success didn't erase the wedding disaster of the previous summer.

Shaye smiled encouragingly. "Jillian and I will be throwing Sophie a baby shower at the end of the month. We would hire you in a heartbeat."

Jill sat close enough to take part in the conversation. "Aidan and his partner Mike need someone to plan an appreciation cocktail party for the financiers of a new shopping mall. The job's yours, if you want it."

Three jobs offered in under a minute. Beth couldn't believe the turn of events. "This is unexpected." Her voice was soft with emotion. "Let me give it some thought and get back to you."

"Deal," said Shaye. She crossed her fingers. "I'm hoping you'll agree. Barefoot William doesn't have a party planner, but we do a lot of celebrating. You'd have a steady clientele."

Halo showed his support. "Planning parties is a great opportunity. You wouldn't be out of a job when you're done working for Ry man. Maybe you could rent his cottage when he heads back to Richmond."

Beth was overwhelmed. "Maybe . . ." was all she could say.

"Or she could start up her business in Richmond," Ry suggested.

"We need her here more," said his sister.

"I beg to differ, I need her—" Rylan stopped himself from saying more. A muscle flexed in his jaw.

Rylan needing her? Didn't make sense to Beth. Whatever had he meant? There was no way of knowing. He'd clammed up.

A curious silence settled over the group. All eyes were on Rylan and Beth. She wasn't used to being the center of attention. Color climbed into her cheeks. She grew uncomfortable. Ry kept his composure. The man was rock solid.

Shaye yawned, stretched, commented, "It's getting late. Time to call it a night."

Halo glanced at his watch. "It's only nine o'clock."

Shaye moved him along. "Past your bedtime."

He pulled a face. "You kicking us out?"

She nodded. "Rylan's too polite, so I'm speaking for him." She turned to her granddad. "We're leaving."

Frank was nodding off. Her husband Trace helped him to his feet.

Ry stood then, too. Beth shared his spotlight when the guests thanked him and filed out. She was treated as half a couple. It felt nice.

Halo and Landon were the last to leave. They hinted at an invitation to lunch the next day, to help finish off the leftovers. Ry shook his head and suggested Molly's Diner for their next meal. They looked disappointed.

Beth gave in. "A plate to go?"

The men grinned like little boys.

Halo pushed by Rylan and held the kitchen door for her. Landon was right behind him. Atlas met them with a woof and a wag.

"Where's Rue and the weenies?" Landon asked.

"Sleeping," Beth guessed. "Atlas likes the action; they're lights out."

"I want a clean plate, one that Atlas hasn't licked," said Halo. "I've caught him with his head in the sink and the dishwasher. The boy goes after the last crumb."

Beth located paper plates in the cupboard then opened the refrigerator door. The guys leaned in behind her. Crowded her.

A second later, Rylan put his hands on their shoulders and drew them back. "Let the lady breathe," he told his teammates.

"Atlas gets to stick his nose in the fridge," Halo noted.

"It's his house," Beth reminded the man.

"Atlas is sniffing the tacos," Halo said. "He's going to inhale the cheese."

Landon frowned. "His mouth is too close to the bowl of chow mein."

"Relax, guys," Beth assured them. "There's plenty for everybody."

She chose Atlas over the men to feed first. In the Dane's case, he got a snack. She would have heated the small bowl of vegetarian rice, but he was anxious and ate it cold. Rylan tossed her the drool towel; otherwise her Levi's would've been speckled with rice. Rylan called the big dog to him, so Beth could fix plates for his teammates.

"No, I'm not sharing," Halo said to Atlas on his way to the door. The dog trailed him, nearly tripping him up.

Landon was more generous. He slipped Atlas a meatball. The Dane chewed twice, swallowed. There was a trace of spaghetti sauce beneath his nose. The dog wiped it on Landon's leg.

"Nice manners," Landon muttered.

"You've wiped your mouth on the shoulder of your T-shirt," Rylan reminded him. "Left barbecue stains."

"Brown Bag in Atlanta," Landon remembered. "There were no napkins on the table." He passed Atlas a second meatball before darting out the door. "Your boy needs a bib."

The door clicked, and Rylan locked it behind them. He ran one hand down his face. "It's been a long day, and those two only make it longer."

Beth understood. "They tend to drag things out."

"In everything they do."

She exhaled slowly. "I want to make a final sweep of the yard. Make sure the volleyballs and croquet mallets got put away."

"Two can check quicker than one." Rylan followed her

outside. Atlas crossed the porch behind them, only to turn around. The guests had disappeared. He stood in the doorway instead.

Beth checked the ground closely. She found a shuffle-board disk in the bushes. Ry located a croquet ball at the base of the banyan tree. They were headed back toward the porch when she heard a ticking sound, followed by a *chchch-kutkutkut*. She looked around, trying to locate the source.

Rylan knew immediately. "Sprinklers," he said, right before they both got sprayed. "Automatic timers are set for ten o'clock."

Sprinklers were better than a thunderstorm. Still, they were getting wet. "My blouse." She needed to protect the vintage lace.

He grabbed her hand, and they made a dash for the cottage. He ran ahead of her, taking the brunt of the water pressure. Her blouse was saved, but her hair and jeans were soaked. Water drops darkened the suede on her boots. She hoped they would dry without leaving spots. Rylan stood in a puddle of water on the porch. He slicked back one side of his hair. His eyelashes were spiked. A droplet tipped his nose. The man looked good wet.

He shook himself off like a dog. Then grinned at her. "I learned that from Atlas."

"That's one way of drying off," she said. "We should get out of our wet clothes." The water was cold, and the evening had cooled.

He nodded his agreement. They traipsed into the house, leaving watery footprints on the hardwood floor. Atlas followed, gave them each a sniff and then wandered off. Damp clothes didn't hold his interest.

Rylan stopped at the island and sent her a look. "Thank you for a great day."

She reached for the roll of paper towels on the counter,

tore off several sheets, dabbed her face. "I'm glad it turned out so well," she said, and meant it. "You never know when a good day will turn bad. Fortunately, everyone had left before the sprinklers kicked on."

She recalled the Statton wedding, which was on constant replay in her mind. The bridal party and guests had suffered a thunderstorm. Water was water, whether dropped from the sky or rising from underground sprinklers. Those in attendance had been drenched, bitter, and angry at her. The memory still made her shudder.

Rylan made her feel better by saying, "Had we gotten wet, we would've dried ourselves. Laughed it off." He made it sound so simple. "The sprinklers were my fault. I'd forgotten the lawn service set the timers for Saturday night."

Beth appreciated his calm. His logic. He put everything into perspective. She rubbed her arms, stomped her feet. Her toes grew cold, and she slipped off her boots, right there in the kitchen. Her socks came next. "I need a new pair." Picking up her boots, she headed for her bedroom.

Rylan went behind her, turning off lights. It appeared he was calling it a night. She was close to doing so, too.

"Got a minute, Beth?" he quietly asked from the hallway.

The door was cracked, and her answer carried back to him. "Be right there." She slipped on a fresh pair of orange and green plaid socks with the message *Hug Yourself* across the cuff ribbing. Her wet jeans clung to her legs. She thought to change out of them, but decided instead to see what Rylan might want.

He stood by the stair railing, his arms at his sides. He looked stiff and serious. Slightly worried. He collected himself, said, "I want to run something by you." The words seemed difficult to say. "I need a PA, and you're ideal for the position. But I'd never hold you to the job, if there was something else you'd rather do."

"Like what?" She was confused.

"Something beneficial to you," he specified. "Today's success suggests party planning. Starting your own business."

"You've already pimped me out to your sister."

"I thought it a good idea at the time, although maybe not so much now. Shaye and Jill would hire you in a heartbeat. You would have steady customers."

Her heart slowed. "Are you trying to get rid of me?"

"I'd like you to stay," he admitted. "I also want what's best for you."

There was no doubt in her mind. "I'm yours for seven more weeks," she told him. "That's not going to change. I'll be available to Shaye and Jill part-time, in my off hours."

"You're certain?"

"I'm positive."

"Atlas will be relieved."

A comfortable silence settled between them. They stared at each other with awareness and new understanding. He cleared his throat, continued. "I might let you stay on at my cottage after spring training, rent free. We could call it a bonus. This would be a great place to establish your business. You could work from home."

Home sounded warm and welcoming. Secure. "We'll see," was all she could give him at that moment.

He went toward her then, standing so close she could feel his heat, breathe in his scent. "You've yet to see the entire floor plan. Care to come upstairs?"

Foreplay, she thought. If she climbed those stairs with him, she wouldn't return until morning. *Why not?* Treasured moments were few and far between.

He offered his hand. She took it. They climbed the steps together. Halfway up, she heard the padding of paws and glanced over her shoulder. Atlas, Rue, and the dachsies were on the move. They'd popped their heads around her bedroom door. They watched her and Ry until they reached the second floor. Atlas turned in a circle, whimpered.

"Stay, gang," Rylan called down to them.

Atlas sent them a soulful look before stretching out at the base of the steps. Rue curled up beside him. Oscar and Nathan returned to their dog beds in her room.

"A little privacy is always nice," he said.

Very nice, indeed, Beth thought.

He led her down the narrow hall. They passed a room with workout equipment before entering the place where he slept. He flipped on the overhead light, and Beth took a moment to look around.

There were no surprises. The space was airy and simple. A large window above his bed let the night in. Basic cotton sheets and a comforter made his bed. The headboard fascinated her. Arched and scrolled, it was old and solid. She ran her hand over the heavy metal frame.

Ry satisfied her curiosity, saying, "An iron gate from an old church. Purchased at an auction, sponsoring a homeless shelter."

A short bedside table, corner wardrobe, small computer table and laptop completed the furniture. Sparse, but functional.

She drew a deep breath and sighed. There they stood, both rooted to their spots. She had no idea what to do next. Fluff his pillows? Turn down the bed? Her nerves got the better of her. She shivered, and goose bumps rose.

Ry reached out and briskly rubbed her arms. "You're cold, and need to get out of your wet clothes. I'll warm you up."

The friction made her tingle. With each touch, she grew warmer. The heat from his skin dried her own.

She stood utterly still as he unbuttoned her lace blouse. The glass buttons appeared smooth and delicate against his callused hands. Ever so gently, he slipped it off her shoulders. Draped it over the back of his computer chair so it wouldn't wrinkle. He then went to work on her button fly. He fumbled with the top brass button. She heard him mumble, "Zippers are easier."

She couldn't help but smile and wiggled, assisting him. As he eased the denim down her legs, she stepped out of her jeans. Her underwear wasn't fancy. A plain white bra and cotton bikini panties. The way he looked at her, she felt Victoria Secret sexy.

"My turn," she said, her voice catching. She was curious about his body. Her hands shook slightly as she worked the buttons on his shirt. Pushing apart the sides, she flattened her palms to his chest. Ry shrugged off the shirt with a roll of his shoulders. Her fingers fanned over ripped muscle and the light abrasion of his chest hair. The V of his sharply cut oblique muscles pointed blatantly to his package.

His stance was wide, his legs sinewed. She loosened the drawstring on his board shorts, and they drifted off his hips. He wore navy boxer briefs and a significant hard-on.

For a brief moment their eyes locked, and the air between them warmed. Sparked. Sizzled. His body called to hers.

We have something here, she thought. Something exciting and frightening. Something to be explored. So many possibilities.

He moved closer, and his focus narrowed on her. "I want you. Are you ready for this?"

His words tugged at something deep inside her, and a

shiver passed through her. "I'm here." Right time. Right place. Right man.

He reached for her then, framed her face with his hands. His thumbs lazily stroked her cheeks. He looked so deep into her eyes, he touched her soul.

She slid her arms around his waist and stepped to him. Skin against skin, the heat of his body covered hers. She melted against him.

She barely had time to take a breath before his mouth came down on hers. His kiss was tentative, yet intimate. Wanting, yet waiting. Latent with promise. There was a naturalness to their kiss. A rightness. Her mouth parted beneath his, accepting him, and his tongue swept inside. Her whole body sighed.

All the while they kissed, their hands moved, explored, claimed. Her bra was soon lost to his skillful fingers. He hooked his thumbs over the edge of her bikini panties, and they went missing as well. She stood before him naked and shy. Still wearing her message socks.

"They stay," she softly said, needing the security of the inspirational message. *Hug Yourself* was the motto of her life at the moment. Rylan had become a big part of her.

He had no problem with her socks. "Fine by me."

He didn't wait for her to remove his boxer briefs. He did it himself. "I'm faster," he said, kicking them aside.

She admired his erection. She carefully traced the tips of her fingers along the straining length of him. He closed his eyes. Sucked air. When she curved her hand around his cock and squeezed, he moaned. A raw, strangled sound from deep in his chest. She loved controlling the moment.

Serious, stable, Rylan had lost his trademark calm. His hunger for her was visible when he opened his eyes. His nostrils flared, and he breathed through his mouth. "Condom," he rasped.

He walked into the bathroom, returning with a box. Her eyes rounded. The man was ambitious.

He drew her down on his bed, made her comfortable. Then lay beside her. He kissed her again, deeper and more demanding. Her desire matched his own. He broke their kiss long enough to nibble her ear, to whisper sexy words. She nipped the underside of his jaw; placed soft kisses along his neck.

He was bold and attentive. Romantic and passionate. Hot and needy. His hands and lips seemed to touch her everywhere at once. Her own fingers traced and discovered. She couldn't get enough of him.

Dipping his head, he took one of her nipples into his mouth, licking, suckling, until she felt the draw of his mouth all the way to her toes. They curled.

Each breath became a challenge. Her heart beat faster, and a damp, hot ache settled between her thighs. She felt anxious. Restless. Beside herself.

She twisted. Writhed. Craved.

He rested his palm on her belly, and his fingers stretched low. She was warm and wet when he slipped one finger inside her. She lifted her hips into his touch.

She found him, too. A stroke, a squeeze, a light scoring of her nails. His cock swelled more. His hips jerked. He could only take her handling so long.

"I want you beneath me." He grabbed a condom off the bedside table, ripped the foil packet open with his teeth, and sheathed himself.

She would've liked to do it for him. There was always next time, and the time after that.

Returning to her, he parted her thighs and knelt between them. Leaning forward, he braced himself on his forearms and entered her body in one long, smooth stroke. She gasped, as he stretched and filled her. He was skilled. He knew what she needed. The slow, fluid rock of his hips gave her time to adjust to him. His heat slid over her. Arousal rose inside her. Liquefying her bones.

He held nothing back, drawing her higher until sensation and climax claimed them. She shattered. Her spasms began a breath before his own. Her body clenched around his, holding him tightly to her.

He moaned his release. Deep and ragged. His body shook with his satisfaction. Dropping forward, he rested his forehead against hers. Caught his breath.

Their inseparable moment lingered. She felt a part of him.

Rylan was first to move. He rolled onto his side and slid off the bed. He disposed of his condom. Once back, he drew her to him, held her close. "What a day. What a night," he breathed against her mouth.

She caught her bottom lip with her teeth. "I'd like more night."

"You would, huh?"

She heard the humor in his voice. "If you're able."

"Able again in fifteen," he said.

She gave him twenty.

Midnight crossed into morning. The box of condoms grew lighter. Four a.m. they finally slept. Sated and exhausted. Their hearts and limbs entangled beneath a soft cotton sheet.

Nine

Morning came too soon. They were awakened by a low howl from below stairs. Atlas wanted his breakfast. The Dane didn't have a snooze button.

Beside Rylan on the bed, Beth stirred. She stretched lazily and her naked body brushed his, all warm, soft, and womanly. He liked the feel of her. Her scent. The way her eyelids fluttered when she opened her eyes and focused on him.

She gave him a small, sleepy smile, murmured, "Time for the big boy to eat." She sat up, clutching the sheet to her chest.

He smiled at her modesty after their long night of sex. *Incredible sex,* he thought. The lady was amazing. She'd lost her shyness and sought to please him. He'd pleasured her, too. They'd made love until they were both thoroughly spent.

He liked everything about her. How her lips parted when she moaned his name. How her breasts rose to his touch. How her hips came off the mattress when he entered her. The way her body clutched his in climax. How she sought him in sleep. Snuggling close. Until Atlas reminded them that he was hungry.

She drew her legs over the side of the bed, tugging the sheet with her. She was covered, and he was fully exposed.

His erection invited her back. The look she cast over her shoulder was wistful, telling him she'd love to return. She gave a heart-felt sigh and went in search of her clothes.

"Wear one of my T-shirts," he offered. "Top dresser drawer." One of his shirts would clear her knees. She wouldn't have to wear panties. That appealed to him most.

She chose an old, worn Rogues shirt. The softest in his drawer. She dropped the sheet long enough to slip it over her head. He appreciated her nudity. Her slender shoulders, sleek back, tight little ass, and nice legs. He liked the fact she was toned, but not muscled. Softer did it for him.

She shook out the hem on his shirt and the cotton hung loose. The tips of her nipples remained visible, pointing at him. The shirt rose on her thighs when she moved toward the door. The fabric snuck between her legs like a hand. She had cute knees.

A crawling, scraping sound stopped her at the threshold. Her eyes widened and her lips parted when Atlas appeared in stealth mode. Crouching low, his belly close to the ground, he attempted to sneak up the staircase unnoticed. He was hard to miss. He pushed up to his full height and grumbled, displeased with being kept waiting.

Beth gave the dog a hug, and he buried his nose in her cleavage. Rylan wished he was Atlas at the moment. She quickly collected her discarded clothing. Her bra and panties topped her jeans. Her lace blouse was wrinkle-free.

"Tofurkey breakfast links," she offered Atlas.

His howl of approval echoed off the walls, sounding like an entire pack of dogs. He accidentally knocked her into the doorjamb on his way out.

Beth pulled a face, rubbed her hip. She picked up daily bruises from the Dane. She needed to be wrapped in bubble wrap or quilted Northern.

"Let me kiss it and make it better," Ry suggested from bed.

"You can kiss more than my hip later." She slipped out.
He looked forward to later.

Or much later as it turned out. He had no idea where
the day went. He remembered her feeding the dogs, while
wearing his T-shirt. The sway of her breasts and hips beneath the shirt had left him bone hard.

But he hadn't caught a break. She'd gone on to fix his
breakfast. Brushing against him—on purpose—when she'd
served him.

She'd walked the dogs. A shower, a change of clothes,
and she'd left the cottage . . . to visit his grandfather. She'd
made those plans at the picnic.

Ry knew Frank would be glad to see her. Their card
games would carry over into the afternoon. Ry wouldn't
see her anytime soon.

Unless he went after her.

But he had his own Sunday agenda. Doing absolutely
nothing. He so seldom had a day off, he planned to make
the most of it, stretching out on the sofa and watching
sports until she returned. He figured recaps on basketball
and hockey scores would hold his attention until the actual games started later that afternoon.

He lost his concentration in under an hour. His mind
wandered to Beth so many times, he finally thumped himself on the forehead. What the hell was the matter with
him?

She'd only been gone a short time, yet he was so restless for her that his skin itched. He'd seen his grandfather
yesterday, but what would it hurt to see him again today?
Nothing at all. Ry nodded. Gin or cribbage, he would
challenge the winner. He held his own in dominoes. Once
spring training started, his time would be limited. Might
as well make the most of his free time now.

As the day progressed, he could toss out the suggestion
of furniture shopping. He'd call it a business trip. Beth had

suggested that he go online and check out sites. He wasn't into designer sofas and chairs, but he did require durable. Several local stores were open on the weekends. They'd start there.

If he was smart, he'd take Atlas shopping with him. It would make selecting pieces so much easier. The big boy could stretch out, and Ry could measure the amount of room left for him. On a good day, Atlas left him eighteen inches. If he were lucky.

Rue, Oscar, and Nathan favored their dog beds. They'd never been couch potatoes like Atlas. Maybe he deserved his own sofa.

However, he did like human contact, and might not go it alone.

Ry wanted to discuss his choices with Beth before he finalized any sale. He valued her opinion. Last night, they'd turned the corner from boss and employee to lovers. She was his PA with benefits. But that didn't come close to how he felt about her. Beth wasn't his usual date or sex partner. She was quirky and spontaneous, with a guarded past. He wanted her to open up to him. To trust him. To share her secrets. To be a part of his life.

That thought shook him most. Falling for a woman in a few short days wasn't his style. It took him weeks, sometimes months, to develop a relationship. There was something about this woman that broke his dating rules. She got to him. His heart *knew* her. He played sports on that same gut level. He went with what seemed natural. Intuitive.

He decided to go ahead and feed the dogs lunch before he left the cottage. It was close enough to noon that Atlas and crew wouldn't mind eating early. He had a recipe for Bow Wow Brunch made with oatmeal, yogurt, cottage cheese, and fruit. Atlas liked bananas. Rue favored mangos. The weenies preferred pears. Afterward he'd take them for a walk before he took off.

He rolled off the couch and found Atlas sitting before the abstract painting. It was bizarre to see. He had no idea what held the dog's eye. Perhaps it was no more than a new object in the house. Atlas would angle his head left then right as if trying to understand the work's significance.

Ry patted him on the head as he walked toward the kitchen. "Don't get lost in the symbolism. We all see the painting differently."

Atlas barked, stared a moment longer, then trotted after Rylan. The scent of brunch drew the other dogs. They ate and Ry cleaned up. He missed having Beth in the kitchen with him. Thinking about her took his mind off Atlas long enough for the dog to wipe his mouth on Ry's gym shorts. He left curds of cottage cheese. Ry reached for a paper towel, cleaned himself off.

A walk, a shower, a quick cleaning of his bedroom, and Ry went in search of Beth.

He'd told her she could drive his Range Rover, but it seemed she preferred her PT Cruiser. Today, anyway. The parking lot at the retirement village was nearly full. Families and friends came to visit on the weekends. The place was bursting at the seams with chatter and news.

"Hello, Rylan," an elderly woman said to him on his arrival. Her spine curved into a wicker rocking chair. She faced the window, watching people come and go.

He remembered her. She had attended his speech. "How are you, Cora?"

She rocked her chair slowly, all prim and proper in a collared cream-colored blouse and a brown skirt. "I'm waiting for my daughter." She smiled at him. "I don't get out very often. We're going shopping today. I can't wait to see my Anne."

Time away from the village would be a change in scenery. Those who didn't drive any longer always appreciated a day out. "Enjoy your afternoon."

"Frank and your Beth are in the recreational center." Cora knew their whereabouts.

Ry figured everyone kept track of everyone else. *His Beth.* He liked the sound of it. "Thanks." He located the main hallway, sought the room where they'd played Bingo.

The area was set up for all kinds of games. From playing cards to boxed board sets of Monopoly, Scrabble, Clue, and Chinese checkers. Activities that kept people busy when conversations lagged. Rylan scanned the room, found his grandfather and Beth at a table in the far corner. He approached them.

Her back was to him. She'd pulled her hair into a ponytail. More strands escaped than stayed captured by the band. She wore a tank top and walking shorts. Her red Keds. Her message socks were a dark blue, patterned with white doves. Inspirational script circled each bird. *Fly High* made him smile.

"Gin," he heard his granddad say. Frank laid down his cards.

Beth gave an exaggerated sigh. "You're breaking my bank." She slipped her hand into the side pocket on her shorts and passed him a quarter, which Frank added to his growing stack of coins.

Ry stepped forward, curved his hand over her shoulder. "I'm good for a loan, if you need one."

Beth started, surprised to see him. "What happened to your alone-time? Your TV day?"

The older man saw right through Rylan. "Two is better than one," he said, his expression amused. He collected the cards. "We're wrapping up here. I promised Morton Potter a game of chess."

Rylan hadn't seen Morton when he entered the room. He raised a questioning eyebrow at his grandfather, and the older man winked at him. Silent communication spoke the loudest. His gramps understood. Ry had just been given permission to spend the afternoon with Beth. He was grateful.

"What are your plans for the day?" his granddad asked.

Beth shrugged, and Rylan responded, "Furniture shopping, if she's willing."

Frank gave him a thoughtful nod. "Settling in, are we?"

"My living room consists of a tilted sofa."

"And a great piece of artwork," Beth chimed in.

"Evelyn Wells, the Gallery Walk," Ry said, explaining the purchase of the painting.

Frank reminisced. "The only paintings Emma and I had in the house were those you kids did in art class in elementary school. I still have several of Shaye's finger paintings in a box in my closet. There's a water color picture of a big yellow car from you in there, too."

"It was a school bus, Gramps."

"That explains all the circles in the windows."

"Those were my classmates."

Frank chuckled. "I should've recognized little Larry Canton. The kid had carrot orange hair."

"He still does," Ry informed him. "He owns a used car dealership. I've seen his TV ads."

"So have I," said Frank. "The guy's hair clashed with a red Mustang he had for sale last week."

"Did you save any of Zane's nudes?" Rylan had to know.

His older brother was the first of the four boys to appreciate the female body. Breasts in particular. Every girl he drew had enormous boobs. Including a likeness of his teacher. Two months into the fourth grade, and Mrs. Watkins requested a schedule change. Zane left Art for Shop. He'd carved a great set of knockers in his woodworking class.

"I kept his charcoal drawing of a tornado. The boy was

always interested in storms. Hurricanes in particular." Frank stood then, waved them on. "Furniture Barn is east of town. George Roberts, a third cousin on your mother's side of the family, converted the old barn into a modern showroom. It's good to keep business in the family."

Rylan agreed. "We'll make that our first stop."

His granddad put his hand on Ry's shoulder. "If I don't see you before, we'll meet up after your first game. Beth has agreed to be my guest. She doesn't mind sitting in center field." He had chosen a two-deck section of seats in the outfield. The rest of the Cateses would be seated along the first base line. There was always room for Frank and a guest, if he so chose.

"You could come in closer," Ry reminded him.

"I've got your back, boy."

Yes, he did, Rylan mused. His granddad would be in the first row of the first level behind the center field fence. Ry could glance up and see him. Beth, too. At least the second deck would provide shade for the lower one. "Need binoculars for my at-bat?" he jokingly asked.

"Hit me a homer and I'll see the ball just fine."

"I'll do my best."

Frank hugged them both, then strolled off.

Beth rose from her chair, facing Ry. "Furniture shopping? Are you sure?"

As sure as he was about anything at the moment. He'd be spending time with her. That's what mattered most. He took her hand, tugged her to his side. He kept her close as they crossed the room, then headed down the hallway. None of the retirees tried to detain him. They were too busy chatting with family and friends.

Rylan noticed Cora Salvo was still sitting in the same chair as when he'd arrived.

Beth spied her, too. She'd apparently spoken to Cora

earlier and was aware of her long wait. "Any sign of Anne?" she gently asked the older woman.

Cora stared straight ahead, as if by doing so, her daughter would magically appear. "Not yet, but soon." She sounded hopeful.

A flicker of sadness appeared in Beth's eyes before she blinked it away. "Would you like us to sit with you awhile?"

Cora sighed. "Maybe a few minutes, but only until my Anne arrives."

Beth gave him a helpless look. She wasn't sure what to do, but he did. Releasing her hand, he pulled up two additional guest chairs, angled them next to Cora, and they both sat down.

"What do you and Anne have planned for today?" Beth asked.

"We're going shopping."

"What kind of shopping?" Ry was curious. *Clothes? Grocery?*

"Budget Buy," said Cora. "It's similar to a dollar store."

Older people were on fixed incomes, Ry knew. Social security didn't stretch far. His grandfather was fortunate to have unlimited funds. But then the Cateses owned Barefoot William. Family took care of family.

"What time was Anne to pick you up?" Beth inquired.

Cora was slow to answer. "There's no set time actually. It's whenever she's able. Her divorce was difficult. Anne has her hands full, working two jobs, caring for her children. She gets to me when she can." Cora ran her hands along the curved wooden arms of her chair. "I do love a good rocking chair. A comfortable place to wait."

Rylan felt the sympathy he saw on Beth's face. There was no pity in her eyes, only kindness. He knew she wouldn't let this moment pass without doing something for the senior citizen. Something that would make her day better.

Beth stood. "I'll be right back." She crossed to Reception and spoke quietly with the lady behind the desk. When she returned shortly, her eyes were moist as if holding back tears. She swallowed hard, leaned toward Cora, drawing the woman's attention. "I've spoken to the receptionist. Unfortunately, Anne won't be visiting today."

Cora sighed, sounding defeated. "Well, then, maybe tomorrow."

"Maybe." Beth gave the woman hope. "Rylan and I are going shopping if you'd care to join us."

Cora stopped rocking, her expression thoughtful. "A third wheel?"

"You have a roommate from what I remember," said Beth. "Include her, too."

Cora nodded. "Lana Arnett is my sister-in-law. We're both widowed. We lost our husbands twenty years ago, within a week of each other. We've lived together ever since."

"We're headed to Furniture Barn," Beth told her. "Care to browse with us?"

Cora rose from the rocker. "Think we could make a stop at Budget Buy on our way back?"

Rylan committed. "Easy stop."

"What about the flea market?"

Out of the way, but doable. He gave in. "We can manage that, too." His saw his private afternoon with Beth rapidly becoming an outing for four.

"Let me grab my purse and locate Lana. Shouldn't take more than fifteen minutes." Cora left with a bounce in her step.

"What's her story?" Rylan asked Beth once Cora was out of earshot. Her conversation with the receptionist had prompted the shopping spree.

Beth's gaze clouded when she said, "Anne and her children no longer live in Barefoot William. They moved to Atlanta shortly after the divorce. Cora hasn't fully comprehended that Anne is gone. She expects her only daughter to walk through the door at any moment. It's not going to happen."

"Sorry to hear that," said Ry.

"Yeah, me, too."

He rubbed the back of his neck. "It's going to be an interesting afternoon."

"I think so, too." The look she gave him was warm and grateful and worth his decision to chauffeur the ladies about town.

Cora and Lana met them thirty minutes later. Lana wore a bright green pantsuit and walked with a cane. She moved more slowly than Cora. She wasn't all that steady on her feet, Rylan soon learned. She tipped to the side when she turned too quickly. He offered her his arm for balance, and she grasped his elbow with surprising strength.

Cora sniffed inside his Range Rover while hooking her seat belt. "Do you have a dog?"

Evidence of his crew lingered. "Four," he responded. He expected her look of horror, only to see Cora's smile reflected in his rearview mirror.

She commented, "I grew up with a household of pets. My mother never turned a stray away. The retirement facility allows dogs and cats under twenty-five pounds. Our neighbor has a Pekinese named Pudge. Chubby little guy."

"I have a Great Dane named Atlas," Rylan told her. He relayed several funny stories that had the ladies laughing. One included the big boy riding in the back with his head out the window, panting so hard he shook the entire vehicle.

Once they reached the Furniture Barn, Rylan realized

the ladies saw their outing as more than an hour or two; they were thinking of it as an afternoon affair.

"We don't get out very often," Cora told him. "Transportation is offered at the village to take us to doctor and dental appointments, shopping and the like. But the van's schedule conflicts with our other activities."

Lana agreed. "We can't miss our morning coffee klatch or afternoon Bingo during the week."

Sunday was apparently a free day and they were glad to get out and about. Beth seemed to be enjoying herself as well. She and Cora had circled the perimeter of the barn twice, surveying the furniture. They wove amid the sofas and chairs, sitting and testing several pieces for sturdiness and comfort.

Rylan took Lana to join them at the rockers. All three sat and rocked with different motions.

"I do enjoy a good rocking chair," Cora said, closing her eyes. She appeared about to fall asleep. Same with Lana. Their bodies seemed to sigh on the cushioned seats. Relaxed smiles smoothed the wrinkles on their faces. They looked ten years younger.

"Rocking is soothing," Lana went on to say. "My physical therapist believes motion helps reduce stress and eases arthritis."

"It can relieve constipation, too," Cora added.

More information than Rylan needed to know.

The ladies rocked so long, the owner of the store made them feel further at home by offering them coffee. "Anything to go with that coffee?" Cora asked.

George Roberts grinned. "Chocolate or almond biscotti."

Cora chose chocolate. Lana went with almond.

"We're going to be here awhile, aren't we?" Ry asked Beth when she rose from her rocker and crossed the center aisle to look at couches and chaises.

She touched his arm, smiled up at him. "A little while longer. The ladies are having a good time, don't you think?"

He glanced in their direction. George had drawn a small round table between their rockers for their coffee and biscotti. It looked like a tea party. The two women were chatting with the owner as if they were old friends. "They're making the most of their day."

"I'll make the most of our night."

That appealed to him. "You will, huh?"

"After the movies."

That took him back. "What movies?"

She explained. "Your grandfather mentioned showtime at the pier. Shaye sets up a large screen against the side of the bait shop, and moviegoers bring their own beach chairs. Tonight's a double-feature. Disney's *Frozen* is the first flick; the second, *Anchorman* with Will Ferrell."

A double-feature. Just his luck. Rylan was familiar with the Sunday tradition. "It's tourist season, so it could be crowded."

"We'll need to get there early for a good spot." She already had their night planned.

"The shows will run late."

"I'm yours from midnight till dawn."

Six hours alone with this woman wouldn't be enough. *Days* sounded better. Even *months*. He had no idea what would happen after spring training. The very thought of them going their separate ways tightened his gut.

Beth motioned to him. "Check out this couples leisure massage chair," she encouraged, easing down herself. "Reclining, heated, and vibrating."

There was plenty of room for him, too. He purposely leaned against her. Wanted to feel her against him. She set the digital control, and they reclined. The chair was nearly horizontal when she raised the temperature, then set the dial for vibration massage.

A masseuse couldn't make him feel better, Ry thought. The recliner did it for him. A big perk: sex in the chair. Relaxed, naked, slow, body vibrating sex. His dick liked the idea.

Beth caught the rise in his Levis and laughed at him.

She was as aroused as he was, he noticed. Her nipples tented her tank top. He pressed a light kiss to her lips, which nearly included teeth and tongue. He backed off when George Roberts came to check on them. Beth quickly pressed the off button, and the recliner stilled.

Rylan sat up. "You've got a sale," he told his relative. "How soon can it be delivered?" He wanted to give it a test drive tonight.

George was accommodating. "Later today if you like."

Unfortunately much later, Ry thought. Their agenda included stops at Budget Buy and the flea market. There was no getting around either one. Cora and Lana had their hearts set on shopping. He wouldn't cut their time short.

Anticipation was the best foreplay. For both him and Beth.

"Around five works," he relayed. "Should a Great Dane answer the door, we're not home. Don't leave the furniture with him."

George smiled. "I've heard about Atlas."

"Most of Barefoot William knows him," said Ry. "Few invite him for a play date."

"Does he play rough?" asked George.

"He merely wants to be the center of attention."

George chuckled. "I have an Afghan Hound. Big and in my face."

Beth listened as the men talked dogs. Ry was a good listener. He kept turning the conversation back to George, allowing the man to expand on his dog's personality and antics. People loved to talk about their pets. You could tell by his animated expression that the store owner treated his dog like a child. But then so did Rylan. Atlas was one big baby!

"Rylan might be interested in a sofa, too," Beth told George when the men wound down.

George tossed out ideas. "Leather, fabric, slipcovered, canvas, stain-resistant?"

"Beth?" Ry deferred to her.

She'd seen an attractive dark turquoise leather sofa when they'd first arrived. It was showcased in a living room display at the front of the store. It had a tufted back and cherrywood arms, and would blend perfectly with the textured blue hues in Rylan's abstract painting. The pieces would complement each other.

She crooked her finger for the men to follow her. "This way."

The couch stretched eight feet long. High-backed. The leather was plush. Rylan raised an eyebrow, looked skeptical. "Dog friendly?"

George gave his pitch. "Leather is a lifetime purchase, even with Atlas. Leather wears in when fabrics wear out. You've selected a protected leather with an extra finish. The sofa should be fine. If not, I'll replace it."

Rylan cut her a glance. "Like?"

"Buy."

The deal was sealed. "We'll take the two pieces," Ry told George.

"There may be more." Beth had a further thought. She turned around, looked back toward Cora and Emma. The elderly ladies were still rocking, still sipping their coffee. Still munching their biscotti, while talking a mile a minute.

Her heart gave a tug. "They like the rockers. Neither lady owns one. Cora mentioned she enjoys the rocking chair in the lobby at the village. Lana has a favorite one in the library. She likes to read." Beth drew in a breath, released it slowly, came to a decision. She'd noticed the price on the rockers earlier. They were expensive. Solid mahogany. Fine craftsmanship. She'd received her first paycheck from Rylan, but she might need an advance on next week's. George had his back to them when she rose on tiptoe and whispered, "Any chance of a loan until Friday?"

"How much do you need?"

Her gaze remained on the ladies. She made a quick calculation and told him the amount.

Rylan had a way of reading her mind. "You buy one, and I'll buy the other."

She swallowed hard. "You're sure?"

He glanced at his watch, "They've been rocking for close to an hour. Those chairs obviously have entertainment value."

He took Beth's hand and they maneuvered through the furniture, back to where the ladies sat. She stood beside him, yet far enough back so the rockers didn't mash her toes. Back and forth, Cora and Lana kept up a steady rhythm.

Emotion welled within her when Ry casually asked them, "Do you have room in your condo for a couple rockers?"

Cora tipped up her chin, admitted, "We have very little furniture. We sold our homes and most pieces when our husbands passed away. We combined our finances and invested in a condo at the retirement village."

Their investment was wise, Beth thought. The gated community would protect and keep them safe. A top priority as a person aged. "What type of furniture do you have now?"

Lana told her, "A short sofa which we share when we watch television." She reached over and patted Cora's arm. "We put a bowl of popcorn between us. We're content."

Beth got watery-eyed when Ry inquired, "You'd have room for two rockers if they showed up on your doorstep?"

The elderly women looked at each other, then at him.

Lana's voice shook when she asked, "Showed up on our doorstep by magic?"

"Abracadabra."

Cora dipped her head, yet her tears were evident.

Lana opened her clutch purse and slipped Cora a cotton handkerchief. Both ladies sniffed. So did Beth. She was emotionally vested in these two. Her own cheeks were streaked with tears.

"Thank you," said Cora.

"Bless you," said Lana.

Beth put her hand over her heart, managed a smile. Rylan stepped closer to her. He brushed away her tears with his thumbs, then kissed her lightly on the forehead. Curving his arm about her shoulders, he tucked her into his side. She leaned heavily against him. Sank into his strength and goodness. She had wanted to do something nice for the women, and Ry had helped fulfill her wish.

Definitely *abracadabra*.

"George," Rylan called to the owner. "Two rockers, to go."

"Do you have room in your vehicle or would you like them delivered?" George needed to know.

Rylan narrowed his gaze on the rocking chairs. "There should be room in my Range Rover. Put some padding around the wood, and we'll be good. The ladies can enjoy them tonight."

Cora and Lana got to their feet. They opened their arms to Rylan and Beth. It became a group hug. A heartfelt moment that Beth would never forget.

She was the first to ease back and looked on as the ladies continued to hug Ry. He had an arm wrapped around each one, looking uncertain as to when to let go. They didn't release him until George and one of his employees came to retrieve the rockers. They took the chairs to the storeroom, readied them for the ride to the retirement village.

Forty minutes later, they were on their way. "Flea market or Budget Buy?" he asked the ladies.

Lana and Cora put their heads together and softly conversed.

Lana spoke for them both. "All that rocking made us tired. Budget Buy and then home. We'll save the flea market for another day."

The dollar store was located in a small plaza. They found the parking lot nearly empty. They had the shop to themselves.

Beth loved a bargain. She had fifty dollars left from her payday after buying the rocking chair. She knew how to stretch a buck. She wandered the aisles, browsing with Rylan close behind her.

The ladies shared a shopping basket, filling it with toiletries. They spent five dollars each. Cora chose a bar of lavender soap, hand lotion, a comb, a compact with face powder, and sugar plum lipstick. Lana picked up a tooth brush, paste, and dental floss, a packet of ink pens and a small box of stationery. The ladies were thrilled by their purchases.

They disappeared toward the back of the store, then met up with Beth and Rylan at the cash register. They were smiling ear to ear when they each chipped in a dollar for two final items.

"A gift for you, Rylan," Cora said, handing him a small picture frame. The border was designed with different breeds of dogs. A Great Dane was in the mix.

Ry thanked them.

Beth's present came next. The ladies gave her a pair of

white women's socks patterned with red baseballs. She loved their choice and gave them a hug. Her heart was happy.

Rylan was fortunate to find a parking place close to the ladies' condominium, east of the main entrance. Beth assisted them from the SUV while Ry carefully removed a rocker from the rear of the Range Rover. He hefted it easily and followed the women inside.

Beth remained by the door while Rylan unwrapped the chair. Cora requested he move their short sofa off to the side, then place the new rockers before the TV. Lana immediately sat down and set it in motion. Her eyelids drooped.

Ry left quickly to retrieve the other chair.

Cora took Beth's hand, squeezed it. "I won't be sitting in the lobby any longer. It was too depressing. My daughter can find me in my room should she come for a visit."

Beth leaned down, gently kissed her cheek. "I'll see you again, soon," she promised. She could easily pop in on the same day she played cards with Frank.

Rylan returned with the second rocker and set it next to Lana in front of the TV. Cora sat down and yawned.

Beth and Rylan took their leave. Beth picked up her PT Cruiser, and they headed home in separate vehicles. The dogs greeted them as if they'd been gone for a year. Atlas brought Rylan two tennis ball. They bulged in his cheeks. He wanted to play. Right then, right there.

Beth chuckled. "He looks like he's got the mumps."

"Or a big squirrel storing nuts," said Ry.

Everyone headed to the yard. She dropped down on the grass near the fence. Leaned back. Oscar and Nathan climbed onto her lap. Rue lay close, too.

The game began. "Nice throw, Rylan," she said after he tossed one of the balls.

"Nice catch, Atlas," she complimented the Dane when

he caught it. Atlas wagged his tail, brought the ball to her. Dropped it by her feet.

"Bring it to me, buddy," Ry called out.

The dog nudged Beth with his nose. Twice. She took his hint and gently moved the dachsies off her lap, then pushed to her feet. She picked up the tennis ball and tossed it in the air. Atlas jumped, grabbed it with ease. He returned the ball to her once again.

"What's the deal?" Ry asked. "Can't I play, too?"

She shot him a challenging look. "We're playing keepaway. From you."

"From me?" Rylan was on her in a heartbeat.

He tried to block her throw to Atlas, but she managed to lob the ball over his head. The Dane took off toward the far end of the yard. He barked around the ball in his mouth.

Running back toward them, Atlas did his best to avoid letting Rylan steal his toy. Ry gave chase, but couldn't catch him. Atlas was crafty. For a big dog, he could zigzag like a running back. Ry slipped and fell while trying to grab his tail. Atlas looped around and jumped over Rylan while he was facedown in the grass.

Their antics had Beth laughing. So hard, her stomach hurt. She could barely catch her breath.

Ry pushed up and stalked her. Slow, steady steps, coming her way with intent and purpose. She tried to sidestep him, but he was quick and athletic. He tackled her, taking her down, protecting her fall with his body. She landed atop him. The scent of grass, sunshine, and man surrounded her. Potent and arousing.

His arms closed around her so she couldn't escape. Not that she wanted to. He felt solid and strong beneath her. Her breasts pressed into his chest, her belly into his sixpack, her thigh rubbed his groin with each twist of her body.

"You're killing me," Ry breathed against her mouth. "Stop moving."

She teased him unmercifully, rotating her hips until he could take it no more. She kissed him lightly, teasingly, in contrast to the deeper sexual pleasure of her pelvis. Flush against him, she felt the erratic beat of his heart against her breast. The tightening of his stomach muscles as he held himself together. The flex of his groin as he pushed his sex between her thighs.

"Too many clothes," he growled near her ear.

Rylan didn't have neighbors. Still, there were no further moves to be made in the yard. They were dry humping on the grass, which wasn't terribly satisfying. What if someone showed up out of the blue? The furniture delivery truck could arrive early.

Thump. A tennis ball dropped near Rylan's head. Atlas stood beside them, and if a dog could grin, he was wearing a smile. A big old, toothy, drooling smile.

The heat of the moment was doused with reality.

"We've got company," she said on a sigh.

"Way to kill the mood, boy," Ry said.

Atlas woofed. He wanted to continue to play.

Beth slipped off Rylan and got to her feet. Her breasts ached and her body pulsed. She wished they had time to sneak upstairs, to make love, but time was not on their side. The rumbling of a truck came down the street, brakes grinding as it pulled into the driveway.

Rylan pushed up, the bulge in his jeans significantly large. Painful, too, from the look on his face. He shifted. "I need a minute. You get the door."

Atlas went with her. He sniffed the strangers before allowing them entry. It took three men to lift the turquoise couch up the outside steps, onto the porch, and into the living room. They were careful not to scrape or scratch the leather.

Once the new sofa was placed, Atlas stared it down. He then settled on the old couch, claiming it as his. Head to tail, he stretched the full length. His tail thumped.

The massaging leisure chair came next. Beth had the men angle it before the television. Rylan liked his shows. There'd be no better way for him to relax. Her, too, when she snuggled against him.

The men departed just as Rylan and the remaining three dogs entered. "My living room looks like someone actually lives here," he said, admiring the setup.

"It's definitely taking shape," she agreed.

"Should you stay on after spring training, start your business here, you'd be quite comfortable. Don't you think?"

Her heart squeezed at his question. She hadn't thought beyond the moment. The idea of his leaving and her staying behind gave her pause. She bit down on her bottom lip, tried to remain positive. She'd taken the job knowing it was for eight weeks. Nothing more, nothing less.

What she hadn't planned on was becoming attached to his dogs. Atlas was a big kid at heart. She adored sweet Rue and the dachshunds, too. And Rylan Cates. She admired the man. She loved working for him. Having sex with him. Yet there'd been no mention of a future together. Not even a hint.

She wasn't in a position to commit to anyone. Not yet anyway. Her life was unsettled. She had unfinished business to resolve—which included her stepmother and stepsister. She was almost strong enough to face them again. Once her past was cleared, she could breathe easier.

"Beth?" Ry came to stand beside her. "You like my cottage, don't you?" He sounded uncertain. He realized she hadn't answered his initial question.

"I love it here," she assured him.

Atlas rolled off his sofa, stretched. He gave Beth his *I'm hungry* look.

She realized it was his dinnertime. "Hamburgers?" she offered, thinking of the container of organic ground sirloin in the refrigerator.

Atlas had a big vocabulary when it came to food. He understood *hamburger*. He trotted to the kitchen. Sat before the stove.

"You should try your massage chair," she said to Rylan as she followed the Dane.

He shook his head, held her gaze. Grinned. "I'll wait until we can vibrate together."

Something to look forward to. Her heart lightened. She would enjoy her time with this man, take one day at a time. There was no point in worrying about tomorrow or the end of the month. Her life would take care of itself. It always had. Somehow.

Ry joined her in the kitchen. "Supper or junk food at the movies?" He grinned, already knowing her answer.

She told him anyway. "Junk food."

He made himself a natural peanut butter sandwich on rye, pulled up a stool, and sat at the island while she cooked the dogs' meal.

"I could've made that for you," she said.

"Atlas would've never let you feed me first," he joked.

"Probably not," she agreed. She and the Dane were joined at the hip. He allowed her to shift an inch, but was then back beside her.

She and Rylan took the dogs for a long walk afterward. They'd be leaving for the movie shortly, and wanted to tire the gang out. Returning home, Rue, Oscar, and Nathan dragged themselves up the front steps, but Atlas got his second wind. He was bouncing off the porch railings.

Ry raised an eyebrow. "What did you put in the hamburger?" he asked, as he let the other dogs in the house.

"Cookbook ingredients only. The other dogs weren't affected."

"My big boy's restless."

"Yeah, he's wound pretty tight." She tugged on Atlas's leash. "We'll walk a little longer. Maybe that will calm him."

"He needs to run."

"I'm not a runner, but I can walk really fast."

He smiled at her. "I bet you can." He took Atlas's leash from her. "You get ready for the movie, and I'll race the boy around the block."

Beth watched as they took off. She heard Rylan say, "Stay close," when he unclipped the leash from the dog's harness. Atlas had the freedom to run flat out.

Ry's concept of *stay close* and Atlas's own were miles apart. The Dane rounded the corner a half block ahead of Rylan. Atlas was speeding.

Concerned, she walked down the driveway, continued on toward the corner. She would catch him as he came charging toward the cottage. What she hadn't expected was not only Atlas, but a group of neighborhood kids on bicycles joining his race. He'd picked up friends on the street. The young boys were bringing him home.

Atlas ran right to her, sliding into her as a baseball player would a base. He knocked her down, though not hard, then tried to sit on her. Way too uncomfortable! She pushed him off. Having delivered Atlas, his entourage turned their bikes around and pedaled off.

Rylan made an appearance moments later. He jogged toward them, all hot, sweaty, and frowning. Atlas took his look for what it was. He was about to get a reprimand. He ducked behind Beth.

"Can't hide behind her, guy. I can still see your tail."

Beth looked behind her. "Just his tail?" She was short and slender. Atlas was a horse.

"Teasing you only," he assured her. His voice was deep,

stern when he addressed Atlas. "You took off and didn't mind me. I don't like that."

The Great Dane stuck his head around Beth, talked back, grumbling low, arguing.

"I heard Billie whistle for you," Ry acknowledged. "You shouldn't have responded. No discipline."

Full out grousing came from Atlas—which Ry didn't tolerate. "Inside. *Move it.*"

Atlas looked at Beth in hopes she'd take his side.

"In." She stood by Rylan.

The Dane hung his head, slumped his shoulders, dragged his butt all the way to the door.

"I feel bad for him," Beth said. "Besides, you were the one who let him off his leash."

Ry came to a dead stop, cut her a look. "Are you siding with Atlas?"

She picked up her pace. "Maybe . . ."

"Don't make me chase you, too."

"I'll let you catch me."

He did so on the porch. She turned the doorknob, let Atlas slip in before Rylan shut the door on her. He trapped her between the cottage and his body. She felt the wooden siding at her back, and his erection at her front.

He claimed her mouth with an instant wanting that weakened her knees. He skimmed his hand up her middle, cupped a breast. Left her nipple hard. He worked his knee between her thighs. Making her wet.

She clung to him. Humped him. Her breathing heavy.

He wrung out her passion. Only to step back.

Dazed, her vision blurry, she stared up at him. "That's it?" she managed.

"For now." She hadn't expected his grin, but there it was, satisfied and wicked. "Side with Atlas, and I'll leave you panting. Side with me, and I'll make you come."

He'd drawn her nearly to the edge, to that moment when her body ruled her mind, and she couldn't remember her name. The man had left her hanging. How unfeeling could he be?

She made a fist and punched his arm. "Jerk," That didn't sound angry enough. "Asshole." That was better.

He snagged her hand midair before she could slug him again. He kissed her palm. A touch of his lips, a flick of his tongue. Her skin heated. Her stomach softened. He trapped her within her own need once again. Left her all alone and longing for him. She would make him pay. Later, after the movies.

Ry glanced at his watch, noted the time. "Sunset in thirty minutes," he predicted. He gave her a slow once-over. "I need a quick shower after my run."

She waited for an invitation to join him. He held back and stepped around her. There was purpose in the way his arm brushed her breast, the way his hip bumped her own. She set her back teeth and entered the cottage behind him.

Atlas awaited them. A dozen toys littered the foyer. He tilted his head, looked at Rylan.

"How sorry are you?" Ry asked him. "These aren't even your best toys, buddy."

The Dane took off in a flash. He skidded around the corner between the living room and hallway, and they heard the sound of a door opening. He'd gone into the closet where his toys were stored.

He returned a moment later, and Beth swore she heard him sigh. He laid the sockie toy she'd made for him at Rylan's feet.

The gesture was significant. A peace offering. Beth's chest tightened.

Ry hunkered down, picked up the balled socks. "You're most prized possession," he noted. "Forgiven."

Atlas had heard the word more than once and knew he

was off the hook. Rylan barely managed to stand before Atlas rose on his hind legs, put his paws on Ry's shoulders, and licked his chin.

"Definitely a shower." Rylan gave Atlas a knuckle-rub on the head.

Atlas was an Indian giver. The second he dropped back down, he retrieved the socks, took off for the old couch, and stuffed his sockie toy in one corner.

Ry shook his head, went to clean up. Beth decided to change clothes, too. She chose a pale blue tank top and her new Levis. Rylan had fumbled with the button fly the night before. She'd do her best to slow him down again tonight. Let him sweat a little.

Rylan came downstairs in a Barefoot William T-shirt, board shorts, and leather sandals. His hair was damp. His eyelashes spiked. He turned on the TV for the dogs. To keep them company. He set the digital clicker on the bookshelf. "I don't dare leave the remote with Atlas. Not too long ago, he hit a button while I was away, and I came home to pay-per-view porn."

They left the house. Ry made one additional stop in the garage. He collected the beach chairs and loaded them in the SUV. Parking was scarce when they arrived at the beach, and they were forced to walk a few blocks. The night air was cool, but comfortable. They stopped at a kiosk on the boardwalk and loaded up on soda and snacks.

Beth couldn't believe they were going out together. He hadn't called it a date, but it felt like a date. She was happy, very happy. She wasn't sure what she'd expected at the pier, but the number of people surprised her. There were both families and couples. Chairs were snugged tightly together with armrests overlapping.

"It's better than the drive-in," Ry said as they maneuvered the narrow path along the railing. He knew nearly everyone, and his friends made room for them.

Beth looked around for Shaye and saw her setting up for the movie. Her husband Trace was by her side.

Full darkness descended. *Frozen* started at eight sharp. The crescent moon didn't interfere with the movie. Neither did the lapping of waves along the shoreline overshadow the soundtrack.

This is better than any movie theater, Beth thought when Rylan reached for her hand. Their fingers laced. She felt comfortable with this man.

Numerous parents and children left after the Disney animation ended. Bedtime beckoned for those facing school on Monday. It was mostly adults who lingered for *Anchorman.* Couples sat closer. Kisses were exchanged.

Ry leaned over and nuzzled her ear. His voice was low when he asked, "Do you have plans for after the movie?"

"Possibly," she answered.

"With me?"

"No, with Atlas."

"You're going to make me beg, aren't you?"

"Bow-wow, big boy."

Ten

Rylan *barked* for Beth's benefit when they entered the cottage. He was begging for her attention, and he got it. His dogs joined in. Their howling chorus echoed off the living room walls.

Beth covered her ears, laughed. She gave the dogs each a treat to calm them down. Atlas got two. Rue and the dachsies soon settled on their dog beds in her bedroom. The Dane took to his couch. Snoring told them that he slept. Deeply.

The night finally belonged to Rylan and Beth. He had plans, which included condoms. He took the stairs to his bedroom, scored a handful of protection, stuffed the latex in his pocket.

Once back in the living room, he located the television remote on the bookshelf, then made his move on Beth. He pulled her down beside him on the massage chair. They fit just fine.

He eased his arm about her shoulders, and she curved into his side. He liked her initiative. The way she stretched her arm across his chest, hugging him. She crossed one leg over his, rubbing her knee high on his thigh. A sexual tease.

The lady fascinated him. She'd been shy and vulnerable when she first arrived in Barefoot William. A week at the cottage, and she'd slowly come into herself. She had a ways to go. Still, he found her funny and snarky. She put him in his place—which no woman had before.

Baseball groupies tended to fawn and favor whatever a player wanted. They were accommodating. Embarrassingly so. Beth had a mind of her own. She told him what she thought, and he listened.

Satisfied with her closeness, Ry flicked on the TV and channel surfed, looking for a show they would both enjoy. They liked westerns, and he settled on *Butch Cassidy and the Sundance Kid*. But ten minutes into the show, he was far more interested in Beth than with Butch, Sundance, and the Hole-in-the-Wall Gang.

She'd begun touching him lazily, taking pleasure in turning him on. Her hand flattened on his abdomen, and her fingers found their way beneath the hem of his shirt. The tip of one finger circled, dipped into his navel, and then skimmed upward. Over the tight flesh on his ribs to his male nipples. His muscles flexed. He grew hard.

He wanted her bad. It had been a day of tease and touch. She'd landed atop him in the yard earlier. He'd later pressed her against the side of the house. They'd held hands and snuck kisses at the outdoor movie. He wanted to complete what they had started.

There was a time to think about doing something, and a time for actually doing it. He lowered the sound on the TV and tipped back the massage chair. He set the dial on low heat and medium vibration. Her body hummed when he rolled on his side and faced her.

He pressed soft kisses to her forehead and cheek. "I've been waiting for you all day," he breathed against her mouth.

"There were lots of delays," she agreed.

"Too much going on." He nipped her chin. "This is our moment. Let's get naked."

She liked his suggestion. They reached for each other, and their clothes came off without resistance. He managed her button fly with newfound ease. There was no modesty. Only appreciation. Anticipation ran high.

The moment his mouth came down on hers, every hard muscle in his body went into overdrive. He was hard-wired for this woman. He lost control, and she let herself go, right along with him. They were wild for each other.

Feel. Respond.

His kiss stripped away her common sense.

Give. Take.

He lost all thought to sensation.

His mouth devoured hers. Yet she was the first to slip him her tongue. He sucked it deeply into his mouth. They tangled.

Their naked bodies pressed, rocked together.

He felt oneness with this woman.

Tension sparked electric. An urgency skittered across their nerve endings. She dragged her hands down his back, stroked his buttocks. Then skimmed her fingers over his hip, dipped lower, and found his sex. She stroked him, cupped his balls, squeezed. He nearly came in her hand.

Shifting, he rolled her beneath him. He kissed down her body. Back up again. His breath glazed her skin. Her body pulsed against his mouth. Her taste drove him crazy.

He bit her inner thigh.

Left a hint of a love bite on her belly.

Her full breasts, the dusky tips, were next. He closed his mouth softly around her, tugging with his lips. He blew gently where he laved, and watched her shiver.

She strained against him. Wanting him.

He was there for her. He leaned over the side of the chair, shook out his jeans, and the condoms fell from his pocket. Scooping one, he allowed Beth to sheath him. Her fingers trembled. He swallowed hard.

Once fitted, he parted her thighs. He pressed into her. Her fingers dug into his shoulders as she rose to meet him. He drew back and rocked forward, moving in tight. Locking them together.

The sensation of being inside her while looking into her eyes transcended time. The blue mirrored the intensity he felt. Sensation coursed through him and into her. Their bodies throbbed. Ached. They were anxious. Impatient.

It became a race toward fulfillment.

Their eyes closed to everything but the moment.

He held nothing back, thrusting into her with a steady, insistent rhythm. His head swam. His chest burned. He could barely draw breath.

She gave him complete and utter surrender.

Their pleasure found voice. She moaned. He growled.

Their orgasms rose on a sexual swell.

His climax followed hers.

They drifted down, sated, satisfied. Sleepy.

They gathered their clothes, and closed out the night in his bedroom.

Morning came too soon. Rylan sensed something wrong when he first wakened, and he soon realized what caused his concern. Beth wasn't in his bed. The side where she'd slept was neatly made. Pillows were stacked and the sheet and comforter were straightened. He glanced at his bedside clock. The alarm had yet to sound, but only by ten minutes.

Spring training started today. The first practice was at nine. His body felt loose and alive. Fluid after sex.

He had Beth to thank for a great night in bed. The lady had stamina for someone so small. He couldn't get enough of her. Sadly, from now on their time together would be limited. His involvement with the team took priority.

He would look forward to his nights with her. He did

plan to spend one or two evenings at Driftwood Inn, just to make sure the ballplayers kept it sane. He didn't want them getting out of hand—which Halo and Landon had been known to do. Zoo, too. They were always ready to party. Cards, drinking, women. Rylan needed to be around to make sure they didn't embarrass themselves. More than normal. There'd be no repeat performances of his teammate's skinny dipping in the hotel pool or playing strip poker at the bar. Videos went viral, and they didn't need that kind of publicity. Not in his hometown, anyway . . . if it could be avoided.

He grabbed a shower, dressed, and headed downstairs. He found Atlas and gang at their bowls eating breakfast. Some kind of pasta, he noted, as the big dog had a shell noodle stuck to his nose.

"What can I fix for you?" Beth was standing at the sink. Her cheeks pinkened when she turned to face him. Her smile was soft. Her eyes very blue. A yellow bandana captured her curls. She wore his Rogues T-shirt with the hem tied in a knot at her waist.

He'd hoped for her bare ass, but got cutoffs instead. Win some, lose some. "What's on the menu?" he asked, as he drew a stool to the island, sat down.

She opened the oven door and a delicious scent escaped. "Organic banana almond bread." She took the pan from the oven, set it on the counter to cool. "I can also make oatmeal with brown sugar and slice fresh fruit."

It all sounded good. Oatmeal stuck to his ribs. Had he been there by himself, he would have gone with rye toast and headed out the door. Beth's offering was so much better. He was damn hungry after their marathon night of sex. She poured him a cup of coffee. Went on to prepare his food. She served him before the dogs were done eating. Atlas barked for seconds.

Beth was ready with the drool towel when the Dane

finished. She shook her head when she picked up his bowl and held it up for Ry to see. "I hid one pea in his veggie pasta to see if he'd eat it. He didn't."

"He has discriminatory tastes."

"It's a tiny pea." She was amazed. "Rue and the dachshunds love them."

"In truth, Oscar not so much," Ry corrected her. "He spits out more peas than he eats, then scoots them behind his bowl."

"Little sneak," Beth said to the dachsie. She cleaned up those he'd pushed aside.

"What do you have planned for today?" Ry asked her.

She fixed herself a bowl of oatmeal and joined him at the island. "I had early morning texts from Shaye and Dune. They'll be by the house around ten. Shaye to pick up her croquet set. Dune will dismantle the volleyball net."

"Don't let Atlas help Dune," Ry warned. "He's gotten himself wrapped in the netting and chewed his way out."

"Grocery shopping is on my list. We need condoms."

He grinned at her. "We?"

"You use them with me." She tapped her spoon on the edge of the bowl. "I saw on your monthly calendar that you plan to host a dinner for the starting lineup the first week of spring training. I'll make a reservation, if you like. Time, place?"

Dining with his teammates built camaraderie. Disagreements and arguments were left in the parking lot. They'd bond over beer and barbecue. It was two hours of live and let live. A night of sarcasm, raw humor, and boasting. Too much food. Way too much drinking.

He debated the restaurant. "Chubby's or Pitmaster are both good. See if one will provide a private dining room. The guys can get loud. I don't want to disrupt other diners."

"You also had dog beach pinned to today's date," she said.

Dog beach drew Atlas's attention. He'd been lying at Beth's feet and popped his head up, listening. Attentively.

Rylan finished off his oatmeal before saying, "There's a really neat cove at the northernmost point of Barefoot William. Private family property. Two fenced acres. A crescent-shaped coral reef protects swimmers from danger. The water is only ten feet deep, shallower than most swimming pools. The dogs will have time to swim before it gets dark. They can eat afterward."

Her eyes widened. "We'll have the beach to ourselves?"

He nodded. "Send out a text to my family members, reserving beach time at six. I like to warn them that we're coming. Atlas gets really excited when he sees other dogs. He goes beyond a simple greeting and tackles them."

"Do all the dogs swim?" she asked.

Rylan grinned. "Rue loves the water. The dachs run from the incoming waves, then chase the outgoing ones. Atlas"—he rolled his eyes—"floats like a barge, heavy and unmoving. That's if he'll go in the Gulf. They all wear canine float coats."

Beth chuckled. "This I have to see."

"We'll take the Range Rover. I'll lower the backseat into a deck. Toss in rubber mats, and we're good to go. Tomorrow you can take the SUV to a car wash. Have both exterior and interior cleaned." He glanced at his watch. "Time to take off."

He rose, gathered his coffee cup, bowl, and plate and set them in the sink. He turned and found Beth staring at him. Her eyes were a vivid blue. Her expression soft, wishful.

There was no denying her look. He knew in that instant that she cared for him. *Really* cared. Possibly even loved

him. Where were they headed? he wondered. Beyond today. He couldn't wrap his head around tomorrow.

They were physically compatible. Unbelievably so. He'd
never been so hot for a woman. He enjoyed her mind and
wit. But one obstacle still stood between them. Trust. He
awaited the day she could speak of her past and not cringe
or withdraw. Once the air was fully cleared, they could
move forward.

He crossed back to her, tipped up her chin, and kissed
her. Flecks of brown sugar dusted her bottom lip. She
tasted sweet. "See you later."

The dogs trailed him to the door. He had always made
a big production of telling them good-bye. He never
wanted to leave without their knowing he would be back.
He gave them his word. They wagged their tails, promis-
ing to be good.

He drove the McLaren to the stadium. The sports car
hummed with a similar vibration to the massage chair. He
pictured Beth naked and beneath him—and nearly ran a
red light. He hit the brake. Hard. Skidded to a stop. He
cleared his head, focused on baseball.

He parked in the players' lot and made his way to the
locker room. Pitchers and catchers preceded the fielders'
arrival. They already had a week of warm-ups and work-
outs under their belts. His teammates were all in attendance. No stragglers today. Anticipation burned the air.
Their restlessness was tangible. The guys were ready to
play ball.

The players greeted him with high-fives and thumps to
his back. Ry noticed the starters' asymmetrical haircuts.
Zoo had gone with a Mohawk. No one cared. His head
was still shaved.

Ry located his locker, changed into his practice uniform. He felt Halo staring at him, *really* giving him the
eye, and looked up. "What's on your mind?"

Halo smiled, too broad and too knowing. "What's on your chest, bro?"

Ry glanced down. He'd yet to button his jersey. Heat circled his neck when he spotted what Halo had already seen. The hickey near his left nipple. He hadn't noticed the love bite during his morning shower. But damn if it wasn't there. A definite bruise. *Beth.*

He kept his cool, buttoned up, and covered with, "Atlas jumped on me."

Halo knew his hickeys. He told Ry so. "That's not a paw print. Those are lips."

Rylan dropped down on the bench and put on his cleats. Halo took a seat, too, a bench away. Landon wandered down the aisle, looking for eye black, the grease applied under the eyes to reduce the glare of the sun. He found a stick on the top shelf in Halo's locker. Lifted it without asking.

Halo didn't call him on it, his gaze held on Ry. "Our captain got lucky," he said louder than was necessary.

That drew every eye in Ry's direction. Landon raised an eyebrow, asked, "With who? One of the girls from the picnic? The redhead, white tank top, black bra was hot."

"So was the green-eyed blonde in the blue sundress. Stacked . . . heels," said Halo. "Renewing old acquaintances, dude?"

Rylan made it a rule not to discuss his dates. What he did in bed, stayed in bed. Sheet pulled to the chin.

Zoo joined them. "Share, Ry-man."

Rylan kept his voice even. "Why do you care?"

"Sex sets up home runs," said Halo. "A satisfied man hits for the fence. We'll see how well you do in batting practice."

Rylan planned to bunt.

Zoo rubbed his chin. Observant. "You're particular about who you date. She must be special."

"Bet he's serious about her," said Landon.

Their speculation went on and on. They brought up every single woman from the picnic, except one.

Halo named her. "Beth?" he asked, his tone more amused than serious.

"No way," said Landon. "Not our Beth. Ry-man doesn't date his PAs."

"*Our* Beth?" Rylan hated to share her.

"*Your* Beth," said Zoo, suddenly smug. "You were watching her without looking at her throughout the picnic. Male radar." He was too damn perceptive.

Rylan stood, scored his baseball cap and glove from his locker, got ready to leave. "Don't make more out of our relationship than is there," he said, not wanting to discuss Beth further.

"So it's okay if I ask her out then?" Zoo was being a dick.

Ry shot him a dark look.

The left fielder chuckled. "I thought so."

"Son of bitch," said Halo. "I never saw that coming."

"Will she return to Richmond with you after spring training?" asked Landon.

Rylan hadn't thought that far ahead. They'd touched on her staying in Barefoot William and starting her own business. Living at his cottage. They hadn't moved beyond that point. Not yet, anyway. "I'll let you know in seven weeks," was as far as he could commit.

Halo huffed. "Updates would be nice."

Landon agreed. "E-mail or text."

Rylan ran his hand down his face. What the hell? He knew his teammates were taken with Beth, but when had they become her guardians? Surely they didn't expect him to check in daily. They would dog him worse than Atlas. Making sure he did right by her.

All because of a hickey.

Rylan changed the subject. "When are you getting your tattoo?" he asked Halo.

The right fielder patted his abdomen. "After practice. Four of us are getting inked. Want to make it five?"

"I already have plans."

"I could change mine and join you."

"You're not invited."

"Give my best to Beth."

The locker room cleared. Practice went well for the first day. It was seventy degrees and breezy. Everyone worked up a sweat. Lunch was catered in, and they ate in the locker room. The tattoo discussion was ongoing. Lots of suggestions were tossed out. The guys were vain when it came to inking their groin. They wanted unique and authentic, and something to impress the ladies.

Ry didn't find *Bone Ranger, Yardstick, Steelix,* or *Keeping Score* all that remarkable. Images of a fiery baseball or a babe straddling a base weren't much better.

The other guys were already set on their tats. Rylan hoped there'd be no regrets. They couldn't erase the ink. Their tattoos would last beyond their baseball careers.

Four o'clock came, and the men took off. Some together, others alone. The tattoo group climbed into Halo's Hummer. The players believed the groin tattoo was a rite of passage necessary to be a Rogue. Those who'd gone before all had ink.

The greats, such as Risk Kincaid, one-time center fielder for the Rogues and present managing general partner and co-chairman for the team, was inked with *Bad to the Bone.* Jesse Bellisaro, previous third baseman and current vice-president, had *Legendary.* Psycho McMillan, one of the most talented right fielders ever to play the game and current senior VP and general manager had *Stands on Command.*

The groin was sensitive. Whether his teammates went

with script or a picture, they would be sore tomorrow. No doubt bruised. Better them than him, Ry thought. He'd yet to decide on getting a tat. He wasn't as superstitious as Halo and Landon. They believed being inked would win them the pennant.

Rylan arrived home to find Beth harnessing the dogs. Harnesses meant walks or rides in the Range Rover. Either way, they were excited.

"I thought to have them ready when you got home," she said.

"Let me change into a pair of board shorts, and I'm good to go." Instead of immediately heading upstairs, he closed in on her. He pulled her to him, kissed her soundly. He felt her smile against his mouth. "Did you have a good day?"

"Mm hmm." She nipped his bottom lip. "You?"

"Better than expected," he admitted. "The guys were cooperative. Psyched for the season." He rested his forehead against hers. "I'm ready for the beach."

"Me, too."

Rylan was upstairs and back down in twenty minutes. He looked forward to spending time with Beth. No place was as fun and relaxing as the beach. She had a stack of towels ready to go and had thoughtfully remembered a big plastic bowl and a gallon container of spring water for his dogs. Rylan didn't want them drinking salt water from the Gulf. It always made Atlas puke.

Once in the SUV, Rue and the dachsies lay down. Atlas paced the small space, barely able to turn around. He became Ry's co-pilot, looking over his shoulder.

"You're blocking my rearview mirror," Rylan told him.

Atlas transferred sides and rested his chin on the back of Beth's seat. Sniffed her hair.

Beth enjoyed the passing scenery.

Twenty minutes on the main highway, and Rylan

turned down a dirt track into the woods. He drove slowly. Dense clusters of palm trees and pine tested his maneuvering skills. The back road had as many dips and climbs as a rollercoaster. A sharp right, and the SUV emerged on a strip of compact sand. A locked gate was just ahead. Ry had a key so they could enter.

He parked inside the chain-link fence. The dogs were up, but Rue and Atlas were the only two tall enough to look out the windows. The dachs bounced in place. They sensed they were at the beach and wanted to explore.

The secluded area had been cleared. Only sand and minimal grass remained. The reef protected the cove from choppy water so the surface was smooth. Gentle waves frothed the shore.

Beth assisted Ry in releasing the dogs. Each one had to be fitted with a life jacket. Atlas wouldn't stand still. He bucked until Rylan was forced to wrap his arms around his belly while Beth secured the straps. Water safety was important.

Afterward, wanting to be helpful, she asked, "What would you like me to do? Which dogs should I watch?"

The golden retriever was already in the water, paddling like a pro. Oscar and Nathan chased the waves, barking when water washed over their paws. Atlas ran along the shoreline, howling at Rue, calling her back. He was too chicken to swim and didn't want her to, either.

"Lay out the towels and get comfortable," Rylan suggested. "The area is contained. The dogs have been here before. They'll swim or play, get some exercise. Keep an eye on the weenies. Atlas creates waves. A big one could flip them."

Sitting sounded good. She would prepare their rest area, but first, she watched him tug off his T-shirt. When he dropped it on the sand, her eyes widened on his chest. Her breath stuck in her throat, and she started to cough.

"You okay?" he asked her, ready to pat her on the back.

"Hickey," she finally managed.

"So I've been told."

"By?" she hated to ask. Hated to know.

"Halo. The man has the eyes of a hawk."

She buried her face in her palms, embarrassed. Ry came to stand before her and circled her wrists, lowering her hands.

"Bruises heal. Look at your face, back to normal."

"I hadn't meant to leave a mark. Not one so visible, anyway."

"I got you, too," he reminded her. "Inner thigh. Belly."

"Your bites were more controlled." She sighed heavily. "I left the imprint of my mouth."

"A very sweet mouth it is." He kissed her then, with just enough warmth to catch her interest, but not enough heat to leave her wet. They'd share the fire later.

"Did your teammates notice my love bite?" she asked, half-afraid of his answer.

"Noticed and harassed me." He shrugged, logical and practical. "I don't care. We're together, that's all that matters to me."

"To me, too."

Atlas's whining soon separated them. The big dog was beside himself. Rue was still swimming, and he couldn't get to her. He could join her if he tried, but he wasn't trying very hard. He wanted her to come back to him, instead.

"He'll follow me out," Rylan said as he moved toward the waterline. Atlas had his eye on him.

Beth admired Rylan's backside. He wore black board shorts low on his hips. His shoulders were broad; his back, muscled. She liked the dimples above his butt; the sinew of his calves.

The man was hot. Sexy. Edgy. He had a big heart. He

was also competent, patient, and protective. Extraordinary. Rylan Cates was an all-around good guy. She hadn't known any other man who had his qualities.

She shook out the towels, which soon covered the ground like a blanket. She heard Ry whistle for Atlas. Shading her eyes against the sun, she caught the Dane's response. Atlas was having a bad day. He grumbled at Rylan. He wanted to play, but had no one to play with. He looked at Beth, then back to Ry, who was swimming out to the retriever.

Atlas groused, and if a dog could have said "shit," he would have. It sure sounded that way to Beth. She couldn't help but smile when he tiptoed into the water, high-stepping the low waves. He got wet to his knees, then bellyached. Loud and pitiful.

Her heart went out to him. She didn't have a swimsuit, but neither did she mind getting wet. She waded in beside him, wearing a tank top and cutoffs. He gave her a cartoon grin, relieved he wasn't alone. She grasped the handle on his float coat and gave a tug. He balked. A second gentle pull, and he walked with her. Until the water hit his chest. He sniffed a wave and got a nose full of salt water. He shook his head, and she got sprayed.

"Be careful, Beth," Rylan called to her. He was treading water near Rue. "If Atlas dives in, he'll drag you with him."

His words reached her too late. Atlas decided *it was time,* and he took the plunge. Her wrist twisted, got caught in the strap. She was unable to release the handle. The water wasn't deep. No matter, he dragged her butt along the sandy bottom until Rylan saved her. He freed her hand, then pulled her up against him. The water surrounded her shoulders.

He brushed her hair out of her eyes, was quick to ask, "Are you okay?"

She took a deep breath, sighed against him. She wouldn't mention the amount of sand in her crack. "I'm fine," she assured him. "Atlas was being such a baby, I forgot about his strength. I should've been more careful. My fault."

She glanced over Rylan's shoulder and saw that all was now right in Atlas's world. The Dane floated near Rue, just beyond his comfort zone. He couldn't stand, but he could bob. He was doing a lot of bobbing. He held his head high.

The dachshunds had chased their last wave and were stretched on the towels. Both Ry and Beth kept one eye on Rue and Atlas, and one eye on each other. She liked being wet and slippery with this man. She tasted sunshine and salt on his lips when he kissed her. He stroked down her back, cupped her bottom, and lifted her against him. Her thighs hugged his hips. Her ankles hooked behind him. She fit her sex to his . . .

Whatever might have happened, did not. Rue brushed against them as she paddled toward shore. She was struggling, breathing heavily, and they soon realized why. She gripped the extended canvas handle of Atlas's life jacket in her mouth. She was towing him to shore.

Beth quickly slid off Ry, which freed him to help the golden. Rylan got them both to shore without mishap. Atlas licked Rue's face, showing his appreciation. Beth followed them to shore, poured fresh water in two big bowls. The dogs took a long drink.

Atlas took up more than his fair share of the towels when he lay down. Beth and Ry sat on the corners. They let the breeze dry them.

"They're going to need baths when we get home, aren't they?" She was thinking ahead.

Rylan nodded. "We'll make it quick. They're tired out.

Even Atlas." He raised an eyebrow, asked, "One or the other. Stay a while longer or head home?"

"Stay for the sunset."

He made her comfortable. He sat back, bent his knees, and eased her between his thighs. Fully against him, her shoulders pressed his chest. Her bottom snugged his groin. The position should've been soothing, relaxing. But how could she sit still with his erection primed at the small of her back?

She took several deep breaths and felt the smile in Rylan's lips when he kissed her neck. They were so aware and into each other, they nearly missed the sun closing out the day.

Orange, gold, and pink soon colored the sky. The reflection was captured on the water and sand, encompassing the dogs. Tangerine tipped Atlas's ears. Rue's tail turned rose pink. A coppery-gold tagged the dachsies' long noses. Dusk deepened around them as the sun waved good-bye.

He nuzzled the soft spot behind her ear. "Should we grab takeout or cook at the cottage?"

"I prepared food ahead of time. My version of an organic shepherd's pie for the dogs. A Caesar salad for us."

He bit her earlobe, and her whole body shivered. "Forethought. I knew there was a reason I hired you."

"You trusted Atlas, and he liked me," she reminded him. "That's how I got the job."

"Either way, having you with us is a smart move."

"Think so?"

"Know so."

Beth took in the dogs, lying around her. "We need to get them home. Eat, bath, bed."

"Sex." Ry pushed to his feet, pulled her up beside him. He then picked up Oscar, and she lifted Nathan. They set the dachsies in the back of the Range Rover. Rue came slowly. Ry gave her a boost. Atlas had yet to leave the towels.

"I'm not carrying you, big guy," Ry called to him.

Atlas lifted his head, dropped it back down.

"Is he that tired?" Beth asked, concerned.

Rylan stood with his hands on hips. "Lazy. He sees us carrying Oscar and Nathan and wants to be carried, too."

"There's a difference in size."

"He doesn't see it."

"Treat, Atlas," she called to him. She'd learn to pack snacks, in case he got stubborn. She wasn't above a bribe. She opened the passenger door and found the canister of sweet potato biscuits.

Atlas was beside her before she could lift the lid. She gave him two, only to have him stick his nose in the canister and inhale two more. He'd had plenty. She gave Rue and the dachsies one treat each.

"Pack it in, Atlas." Ry patted the back deck, encouraging him to jump. On his own.

The Dane made a feeble attempt, which forced Rylan to lift him the rest of the way. Ry scrubbed his knuckles over the big dog's head. "Spoiled."

Atlas gave him a toothy grin.

Beth secured the towels and dog bowls. Stored them on the floor beneath her feet. They were soon headed home. She leaned back against the seat. Glanced at Rylan. "One or the other. Day or night?"

His look gave her goose bumps. "Night."

"Massage chair or bed?"

"Both have been good to me."

"Lover or best friend?" Her voice trembled slightly.

"I want my best friend to be my lover," he said slowly, thoughtfully. "I want companionship and caring with my hot sex."

She liked his answer. "Live-in roommate or marriage?" The question was important to her.

"Atlas plans to be my best man someday. It'll be a walk down the aisle when the time comes." They'd reached the cottage. He parked and turned the game around with a question for her. "Big wedding or small?" he wondered.

How to answer without sounding sorry for herself. She inhaled. "I have no one to invite, Rylan."

He exhaled, told her, "My relatives are numerous. We're all tight. They'd fill a church. Standing room only."

"How fortunate for you."

"I do consider myself lucky."

They climbed from the SUV, unloaded the dogs. Baths were easier than on the evening when Atlas had popped her in the cheek. They wanted to eat and sleep. Being co-operative got them to their goal. They were scrubbed down and toweled dry in under an hour.

Beth warmed up their dinner, and they ate. There were yawns and their eyelids drooped. Fresh air and exercise had tired them out. They would sleep well tonight.

She served Rylan a Caesar salad and green iced tea at the counter. She snapped her fingers, remembering the team dinner reservation. "Pitmaster, seven p.m. tomorrow. Private dining room seats twelve, you'll be fine with nine. Zoo asked if he could bring a date, I told him no. It was guy time."

"What will you be doing while I'm eating ribs?"

"Party planning with Shaye and Jill. They're coming by the cottage to discuss the boardwalk luncheon and Sophie's baby shower. I hope you don't mind."

"Did you clear it with Atlas?"

"I'll convince him with a batch of peanut butter bark. He likes the crunch."

Ry stared at her for a long moment.

She thought she might have salad on her mouth and dabbed her napkin to her lips. Nothing.

His smile came slowly. "You look happy. Confident."

That got her attention. "Confident. How so?"

He set down his fork, rested his elbows on the edge of the island. "You looked as if you were running for your life when I first interviewed you. As if your past was gaining and you couldn't outrun it."

Her throat felt dry, and she took a sip of her tea. "You were so serious. So perceptive. You saw through me."

"We all have something in our lives that needs to be fixed. I've learned to recline and unwind. A Band-Aid covers a cut or a scratch but not pain. Someone hurt you. I saw it in your eyes."

"It's not important."

"It is to me."

"I'm not sure I'm ready to talk about it."

He reached across the island, took her hand in his. "I'm here whenever you are."

"I'll find you when the time's right."

"Atlas will pressure you to tell him first. Don't."

"Deal." She finished off her salad.

He drank the last of his iced tea.

They cleaned up together. It was early, but they both yawned. He turned off the first floor lights, and they took the stairs to his bedroom. They showered together, soaping each other to orgasm beneath the pulsing spray. Clean and spent, they crawled into bed. It was a night of pillow talk and light kisses. And a solid eight hours of sleep.

Eleven

The next week settled into a routine. Rylan went to the stadium and Beth took care of his dogs and household and became involved in party planning. He liked seeing her so excited. She always took care of him first, overseeing his commitments and obligations. She visited his grandfather often. They played gin and, on occasion, she beat Frank at his favorite card game. She banked the quarters she won in a capped mason jar. The jar was half full.

Rylan heard through his granddad that Beth's party skills had reached ears at the retirement village. He had Shaye to thank for that. She'd spread the word.

Beth had been invited to their Social Committee Meeting. She'd willingly attended. The group was busy planning Grace Mayberry's ninety-seventh birthday bash. Grace wanted a blowout. Lots of glitz, she'd told them. The committee had more ideas than money. Their budget didn't stretch far.

Beth suggested the women should get together and bake the cake. A homemade dessert always tasted better than store bought. Cora Salvo offered to purchase balloons at Budget Buy, but the eighty-year-old residents didn't have the huff and puff to blow them up. They would rent an electric air pump. The store also sold sparklers, rhinestone tiaras, and retired disco balls. There'd be lots of glow and glitter.

His sister Shaye and sister-in-law Jillian kept regular hours at the cottage. They listened to Beth's ideas. Took notes. The lady was creative, imaginative, and could throw a party.

Halo and Landon came and went like a revolving door. They visited way too often. Rylan saw them at the stadium during the day. Then they'd land on his doorstep two hours later; settle in for the evening. They sat on his new turquoise sofa and watched TV. Beth made them popcorn. Why couldn't they go to the movies? Ry wondered. When had they last dated? Women flocked to spring training. The players had their pick. Instead, both men flirted outrageously with Beth. She was more embarrassed than flattered. Her face had gone from bruised to a permanent blush.

Atlas didn't mind their company, as long as the men stayed off his couch. He stuck his face in Landon's popcorn bowl and ate his fair share. No butter, unsalted. Landon got him back, going to the refrigerator and eating a handful of his cheese star treats. Atlas growled at him.

Rylan was drilled with twenty questions every time he entered the locker room. How was Beth? What were her plans for the day? He stopped answering them. He valued his privacy. The men were intrusive.

He stood before his locker. Breathing deep. Getting in the zone. The Rogues first exhibition game was against the St. Louis Colonels. He was ready, and as far as he could tell, so were his teammates. They were as focused as they were cocky. That would play to their advantage.

"Ry-man." Halo spoke to him from his neighboring locker. "When are you taking us to dinner again? Good times, bro."

Good? Ry swallowed the urge to question the man's sanity. Boozing and rowdy described their recent night out. They'd pigged out on barbecue. Drunk the bar dry. Rylan had called for cabs to take the men to Driftwood Inn. They'd been in no condition to drive, despite Halo's argument he could walk a straight line—which he could not.

The taxis had arrived within twenty minutes, but not before his teammates had had a chance to show off their tattoos. Rylan saw more than he'd ever wanted to see. Their tats reflected their personalities.

Halo's in particular stood out. He'd been *supersized*. Zoo had warned him it could happen at any time. It had. His buddies had paid him back for their haircuts. He'd wanted *Caution: Hard and Hot* inked near his left hip. Small, yet readable. Zoo had demanded big. Put on the spot, Halo ended up with a street-sign size tat on his abdomen. It was visible from a block away. He was still proud of it, saying that more people could see it from a greater distance.

Landon had gone with a sword with the word *Invincible* on the blade.

Zoo went with an image of a Hellhound. A mythical black dog with red eyes. Tenacious and vicious. A testimony to his baseball skills.

First baseman Jake Packer chose *Who's on First?* Not very original, but appropriate.

The remaining five starters had yet to commit to a tattoo. They had a few weeks to finalize their decision. Ry had no plans to get inked. Halo continued to toss out suggestions. A Flying Monkey. Tasmanian devil. Batman. Captain Marvel. Elmer Fudd. Ry wasn't going there.

Rylan raised the future dinner beyond the right fielder's reach. "I'll extend a second invitation should we win twenty-five of thirty exhibition games." Challenge issued.

Chances were good he wouldn't be buying another meal. However, if it happened, the Rogues would have survived one hell of a spring training.

Halo whistled beneath his breath. "You're asking a lot, dude."

"I don't ask anything we can't deliver." Ry added incentive. "Kick preseason ass, and I'll pay the owner to close Pitmaster to all but the team."

Halo grinned then. "You think you're safe, don't you? That we won't man up and bring it home."

"Prove me wrong."

They headed for the home dugout. Took the field, warmed up. At 1:05 a local vocalist sang the national anthem. The introduction of players followed. The stadium rocked. The Rogues had incredible fans. Win or lose, they were supportive. The crowd never left games early, not even when the team was significantly behind. They sat, waited, cheered even louder. They believed Richmond could rally in the ninth. It had been known to happen.

Thousands of Richmond fans had followed the team south. They took up a huge section of the stadium. Local residents filled the remaining seats. The umpire gave the signal to start the game, and the Rogues took to the field.

"I'm already tasting barbecue ribs," Halo said as he jogged beside Rylan toward the outfield.

They parted at the dirt baseline between first and second. Halo went right; Rylan to center. Ry glanced up, scouted the upper deck, spotting his grandfather and Beth. She jacked his heartbeat. His granddad nodded and Beth smiled. Ry got down to business.

The Colonels were the Rogues' biggest rivals. Rylan knew most of their seasoned players. Their roster hadn't changed much since he'd been traded two years earlier. The men were solid, strategic, and serious. A St. Louis batter would wait for the perfect pitch, whereas the Rogues took chances. Young hitters were impatiently aggressive. Some of their gambles panned out, others came up short.

Top of the first, and St. Louis loaded the bases. They gained two runs before Richmond closed out the half inning.

The Rogues took their bat. Halo Todd led off. He stood in the on-deck circle and took several practice swings then approached home plate. All strut and purpose.

There was a man tasting barbecue, Rylan mused as Halo slammed the ball down the left field line for a double.

Landon batted second. He hit a fly ball to center for the first out. Halo advanced to third. Ry came next. His hometown stood behind him. He wanted to make a good showing. He picked a point in center field and mentally aimed for the stands.

Ball one was thrown high and buzzed his chin. Ry didn't flinch. Didn't show emotion. He held his stance. Set his jaw.

"What the fuck?" Zoo called from the dugout.

"Back off," came from Will Ridgeway.

His teammates moved to the railing.

Ry was aware that a fight in the first inning would make national news. Something to be avoided. He stared hard at the pitcher until the man blinked and went into his wind up. He was one of the only pitchers in the league to throw three changeups in a row. He threw a power sinker for strike one. Rylan predicted his next pitch and smoked the ball to center. The ball dropped short of the fence, yet was out of reach of the center fielder. Halo made it home. Ry landed on third.

Zoo next laid a high breaking ball over the third baseman's head. He sprinted to first. The left fielder scooped the ball. His throw to home was off the mark, and Ry slid in safe. The score was now tied.

A team was only as strong as the middle of its batting order. The Rogues had power.

"Nut up," Halo said to Jake Packer when the first baseman took his bat.

The Rogues had three straight hits, adding one run, before two additional outs sent them back on defense.

The afternoon progressed. The innings brought errors, miscues, and two minor infield collisions. The Colonels suffered both injuries.

Seventh inning stretch, and the Rogues started taking beer bets as to who would nail the first home run. Halo placed a six-pack on himself. Zoo and Landon favored Rylan. They wagered a case of Coors.

A flock of big, black crows collected on the power lines during the top of the eighth. It started to look like a scene from the Alfred Hitchcock movie *The Birds*. Their cawing grew louder. One crow swooped down near Halo. Halo waved his arm, avoided the dive.

"What's going on over there?" Rylan called to him between batters. All the action was taking place on the infield. "You have birdseed in your pockets?"

Halo admitted to, "Sunflower seeds. Shit, I dropped a few."

"How many is a few?"

"Half a pack, give or take."

"Grind the ones you've dropped into the ground," Ry told him. Crows could be aggressive. Birds fighting over food would not be pretty.

"They're going to peck my eyes out." Halo covered his face when several dive-bombed him all at once.

"You're wearing sunglasses, dumbass." Ry had little sympathy for the man.

The first base umpire noticed the flock. The crows were ominous. The situation bizarre. Ry had never seen anything like it. What he hated most was the bird poop. They'd soon have a mess if the crows weren't moved.

The ump came to a decision and called time-out. The Rogues headed to their dugout. A few birds trailed after Halo. The ground crew came out and scattered the crows. It took twenty minutes. Halo left the remainder of his sunflower seeds in the dugout when he returned to the field.

The game continued. Rylan made a major save at the top of the ninth. The Colonels' shortstop pounded the ball to center. Ry tracked it and ran full-out to reach it. He completed the backhanded catch at the warning track. He held up his glove, gave an air punch.

Next batter, and Zoo lost a high fly ball to the sun in left field. He scrambled to retrieve it. The St. Louis player ran the bases like an Olympic sprinter. He slid home.

Angry with himself, Zoo kicked dirt along the baseline.

The score was tied when the Rogues returned to the plate. It was once again the top of the order. Excitement pressured the Rogues to score. The stadium was jumping. Fans wanted a home run and would settle for nothing less.

Halo grunted when he smacked a fastball right into the glove of the shortstop. Zoo called him *bird brain*.

Landon went down on strikes.

Rylan took a slow walk to home plate. There seemed to be an atmospheric shift when he dug in at the plate, and the crowd held its collective breath.

He went to full count, three balls and two strikes, before a curveball hung over the plate long enough for him to connect. It was a beauty. He found the sweet spot and crushed the ball into the upper deck in center. Long and gone. He rounded the bases, crossed home. His teammates emptied the dugout, congratulating him. Not quite the World Series, but an exhibition win, nonetheless. A great way to start preseason.

Halo pointed to the jumbotron, just as a picture of his granddad appeared. Frank was standing, his glove extended as he caught the home run ball. Beside Frank, frozen in the moment, Beth reached out, too. Her eyes were wide, her lips parted. Her curls sprang from all sides of her baseball cap. She was Frank's backup had he missed or dropped the ball.

Rylan would never forget that moment.

He ducked into the dugout. Drank a plastic glass of Gatorade. Fan applause drew him out for a second wave to the crowd. They were supportive. They would return to the park tomorrow when the Rogues faced the Atlanta Braves.

Local press covered the game. Rylan answered his fair share of questions. Halo and Landon replied to a few directed to Ry, as well. The guys liked being interviewed. They felt their responses should be chiseled in stone.

Family and close friends met Ry at the locker room exit. They approached him with hugs and fancy fist bumps. A few fans snuck by the guards. They requested autographs and a photo. Rylan was obliging.

Through it all, he scanned the crowd for Beth. He found her standing on the sidelines. She looked out of her element. Not certain what to do.

She wore her baseball cap backward. She looked good in her Rogues T-shirt and shorts. Her red Keds. Sunburn slanted off her nose. Her smile was shy. Her hands were clasped before her. He excused himself. Walked toward her.

Beth's heart rate ramped up. Rylan was coming her way. His hair was damp from his after-game shower. He looked sexy and composed in his black polo and khakis. His leather sandals. This was a different man from the player she'd seen on the field a short time ago.

His attitude and uniform had turned him into a warrior.

His game face was fierce and intense. His body solid and strong. He'd looked as good jogging toward center field as he did returning to the dugout. She hadn't taken her eyes off him.

He shook hands with dozens of people before he reached her.

The world around her quieted when they met. It became just the two of them.

Her voice sounded breathy when she said, "Nice hit. Good game."

He tipped up her chin with his finger, leaned in, and kissed her full on the mouth. A claiming kiss that told anyone around them that they were a couple. She liked being part of him.

Halo had the balls to interrupt them. He wore his Cates T-shirt. He still thought he was family. He tapped Rylan on the shoulder. "Pulled pork. Maple syrup baked beans." He moved on.

Ry kissed the tip of her nose before he straightened and explained what he'd added as incentive to the preseason. "We won today, and Halo's already salivating. He has food on his mind as often as Atlas."

Beth smiled. "It's good to have a goal."

"What are your plans for the rest of the day?"

"A stop by Galler-E. Evelyn sent me an e-mail reminder. The progressive wedding photo is framed. It's been ready for several days now."

Rylan ran his knuckles along his jaw. "One or the other, Beth. You haven't had time to get it or you've avoided picking it up?" The man was perceptive.

She was honest with him. "Little of both."

"Want me to get it for you?" he asked. "Or we could go together, if you like."

That would be the easy way out, but it was a moment she had to face. The photograph brought back too many memories. Disturbing, painful memories. "The gallery is on my way to the car wash. The dogs left sand in the back. You need a new air freshener, too."

"The pine scent has faded."

"I was thinking spring breeze."

"Works for me."

"I'd better get going, then."

"I'll see you around six. I want to spend some time with my granddad. Shaye brought him to the game, and I'll take him home. We may even stop somewhere for a beer. Toast today." He kissed her again, light and lingering, but still a turn on.

Zoo closed in on them. "Can I get a kiss, too?"

Beth eyed him. "From me or from Rylan?"

Zoo laughed out loud. "The man hit a homer. He deserves more than a kiss tonight, babe." He disappeared between the parked cars.

"One of Zoo's better suggestions," said Rylan. "He specializes in bad taste."

Frank worked his way toward them. He smiled at Beth. "Thank you for sitting with me today. I enjoyed your company."

"We had the best seats," she agreed. "I liked the center field view."

A few more comments, and they soon parted ways. Beth walked to the Range Rover. She watched over the hood as Rylan assisted Frank into the low-slung sports car. The older man had to bend, and Beth was certain his bones creaked. Two attempts, and he was seated, his seat belt hooked.

She followed the McLaren from the lot. Ry went north, and she went south to the boardwalk. She had no problem finding a parking place. Everyone in town must've been at the ball game. She pulled against the curb in front of the gallery. Stepped from the SUV.

She stood before the main window and stared equally as long at a beautiful floral water color inside as she did at her own reflection. She looked different, but the same, she thought. She'd avoided mirrors for a long, long time, but was no longer afraid to look at herself.

Whether long or short, her hair would always be wild. She'd inherited her mother's curls. Also the color of her eyes. The slight cleft in her chin was from her father. She carried both of her parents with her. That was a gift.

She entered Galler-E, and Evelyn Wells waved at her from across the room. She and her associates were evaluating an oil painting. Passion lifted off the canvas of a French boudoir. The private lady's bedroom was an exotic blend of black and white with shades of gray and gold. A sheer, three-paneled screen picked up the silhouette of a naked woman. The shadow of a shirtless man sat on the bed. Their bodies curved with sexual intent.

The composition was as sensual as the satin sheets on the bed, Beth thought. Romantic as the book of poetry on the bedside table. The artist had a lover's heart. The work was moving and meaningful.

She inched toward the painting, not wanting to be noticed, just hoping for a better look. The piece made her insides go soft. She felt the depth of the love between those two. Knew they were soul mates.

It was a painting to be shared. To be hung over a married couples' bed. She thought of Rylan, and somehow knew that he would appreciate the composition. The price was beyond what she could afford. That didn't mean she couldn't admire it a moment longer.

"It's quite remarkable, isn't it?" Evelyn commented when she joined Beth a short while later. "Sultry. Inspiring. Observers reactions will vary. Whoever views the painting can decide if the man is about to take her to bed or if she's already been satisfied. The perfect wedding gift."

"For some lucky bride and groom," Beth agreed, sighing.

The gallery owner gave her a look of understanding. "Your photograph awaits you. The dreariness of that rainy day has been lifted with the colorful turquoise frame."

Beth followed Evelyn to her office. Wrapped in a thick protective mailer, the photo was Beth's for the taking, although the mailer appeared thicker and heavier than when she'd initially left it with Evelyn.

"There are two framed photographs inside," Evelyn explained when she handed them over to Beth. "Gerald deVasi visited my shop a day or two after the Gallery Walk. He introduced himself, and we sat and had tea. I looked through his portfolio. Your photo was being framed at the time, and Gerald showed me a second black-and-white image from the same series. The single picture spoke to me. I acquired it with the sole purpose of giving it to you." Her brow creased. "I believe when you see it, you'll understand."

Beth's hands trembled. "Should I open the package now?"

Evelyn shook her head. "Alone might be better. It brings your past into perspective, Beth. Sometimes Mother Nature carries karma to the extreme. She has a wicked sense of humor." Evelyn gave her a gentle hug. "Find peace in your heart. You deserve it." She escorted Beth to the door.

Beth unlocked the Range Rover, set the elongated mailer on the backseat. The car wash was next on her list. Rylan had an account with Wally's Wash and Shine. Apparently he used their services often. She got out of the SUV while it passed through the automatic conveyer. Employees took a vacuum to the inside at the exit.

"Atlas," she heard one of the young men say. Then smile.

Afterward, she headed home. She grabbed the two photos, carried them into the cottage. Atlas met her at the door with his usual bark, demanding she share her day. She'd grown used to talking to the dog. His ears flickered as if he understood every word she said.

He followed close behind her when she walked to her bedroom. There, he sat on the end of her bed. She laid the mailer across her lap. Held it until she was ready to open it. The air seemed charged with an undefined sympathy. The feeling held as she slipped off her red Keds and stared at her burgundy and pink message socks. *Forgive and Forget* was scripted across her toes in gold thread. She took the sentiment to heart.

The photographs were carefully stacked with bubble wrap between them. She recognized the top framed photo. The image of the Statton wedding made her cringe. The expressions on the faces of the bridal party and guests were still as hateful as she remembered.

She was suddenly curious about the second photograph. The transparent plastic hinted at another gathering. She pulled the wrap away and was transported from the wedding to a lawn party. Summertime. The decorations indicated a Fourth of July Celebration.

She immediately understood the significance of the photograph. The evidence was clear. Different day. Same rain. Black clouds swarmed the sky, and a storm let loose on the Stattons and their guests once again.

People stood damp and dismayed in puddles up to their ankles. There in the forefront was the hostess. Mrs. Statton wore the same expression as she had in the wedding photo. The matron's lips were as pinched as a prune. Her daughter appeared to be screaming or cursing at being drenched. Beth could hear her displeasure.

It seemed the same cast had assembled to reenact the drama of a spoiled party. The only person missing from the second photo was her, Beth realized. She'd been hiding in the corner of the wedding picture. Her shoulders slumped, her hands over her face. Fractured by the outcome.

Mother Nature was not one to be told what to do. She'd drowned the Stattons twice. Some people carried a dark cloud over their heads. The thought released the harshness in her heart—the part of her that had carried their baggage and blame for something that was never her fault. They'd been mean to her. Had hurt her with words and actions.

Not nice coming from family.

Her stepmother and stepsister had bruised her soul.

She was about to place the photographs in her suitcase when Rylan appeared down the hall. She hadn't heard him come home. The man had stealth. He studied her from the doorway. "You look sad," he noted. "Do you mind if I sit with you or would your rather be by yourself?"

She patted the end of the bed. "Join me."

Atlas gave Rylan very little room to squeeze in. Ry fused himself against her.

She liked the feel of him. She held up the photographs, side by side. "Compare the two pictures. Tell me what you see."

He narrowed his gaze. "More rain, more gloom and doom."

"What else?" she asked.

It didn't take him long to pick up the Stattons in both photographs. The guest list was identical. Invitations sent to the influential and prominent. A minute or so later, Rylan had figured it out. "Everyone's angry in both photos, but the sad woman is missing in the second one. She became invisible."

"Yes, I did."

"You?" He was disbelieving.

She'd been heavier in the photo. Her hair longer. Yet

there was no denying her identity. She cleared her throat and spoke of her past, not leaving out a single detail. Her heart lightened. She felt suddenly free.

"Holy shit," Rylan said when she'd finished. "Those people were assholes." He seldom swore. The fact that he was upset on her behalf soothed her.

Atlas growled, too, chiming in.

Beth ran her finger around the corner of the framed photograph. "I never understood why my dad married Luella Statton."

"Cruella," Ry teased her.

Beth smiled. "My father's family came from old money. A long pedigree. His parents didn't approve of my mother. She was middle class. Free-spirited. Bohemian. Yet she made my father happy. She would dance down the side-walk. Dip her toes in public water fountains. Offer a stranger an ice cream cone. Laugh with zest."

She paused, thoughtful. "My dad lost his inheritance when he married Mom. He still had the family name, just no money.

"Luella was just the opposite. She was new money, but with few social connections. My father's name interested her most. She gave him time to mourn my mother's pass-ing, then pounced on him with intent and purpose. His parents were all for his second marriage.

"Once they were wed, she put on a good front for his benefit. Pretending to like me. To guide me. All the while setting me up for every possible failure. She used me as a scapegoat when it rained at my stepsister's wedding. Words hurt. I lived with the blame. Then with the shame when the groom accused me of being his mistress. People were quick to believe him. He was a Wentworth, of the hotel Wentworths. Everyone thought the worst of me. Luella swore that wherever I went, she would ruin me. She has a far-reaching arm.

"I grabbed my mother's battered suitcase and packed a few items. I traded in my car and headed south. It was a little scary."

"You're not scared now."

"I'm feeling pretty secure, actually." She stood then, took the photographs to her closet, and faced them toward the wall. She had come to grips with what she couldn't change. Her future had immense possibilities.

Ry reached for her when she returned. He eased her down on his lap and held her gently.

Her body warmed. "Did you enjoy your time with your grandfather?" she wanted to know.

Rylan rubbed the back of his neck, thoughtful. "I was ready to talk sports, to discuss the game. Instead, Gramps took a walk down memory lane."

"That surprised you?"

"A little. He got melancholy, more than usual. He talked about his wife Emma. How he knew from their first meeting that she was meant for him. I quote him now. 'Emma Loraine Halverson was the prettiest thing a man could see on a summer day.' "

"How lovely." Beth was a romantic. "When did they meet?"

"She'd ridden the train into town with her family. They were on vacation. He became smitten with her when he saw her at Milford's Soda Shop, sipping a strawberry milk shake with whipped cream and a cherry. Emma reminded him of sunshine with her honey blond hair, light blue eyes, and warm smile."

"I bet you have her blue eyes."

"So I've been told," Ry said, then continued with the story. "My grandfather walked over to Emma and asked if he could 'sit a spell.' His exact words. She lowered her eyes and nodded. Sweet and shy. He ordered a double-dip vanilla ice cream cone, but was so nervous he could barely eat it. He kept wiping his face with a handkerchief."

Beth's heart swelled. "He was trying to impress her."

Ry nodded. "He apparently did. After a chaperoned movie and a slow stroll on the boardwalk, Frank asked her to marry him. They'd only known each other a week. Emma's parents returned to Ohio, and she stayed in Bare-foot William. He loves her as much today as he did back then."

Beth's voice was barely above a whisper when she said, "Love can be unexpected." *And hard to pin down.* Relationships were new to her. She had feelings for Rylan, yet had no idea where she stood with him. They had great sex. Had a lot in common. But never spoke of commitment. Perhaps it was too soon. Perhaps she expected too much from him.

Atlas didn't let her dwell too long. He nudged her with his nose. The boy was hungry. She pushed off Rylan's lap, and he let her go.

"To be continued," he said.

They progressed at the same pace for the next two weeks. Beth camped at the cottage with the dogs. Rylan spent one night a week at Driftwood Inn. He'd heard from the hotel manager that his teammates kept early hours, which surprised the hell out of him. They arrived at the stadium with fewer hangovers and more focus than before.

Playing in the Grapefruit League, the Rogues faced other teams with spring training facilities along the Florida coast and in the center of the state. Their schedule in-cluded traveling, with three out-of-town games each week. Beth missed Rylan when he was gone, but he would text or call her.

Beth followed their schedule online. They played the

St. Louis Colonels again in Port St. Lucie. Miami Marlins in Jupiter. Minnesota Twins in Ft. Myers, and met up with the Phillies in Clearwater. Additional teams arrived in Barefoot William, wanting to steal the Rogues' preseason standing. The Rogues were playing well. Rylan was pumped.

The night of Grace Mayberry's birthday, he held Beth close when they slow danced to a collection of Big Band Music. "We've won twelve of sixteen games thus far. Halo believes thirteen additional wins are within our reach. I usually give the team pep talks before each game, but Halo's taken over. He's long-winded."

That same night, Morton Potter taught Beth to cha-cha. Ry's grandfather instructed her on the swing. They were always a beat behind the music. Rylan did the box step with Grace and Cora Salvo. Then a spry Alva Madison taught him to jitterbug.

Rylan should've lived in the nineteen forties, Beth thought. He was that good.

Their gift to Grace was a large sand globe. It was similar to a snow globe, but filled with sand, colorful seashells, a starfish, and sea urchin. The sand had specks of gold glitter, and the globe would sparkle in the sunshine when she set it on a window ledge. Grace liked sparkle.

Beth stared at the calendar one Monday morning and wondered where the time had gone. She had only two weeks left with Rylan. They shared laughter at the cottage and a lot of sex. Atlas obeyed her on a good day. He went as far as to retrieve his drool towel so she could wipe his mouth. The other dogs were committed to her, too. She still took them for long walks—she liked being outside in the fresh air. Rue would keep Atlas in line when the big boy acted up or copped an attitude. Oscar and Nathan took Beth's side as well. Atlas felt they'd defected and told them so. By grumbling for an entire block.

She and Rylan had yet to discuss the end of her employment. She hoped to broach the subject tonight. If she could find a quiet moment with him. Shaye and Jill had contacted their friends, and her phone rang nonstop. People sought her for children's and upcoming holiday parties. A German shepherd's birthday. She agreed to the job, but only if Atlas was on the guest list. The dog's owner hemmed and hawed, but finally gave in. Ten dogs would be invited to a backyard romp, needing supervision. Piece of organic canine cake.

She was waiting to finalize any other dates until her future was decided. She dreaded the day Rylan and his dogs pulled out of the driveway, heading for Virginia. Leaving her standing on the porch.

She was conflicted. Could she stay at the cottage without him there? Doubtful. He hadn't mentioned taking her with him. He had a permanent PA in Richmond. Beth had been his live-in fill-in.

She heard the front door open and close and knew he had arrived home. The team had played Houston in Kissimmee. He'd sent her a text, indicating heavy traffic had held up the team bus.

He called to her. "Beth, do you have something to tell me?" His voice was wary. He'd spotted the baby crib set up in the living room.

She burst out laughing when she came from the kitchen and saw his face. He looked nervous and apprehensive, but smiling, as if taken with the idea.

"Not *our* crib," she told him. "It's for Sophie's baby shower. The guests can stack their gifts inside, and she can take the crib home with her when she leaves."

"Nice touch," he said, then took a moment before asking, "One or the other. Big family or small?"

"What size are we discussing?"

"One to a dozen."

She'd grown up an only child. It would've been fun to have a brother or sister. Less lonely after her parents passed away. "Two, maybe three kids."

"I'm used to a big family," he said easily. "Holidays bursting at the seams. Buffet tables and football."

"I'm used to being alone. A take-out dinner for one." It wasn't a pity party, so she added, "I've made a lot of friends in Barefoot William. I'll miss them when I'm gone."

Rylan stilled, suddenly becoming a man of stone. "You're going, when? And why? Do you already have one foot out the door?" His voice was deeper than usual; his concern evident. "I thought you'd planned to start a business here."

"I'm weighing my options, still giving it some thought."

He took a deep breath. "Look—"

His iPhone rang, and he pulled it from his jean pocket. He stared at the screen, said, "I have to take this. It's my assistant Connie." He crossed to the turquoise couch, tapped the screen, and settled in for the call.

Atlas came to stand beside Beth. Nudged her hand with his nose. She patted him, uncertain whether she should stay in the room or go. She had work to do in her office and headed for the hallway. Ry held up his hand, signaling her to stay.

She leaned against the far wall. Atlas rested against her leg. She listened, wondering over his conversation. He soon disconnected, ran one hand down his face. "Connie got married not too long ago. She just found out she's pregnant. She won't be returning to work. I have a PA position open in Richmond." He grinned at Beth. Teased. "Care to apply? I'd give you a good recommendation."

He was offering her a job, but not a commitment. Her heart squeezed. It was a setback. She wasn't certain which would be worse—to have him leave town or for them to take up as they were in another city. She suddenly wanted more.

She loved this man, but he had to want her, too. She wasn't good at dropping hints. She'd hoped he would step up and propose. That is, if he wanted her as much as she needed him. It had to be a two-way street.

"You can leave an application on my desk." She kept her voice light, even.

"Will you fill it out?" He was serious.

She was honest. "I have no idea what I'll be doing in an hour, much less at the end of next week."

Rylan frowned. "Make plans, Beth." What the hell was she doing to him? he wondered. The offer that had started as a joke had turned on him. Bit him in the butt. He'd been relieved and extremely pleased when Connie gave him her notice. As of today, he was without a personal assistant.

But hiring Beth as his Richmond PA had never been his real intention. He wanted a lifetime with this woman. His only concern was that he wasn't sure she was ready for him. She'd just come to grips with her old life. He wanted to be part of her new life. He'd played the PA card in hopes of getting her to Virginia. He wanted her with him, however he could get her there.

Damn if she hadn't taken offense over his job offer. Her gaze had narrowed, and her voice had chilled. He was marriage minded. But were their heads in the same place? She'd given no indication she was serious about him. All he needed was a hint. One tiny clue.

Atlas sensed the shift in mood. He didn't like it in the least.

Uncertainty claimed them. The air flattened. He could barely draw breath. The Dane had his own solution. He took Beth's hand in his mouth and gently tugged her toward Ry.

"Seriously?" he heard Beth say, but there was humor in her voice. She didn't resist.

Rylan was quick to take her hand once Atlas dropped it. "Atlas the Matchmaker." The big boy believed they belonged together.

Ry realized then what a big part Atlas had played in bringing them together. He had been annoying. Relentless. And he'd fixed Rylan up with the perfect woman. He'd sensed the rightness between them all along. Smart dog.

Atlas barked then, confirming that matchmaking was his purpose in life. Ry scratched him behind the ear.

His grandfather believed in love at first sight. He and Emma had gone the distance. The years had been good to them. Frank's thoughts were the same as Rylan's own. A man's destiny was written with one woman. Beth brought a laid-back easiness to his life. They had fun together, and so much more.

Ry has always believed in the power of three. One more sign that this was the right moment . . .

He set his back teeth when Halo and Landon walked through the front door without knocking. They thought they lived in his house. What the hell could they possibly want? Halo carried a plastic bag. Landon held a beer. He took a long sip.

Ry tightened his grip on Beth's hand, eased her closer to him. Feeling possessive. "Can I help you?" he gritted out.

His teammates ignored the sarcasm in his voice. *Par for the course,* Ry thought. Both men wore *new* Cates family T-shirts. Different color. Bolder print. "Are you manufacturing your own shirts now?" he wanted to know. "Do you have a side business?" He hoped they weren't selling specialty tees on the boardwalk. Everyone he passed would claim to be his relative. His actual family would not be happy.

"I got a tear in my other shirt," Halo informed him.

"I added too much bleach to my laundry," said Landon. "My shirt turned white, and the lettering faded."

Faded was good. White T-shirts worked for Rylan. The guys were inventive. They must have placed a recent order with a T-shirt company. No doubt paid a high price for overnight delivery.

"Moving on," Ry said, hinting that they get to the point of their visit.

"Two things," Halo told him. "First, Will, Brody, and Sam are getting tats tonight. Hank tomorrow. You in or out, dude?"

Ry made them wait for his answer. A minute passed before he said, "In." He'd made his decision only moments before. It felt right. He was sticking to it.

Landon appeared stunned.

Halo disbelieving. He backed up a step. "You're sure?"

"Positive."

"What are you going to get?" Landon was curious.

"That's between Beth and me." He kept it private, seeking her approval.

Halo pumped his arm. "Total team unity." He was psyched.

He then tossed Beth the plastic bag, which she caught with one hand. His smile curved. "For you, babe. We like you. Be part of our family."

She looked suspicious. And a little confused. She released Rylan's hand and clutched the bag to her chest. "I don't understand."

Landon winked at her. "You will when you open our gift."

What had they done? "You shouldn't have," Ry said, his tone wary.

"But we wanted to." Landon sounded sincere.

Beth fumbled with the knot Halo had tied in the plastic. "What, no gift wrap?" she kidded him.

"No time," Halo returned. He watched her intently.

"Don't worry, Ry-man," Landon reassured him. "We're not staying. We only wanted to drop off her shirt."

"My shirt . . ." Beth's voice trailed off as she removed it from the bag. She held up a light gray tee with blue script. Her eyes watered and there was a catch in her voice when she said, "Hello, my name is Beth Cates."

Silence, heavy and profound, settled in the living room. There was significance to their gift. Rylan understood and was actually grateful. Here was his third sign. He'd never expected Halo and Landon to offer the opportunity for his marriage proposal. But they had. He would take it.

Ry nodded toward the door, nudged. "You were just leaving?"

His teammates grinned then, devious and knowing. "Take care of unfinished business, Ry-man," Landon advised.

"Welcome to the family, Beth, babe," Halo said.

Both men pushed Ry aside to hug her. Bear hugs that smothered and left her breathless.

The second they released her, she again took Rylan's hand. "Have a nice night," she said as they turned to leave.

"You have a better one," were Halo's last words. The door closed behind them.

Beth clutched the shirt to her chest. Her eyes were bright, and one tear escaped.

Ry gently brushed his thumb over her cheek. "The shirt makes you happy?"

She looked at him. "It means a lot."

Ry pursed his lips. "Beth Cates sounds good to me. How about you?"

"A name I could live with."

"For the next hundred years?"

"That I could manage."

"One or the other. Love me or love me not?"

Her voice broke. "Love you, always."

"I love you, too."

Atlas woofed. He loved them both. Rue and the dachsies entered the living room. Yawning. They'd slept through the excitement, but were awake now. They sat beside the Dane. Wagged their tails and looked on.

Ry pulled her close, took her mouth in a sealing kiss. "Let's make it official. Marry me, Beth Avery."

"I'm yours, Rylan Cates."

His heart felt light. He'd never been happier. He chuckled when he told her, "I'm glad you agreed, since I already purchased your wedding gift."

They stood so close, he felt the skip in her heartbeat.

"What did you buy?"

He hadn't planned to tell her, had hoped to surprise her, but the delight and eagerness of her expression made him relent. "Evelyn Wells texted, sending a picture of a painting you'd admired. A bedroom scene."

"The boudoir." She knew the one. "It was so expensive."

"You're worth it."

"I'm worth it . . ." Her voice was no more than a whisper.

She fought back tears. Her body softened against his.

She'd had her share of dark days, Rylan knew. He'd never let anyone hurt her again. "We'll hang the painting on the wall above our bed. Our inspiration."

"It's very sexy."

"So are you." He kissed her until her knees went weak and he was so hard he hurt.

It was Beth who broke their kiss, breathed against his mouth. "A tattoo, huh?" she questioned him. A smile was on her lips. "Who changed your mind?"

"You did."

Her surprise was evident. Wide eyes. Parted lips. A catch in her throat. "How so?"

"I'm giving permanence to us." He took her hand, settled it over his right hip. Her fingers touched the hollow of his groin. "My tattoo. *Married.*"

"I like your choice."

"I thought you might."

Atlas sensed all was well in the world. He howled, loudly. The other dogs joined in. They were serenading his fiancée.

They all seemed to agree—there was no one like Beth. And she was theirs.

Don't miss the next charmingly quirky tale in
Kate Angell's Barefoot William series, *No, No . . . Yes!*
Please read on for a glimpse of Halo Todd's story,
available next spring.

"*B*e *my boyfriend for one hour.*"
    Halo Todd stared at the woman dressed in the
chicken costume. At least, he assumed she was female.
Feminine voice. Short in stature. Indeterminable age. She
wore a padded yellow, feathered jumpsuit with orange leg
covers and spiky chicken toes. The head cover had a red
wattle. A sharp black beak.

Six-fifteen a.m., and she paced outside Jacy's Java, a
popular coffee shop in historic Richmond, Virginia. Brick
buildings and sidewalks. Gas streetlights and narrow av-
enues. A hint of dawn was on the horizon.

He'd purchased a double espresso in preparation for
his drive south. The Rogues were about to begin spring
training in Barefoot William, Florida. He played right
field. It was the first week in February, and the morning
was bleak. Fifty degrees. Overcast skies. A stiff wind blew
from the north, ruffling the chicken's feathers.

Who the hell was she? He scratched his head, asked, "Do
I know you?" He had, on occasion, slept with women and
not known their names. He would have remembered a
chicken.

She shook her head, and the red wattle beneath her chin
quivered. "We've never met."

"Why me?" he asked. Amused. He wondered if his

teammate Landon Kane was pranking him. But there was no one on the street corner other than him and the chick. No one hiding behind a parked car. No one recording a video for YouTube, as far as he could tell.

The woman clapped her hands, stomped her feet. Shivered. A few feathers flew. Apparently the costume wasn't as warm as it appeared. "My boyfriend broke up with me last night," she said on a sigh.

Her man must not be into chickens.

"You're the biggest guy to walk down the street," she went on to say. "The last male costume for matching couples at Masquerade was an extra-large rooster. Cocka-doodle-do me?"

His mind went to the gutter. *Cock-a-doodle-do her* sounded kinky. He had no idea what she looked like. Other than that her eyes through the slits appeared green. Her mouth was hidden beneath the beak. His curiosity got the better of him. "What's with the costume?" he asked.

"Go Big or Go Home."

"The game show?" No way, Jose.

"I have tickets. I stood in line for three days."

Go Big or Go Home was a popular television show. He'd watched it on occasion, during the off-season. Seated on the sofa in his condo while sipping a beer. The show got funnier as he worked his way through a six-pack. He'd be cheering for his favorite contestant when he crushed the last can in his hand.

Challengers lost their inhibitions. They made spectacles of themselves. Jumping, shouting, and waving signs to get the host's attention. Alex Xander encouraged them to riot. The louder, the crazier, the more out of control, the better. The costumed audience fed into the frenzy.

Halo was familiar with wild and crazy. Raising hell. Sleeping around. Calling a friend for bail money. He lived the moment. Controlled his own chaos.

A game show would flip his competitive switch. Winning was important to him, in all aspects of his life. He would have to abide by their rules. He'd have no say in the matter. The show was based on challenges. The contestants played games. Some were mental; others physical.

Each day had a different theme, which varied from midway at the fair to three-ring circus, haunted house, rodeo and jungle madness. No one knew the activity until the curtain went up. He'd be at the host's mercy. He had no desire to make a fool of himself. Even in a costume.

"So, what do you say?" the chicken pressed, sounding hopeful. "Sixty quick minutes."

Quick minutes? It would be the longest hour of his life. One he could never get back.

"The television studio is six blocks east." She rolled back the orange mitt on her hand, glanced at her watch. A big faced Minnie Mouse on a red band. She had kid in her. "The show films in the morning and airs in the afternoon. We have less than an hour to sign in. As it is, we'll be stuck standing in the back row."

The last row wasn't far enough back for him. "Sorry, I can't help you."

"Can't or won't?" she stood up to him. Chicken was brave.

"Won't." He was honest with her.

She pointed a hand claw at him, said, "The show's in its tenth season. This is anniversary week. Friday is for couples only. Winners take home cars, jewelry, and dream vacations. Fifty thousand dollars is the grand prize." She spread her arms wide and her chest puffed. He glimpsed the outline of her breasts for half a second. Small, high, and firm. A-cups. "Anything you'd ever want," she tempted him.

Don't miss any of Kate Angell's Barefoot William novels!

No Tan Lines

"Hot, sexy and smart!"
—Carly Phillips, *New York Times* bestselling author

There's a place where the ocean meets the shore, where kicking off your shoes and baring some skin is as natural as sneaking under the boardwalk for an ice cream cone and stolen kisses.

But life isn't all a beach for Shaye Cates, even if her idea of an office is a shady umbrella at the water's edge equipped with cell phone and laptop. Steely-eyed Trace Saunders is the incredibly irksome fly in her coconut tanning oil. And running a kids' softball team with her longtime rival is going to have everyone in her little Florida town buzzing. Her scads of laid-back relatives and his whole uptight clan know that Shaye just wants to play ball while Trace thinks only of business. But beneath the twinkling lights of the ferris wheel, the magic of sea and sand can sweep away every inhibition . . .

Suddenly, it's summertime, and the lovin' is easy.

No Strings Attached

*Balmy ocean breezes . . . sweet coconut oil . . . glistening
tanned bodies. There's no better place for romantic sparks
to fly than at the beach.*

As a professional volleyball player, Dune Cates attracts
scores of pretty women who flock to his side. But only
one has managed to get under his skin—Sophie
Saunders. Unlike the skimpily-clad beach groupies,
Sophie marches to a beat all her own. And though she's
afraid of the surf, burns in the sun, has two left feet, that
doesn't stop her from trying every daring sport available
on the boardwalk. Dune knows Sophie spells trouble,
and he should keep his distance, especially since he's a
no-strings-attached kind of guy. But he can't ignore an
overwhelming instinct to protect her. And with the
promise of ice cream sandwiches, merry-go-round rides
and dreamy sunsets, it's only a matter of time before
Dune gives in to the temptation of Sophie's soft lips.

Love is always sweeter in the summer.

No Sunshine When She's Gone

Life's a Beach

Though his family owns the charming beachside town of Barefoot William, Aidan Cates is as down-to-earth as the locals. He's also practical to a fault and doesn't believe some psychic on the boardwalk can predict *his* future.

Jillie Mac is as free as an ocean breeze, so when the hot stranger and his date mistake her for a fortune-teller, she's ready to have some fun. But one devastating secret told, one mistaken identity revealed, and numerous long summer nights later, it's Jillie and Aidan who discover that sometimes love comes with a simple twist of fate.